rave reviews for
the winemaker's wife

"Love and betrayal, forgiveness and redemption combine in a heady tale of the ever-present past. . . . Fantastic!"

—Pam Jenoff, *New York Times* bestselling author of *The Lost Girls of Paris*

"A heart-wrenching story about how one decision can change our lives, perfect for fans of *The Nightingale*."

—*PopSugar* (The 34 Best New Books to Put in Your Beach Bag This Summer, 2019)

"A suspenseful story of the Champagne region in World War II."

—*Tampa Bay Times*

"What could be better than a story of champagne, secrets, lies, and history from a writer as compulsively readable as Kristin Harmel? Pick up this epic and heart-wrenching World War II tale immediately!"

—Alyson Noël, #1 bestselling author of *Saving Zoë*

"Unfolding in multiple viewpoints, the writing is atmospheric and rich. . . . Harmel's touching story of love and loss in World War II France will appeal to fans of Pam Jenoff and Kate Quinn."

—*Library Journal*

"Keep a good supply of tissues close, not just for the reading of this gorgeous work but for that moment when the story ends and your heart soars with the beauty of the telling."

—Kelly Harms, bestselling author of *The Overdue Life of Amy Byler*

"With exceptional skill, Kristin Harmel constructs *The Winemaker's Wife* between the past and the present, giving equal weight and importance to both. . . . Once you start reading this moving novel, you will not be able to put it down until you reach the last page."

—Armando Lucas Correa, *USA Today* bestselling author of *The German Girl*

"The lives of several strong women intervene in a complicated historical tale of love and war. . . . This World War II novel takes a unique approach."

—*Booklist*

"Written in heart-wrenching prose, *The Winemaker's Wife* is a complex story of love, betrayal, and impossible courage. . . . I couldn't turn the pages fast enough and savored every moment at the same time."

—Anita Hughes, bestselling author of *Christmas in Paris*

more praise for the work of kristin harmel

The Book of Lost Names

"A fascinating, heartrending page-turner that, like the real-life forgers who inspired the novel, should never be forgotten. A riveting historical tale that I devoured in a single sitting."

—Kristina McMorris, *New York Times* bestselling author of *Sold on a Monday*

"Harmel brilliantly imagines the life of a young Polish-French Jewish woman during the depths of World War II. . . . This thoughtful work will touch readers with its testament to the endurance of hope."

—*Publishers Weekly* (starred review)

"Not since *The Nightingale* have I finished a book and been so choked with emotion. . . . Sweeping and magnificent."

—Fiona Davis, *New York Times* bestselling author of *The Lions of Fifth Avenue*

"A heart-stopping tale of survival and heroism centered on a female forger who risks everything to help Jewish children escape Nazi-occupied France."

—*People* (The 20 Best Books to Read This Summer, 2020)

The Room on Rue Amélie

"Harmel writes a poignant novel based loosely on the true story of an American woman who helped on the Comet Line, which rescued hundreds of airmen and soldiers. This compelling story celebrates hope and bravery in the face of evil."

—*Booklist*

"*The Room on Rue Amélie* is a World War II story of courage against all odds and fighting for what you believe in."

—*PopSugar* (31 of the Best New Books You Should Read This Spring, 2018)

"Reminiscent of *The Nightingale* and *Map of the Heart*, Kristin Harmel's *The Room on Rue Amélie* is an emotional, heartbreaking, inspiring tribute to the strength of the human spirit and the enduring power of love."

—Mariah Stewart, *New York Times* bestselling author

"Harmel injects new life into a well-worn story . . . about the struggle to find normalcy amid the horrors of World War II. . . . This is a celebration of those, like [her protagonist] Ruby, who found the courage to face life head-on."

—*Publishers Weekly*

"Set against all the danger and drama of World War II Paris, this heartfelt novel will keep you turning the pages until the very last word."

—Mary Alice Monroe, *New York Times* bestselling author

"Heartbreaking and uplifting . . . readers will be completely absorbed by Harmel's storytelling."

—*RT Book Reviews*

"The strong and courageous inhabitants of *The Room on Rue Amélie* occupied all my time until the tender and powerful final pages. Beautifully written, Kristin Harmel's latest is an unforgettable exploration of love and hope during the darkest of moments."

—Amy E. Reichert, bestselling author

"Recommended for fans of World War II historical fiction."

—*Library Journal*

"Harmel's poignant novels always tug at the heartstrings."

—*B&N Reads* (The Best New Fiction of March 2018)

When We Meet Again

"Harmel . . . authentically weaves American history into this engaging novel. An appealing family saga that connects generations and reaffirms love."

—*Kirkus Reviews*

"Centering on a lesser-known facet of American history, *When We Meet Again* is a gripping novel of history, art, and the power of love. Kristin Harmel's work is always riveting, but her storytelling reaches new heights with a tale that is layered, complex, and satisfying to the last page."

—Michelle Gable, *New York Times* bestselling author

The Sweetness of Forgetting

"Kristin Harmel writes with such insight and heart that her characters will stay with you long after you've finished her books."

—Emily Giffin, *New York Times* bestselling author

"Kristin Harmel . . . has a way of bringing the reader into her stories in such a powerful way that they can often forget they're reading at all. *The Sweetness of Forgetting* may just be Harmel's best book yet."

—Lisa Steinke, SheKnows Book Lounge

"Absolutely enthralling. . . . Readers will remember *The Sweetness of Forgetting* long after the final page is turned."

—*Fresh Fiction*

the winemaker's wife

KRISTIN HARMEL

POCKET BOOKS
NEW YORK LONDON TORONTO SYDNEY NEW DELHI

Pocket Books
An Imprint of Simon & Schuster, Inc.
1230 Avenue of the Americas
New York, NY 10020

First Pocket Books paperback edition August 2021

POCKET and colophon are registered trademarks of Simon & Schuster, Inc.

For information about special discounts for bulk purchases, please contact Simon & Schuster Special Sales at 1-866-506-1949 or business@simonandschuster.com.

The Simon & Schuster Speakers Bureau can bring authors to your live event. For more information or to book an event, contact the Simon & Schuster Speakers Bureau at 1-866-248-3049 or visit our website at www.simonspeakers.com.

Manufactured in the United States of America

10 9 8 7 6 5 4 3 2 1

ISBN 978-1-9821-7877-2
ISBN 978-1-9821-1231-8 (ebook)

To Jason and Noah.

You teach me again and again what love really is.

It is not tolerable, it is not possible, that from so much death, so much sacrifice and ruin, so much heroism, a greater and better humanity shall not emerge.

—*General Charles de Gaulle,*
leader of the French Resistance,
speaking about the impact of
the Second World War

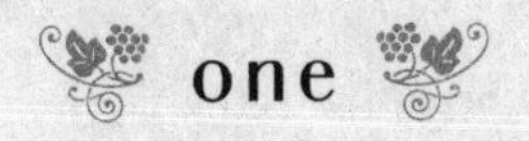

one

MAY 1940

INÈS

The road snaked over the lush vineyards of Champagne as Inès Chauveau sped southwest out of Reims, clouds of dust ballooning in the wake of her glossy black Citroën, wind whipping ferociously through her chestnut hair. It was May, and already the vines were awakening, their buds like tiny fists reaching for the sun. In weeks they would flower, and by September, their grapes—pale green Chardonnay, inky Pinot Meunier, blueberry-hued Pinot Noir—would be plump and bursting for the harvest.

But would Inès still be here? Would any of them? A shiver ran through her as she braked to hug a curve, the engine growling in protest as she turned down the road that led home. Michel would tell her she was driving too quickly, too recklessly. But then, he was cautious about everything.

In June, it would be a year since they'd married, and she couldn't remember a day during that time that he hadn't gently chided her about something. *I'm simply looking out for you, Inès*, he always said. *That's what a husband is supposed to do.* Lately, nearly all his warnings had been about the Germans, who'd been lurking just on the other side of the impenetrable Maginot Line, the fortified border that protected France from the chaos besetting the rest of Europe. *Those of us who were here for the Great War know to take them seriously*, he said at least once a day, as if he hadn't been just four years old when the final battle was waged.

Of course Inès, younger than Michel by six years, hadn't yet been born when the Germans finally withdrew from the Marne in 1918, after nearly obliterating the central city of Reims. But her father had told enough tales about the war—usually while drunk on brandy and pounding his fist against the table—that she knew to be wary.

You can never trust the Huns! She could hear her father's deep, gravelly voice in her ear now, though he'd been dead for years. *They might play the role of France's friend, but only fools would believe such a thing.*

Well, Inès was no fool. And this time, for once, she would bring the news that changed everything. She felt a small surge of triumph, but as she raced into Ville-Dommange, the silent, somber, seven-hundred-year-old Saint-Lié chapel that loomed over the small town seemed to taunt her for her pettiness. This wasn't about who was wrong and who was right. This was about war. Death. The blood of young men already soaking the ground in the forests to the northeast. All the things her husband had predicted.

She drove through the gates, braked hard in front of the grand two-story stone château, and leapt out, racing for the door that led down to the vast network of underground cellars. "Michel!" she called as she descended two stone steps at a time, the cool, damp air like a bucket of water to the face. "Michel!"

Her voice echoed through the tangled maze of passageways, carved out of the earth three-quarters of a century earlier by her husband's eccentric great-grandfather. Thousands of champagne bottles rested on their sides there, a small fortune of bubbles waiting for their next act.

"Inès?" Michel's concerned voice wafted from somewhere deep within the cellars, and then she could hear footsteps coming closer until he rounded the corner ahead of her, followed by Theo Laurent, the Maison Chauveau's *chef de cave*, the head winemaker. "My dear, what is it?" Michel asked as he rushed to her, putting his hands on her shoulders and studying her face. "Are you quite all right, Inès?"

"No." She hadn't realized until then how breathless she was from the news and the drive and the rapid descent into the chill of the cellars. "No, Michel, I'm not all right at all."

"What's happened?" Michel asked while Theo regarded her silently, his expression as impassive as always.

"It has begun," Inès managed to say. "The invasion, Michel. The Germans are coming!"

A heavy silence hung in the damp air. How long would it be before the quiet of the cellars was punctured by the thud of goose-stepping boots overhead? Before everything they'd built was threatened, perhaps destroyed?

"Well then," Michel said at last. "I suppose it is time we finish hiding the champagne."

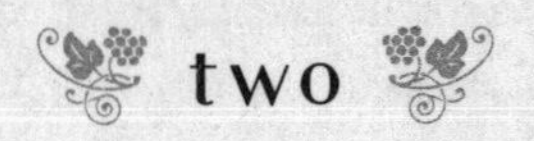

two

JUNE 2019

LIV

Liv Kent's left hand was naked. Or that's how it felt, anyhow, each time she looked down and saw the empty space where her wedding ring had been for the past twelve years. And though she'd taken it off three months ago, five weeks after Eric had announced he was leaving and wanted the paperwork done as soon as possible, it still startled her sometimes, the absence of something she'd thought she would have forever. But then, there were a lot of things she'd thought she could count on.

"Thanks for being cool about this," Eric said as he carried the final cardboard box of their shared belongings into her small one-bedroom apartment, the one Liv had moved into after they'd separated. It felt strange to have him here, filling space that would never belong to him. Part of her wanted to scream at him to get out, but another piece of her, a piece she was utterly ashamed of, wanted to beg him to stay. The speed at which their marriage had disintegrated had left Liv feeling as if the ground had opened up beneath her.

"Cool?" she repeated as he gazed around, taking in the apartment she'd filled with furniture they used to share. His eyes lingered on the distressed leather couch anchoring the room, and she wondered if he was thinking, as she suddenly was, of the day they'd bought it, the way they'd argued about the expense, the way they'd fallen onto its unforgiving cushions afterward to make up, sweaty and tangled up in each other. Then again, maybe he was just thinking that he was glad to have a fresh start, with none of the items they'd purchased together infringing on his new life.

His eyes moved back to hers. "I just mean I know this hasn't been easy." He rearranged his features into a mask of somber sympathy, and Liv felt a spike of annoyance, which was better than the sadness that had been swirling through her like a storm since they'd officially signed their divorce papers that morning. "I really am sorry about the way things turned out, Liv, but we just wanted different things."

All Liv could manage was a noncommittal, "Mmmmm."

"I do want what's best for you. You know that, right? I'll always care about you."

"Just not as much as you care about yourself." Liv couldn't resist. "Or your new girlfriend."

Eric sighed. "Don't be angry, Liv." He set the cardboard box down on the floor and brushed his hands off. "I'd like to think that someday we might even be friends."

Liv snorted, and for a second, Eric's sympathetic look slipped, and his forehead creased in annoyance, giving Liv a glimpse of the man she now knew lurked beneath the carefully curated exterior, the one who blamed her for everything that had gone wrong between them. Liv had wanted to have a baby, to build a family, and Eric had been seemingly happy to try. But then, after more than a year of disappointments, she had been diagnosed with premature ovarian failure. They'd tried three rounds of in vitro using donor eggs before Eric had abruptly announced he was done—done with trying for a baby, done with trying to understand Liv's sadness, done with their marriage. Of course, Liv later found out that by then he had already started dating a twenty-four-year-old named Anemone, one of the administrative assistants at the Bergman Restaurant Group, the company he managed. "Friends, huh?" Liv finally replied. "Sure. Maybe you and I and your girlfriend can set up a weekly dinner date. That sounds cozy."

"Liv, I know you're angry. But this isn't Anemone's fault. You and I just outgrew each other. We weren't meant to be together anymore."

"And you were meant to be with a millennial vegan whose hippie parents named her after a species of jellyfish?"

"An anemone is actually a sea polyp," Eric corrected without meeting her eyes. He shrugged with exaggerated helplessness. "What can I say, Liv? She gets me."

"What exactly does she get? That you're a complete cliché? That you're the walking embodiment of a midlife crisis? That someday, when Anemone becomes inconvenient for you, you'll bail on her, too?"

Eric sighed and Liv saw pity in his eyes, which made her feel even worse. "Liv, be honest. Did you even love me anymore by the time we split up?"

She didn't answer, because how could she explain that she would have loved him forever if he'd given her the chance? That was what you were supposed to do with the people you promised your life to. It was just that by the end, she hadn't particularly *liked* him. But she'd been willing to work through it, to try to find her way back to who they'd once been. Her own parents had never gotten that chance; her father had died when Liv was just a baby, and her mother had flitted from relationship to relationship ever since. Liv had always vowed that her life would turn out differently. But maybe we were all doomed to repeat the mistakes of those who came before us, even if we knew better.

The thing was, Eric was right. They didn't belong together. Maybe they never had. And maybe going their separate ways was the best thing they could have done. But it still felt like he'd failed her when she needed him most.

When the silence had dragged on for too long, Eric spoke again. "So what are you going to do now? Are you going to try to get back out there into the workforce? You know you can ask me for a letter of recommendation if you need one."

Liv bit her lip, hating him a little for the way he was looking at her, like she was pathetic. It had been his suggestion, a year ago, that she quit her job as the VP of marketing at Bergman, the place they'd met fifteen years earlier. They'd worked side by side for a decade and a half, him rising through the ranks in the finance department while she rose to the top of the marketing department. They had been the perfect power couple—until they weren't.

Look, if we're doing in vitro for a third time, maybe you should just stay home and focus on that, he'd said last June. *Besides, once we have the baby, you'll want to take a leave of absence anyhow, right?* She had reluctantly agreed, but she saw now that following his advice had been a mistake, that it had been the first step in him ushering her out the door of her own life. The result was that when the bottom had dropped out, she was left with nothing—no child, no husband, no job, no savings. She was utterly adrift. "I'll figure it out," she mumbled.

"At least you've got your grandmother in the meantime." Eric's lips twitched. "I'm sure she's helping you, right?"

"She's been generous," Liv said stiffly. "I think she realizes she gave me some bad advice." Grandma Edith—her father's eccentric, wealthy mother, who lived in Paris—had been the one to insist on a prenup before Liv had married Eric, one that stipulated that if the marriage ended, neither was entitled to anything that originated with the other. It had obviously been intended to keep Eric from getting his hands on what would one day be Liv's inheritance, but since Grandma Edith was still alive, and Eric was making mid–six figures while Liv was unemployed, the document now seemed like an insane mistake. At least Grandma Edith had offered to pay for Liv's apartment while she figured out her life, but Liv felt guilty enough for taking the money without Eric rubbing it in.

"And yet she was so sure of it at the time." He chuckled. "Anyhow, Liv, I've got to get back to the office. But let me know if you need anything, all right? I guess I'll see you around."

He didn't wait for a reply. He left without a look back, and as Liv closed the door behind him, she had the sense she was finally shutting out the past and stepping into an uncertain future.

An hour later, Liv had finally worked up the courage to open the final box Eric had delivered. She felt as if she'd been punched in the gut when she sliced through the tape, lifted the flaps, and realized it contained their wedding album and two shoeboxes full of pictures from their life together, pictures that obviously meant nothing to Eric anymore. She flipped through the ones on top—honeymoon photos in which she and Eric held coconut drinks while standing on the beach in Maui, beaming at each other—before jamming them back into the box and backing away as if their mere proximity could wound her.

There was a sharp rapping on the door, and Liv looked up. She wasn't expecting anyone, and she'd only given her new address to a handful of people. Her sole friends during her marriage to Eric had been her coworkers at Bergman, and when she'd left her job last year, none of them had stayed in touch, which had only added to her feeling of being erased from her own life. Had Eric come back to discard another box of memories? She considered not answering, because she didn't want to face him again, but then there was another knock, louder and more insistent this time.

When she stood and peered out the peephole, she had to blink a few times to process what she was seeing. There, in the dimly lit hall, stood her ninety-nine-year-old, impossibly spry grandmother, white hair wound into a meticulous bun, gray tweed Chanel jacket perfectly tailored, black slacks impeccably cut. "Grandma Edith?" Liv asked in disbelief as she opened the door.

The old woman pursed her lips, her penciled-in eyebrows knitting. "Honestly, Olivia, is that how you dress when I'm not here to supervise?" The dig sounded almost polite wrapped in Grandma Edith's soft French accent. "Have I not taught you better than that?"

"I, uh, wasn't expecting you." Liv looked down at the torn

jeans and ratty sweatshirt she'd changed into after Eric had left, perfect clothes for moping in. "*Should* I have been expecting you?"

"Well, I am here, am I not?"

"But . . . what are you doing in New York?" When Liv had last spoken with her—three days earlier, when Grandma Edith called to crisply ask when the divorce would be final—there had been no talk of a transatlantic trip from Paris. Considering Grandma Edith's age, a flight to New York should have merited at least a mention.

"Well, I have come to get you, of course. Aren't you going to invite me in? I'm dying for a martini. And do not dare tell me you are out of gin. I would have to disown you immediately."

"Um, no," Liv said. "I have gin." She stepped gingerly aside and watched as Grandma Edith swept past her. She wondered fleetingly why they never hugged like normal people did.

"*D'accord*. Have you any blue cheese olives on hand?" Grandma Edith asked over her shoulder as Liv followed her in and shut the door. It was then that Liv realized Grandma Edith didn't have anything with her aside from her familiar Kelly bag.

"Where's your luggage, Grandma Edith?"

The older woman ignored her. "I would even take a garlic olive in a pinch."

"Um, I think I just have regular ones."

Grandma Edith harrumphed but seemed to accept this as she settled onto Liv's living room couch.

Liv was silent as she prepared her grandmother's drink, a task that had been hers from the time she was nine. A healthy dose of gin, a splash of dry vermouth, a few drops of olive juice, shaken with ice, and then strained.

"You really should chill the glass first, Olivia," Grandma Edith said in lieu of a thank-you as Liv handed over her drink. "Aren't you going to have one, too?"

"It's two in the afternoon, Grandma Edith. And I'm still trying to figure out what you're doing here."

The older woman shook her head. "Honestly, need you be so uptight?" She took a long sip. "Very well. If you must know, I'm here because today's the day you are officially free of that soul-sucking *salaud*. I hate to say I told you so, but . . ."

"So you've come to gloat."

Grandma Edith took another swallow of her martini, and Liv noticed fleetingly that her grandmother's hand was shaking. "I most certainly have not," she said. "I have come to help you pack your bags."

"Pack my bags?"

Grandma Edith sighed dramatically as she stood and beckoned Liv toward the bedroom. "Well, come on, then! We are already behind schedule."

"For *what*?"

"For our flight."

Liv just stared at her.

"Enough wallowing, now, Olivia. Our plane leaves in four and a half hours, and you know how security is at JFK."

"Grandma Edith, what on earth are you talking about?"

"Try to keep up, dear." Grandma Edith rolled her eyes and drained the rest of her martini. "We are going to Paris, of course."

three

MAY 1940

INÈS

The cellars beneath the Chauveau property were dark, dank, humid. The arched brick walls, carved into soft chalk and limestone, held the wetness in, had done so since Michel's great-grandfather had begun constructing them seven decades earlier, and because of that, they were the perfect place for champagne bottles to sleep on their way to becoming something great.

Inès knew this because Michel had told her the history of his family's property when he'd first begun courting her a year and a half ago. His father's family had been *vignerons*, winegrowers, since the sixteenth century, but it was only in the early 1800s that they'd begun to toy with the idea of producing their own wine. In nearby Reims and Épernay, and even the commune of Aÿ, massive champagne houses were making a fortune, while growers in the small villages still lived like peasants. When Michel's great-great-grandfather married the daughter of a textile magnate in 1839, there had finally been some money to purchase equipment and supplies.

The business had evolved slowly, and nearly stalled when Michel's eccentric great-grandfather became obsessed with building a network of caves underneath their property to rival the chalk-carved *crayères* of the great houses of Reims. The tunnels he had constructed, beginning in the 1870s, were so twisting and complex that during Inès's first week living at the Maison Chauveau, she'd gotten lost belowground for hours, a terrifying ordeal. Michel hadn't found her until well after nightfall.

"The tunnels go on for many kilometers and are quite confusing," he'd told a sobbing Inès as he led her into the evening air. "Don't worry, darling. You'll learn." Of course, Michel knew every centimeter of the maze by heart, had played hide-and-seek in the twisting caverns as a boy, had carved his name into the chalk portions of the walls alongside the names of his ancestors, had huddled there while bombs shredded the earth overhead during the Great War.

But even a year after that first frightening experience, Inès still wasn't accustomed to the dark stillness, the way the aging bottles crowded the caves like silent little coffins. She hadn't gotten used to the constant chill, as if the seasons aboveground ceased to exist, and she had never adjusted to the way the wind sometimes howled at the main entrance to the caves, a sound that made her think of the ghosts and wolves of fairy tales.

This was supposed to be a fairy tale, Inès thought with a pang of regret as she paused now to rub her throbbing shoulders. When she'd first met Michel, in November 1938, they'd seemed a perfect match; he had been entranced by her youth and her optimism, and she had been equally moved by his solidity, his wisdom, and his fascinating role in making a champagne that everyone in France knew of. It had all seemed so magical. Who would have thought that a mere eighteen months later, she would be wearing work boots and sliding twenty-kilo cases of wine toward the secret cave Michel's parents had constructed during the Great War to hide their valuables?

It was an ingenious installation, and the first time Michel had shown it to Inès, just after France had declared war against Hitler's Germany in September, her jaw had dropped; she never would have guessed there was an enormous storage cave lurking behind what looked like an impenetrable wall. A hidden door swung out from a hinge concealed between bricks, and when it was closed, it looked as if it was part of the decades-old stone and chalk tunnel. There was even a specially ordered Madonna, designed to appear permanent, in front of it, although the statue of the virgin was deceptively easy to move. Inès knew that be-cause she'd had to do so herself earlier that morning in order to access the hiding space, where they'd been slowly concealing bottles for months.

Alone in the caves, her arms and back aching, she felt a chill of foreboding. In January, as they'd lain in bed together one stormy night with the wind lashing the vines outside, Michel had predicted a terrible year for Champagne—a bad harvest, a shadow cast over their whole region. Inès had thought he was just being a pessimist, but now that the Germans were over the border, she wondered if he was, as usual, right about everything. While she respected his intellect, sometimes his inability to err could be stifling. It left no room for Inès to have thoughts or opinions that differed from his.

"Inès? Are you here?" A voice wafted down the narrow stone stairway from the main entrance to the cellars, which was behind a wooden door tucked into a stone wall behind the château where Michel and Inès lived. Inès closed her eyes briefly. It was Céline, the wife of Michel's *chef de cave*, Theo Laurent. "Michel said you might need some help."

"Yes, I'm here!" she called back, trying to sound friendly. She scratched her left forearm, a childish habit her mother had tried to break her of, telling her it was unladylike, that the harsh red streaks her fingernails left were unbecoming and juvenile. Still, the nervous tic returned whenever she was on edge. "I'm just headed back to the cave where the last of the twenty-eights are stored."

"*C'est bon.* I'll be right there." She could hear heavy footsteps on the stairs; Céline had ditched her stylish mules months ago, when the Marne was emptied of its men, and now wore work boots nearly every day. She was stronger than Inès, and more sure of herself, and Inès often felt like an inexperienced little girl next to her, though they were only a year apart.

Inès tried to pitch in, too, but she didn't have the same knack for it that Céline did, and she was often left in the dust—literally. Inès had no palate for tasting, though she tried; no skill for the bottling of blended wines; and no finesse for the racking of bottles, which had to be done with a sure hand. She suspected that the others thought she was just lazy, but the truth was, she was hesitant and unsure, and each time she broke a bottle, she lost a bit more confidence. She was useless.

The irony was that not so long ago, that's exactly how Michel had wanted her to be. When he had proposed marriage to her a little more than a year earlier, he had told her he would take care of her, that he didn't want her lifting a finger.

"But you see, I'm happy to help out," she had tried to explain.

"It's my responsibility to take care of you now," Michel had said, cupping her chin gently with a calloused hand and looking into her eyes. "You won't have to work."

"But—"

"Please, my dear," he had interrupted. "My father never had

to ask my mother to bother herself with the champagne production, and I don't want to ask you to, either. You'll be the lady of the house now."

But then war had been declared that September, and the draft had stolen their workers. Michel had slowly changed his tune, at first asking her to do small tasks with mumbled apologies. She made sure to let him know at every opportunity that it was perfectly all right, and that she truly wanted to pitch in. But as the autumn dragged into winter and the labor shortage began to take a toll on their production schedule, he had implored her to take on more and more responsibilities. She scrambled to do everything he wanted, but there was often a learning curve, and as the months wore on, she could feel the heat of his deepening disappointment in her.

She pasted on a smile as Céline rounded the corner now. Even in faded trousers and muddy boots, Céline was beautiful, which annoyed Inès, though she knew that was irrational. But then Inès looked more closely at the other woman, and even in the darkness, she could see that Céline's eyes were rimmed in red.

"Are you all right?" Inès asked.

Céline immediately ducked her head, hiding her face behind a curtain of long brown hair. "Oh yes, just fine."

"But you've been crying." Inès knew she was being tactless, but it simply didn't seem fair for Céline to pretend that everything was normal when clearly, above their heads, it was all falling apart. Then again, in the year since Inès had married Michel, the two women had never really become friends, though Inès had tried. Céline was quiet and serious, always tromping around with a frown on her face, while Inès did her best to look on the bright side. A month after Inès had arrived at the Maison Chauveau, she'd overheard Céline whispering to Theo that Inès's constant optimism grated on her because it was so unrealistic. After that, Inès had at least understood the exasperated looks Céline sometimes cast her way.

Céline drew a shuddering breath. "Yes, well, I'm worried about my family, Inès."

"Oh." Inès was temporarily at a loss. "Well, I imagine they're all right. I'm sure the Germans aren't harming civilians."

Céline made a sound somewhere between a laugh and a sob. "Inès, don't you remember that my family is Jewish?"

"Well, yes, of course." The truth was that Inès didn't think about it much. It had come up in conversation a few times over the past few months, when there were news reports of Jewish roundups in Germany. Céline's father and his family were Jews, but Inès knew that Céline's mother—who had died two years earlier—had been Catholic, and that Céline hadn't been raised to be particularly religious at all. "But you mustn't worry. This is still France, after all."

Céline was silent for long enough that Inès thought perhaps

she had no reply. "Do you really think that will matter when the Germans have control of things?"

Inès bit her lip. Céline didn't have to look at every situation as if it were the end of the world. "There's no word of anything happening to Jews here," she said confidently. "You'll see. It will be fine."

"Right." Céline turned away without another word. Inès watched as she bent, lifted a crate of twenty-eights from the floor, and trudged down the tunnel toward the hidden cavern.

Inès grabbed a crate of her own and hurried after her, her back aching in protest, her underused biceps burning. "You're from near Dijon, though, right?"

"Yes, just to the south, Nuits-Saint-Georges."

"Well then, your father and your grandparents are much farther from the Germans than we are, yes?" Inès knew that Dijon was some three hundred kilometers south of Champagne. "They're probably already heading south." Michel had explained that hundreds of thousands of refugees were clogging the roads as the Germans approached.

"No." Céline didn't look at Inès as she placed her crate on the stone floor of the hidden cave. "My father manages a winery, and nearly all his workers were sent to the front. He felt he could not leave. He's quite loyal to the owner, who has been good to him. My grandparents decided to remain with him."

"Well, surely they will be fine."

"Surely they will be fine," Céline repeated, but Inès could hear the bitterness in her tone, the fear, so she went silent and returned to her bottles.

Inès supposed she would be worrying about her own relatives, too, if she had any left. But both of her parents had died when Inès was just sixteen—her father felled by a stroke, her mother by a heart attack two months later. There were no siblings, no extended family; Inès was entirely alone. Thankfully, her dear friend Edith's family had taken her in, and Inès had found a home again.

It made sense, then, that in early 1938, when Edith had fallen in love with a young restaurateur named Edouard Thierry, who had inherited his family's brasserie in Reims, Inès would accompany her to Champagne. She had no reason to remain in their hometown of Lille, and though she resented Edouard at first for taking Edith away, she was surprised and moved by his offer for her to come and stay with them in his large apartment, situated just over the brasserie. *You are her dearest friend*, he had said solemnly as she wiped her tears away after their modest wedding at the baroque-domed Église Sainte-Marie-Madeleine in Old Lille. *Of course you will be with us for as long as you like.*

She hadn't believed at first that he actually wanted her there, but he'd been a genuinely enthusiastic host, often including her in social engagements and sometimes even asking her opinion about world affairs. He'd even let her help out behind the brasserie's bar on occasion to make a bit of money. When Edouard brought his old friend Michel Chauveau around for dinner one cold evening in the fall of 1938, announcing that Michel was a *very* eligible bachelor, it seemed predestined that Inès would fall in love with him.

"Oh, Michel is so handsome!" Edith had exclaimed later that night, clapping her hands as Edouard walked Michel out, leaving the two women alone. "Don't you think, Inès?"

Inès had smiled, her heart still fluttering. "Did you see his eyes?" They were a piercing blue, the kind that could see right through you. He was tall, solidly built, with sandy blond hair and sharp features, and though his suit was a bit outdated, he wore it well.

"His eyes?" Edith had repeated with a laugh. "I noticed only that they were focused on you all night, my dear friend. And how could he resist? You're beautiful." Edith had a way of making Inès feel that way. She had always been that kind of friend, the kind who lifted you up when you were down. "Can you believe he owns the Maison Chauveau?" Edith added, raising both eyebrows meaningfully.

"And yet he was so modest," Inès said. He had come bearing chilled bottles from three different Chauveau vintages, but he deflected Inès's questions about his champagne empire gracefully, turning the attention back on her, asking her about her life in Lille, her friendship with Edith, and whether she'd yet had a chance to tour Champagne.

Later, she and Edith agreed that he had been asking her for a date. Like Edouard, he was several years older than Edith and Inès, and more serious than they were, too. Inès supposed it was because he and Edouard had both been forced into their family businesses early; they had taken on responsibilities she could barely imagine when they were in their early twenties.

"I haven't ventured beyond Reims yet," Inès had told him. "But I would love to see the countryside."

"Would you?" Michel smiled, and Inès's stomach fluttered. He had called on her the following week, and by the spring, they were engaged. They married the first week of June, for there was no reason to wait; like Inès, Michel had no living family.

It had all seemed so very dazzling at first. Inès was the new wife of the owner of a prestigious champagne house! She would be living in the midst of rolling vineyards! She would drink bubbly every night!

But the reality was quite different. Once Inès and Michel were wed, they rarely went into Reims; the picturesque scenery became mundane after a while; and even the nightly bottle they opened with dinner began to feel repetitive.

The biggest problem, though, was that Inès no longer had Edith to gossip with on a daily basis, or even Edouard to engage her in conversation, now that she was no longer living with them. Michel was even more introspective and serious than he had seemed during their brief courtship; they often spent entire meals in complete silence as he ruminated about problems with the production schedule or issues with growers—neither of which he wanted to discuss with Inès.

Inès had imagined that she and Michel would go back to Reims often to see their friends, but though the small city was only forty minutes from Ville-Dommange by car, it might as well have been in another country. The demands of champagne production kept Michel busy from dawn until dusk most days, and he didn't like her taking the car without him. Inès was effectively trapped in a place that still didn't feel like home.

And though Inès had met the burly, dark-haired Theo and his strong, elegant wife, Céline, on her first visit to the Maison Chauveau and imagined they might become her friends, that hadn't happened, either. Theo was so immersed in his work that he could vanish for weeks at a time, while Céline was as quiet and solemn as Michel. The more Inès tried to bond with her over gossip or news from town, the more Céline seemed to withdraw.

Now, with war looming on the horizon, Inès felt more isolated than ever. In the depths of the cellars, she and Céline should have been sharing their fears about what was to come. Instead, they worked in silence, the only sound the quiet thud of each crate landing in its new hidden home.

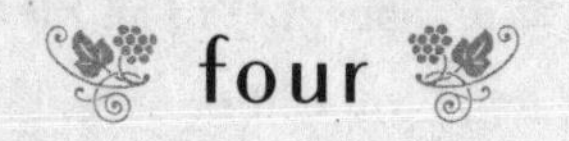

four

JUNE 1940

CÉLINE

On a Friday morning in June, days after the Germans had finally marched into the Champagne region, Theo came rushing into the small cottage he shared with Céline, his face flushed.

"They are finally here in Ville-Dommange," he blurted out. "The Germans. Come quickly."

Céline felt a surge of fear. She had known this was coming, for the Germans had been pillaging the towns around them since they'd swept in earlier that week. She'd been holding out hope that somehow their small village would be overlooked, but of course that was silly. The conquerors would want their reward—in this case, the endless bottles of fine champagne that huddled in the dark cellars beneath the countryside. But what if the Germans were after something else, too? What if they were coming because they knew Céline was half Jewish? "Should I hide?" she asked.

"This isn't about you," Theo said instantly, his dark brows

drawing together. "It is happening to all the champagne houses. Come, Céline. We are not in danger as long as we do what they say. And right now, Michel needs us."

Céline couldn't say no to that, not after the kindness Michel had shown them. When Theo had applied for the job of head winemaker at the Maison Chauveau four years earlier, just after marrying Céline in Nuits-Saint-Georges, he'd already been turned down from several larger champagne houses in Reims because he'd learned his trade in Burgundy rather than in Champagne. But Michel hadn't cared at all about his lack of pedigree. "You are a skilled winemaker; that much is clear," he had said after reviewing Theo's references and doing several rounds of tasting and blending with him. "Any house would be lucky to have you."

And that had been that. Michel had offered them the former caretaker's cottage, just fifty meters to the right of the main house, as part of Theo's salary, and Theo had accepted. Since that day, Michel had been generous to a fault, treating the Laurents like family, inviting them every so often to Sunday dinners in the much grander main house, even including them in holiday celebrations. He and Theo had been almost like brothers for a time, although since war had been declared in September, Céline had seen a growing distance between them. Theo wanted to pretend that nothing was happening, while Michel was determined to look the future square in the eye, even if it was frightening and uncertain. Céline would never say so, but she thought Michel was right, while her husband was being shortsighted.

And so, despite her hammering heart and clammy palms, Céline smoothed back her hair and forced a smile. She was already dressed for the day in dungarees and work boots, a white cotton blouse buttoned over her camisole. She had planned to accompany Theo to a nearby vineyard to inspect some of the early buds, though it was clear that would have to wait. "Very well," she told Theo. "Let's go."

He grasped her hand, squeezing her fingers too hard, and pulled her out the door. Down the lane, less than a kilometer away, Céline could see a small caravan of military trucks, dust swirling around them as they approached. The hum of their engines cut through the morning stillness, a low and insistent buzz of warning. "*Merde*," Theo muttered. "They're here sooner than I thought they'd be."

Theo and Céline ran to the main house. The door was already open, Michel and Inès waiting for them just inside, their faces pale. "What will we do?" Inès asked as soon as they entered. For once, she looked undone, her dark auburn hair swirling untamed and wild. She was in black T-strap heels and a long blue dress with a fitted waist, somehow still delicately pretty in the midst of all the chaos. Inès looked from Theo to Céline and then back to Michel. "We have to do something!" She put her palms on her cheeks and then ran her nails down the lengths of her arms, as if she didn't know what to do with her hands.

"We wait," Michel said, closing the door. The dark stillness of the front hall engulfed them. "We wait, and we see what they want."

Less than a minute later, after the squealing of brakes and a cacophony of rough laughter and deep voices outside, there was a heavy knock on their front door.

"Calm," Michel reminded them, and then he swung the door open to greet their invaders. Céline could see three German soldiers, all in full uniform, two toting long rifles, standing on the step, and behind them, a half dozen more. They were young, perhaps in their early twenties, except for the broad-shouldered man in front, who appeared to be closer to forty. His hand hovered over the holstered pistol at his hip.

"Hello," Michel said evenly, as if answering the door to Germans was an everyday occurrence. "How can we help you?"

"Help us?" The older man snorted. "You can *help us* by showing us where the entrance to your champagne cellar is."

Michel didn't reply right away, and in those frozen few seconds, Céline studied the man. He was tall, dark-haired, with a narrow mustache, small eyes, and refined, almost elegant features that were currently arranged in a sneer. His forest green uniform jacket with its rigid black collar was cinched with a brown leather belt and adorned with bronze buttons, medals, and a Nazi insignia. His pants were gray, and below them, his black jackboots gleamed in the sunlight. Despite the heat of the morning, there wasn't a single crease on him. He was an officer, she realized, in charge of the others. His French was perfect, hinting at some level of education and grooming.

"Certainly," Michel replied evenly. "Might I ask what you're looking for?"

"You may not."

Michel and Theo exchanged looks, and then Michel stood back, ushering the soldiers inside as if they were honored guests. He led them through the house and out the back door, and it was only then that Céline realized that the small secondary entrance to the cellars, the one Michel's great-grandfather had installed in the kitchen in case the family needed a quick route to the cellars, had been hidden behind a large armoire. Instead, Michel—with Theo a few steps behind him—seemed to be taking the soldiers to the main entrance in the stone wall that separated their garden from the vineyards beyond. When Michel's great-grandfather had constructed the elaborate tunnels to rival the crayères of the larger champagne houses, he had also installed an imposing entryway made of stone, closed off by an ornately carved wooden door so it looked as grand as possible. "Stay here," Michel warned over his shoulder, looking first at Inès and then at Céline.

But the officer placed a firm hand on Michel's forearm and glanced back at the women. He smiled, and there was something about the expression—cold and lupine—that chilled Céline to the bone. "No," he said, "I think the women will come with us, too."

Céline didn't resist when Inès grabbed her hand, lacing her tiny, childlike fingers through Céline's longer, narrower ones. Together they followed their husbands through the imposing cellar door and down the narrow steps, their hurried footsteps clicking on the stone like the insistent tap of woodpeckers. One of the soldiers whistled in appreciation as the first cave full of bottles came into view, but the man behind him nudged him and said in German, "Oh, come on now, this is nothing compared to Veuve Clicquot Ponsardin."

Céline understood, because her mother, who had grown up near the German border, had taught her German at home when she was a girl. But she played dumb, keeping her eyes wide and her expression neutral. She knew that she was at an advantage, however little it might be worth, if the Germans felt they could speak openly in front of her.

"Well? Where are your 1928s?" the officer asked, looking around suspiciously. "And your thirty-fours?"

"We have only a hundred odd bottles left of each vintage." Michel met the officer's gaze. "But if you'll follow me, they're just this way."

The officer narrowed his eyes, but he allowed Michel to lead the group down the main tunnel to a cave on the left, where Céline knew Michel had deliberately left out a few racks of the best wines. A total absence would be suspicious; a shortage could be explained by saying that the remaining bottles had sold. "Here we are," Michel said, waving his arm toward the room. "Just on the floor there to the right."

"Hmph." The officer beckoned one of his men, and together they lifted up one of the crates and pulled a bottle out. It was indeed a twenty-eight, one of the most valuable of their collection. Behind the Virgin Mary nestled into the curve of the hall, its sisters lay silently in wait. "Where are the rest?" the officer asked, turning to Michel, his expression hard, his right hand drifting toward his pistol again.

"Oh, we've been nearly sold out for a long time. Twenty-eight was a very good year, you know. Very in demand. Thirty-four, too." Michel furrowed his brow. He was a far better actor than Céline had realized. "Please. Take what we have. You'll have no quarrel from me."

The officer gestured to two of his men, who scrambled to begin grabbing bottles. "That will do. Now leave us to it."

"Certainly." Michel took Inès's hand and began to walk briskly back toward the stairs. Céline and Theo followed. The four of them were silent until they'd made their way back upstairs, across the back garden, and into the kitchen of the main house.

"Michel, you practically *thanked* them for looting our cellars!" Inès cried as soon as they were alone.

"What is it I should have done, Inès?" Michel sounded weary. "It's anarchy out there. We have to plan for the future, and if they think we're hiding something, they'll tear our caves apart."

"But did you have to be so . . . submissive?" Inès demanded, her voice rising an octave in indignation. "This is our property!"

"Inès!" It was the first time Céline had heard Michel raise his voice. He raked his hand through his hair as Inès blinked at him like a wounded doe. "Darling," he said more calmly. "This is the worst of it. We wait out this storm, and the German authorities will be in control of their men in a few days. Until then, we just have to survive."

Inès opened her mouth to reply, but she was interrupted by a voice behind them. "It seems you French are wiser than you look." They all whirled around and saw the German officer framed in the sunlit back doorway, a cigarette in his hand trailing a sinewy ribbon of smoke. "Your only job now is to get by. *Verstanden?*"

No one answered, so after the silence had ticked on for too long, Céline replied for all of them. "Yes, sir. We understand. You'll have no trouble from us."

The officer smiled slightly, which made him look even more

dangerous, more sinister. Or maybe it was just the way he was suddenly studying her that was so unsettling; it was as if he was noticing her for the first time. His gaze lingered on the top buttons of her blouse. She resisted the urge to flinch, to cower, and finally, his eyes traveled back up to her face. "I'm glad to hear it," he said.

Céline swallowed hard as the officer turned his attention back to Michel. "Now. What is in that smaller house?" He gestured toward Céline and Theo's cottage. "My men wish to see."

An hour later, both homes had been emptied, along with dozens of cases of the Maison Chauveau's best champagne. Michel had insisted they all remain passive as the Germans grabbed furniture, ripped generations-old tapestries from the walls, raided their pantries, and carried out precious loaves of bread, jars of jam, cans of coffee. The Germans took everything—armchairs, blankets, mattresses—even the old grandfather clock that had stood watch for more than a hundred years in the parlor. They piled it all in the garden outside the main house, crushing the bed of red peonies Inès had stubbornly tended even after Michel had insisted they'd need to convert all remaining tillable soil to vegetable gardens. It was a moot point now.

Atop the pile, Céline saw the faded quilt her mother had made her to celebrate her marriage to Theo, and she felt suddenly furious. What would these men need with something so personal? It was the middle of June; the nights were warm enough. No, the quilt represented something worse—a need to plunder for the sake of plundering. She blinked back tears; she knew she should be more concerned about the loss of furniture, of canned and jarred food that would have taken them through the winter. But the quilt was one of the last things she had to remind her of her mother.

The men poured out from the houses, having finally taken everything of any conceivable value. As the men loaded up the trucks, the officer in charge strolled over, his thumbs hooked in his belt.

"We will be back for more champagne when we need it." There were crumbs on his mustache, a smear of jelly on the right side of his chin. "All you have belongs to Germany now."

Michel coughed and pressed his lips into a thin line.

The officer studied him. "*Wir werden uns wiedersehen,*" he said, his tone menacing. No one responded, and he looked amused by their lack of understanding. Céline made sure to keep her expression neutral, and when the officer's gaze landed on her again, lingering for long enough that she could feel Theo tensing beside her, she forced herself not to blink, not to flinch, until he finally turned on his heel and strode off.

And then, as quickly as they had arrived, the Germans clambered back into their trucks and pulled away with their spoils, hooting and hollering until they were out of sight.

"What did he say?" Inès asked, her tone bordering on hysterical, once the convoy was finally gone. The sudden silence felt ominous. "Does anyone know what he said?"

"He said we will meet again," Céline replied. There was no need, though, to translate the intent behind the words. They were a threat, and even in the heat of the warm Champagne sunshine, Céline's blood felt like it had turned to ice.

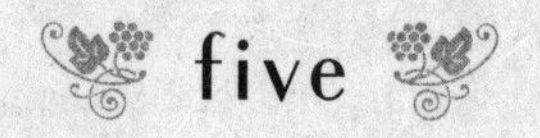

five

JUNE 2019

LIV

"You need to snap out of it," Grandma Edith said as Liv stared out the window at the dark sky over the Atlantic, wondering when she'd see the first rays of dawn over the eastern horizon.

Liv turned, surprised to see her grandmother sitting up, studying her in the muted lighting of their first-class cabin. They had boarded the Delta flight hours ago, but Liv hadn't been able to sleep, despite the fact that the lie-flat premium seats were even more comfortable than Liv had imagined they'd be.

"I didn't know you were awake, too." Liv put a hand on her grandmother's arm. It was cold, covered in goose bumps, and Liv instinctively reached for the blanket that had slipped to her grandmother's lap.

"Leave it," Grandma Edith said, pushing Liv away. "I'm fine. But you aren't. You're wallowing."

"I'm not wallowing. I'm just sad."

"About that good-for-nothing Eric?"

Liv picked at her thumbnail. "About the fact that I don't even know who I am anymore."

"Oh for God's sake, Olivia, I hope you're not telling me that you had your identity tied up with that good-for-nothing. I know that after your father died, your mother went through husbands like other people go through cartons of milk, but I thought you were better than that."

Liv gave her a look. "I just meant that this whole thing blind-sided me, and now I feel a little lost, okay? I'm forty-one with no husband, no kids, and no job. It's not where I thought I'd be."

"Yes, well, if you let Eric take everything from you, then he wins, doesn't he?" Grandma Edith shook her head and pushed her call button. "And that would be a disappointment indeed."

Liv chewed her lip as a flight attendant approached, her mascara smudged, her hair flattened on one side. She'd clearly been sleeping, but Grandma Edith didn't seem to care as she crisply ordered a gin martini and some pretzels. The flight attendant delivered the order a moment later with a yawn and shot Liv a questioning look. Liv could only shrug. No one ever seemed to know what to make of the diminutive French nonagenarian who drank like a 1960s advertising executive.

"Now, where were we?" Grandma Edith asked after she'd taken a long sip of her cocktail, her third since boarding. Clearly the secret to the old woman's longevity was an unwavering commitment to pickling her liver. "Oh yes, your malaise. It's not terribly becoming, dear. My mother always said that a lady should find a way to solve her problems without complaint. I think that was very good advice, though I admit I didn't always adhere to it."

"With all due respect, Grandma Edith, maybe your mother never had to deal with infertility and a husband who couldn't stand the sight of her anymore."

"No, dear, she only had to deal with the violent death of her brother in the First World War, terrifying nightly bombings while the Germans ransacked France, and my father returned from Verdun half blind and full of misplaced anger."

Liv stared at her. "Grandma Edith, I'm so sorry. I had no idea your family had gone through all that."

"Yes, well, some things are best left alone. The point is, many people lose more than they can imagine, and they still find a way to carry on." When she lifted her martini again, her hand was trembling. She glanced at Liv, and then she looked past her, her gaze very far away. "I found a way, Olivia. And you must, too."

Paris was bustling, even though it wasn't quite eight in the morning as their chauffeured car wove through the narrow streets of the seventh arrondissement. Liv gazed out the window at the boulangeries already crowded with people, the florists just setting up for the day, the fromageries with their overflowing displays of cheeses. Liv cracked the window and breathed in deeply, inhaling the familiar mélange of yeasty bread, faint cigarette smoke, and flowers—a combination that was uniquely Parisian. She had been here so many times as a child that the scent should have triggered happy recollections of running through the Tuileries gardens with her grandmother strolling behind her, a cigarette pinched between two narrow fingers.

Instead, the memory that dug its claws into her was of a more recent trip, one she took with Eric right after he'd proposed thirteen years ago. She couldn't marry him in good conscience without Grandma Edith's approval. It was supposed to have been a mere formality, but Grandma Edith had disliked him from the start for reasons Liv couldn't fathom. Eric hadn't liked Grandma Edith much, either; he'd told Liv on their first morning there that the old woman seemed too showy.

"I think she just lives comfortably, that's all," Liv had protested. "Besides, you know how generous she always is with me."

Eric had rolled his eyes. "Yeah, well, it must be nice to be rolling in money she didn't actually earn."

"What are you talking about? We have no idea where her money comes from."

"And you don't think that's weird?"

Liv shrugged. "I think it's old-fashioned. She always says it's vulgar to talk about finances."

"Well, regardless, she doesn't seem to believe I'm worthy of a cent of her fortune."

"What?"

"You're going to tell me that having me sign a prenup wasn't all her idea?"

Of course, it had been Grandma Edith who had insisted on the document, which seemed pointless to Liv. But the older woman was generously paying for their wedding, and acquiescing to the request seemed a small price to pay to keep the peace. "Look, does it matter? It's not like we're going to get divorced. I love you."

Later, when Eric had been in the shower, Liv had broached the subject with Grandma Edith. "You *do* like him, don't you?"

It had taken Grandma Edith a long time to meet Liv's gaze. "No, not particularly."

"But you barely know him! How can you possibly say that?"

"A lifetime of experience, dear. When you know, you know."

"Well, you're wrong! And it's not your place to be judging the person I love!"

"Someone has to be the voice of reason," Grandma Edith replied, looking her in the eye. "And your mother is too busy gallivanting around with her boyfriends to say a thing."

"Maybe she just respects my point of view more than you do."

"Or maybe she hasn't realized yet that matters of the heart can make you both blind and stupid." Grandma Edith shrugged while Liv seethed. "But it's your life. Marry him if you want. Just don't say I didn't warn you."

Now, nearly a decade and a half later, the words still rang in Liv's ears. "Grandma Edith?" she asked softly as the car turned right on the rue Fabert and the gold dome of Les Invalides came into view.

"Hmm?"

"How did you see through Eric so quickly when I first brought him here to meet you?"

"You are in Paris, and still you are thinking of him?" Her grandmother clucked her disapproval. "Let him go."

"I have," Liv said. "Honestly. I just—I don't know how I got it so wrong when you knew exactly who he was right from the start."

Grandma Edith shifted in her seat, her eyes watery. "It's not your fault, Olivia, not really. When you're young, you see only the future. When you grow older, you see the past." She turned to stare out the window. After a long pause, she spoke again, her voice quivering in a way Liv had never heard before. "And the past has a way of showing you things clearly, whether you like it or not."

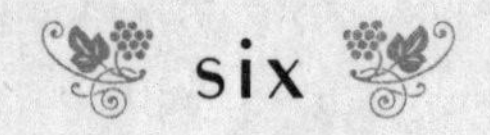

six

SEPTEMBER 1940

INÈS

The grapes themselves were the first to resist the Germans, dying on the vines or simply committing suicide in the middle of the night by falling to earth in the darkness. Grape moths and harvest worms had invaded along with the German army, destroying so much of the year's crop that the champagne houses were already counting their losses before a single piece of fruit had been pulled from the vines.

On the first morning of the harvest that year, Inès and Céline accompanied Michel and Theo to one of the vineyards that supplied many of their Pinot Meunier grapes, and Inès watched with growing unease as children and old men did the work that in years past had belonged almost wholly to strong, able-bodied laborers.

The harvesters worked in pairs, cutting clusters of plump black grapes from the vines with secateurs and placing them into small baskets, which were then carried by some of the school-aged children to large wicker bins called *mannequins*.

"They are not working quickly enough," Theo muttered, exchanging worried glances with Michel.

"We should help," Céline said.

"*Non.*" Theo turned away. "You will need to save your strength. We have our own to harvest, too."

"Yes, we should return to our domaine," Michel said. "This batch should begin arriving soon. We must prepare."

Inès knew that the grapes that were being clipped now would go to the press in their cellars by that afternoon, their juice extracted by machines that held four thousand kilos of fruit at a time in circular baskets. Plates would be lowered, crushing the fruit and forcing their juice down the sides and base of the press. The first hundred liters or so, full of impurities from the skins, would be discarded, and then the cuvée—the juice richest in sugar—would begin to flow into open tanks. Once two thousand fifty liters had been extracted, a final pressing or two would produce five hundred additional liters of a fruitier liquid called the *taille.* All the runs would be clarified and brought deeper into the caves for finishing.

There, Theo would start the fermentation process, and by November, the wine—still without its sparkle—would be racked to age, awaiting a series of tastings by Theo and Michel, who together would decide on the final blend that would make up the champagne from the 1940 harvest. It was a fascinating, complex process filled with lots of strict rules and regulations Inès was still trying to understand.

"I'm worried," Inès said from the passenger seat as they rode home, all four of them crammed into Michel's Citroën. "The workers were losing so many grapes."

"It was a doomed harvest from the start." Michel's tone was grim, his knuckles white as he gripped the steering wheel. "Anyhow, they were doing their best. Now we'll have to do the same."

There was silence for a moment.

"But what will we do if we don't get as many grapes as we expected we would?" Inès asked.

Michel looked at her in the passenger seat. "We will make do."

"But *how*?" Inès persisted.

In the back seat, Theo cleared his throat, and Michel glanced at him before turning to Inès. "Darling, it's not your concern."

"But *of course* it is," Inès persisted, though she could see her husband's face darkening. "Why won't you talk to me about any of this, Michel? I just want to help. The Maison Chauveau is my future as much as it is yours."

She'd meant the words as an expression of solidarity, but as he shook his head, he only looked angry. It seemed to be his default reaction to her most of the time these days.

It hadn't been like this at the beginning. Michel had seemed enchanted by her inexperience. When she'd asked questions, he'd been happy to answer, explaining complicated steps of the champagne-making process in a way that allowed her to understand.

But things had begun to change just after war was declared. Now, when she inquired about something, he usually answered curtly, dismissively. She knew he had a lot on his mind, but it hurt. She missed the way they'd once laughed together, confided in each other, but that had only lasted for the first few months of their marriage anyhow. What if that had never been real, and this was what the future had in store for her?

"You'll just have to trust me, Inès," Michel said at last, his voice tight. "I have it handled."

"But—" Inès began.

"I'm sure we will make the best of what we have at the end, Inès," Céline interrupted from the back seat. "We'll be able to salvage something beautiful. We always do. You needn't worry."

Inès wondered if she was imagining the condescension in the other woman's tone. And who was she to speak for Michel and Theo, as if she was one of them, three against one? "Yes, thank you, Céline," Inès said stiffly. "Quite helpful." She turned to stare out the window so no one in the car could see the tears of frustration in her eyes.

Back at the Maison Chauveau twenty minutes later, Michel and Theo headed for the cellars to make their final preparations to receive the grapes for the press, while Céline accompanied Inès into the main house. Despite the shortage of available food, they'd managed to assemble the ingredients for a giant vat of rutabaga and turnip soup and several loaves of bread to feed the workers who would arrive the next day to begin harvesting on the Maison Chauveau's own plots.

They started off working side by side as they peeled and chopped the vegetables, the only sound the steady *slip-slip* of their knives.

"I'm sorry if I offended you earlier," Céline said, breaking the uneasy quiet between them.

Inès didn't look at her. "Yes, well, I don't think I'm wrong to be worried."

"You're not."

"Then why does Michel jump down my throat every time I say a word these days?" The question was meant to be rhetorical, so Inès was surprised when Céline spoke again.

"He's under a lot of pressure, Inès."

Inès gritted her teeth and attacked the turnip she was holding with a vengeance. "I realize that, Céline. You don't actually need to explain my husband's state of mind to me."

Céline didn't say anything for a few seconds. "I'm sorry. I didn't mean to overstep."

"Of course you did." Inès set her knife down. She had tried

for more than a year to be as pleasant as possible to Céline, in hopes that the other woman would finally view her as a peer, but she was sick and tired of playing nice while everyone else walked all over her. "You think I'm a fool, Céline. You think I don't care about what's happening here, but I do. I know I'm not as good at helping out in the caves as you are, but I'm not the useless idiot you like to believe I am." Inès choked on the last words as she swallowed a sob.

Céline sighed. "I don't think you're useless, Inès. I think . . . I think you're just new at this. It's a lot to learn."

"I'm trying, Céline, I really am."

The silence that descended felt awkward, uncomfortable. Inès returned to peeling vegetables, her eyes stinging with tears she refused to cry in front of Céline.

"Look, I'm sorry," Céline said after a while. "I haven't always been very fair to you."

Inès looked up. "No, you haven't. I know we don't have much in common, Céline, but I used to imagine that you and I would rely on each other one day. After all, we're stuck out here in the middle of nowhere together. Michel never seems to listen to me anymore, and, well, it would be nice to have a friend."

"We're friends, Inès."

"Are we?"

"Of course." But Céline didn't look up or offer anything else, and as Inès lapsed back into uneasy silence, she felt even more estranged from the woman beside her than she had before.

By the time the vines had fallen into their late autumn slumber and the mornings sparkled with frost, Inès was exhausted. She rose each day before the sun and followed Michel sleepily into the caves, where they affixed labels to bottles from the 1936 harvest and prepared shipments, though it was hard to know when they might have regular clients again.

One night in November, long after darkness had fallen, Michel came up from the caves, his cheeks flushed and his eyes wild. "Klaebisch is coming in the morning," he announced to Inès, who was standing in the kitchen, frowning into their nearly empty cupboard. "Emile from the commission just sent a messenger to inform us."

"What does he want?" Inès asked. Otto Klaebisch was the newly appointed German overseer of wine production in Champagne, the *Beauftragter für den Weinimport Frankreich*, a man they had dubbed the *weinführer.* His arrival in Champagne that July had been somewhat of a relief, for it had put an end to the cellar looting. Besides, he came from a good family that had been involved for a long time in the wine trade; he had even been born in Cognac, where his parents had been brandy merchants before the Great War. If Champagne was going to be ruled by an invader, it might as well be someone who understood their work, their way of life. But Champagne's taste for him had quickly soured when he requisitioned Bertrand de Vogüé's personal château at Veuve Clicquot Ponsardin and moved right in.

"No doubt to demand more wine," Michel said through gritted teeth.

"And what will you say?" Inès asked.

"I will do my best to accommodate him."

Inès clenched her jaw. "They cannot do this."

"Inès, of course they can." Michel sounded weary. "This will be a long war, and we must do what we can to survive. We've talked about this, yes?"

"Yes," Inès mumbled, knowing she'd once again said the wrong thing.

The next morning, Inès and Michel rose even earlier than usual to finish labeling the last of their bottles so they would be ready by the time Klaebisch arrived. Inès changed into a pale green dress that swished against her calves, pulled her hair back into a low chignon, and swiped on a bit of lipstick. Before the war, this was how she had always looked—elegant, put together, fashionable. Now, it had been so long since she'd dressed nicely that she barely recognized herself in the mirror.

"You are making much effort for our occupiers," Michel said with a frown as she emerged from their bedroom to stand beside him in the parlor.

"Don't you think it's important that he take us seriously?" Inès asked, smoothing her dress. She felt suddenly self-conscious when Michel didn't answer. "Are Theo and Céline joining us?"

Michel shook his head. "I thought it better if Klaebisch does not meet Céline. The German opinion on Jews, well . . . Céline's situation might be less secure than ours."

"But she doesn't fall under the *statut des Juifs*," Inès pointed out. In October, the French government had issued restrictions on Jews, but only those who had at least three Jewish grandparents. Céline had just two.

"But who knows when the Nazis will change their mind? It's better to be cautious."

In truth, Céline's absence would be a relief; Inès wasn't sure she could take any more of the other woman's brooding silence. In the past few weeks, Céline had withdrawn into herself even further, talking only to Michel and Theo curtly about wine production. Inès wondered how on earth Theo managed to bear her coldness behind closed doors.

Herr Klaebisch arrived promptly at eight in the morning, accompanied by two German soldiers who hung back and mumbled to each other. The weinführer was a tall man, his black hair greased, his jowly face punctuated by a wide, beak-like nose. His hooded eyes seemed to glint in the morning light as he gazed around their house, taking everything in. "Thank you for receiving me," he said, his French as impeccable as that of the beady-eyed officer who had led the looting of their house in June. "You will show me to the cellars now?"

Inès trailed along after Michel and Herr Klaebisch, surprised to hear the almost friendly conversation between the two. The weinführer was asking about the composition of the local soil, and Michel was expounding about how the sand mixed with the native chalk in the vineyards west of Reims helped keep the vines moist, even in dry weather. Inès couldn't help but think that the German must already know this; he'd been in Champagne for months and in the wine trade for years. But he seemed to be listening intently.

"And yet the harvest this year was a failure," Klaebisch said mildly as they descended into the cool darkness. "We must do better next year. This region is very important to the führer."

"But of course you understand that when our labor force is taken away, it is impossible to get the most out of the vineyards, *oui*?" Michel replied. "You know that this year's yield was down by eighty percent. Here, we are doing the work of many men to make the champagne. Even our wives are helping with the labor."

Klaebisch didn't respond for a long moment, and Inès feared

that Michel had overstepped. But then they reached the bottom of the stairs, and the weinführer cleared his throat. "Monsieur Chauveau, I understand your plight, but in wartime, we all must make do with less, *ja*?"

"Of course."

"Then I imagine you will find a way. I have always found the French very resourceful." As Klaebisch made his way down the narrow hall that ran the length of the main tunnel, the thud of his boots echoed in the heavy silence. He walked the rows of racks, pausing to peer at bottles here and there, but he didn't say another word, and neither did Inès or Michel. As he drew closer to the statue of the Virgin Mary that guarded the false wall, Inès forced herself to breathe normally. She couldn't help a small sigh of relief when Klaebisch finally turned back toward the cellar exit without noticing anything amiss.

"A beautiful collection," he said once they had all ascended the winding stairway and exited into the chilly morning. He pulled a small notebook from his pocket and jotted something down, squinting at the page and pursing his lips. Finally, he looked up. "I understand you oversee the production with the help of a *chef de cave* named Laurent?"

"Yes, Theo Laurent."

"I should like to meet him. Perhaps the next time." Klaebisch didn't wait for a reply. "In any case, we will begin with a thousand bottles of your 1935 *cuvée de prestige* and an equal amount of your thirty-six. Prepare them for shipment immediately. Reichsmarschall Göring will be quite pleased indeed."

He gestured to the soldiers, who were still lingering by the front door, and together they left in silence. Inès and Michel watched from the front drive until their truck disappeared behind the hills in the distance.

By the new year, a small rebellion against the Germans had begun. Soon after his arrival, Herr Klaebisch had met with the Commission de Châlons, the regulatory body for the champagne houses, and ordered 350,000 bottles of champagne each week from across the region, paid for with inflated marks, all to be stamped *Reserved for the Wehrmacht*. Only after those orders were met were the houses allowed to sell champagne to their own countrymen, but there was never enough left to make much of a profit. Now, winemakers were using dirty bottles, bad corks, and second-rate cuvées in shipments bound for Germany, and some in the region were positively giddy with the idea of pulling one over on the Germans. Inès knew that Michel was proceeding cautiously, but even he couldn't resist the lure of making the Germans look foolish.

"I like to imagine Göring and Himmler dining together in Berlin with one of our best bottles," Michel said one cold evening after he had invited Theo and Céline to join them in front of the roaring fire in the main house for a bit of warmth.

"A thirty-five grand cru," Theo interjected with a gleam in his eye.

"*Bien sûr.*" Michel grinned. "They won't even notice the specks of dirt."

Theo chuckled. "Or the fact that the bottles are actually lousy nonvintage wines from thirty-seven."

"Aren't you worried about getting caught?" Inès asked.

"Everyone is doing it, Inès," Theo said with a shrug.

But a week later, Klaebisch paid them an unexpected visit, arriving by chauffeured car on a snowy afternoon, accompanied by a uniformed German toting a long gun.

"Monsieur Chauveau," he said evenly when Michel answered the door. "I have come to discuss the matter of your treachery."

"I don't know what you mean," Michel said, his voice even, but Inès, who had come to the door behind him, could see a flush creeping up his neck. He glanced quickly at her before turning his attention back to Klaebisch.

"You believe I don't notice what you are doing? What all of you damned Champenois are doing?" Spittle flew from the weinführer's mouth. "Do you think me a fool?"

"Of course not."

"But you do not deny falsely labeling inferior bottles bound for Germany."

The corner of Michel's lips twitched. "I have made sure to treat the German shipments with all the respect they deserve."

The men stared at each other.

"Sir," Inès cut in. "If anything is amiss, it was clearly a mistake. Tell him, Michel!"

Klaebisch tilted his head. "Is this true? You have made a mistake?"

Michel said nothing, and finally the weinführer sighed. "Very well. Perhaps you would like to think about it in prison."

"No, sir, please!" Inès gasped, but Michel didn't say a word as the German in uniform put a rough hand on his arm and shoved him toward the doorway.

"It will be all right, Inès," Michel said over his shoulder as the man hustled him away with Klaebisch following close behind. Inès thought she saw the hint of a smile on Michel's face for an instant, but then it was gone.

"Please!" Inès called after the weinführer. "He is innocent!"

Klaebisch turned to face her, his face etched with exhaustion. "Madame," he said, "none of us are innocent anymore."

In the end, Michel spent just three days in prison in Reims, and he described it afterward as a jolly affair, for the cells were full of winemakers who had been arrested for the same offense.

"Inès," Michel said on the night he returned to the Maison Chauveau, dark circles under his eyes. "You should have seen it. It made me proud to be Champenois."

Inès led Michel to the bedroom, and as she slowly unbuttoned his shirt and pulled him toward her, thanking God that he'd made it home safely, she murmured, "But now that you've stood your ground, you can go back to making bottles normally, right? You've made your point, I think, my darling."

She leaned in to kiss him, but he pulled away. "Inès, this is only the beginning."

She stared at him. What had happened to his talk of remaining passive? "But, darling, you're playing with fire."

"Yes," Michel said, his eyes glimmering with something dangerous. "And what was it General de Gaulle said? 'Whatever happens, the flame of French resistance must not and shall not die.' This is our country, my dear, and I will fight for its honor to the end."

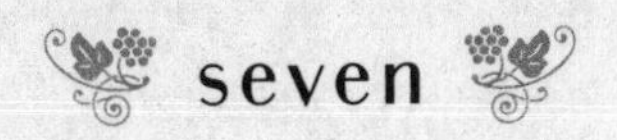

seven

JULY 1941

CÉLINE

On the second Thursday in July, Theo and Michel left one morning to attend the annual meeting of the *Syndicat Général des Vignerons*, the union of winemakers, twenty kilometers south, in Épernay. There was word that Maurice Doyard, who represented the region's growers, had an announcement to make, along with Robert-Jean de Vogüé from Maison Moët & Chandon, who represented the champagne houses.

"De Vogüé has some ideas for how to stand up to the Germans without getting ourselves in trouble," Theo told Céline on his way out the door.

"I hope he's not advocating anything dangerous," Céline said.

"I think it is more a matter of figuring out how to deal with Klaebisch as effectively as possible."

That made Céline feel a bit better, but she knew she wouldn't relax until Theo and Michel had returned. She kissed Theo goodbye, a perfunctory peck on the lips, and headed for the cellars as the men drove off in Michel's Citroën.

Below, Inès was already pulling out barrels from a storage cave and rolling them into the main hall. Since the previous week, inspecting and preparing the barrels for the upcoming harvest had been her main task, an assignment Michel had given her because it kept her busy and took little finesse or skill. Céline hoped that Inès didn't realize this was her husband's logic. As the war had dragged on, forcing them together, Céline had begun to feel a bit sorry for Inès, who did seem to be trying to pitch in. Céline couldn't imagine they would ever truly be friends—Inès was flighty and seemed not to grasp the magnitude of the war at their doorstep—but Céline knew she needed to try harder to be pleasant to the other woman. A sense of lonely desperation seemed to swirl around Inès these days, and at the very least, Céline understood how that felt.

"Where are we?" asked Céline as she approached the storage cave.

Inès wiped her brow; her left cheek was streaked with dirt, her forehead glistening with sweat. "I'm just beginning with these. I'm putting the barrels that need extra attention in the empty cave over there to the left."

"Good." Céline tied her hair back and eyed the barrels Inès had already rolled out. "Shall I start with the ones you filled yesterday?" Each day of the inspections, they had to first knock on the barrels to make sure that the echo didn't sound dull. If it did, the barrel was likely compromised. If the echo pinged instead, as it was supposed to, the barrels were rolled into a cave, where they were washed out and filled with a bit of water. If the water was still there the next day, the barrel was flipped over, to check that the other end was structurally sound, too. It was vital to do this with every barrel, because if any of them had cracked or warped, a great deal of wine could be lost. It was in these vessels that the first fermentation would take place before the wines were moved to bottles to ferment for a second time.

"All right." Inès bent to a barrel and knocked on the top. She then tapped her knuckles down the length of the wood in several places and nodded in approval.

"Here, I'll get that one," Céline said, taking the barrel from Inès and turning it onto its side to roll it. "I'm headed back anyhow."

"Thank you." Inès reached for another barrel. "So where did you learn so many steps of winemaking, anyhow? I've always wondered."

"Oh, I've been working with wine since I was young. You remember that my father is a winemaker, yes?" Saying the words made Céline's heart ache, for she still hadn't heard from him. With every day that passed, she grew more and more worried.

Inès nodded. "So he taught you to make wine before you married Theo?"

"Long before." Silence fell again, and Céline knew she should be trying harder to be pleasant. She forced herself to add, "That's how Theo and I met, actually. Through my father."

"I never knew that."

"Theo apprenticed with my father for a short time to learn how to make sparkling wine. My father is fairly well known in Burgundy for the *vin mousseux* he produces each year." Céline started down the hall with the barrel. "My father could see how talented he was, and he knew Theo aspired to come to Champagne," she added over her shoulder. "I suppose you could say my father orchestrated things between us. He felt Theo had a bright future ahead of him and that he could give me a better life than I would have in Burgundy."

"So you and Theo started to date?" Inès was following Céline down the hall, her eyes wide with curiosity. "And then you fell in love?"

Céline moved the barrel into a storage cave and righted it before answering. "We married quickly, actually, before we really knew each other at all, because Theo was already making plans to leave Burgundy. The union made sense, you see. I was the daughter of a winemaker, and I understood what it would be like to have a life that revolved around wine. And for Theo, I think being married felt like a bit of a relief. He didn't have to worry about courting anyone; he could focus only on his work."

"You didn't marry for love?" Inès looked devastated. "That's so sad."

Céline felt a small surge of annoyance. Did the other woman really think that finding that sort of romance was commonplace? No, love was something you had to work for, and Céline had tried hard over the years. "We love each other now," she answered simply, though she wasn't entirely certain the words were true. The passage of time had only revealed how little they had in common.

"But . . ." Inès said before trailing off with a perplexed expression.

"Honestly, Inès, we're not all as lucky as you and Michel," Céline said. She regretted her tone as hurt flashed across Inès's face, and she tried to soften her words by adding, "I'm only saying that you're fortunate to have fallen in love with someone who fell in love with you, too, right from the start." It had been hard to watch, actually. Céline had always respected Michel, and at times, especially when Theo withdrew into himself to brood about wine production, she had felt a connection with him that startled her. But then he had fallen head over heels for a skinny, gorgeous whirlwind, and Céline had been a bit disappointed. She had always imagined he would marry someone a bit more solid and serious, perhaps someone more like her, someone she could have imagined a true friendship with.

"Yes." Inès went silent, and Céline thought the conversation was over until Inès added in a small voice, "But sometimes I wonder if Michel fell in love only with the idea of me. Like he looked at me and saw what he wanted me to be, but he has been disappointed by the reality."

"I'm sure that's not the case."

"Isn't it?" Inès let out a small, ragged sigh. "It seems I can't do anything right anymore. I can see it in his eyes."

"It's just the war. There's a lot weighing on him." Though Céline felt sorry for Inès, she understood Michel's frustration. He had too much on his shoulders to have to coddle her, though certainly he had seemed eager to do just that when he first brought her home and installed her in the house like a beautiful decoration.

"I know. But that's why I wish he'd trust me to help more. The way he trusts you."

The edge to Inès's voice was unmistakable, but the fact was, Michel and Theo had given Inès several chances. Most recently, they had been desperate for assistance with the disgorgement—popping the sediment out of bottles that had already gone through the riddling process—and they had taught both Céline and Inès how to do it. It was tricky; they had to grab an upside-down bottle and tilt it upright while watching the bubble of gas rise inside. At the second the bubble reached the sediment collected in the neck, they had to snap the cap off with a metal tool called a *pince à dégorger* before quickly plugging the bottle with a thumb. Céline had gotten the hang of it after about three dozen attempts, but they'd had to stop Inès after a hundred or so bottles, because instead of waiting for the bubble of gas inside, it appeared she was simply popping caps at whim, which resulted in far too much wine spilled onto the cave floors.

"Well, you are helping now," Céline said.

Inès sniffed. "Yes, well, anyone can knock on wood and fill barrels with water, right?"

Céline forced a small smile. "It is still useful."

"Yes." Inès's tone was flat. "That's just what Michel says."

They lapsed into silence and worked together for the next few hours without exchanging more than a handful of sentences about where to put the barrels, or what time the men might return.

It was nearly seven o'clock when they heard the rumble of the Citroën aboveground. A moment later, Michel came down the winding stairs. Theo was just behind him, smiling.

"How did it go?" Céline asked, looking up from a barrel and brushing off her hands.

"Wonderfully," Theo replied, and for the first time in months, Céline saw hope in his eyes. "The intention is to have Klaebisch deal with an organization that represents all of us rather than approaching us individually. That way, we all share the burden in a manner that is fair."

"Well, that sounds like the perfect solution!" Inès exclaimed brightly, clapping her hands.

Michel frowned at his wife. "Well, it is a step in the right direction," he said carefully. "But we have also received word that Klaebisch is now requisitioning five hundred thousand bottles a week from Champagne."

"Five hundred thousand?" Céline asked. "How will we keep up with that? If this year's harvest is down, too . . ."

Theo glanced at her. "But this will keep them from breathing down our necks for the more valuable vintages. Trust me, Céline, this is a good thing. The industry is going to survive. It will all be okay."

Michel cleared his throat, and as Céline looked up to meet his eye, she wondered if he was thinking, as she was, that Theo seemed to be missing the point. The war was about far more than whether their wine survived.

"Well, the new arrangement should certainly help, anyhow," Michel said. He looked once more at Céline, and he held her gaze for a split second before turning back to the others. "In any case, let's see how the barrel inspection is coming along."

That night, Theo pulled Céline close as soon as she climbed into bed beside him. She was startled to feel her body stiffen in response, and she forced herself to relax.

"Champagne will survive this." Theo stroked her cheek, his hand rough. She couldn't remember the last time he had touched her this way, and it felt strange, unfamiliar. "The meeting today, Céline, well, it is the first time I've felt that there's truly a solution of some sort," he added. "De Vogüé is a wise man."

"Yes."

"He will take care of us. The wine will be all right." He touched her face again, moved his hips into hers.

She bit her lip but couldn't stop herself from blurting out, "But what about the people? Is it only about the wine for you?"

She could feel him go still, and when he rolled onto his back, opening up a gulf between them, she closed her eyes in the darkness, already angry at herself. He didn't share her fears, and though she was aware of that, forcing the words to the surface could do no good.

"Of course not," he snapped. "But you should care about the wine, too. It is our life, Céline."

"No, Theo. It is the thing we *do*, not who we *are*. If the Germans destroyed the vineyards tomorrow, we would find a way to go on. But what if they destroy my family? What if they already have?"

"Céline, come now. Your family, they are safe. It will all be fine. You will see."

"You can't know that." Céline could see her father's face in her mind, could feel her grandfather's strong hand on her shoulder, could feel her grandmother's warm lips pressed against her cheek. Suddenly, she couldn't be beside Theo any longer.

Without another word, she scrambled out of bed and headed for the bedroom door, pausing only long enough to grab the long sweater that was draped over the chair in the corner.

"Céline, you're being dramatic. Where are you going?"

"I need some air." She made her way in the darkness to the back door of the house, half expecting Theo to follow her, to apologize for his lack of understanding, but he didn't, and she supposed that said a lot.

Outside, the moon was nearly full, illuminating everything. Céline headed for the cellars. She would be alone with the sleeping bottles, and she knew that would bring her peace. Theo didn't believe that she cared about the wine, but she did—deeply. She could feel the hearts and souls of the workers in every bottle. It was just that she cared about their actual lives more.

The inky black darkness belowground felt like an embrace. At the foot of the stone stairs, Céline lit an oil lamp, and the walls around her came alive with familiar shadows. She inhaled deeply and then froze. There was a slight scratching sound in one of the caves ahead and to the right. Was someone there? She stood perfectly still, her heart pounding.

Of course, the smart thing to do would be to turn around and head back aboveground, extinguish her light, hurry back home. But a sudden defensiveness swept over her; the Germans could impose their rules and requisition their bottles, but this hallowed place beneath the earth could never belong to them. It belonged to France, all the years of history that had unfolded here, the way the very earth had wrapped itself around the aging wine and turned it into something magical. Before she could stop herself, she slipped off her shoes and walked as quietly as possible down the narrow passage.

The cellars had gone silent, and Céline told herself that perhaps the sound she'd heard had come from a mouse. Still, she moved forward cautiously, illuminating the first cave to the right. What would she do if she found a German lurking in the darkness? But there was nothing there, nothing but thousands of sleeping bottles.

The next cave held no movement either, and she was just about to shine her light into the third when a voice cut through the darkness.

"Céline?"

She let out a strangled scream before realizing that it was Michel standing a meter and a half in front of her, his eyes wide. "My God, you scared me to death." She put a hand over her heart. "What are you doing down here?"

"I couldn't sleep," he said. "I come down here sometimes when I need to think."

"So do I." Céline looked up at him, alarmed. "I mean, I hope that's all right. I realize these are your cellars . . ."

"Céline, this place is as much yours as it is mine. After all you and Theo have done, all the time you've invested here." He shook his head. "You could have gone south, tried to find a safer place to wait out the war, and you stayed."

"Of course we stayed." Céline didn't know quite how to put it, but she felt rooted here, like she had found the place she was meant to be. She and Theo had never even talked about leaving.

"Well, I am grateful." He gestured into the cave he'd just emerged from. "Now that you're here, would you like to sit for a while? I could use the company."

Céline hesitated. She knew she should probably go back upstairs, leave Michel to his thoughts. That would be the polite thing to do, the appropriate thing. But there was something about Michel's expression, the softness in his eyes, that made her want to stay. "I should—" she began.

"Please," he interrupted. "I would like very much to ask you something."

Céline hesitated before following him into the cave, goose bumps prickling her skin. He gestured to the stone bench along the back wall, and she sat at the far end, leaving plenty of room for him to settle on the other side. Still, when they faced each other in the darkness, the moment felt suddenly intimate. He must have sensed it, too, for he leaned away immediately.

"Is everything all right?" she asked when he still hadn't spoken.

"What? Oh, yes, yes." He raked a hand through his hair, and

she noticed how tired he looked, how worn. Of course they all looked like that these days, but there was something about Michel that seemed different to her, a sadness to his eyes. She wondered if he could see her emotions as clearly as she could see his.

"You said there was something you wanted to ask?"

"Yes. And please forgive me if my inquiry is too personal, but . . ." He trailed off and raked his fingers through his hair again. "I wanted to ask about your family."

Her heart sank. She had expected this, that at some point people would begin asking about her Jewish ancestry. She just hadn't expected it to be Michel. Still, she lived on his property, and she owed him the truth. "Well, yes, my father is Jewish, and although my family wasn't religious at all, of course I'm still considered—"

"No, no," Michel interrupted. Even in the darkness, she could see the color creeping up his neck and rising to his cheeks. "I'm sorry. That isn't what I meant. I know you are half Jewish, Céline. I meant only to ask if you've had any word from your family. Are they all right? I've been worried and didn't know the right way to ask."

To her surprise and embarrassment, she felt her eyes well with tears. She couldn't speak over the lump in her throat, and when she looked up at him again, the deep sympathy and worry etched into his face released the floodgates. Suddenly, she was sobbing.

After a few seconds, Michel inched toward her, tentatively at first and then all the way across the bench. He hesitated before slipping his arm around her, and she leaned into him, her tears drenching his shoulder. Then, she pulled back, mortified. "I'm so sorry," she said, wiping her tears. "I—I don't know what came over me."

"Don't apologize. I didn't mean to make you upset."

"No. It's not your fault. The truth is, I'm very concerned about them. I haven't heard from them at all."

Michel sighed. "Oh, Céline. I was afraid of that."

"I know the communication is terrible right now, but—"

"I have a friend," he interrupted, his voice suddenly low and urgent.

"What?"

"I have a friend who can arrange to have someone check on them. If you'd like."

She blinked at him. He wasn't meeting her eyes. "Well, yes, of course, but I don't want to put anyone in danger."

He smiled slightly. "My friend is in danger all the time. But I know he would be willing to help."

She had a hundred questions, and perhaps a dozen reasons why she should say no, but instead, she whispered, "Thank you."

"It's nothing." Michel held her gaze. "We must all look out for each other, *non*?"

Céline nodded and looked down. She could feel Michel's eyes on her again, and she knew he was waiting for something, but what?

"Theo, he is concerned for your family, too?" he asked after a while, and she looked up, startled.

"What do you mean?"

"I mean that sometimes, I worry he's living in a bubble, that he thinks too much about the wine and not enough about what's happening with the war." Michel hesitated. "I hope you don't think me rude for saying so."

Céline glanced at him and looked away. "The truth is, I suspect he doesn't think much about the things that don't impact him directly." She felt disloyal for saying even that.

"I think perhaps it is the same with Inès."

"She's trying," Céline said after a pause. The conversation she'd had with Inès that afternoon had stayed with her, and though she knew she would never have much in common with the other woman, she was beginning to understand her a bit more now. She owed it to her to stand up for her a bit, didn't she?

"I know. But perhaps she just wasn't cut out for this life, and I've been foolish to expect her to change. I knew who she was when I married her, didn't I?" He shook his head and looked at his hands. "I'm sorry. That must sound like a terrible thing to say about one's wife. It isn't that I don't love her."

"I understand," Céline whispered, and she did, for in some ways, it was just how she felt about Theo.

A silence descended between them, but it felt comfortable,

companionable, and that was reason enough to leave. "I must get back to Theo before he worries," Céline said, standing. "But thank you, Michel. Thank you very much for your kindness." It wasn't just his offer to check on her family that she was grateful for, though; it was the feeling of being understood. She hadn't realized how much she had missed it.

"*De rien.*" He smiled at her, but his expression was sad as she turned to leave.

"Good night, Michel."

"*Bonne nuit*, Céline. I will see you tomorrow."

Five minutes later, after ascending the stairs and making her way in the moonlight to her front door, she let herself in, preparing to explain her long absence to Theo.

But when she slipped into their bedroom, she could hear him snoring softly. He was fast asleep, and as she climbed under the sheets next to him, he didn't stir. She lay beside him in the blackness, staring at the ceiling until morning came.

eight

JUNE 2019

LIV

Already Paris was working its magic on Liv, and as she strolled down the Avenue Rapp late on a Tuesday morning with a fresh baguette, a hunk of Brie, and a *saucisson* tucked into her canvas shoulder bag, she found herself wondering why she hadn't come back sooner.

When Liv was a child, Grandma Edith used to call the magic that was uniquely Paris *le grand soupir*, the grand sigh, which used to make Liv laugh. But now she understood. Somehow the city made you breathe in deeply and exhale, and when you did, some of your troubles fell away.

A long time ago, before she had met Eric, Liv used to imagine what it would be like to move to France, to fall in love, to find a reason to stay. It was a dream that had come more naturally to her than any other vision of her future, perhaps because she had spent every summer here with her grandmother, making it feel like the one constant in her life. After Liv's father had died, her mother had

had a new boyfriend every few months, a new husband every few years, which meant that Liv had moved a grand total of seventeen times during her childhood. So although Grandma Edith had never been particularly warm, it had been comforting to know that when everything else felt unpredictable, France would always be a place to come home to. Liv was surprised to realize that somehow, after all these years, it still felt just the same.

After Liv had spent a few days in the City of Light, Eric no longer lurked at the edges of her every thought, but a new burden had replaced him. She was worried about Grandma Edith. Of course, the older woman had always been strange and a bit flighty, but she was jumpier than Liv had ever seen her, and she'd taken to gliding around the apartment in full makeup and a black silk dressing gown, looking haunted. Every time Liv asked her if something was wrong, Grandma Edith snapped at her to stop projecting.

Maybe her grandmother was right, Liv thought as she took the elevator up to the spacious fifth-floor apartment and inserted the spare key into the ornate lock. When she pushed the door open, she saw Grandma Edith standing in the middle of the living room in a perfectly tailored pale pink Chanel suit, her gray hair newly slicked into a tight bun, her red lipstick immaculately applied.

"Well? Where have you been?" Grandma Edith demanded.

"Just at the boulangerie," Liv said, holding up the baguette. "I thought we could—"

"Well, don't just stand there. Get your things. You can eat your bread on the train, if you must. We're going to Reims." She pronounced it *Rance*, and it took a few beats for Liv to realize that her grandmother was talking about one of the main cities in the Champagne region. Liv and Eric had once talked about visiting—it was only a forty-five-minute TGV train ride from the center of Paris—but they had decided against it for reasons Liv couldn't recall anymore. Still, she'd never heard her grandmother talk of the place.

"But . . . why?" Liv asked.

"I have some business there." Grandma Edith pursed her lips when Liv still hadn't moved. "Olivia, the train leaves at 12:58 on the dot. *Dépêche-toi!* We mustn't be late. I have a car waiting to take us to the station."

"Um, okay," Liv said, confused. She started toward her room.

"Wait!" Grandma Edith called after her. She walked over to Liv, removed her own scarf—white-and-gold vintage Chanel—and tied it around Liv's neck, frowning as she wrapped it just so. She stepped back to admire her handiwork. "There. Now you look almost as if you might belong here."

Less than two hours later, after taking the TGV through a landscape dotted with rolling grain farms, industrial windmills, and tiny villages nestled between hills, Liv found herself in a sumptuous two-bedroom suite in a boutique hotel on the rue Buirette, just a short taxi ride from the Reims train station. The carpets were a plush, spotless cream, while the furniture was ornate and gilded, with invitingly soft burgundy pillows piled everywhere.

"You'll be in there," Grandma Edith said, gesturing to the bedroom on the left as a red-faced porter struggled with a heavy Louis Vuitton case behind her.

"Looks great. So, do you want to go grab something to eat once we get settled?" Lunch would inevitably come with alcohol, and perhaps bribed by a drink or two, her grandmother would explain what on earth they were doing here.

"*Non*. But you go, dear. I have a headache, and I need to lie down."

Liv was startled to realize how pale her grandmother had grown in the past few minutes, even under her layer of freshly applied blush. "Are you all right, Grandma Edith? What can I do?"

"I'm fine." She handed a few coins to the porter, who hurried away with a mumbled *merci*. "Please. Go have a *coupe de champagne*, Olivia. Enjoy yourself." She gave Liv a small smile and then turned and walked into the bedroom on the right, closing the door behind her.

Liv bit her lip. Should she knock, make sure Grandma Edith was okay? Then again, that would likely only result in more accusations about what Liv was doing wrong with her life. Still, she didn't feel right leaving her grandmother alone if she wasn't feeling well.

She pulled her suitcase into her room, which featured a large, polished mahogany, four-poster bed with a crisp white duvet and a pile of pillows matching those in the parlor. The heavy drapes were open, and light spilled in from windows overlooking a street punctuated by long, rectangular fountains, shops, and hotels. Narrow chimneys poked up from angled rooftops, and buildings made of centuries-old stone shared space with large, blockish structures that couldn't have been built more than fifty or sixty years ago. Above the buildings, Liv could see the twin towers of a cathedral that looked like Paris's Notre-Dame. A block away stood a soaring, ornate fountain topped with a winged woman cast in bronze.

As Liv gazed down at the little red awning of the café just below her window, her phone rang. She glanced at the caller ID: *Mom*. She groaned and considered ignoring the call, but her mother would only keep trying. She picked up, bracing herself for a barrage of questions about her divorce. "Hi, Mom."

"Hi, sweetie," her mother chirped. "I'm heading up to New York tomorrow with Stan. Just wondering if you want to meet us for dinner. We have theater tickets on Thursday, but I said to Stan, 'You have to meet my daughter.' "

Temporarily stunned that her mother hadn't asked about Eric, Liv said, "Um, which one is Stan, again?"

Her mother laughed. "The lawyer. Owns the condo at the Ocean Sun in Boca?"

"Oh. Right." Liv was fairly sure she'd never heard of Stan—or the Ocean Sun in Boca—but that would be par for the course with her mother. "Actually, Mom, I'm not in New York right now. I'm visiting Grandma Edith."

"In Paris?"

"In Reims, actually. About forty-five minutes east of Paris."

There was another beat of silence. "Well, what on earth are you doing there?"

"Honestly? I have no idea. She hasn't been acting like herself."

Liv's mother laughed. "And that's a bad thing?"

"Mom, I'm serious. I'm a little worried about her. She seems, I don't know, depressed."

"Honey, I'm sure it's nothing." Liv's mom plunged immediately into a story about something that had happened at the pool at Stan's condo complex the day before, but Liv was no longer paying attention, because out the window, she had just spotted a familiar figure clad in pink Chanel hurrying out the hotel's front door, turning left without hesitation, and slipping into pedestrian traffic on the sidewalk. It was Grandma Edith, but where was she going? Hadn't she just told Liv minutes earlier that she was feeling too unwell to leave the room?

"Sorry, Mom," Liv interrupted. "I have to go."

Her mother began to say something else, but Liv was already hanging up and heading for the door.

Outside the hotel, still panting from running down six flights of stairs, Liv turned in the same direction she'd seen Grandma Edith disappear, but she already knew finding her would be futile. The streets were crowded with people fixated on their cell phones, couples holding hands and leaning into each other, locals walking dogs, children giggling and dashing a few steps ahead of their parents. Liv walked three blocks, then doubled back, turning into the plaza anchored by the fountain she'd seen from her window. She peered into every storefront, every restaurant, but her grandmother had vanished. Puzzled, she turned slowly and walked back toward the hotel.

She tried calling Grandma Edith's mobile phone, but as it often did, it went straight to voice mail. There was nothing to do now but wait for her return. As she turned onto the rue Buirette, she reminded herself that Grandma Edith lived alone and obviously went out by herself all the time. Surely there was no reason to worry.

Back in the suite, she grabbed a book from her suitcase—a mindless thriller she'd picked up at the airport in New York—and settled onto the sofa in the living room to wait. She had checked her emails, scrolled through a few news stories on the

New York Times website, and read the first few chapters of her book when there was a knock on the hotel room door. Liv sighed in relief; her grandmother was notorious for misplacing things and had probably lost her room key. Liv got up and swung the hotel door open, fully expecting to see Grandma Edith rummaging around in her purse, back from her mystery errand.

Instead there was a man there, leafing through a weathered leather briefcase. He looked up with a smile, and his forehead wrinkled in confusion when he saw her. "*Oh, excusez-moi, ce doit être la mauvaise chambre*," the man said quickly, shoving some papers back into his bag as he began to turn away.

Liv quickly translated the French in her head; she was better at understanding than she was at speaking. "*Attendez!* Um, *cherchez-vous ma grand-mère?* Edith Thierry?"

"*Oui.*" The man looked at her more closely, then his eyes lit up. "Wait, you are Olivia?" he asked, switching seamlessly to English. "But of course you are Olivia! Your grandmother has shown me many pictures."

"And you are . . . ?"

"Oh, I'm terribly sorry. I should have introduced myself straightaway." He stuck out his hand. "I'm Julien. Julien Cohn." He was about Liv's age, maybe a few years older, with thick, gray-flecked dark hair that looked like it needed to be trimmed, hazel eyes framed by laugh lines, and a strong jaw dusted with salt-and-pepper stubble.

Liv shook his hand. "And how do you know my grandmother?"

"She is a client of mine. I am here to drop off some paperwork she requested."

"Paperwork? What kind of paperwork?"

"Well, I am one of her attorneys. She mentioned she would be arriving today, and I arranged to come by this afternoon, but perhaps she forgot."

Liv just looked at him. "But why does my grandmother have an attorney in Reims?"

"I suppose that's a question you'd have to ask her." Julien's smile was almost charming enough to distract her from the mystery of his visit.

"Well, you can leave the papers with me if you want. She should be back soon."

Julien frowned. "I'm terribly sorry, Olivia, but I cannot. They're sensitive papers; you understand."

"Oh. Right. Of course." She hesitated, a little stung. "And it's Liv."

"Pardon?"

"I go by Liv."

"Oh, I'm sorry." There was that smile again. "Your grandmother has called you only Olivia."

Liv rolled her eyes. "She refuses to recognize nicknames. She says they're for children and pets."

Julien laughed. "Yes, that does sound like your grandmother."

"You know her well?"

"I do. She's been with my family's firm for, oh, seventy years. Not that I've been around that long, of course."

"Seventy years?" She blinked at Julien, completely lost. "Here in Reims?"

He nodded and raked his left hand through his hair. It was Patrick Dempsey hair, John Stamos hair, the kind of hair normal men didn't get to lay claim to. In the brief silence that followed, Liv found herself glancing at his ring finger as he lowered his hand. His wedding band was thick and gold, claiming him for someone else. She looked up and realized, to her embarrassment, that he was watching her—and that he had clearly noticed what she was doing. He smiled slightly, and she could feel her face heating up.

"Well," he began at the same time she said, "So . . ."

They both laughed, and Julien reached out to shake her hand once again.

"I was just going to say that it was nice to finally meet you, Liv," Julien said, taking a step back. "I'll look forward to perhaps seeing you later in the week."

"Oh, I don't think we're staying very long."

"*Vraiment?*" His forehead creased in confusion. "Are you sure? Because I think your grandmother might have a different idea in mind."

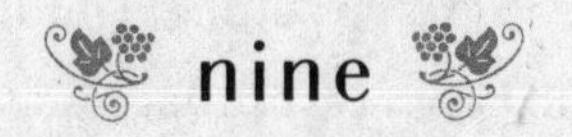

nine

SEPTEMBER 1941

INÈS

The harvest was about to begin, and all of Champagne was abuzz. The grapes this year appeared to be merely average in both quality and quantity, but that was an improvement over the previous year, which was cause for celebration. Beyond that, though it had begun to seem as if Herr Klaebisch's primary purpose as weinführer was to make the lives of the Champenois miserable, he had come through on at least one count: returning a few hundred able-bodied men from labor camps to the vineyards, where they would assist in the harvest and the wine production. De Vogüé's argument that the 1941 vintage would be as poor as the previous year's without enough workers had apparently succeeded.

"It's a relief to have many of the men back," Inès said to Michel over an early dinner on the Wednesday before the first grapes were to be picked. Since he'd returned from his short stint in prison several months earlier, speaking of de Gaulle and resistance, there had been even more distance between them, and she missed him, even when he was sitting right across the table from her. "Perhaps we will have a chance now to spend a bit more time together once the harvest is done."

"Inès, that's hardly the issue." He didn't even look at her. "These men were being forced to work for Germany, and now they're home and safe. We should be thanking God for their freedom!"

"Yes, of course, I know." Inès could feel her cheeks flaming. It seemed that everything she said these days was incorrect or somehow offensive. She scratched her arm. "I only mean that I was hoping we'd have some time to ourselves one of these days. We both work so very hard, and you've been so tired . . ."

"Inès, we're at war. What do you expect?" Michel put his spoon down and sighed. "I'm sorry," he said. "I just worry sometimes that you don't grasp the magnitude of what's happening here."

"I'm not an imbecile, Michel."

"I know you're not. But Céline understands what's going on, and I can't understand why you—"

"So you *are* comparing me to Céline." Lately, whenever Inès dared comment on the way the Germans had impacted their lives, Michel seemed barely able to contain his annoyance, but whenever Céline spoke about the same matters, he paused and listened intently. It was a small thing, Inès knew, but it hurt her just the same.

"Of course not. It's just that the weight on my shoulders feels very heavy right now, and—"

"Then let me help!" Inès blinked back tears, because she'd made the mistake of crying in front of him more than once in the past few months. His response was never to comfort her anymore; it was to turn away in frustration, and she didn't want to lose him again right now. She wanted him to hear her, to understand that she wasn't nagging him. "*I'm* your wife, Michel. I should be sharing the burden."

He stood abruptly. "Excuse me, Inès. I have some things to attend to."

"But . . . you didn't finish your dinner," Inès said in a small voice.

"I'm not hungry," he said, though that wasn't possible. The rations were getting tighter, the food quality poorer. They were lucky to live in the countryside, where they were able to grow some vegetables and keep a few chickens and rabbits, but still, there was never enough to eat. "I'm going to head back down to the caves. Don't wait up."

He was gone before she could say another word. In silence, Inès finished the rest of her soup, and then, after a moment's hesitation, the rest of Michel's, too. As she washed the dishes, Inès glanced at the clock on the wall, the inexpensive one the Germans had left behind when they toted away Michel's generations-old grandfather clock. Five minutes before seven. It was still early, and Inès knew that with nearly an hour of daylight left, and with Michel likely swallowed by the cellars for the remainder of the evening, she'd once again be lonely. It wasn't fair; he wasn't the only one tortured by the war, worried about the fate of the business.

She put the dish towel down, smoothed her skirt, and made a decision. She would go into Reims for the night to see Edith. What harm could that do? Though the main city was only sixteen kilometers away, she hadn't been there in months because the tasks around the champagne house were so never-ending and arduous, and because Michel didn't like her to travel alone. But if he wanted to treat her as if she were useless, she wasn't going to sit around and grovel. Besides, she missed her best friend terribly. More than that, she missed her old life, the one she'd had before Edith had met Edouard, before Inès had followed Edith to Champagne, before everything had become so difficult.

Without giving herself time to rethink the decision, she dashed up the stairs, threw on the first decent dress she could find—a red one with butterfly sleeves and a long A-line skirt that swished at her calves, which she'd bought in 1938 just before she'd left Lille—and added her black two-inch pumps, the soles of which had grown so thin that it was uncomfortable to be on her feet for more than an hour or so. But before she'd met Michel, they'd been the shoes that made men do double takes, and she wanted to be looked at like that tonight. She couldn't remember the last time Michel had gazed at her admiringly.

She drew a line down the back of each calf with an eye pencil to mimic the seams of stockings, and swiped on black mascara and red lipstick, though her supplies of each were dwindling. Her hair was a lost cause, so she clipped it on each side. Grabbing her black handbag, she went downstairs and out the back door.

"Michel!" she called down into the entrance to the cellars. There was no reply, and she wasn't going to waste time trooping around beneath the earth in search of someone who didn't want to be found.

Five minutes later, after leaving a scribbled message on the dining table, Inès headed out the front door, the keys to the Citroën in her hand.

"Inès?"

Inès looked up and saw Céline walking toward the main house. "Oh, hello."

"Is everything all right? Where are you going?"

"To Reims," Inès said without slowing down. She glanced up at the sky; the sun was already hanging low. She'd have to hurry in order to make it to town before darkness fell.

"To *Reims*?" It was as if Inès had just told her she was planning to drive to Berlin. "Whatever for?"

"To see Edith," Inès said. She unlocked Michel's Citroën, slid in, and slammed the door.

Céline stepped up to the window and waited until Inès rolled it down. "Edith?"

"My best friend. You remember her. The one who introduced me to Michel?"

"Of course I know Edith," Céline said, staring at her oddly. "But don't Michel and Theo need the car to visit the vineyards for the harvest tomorrow?"

"I'll be back in the morning." Inès turned the key and the engine purred to life, but still, Céline didn't move. "Yes? What is it?"

"Are you sure it's safe? You know about the German checkpoints . . ."

Inès had heard that the Germans were blocking roads here and there, stopping all traffic and asking the nature of each driver's business. But she didn't have anything to hide. All her papers were in order, tucked neatly in her handbag. "I'll be fine, Céline. I'll see you tomorrow."

Biting her lip, Céline stepped aside. As Inès backed out and pulled down the drive, she glanced in the rearview mirror and saw Céline still standing there, her shoulders stiff as she watched Inès drive away.

By the time Inès drove through the outskirts of Reims forty minutes later, with the color leaching from the sky, she had realized that perhaps Céline was right.

There had been no official checkpoints along the road, but there had been plenty of German soldiers passing by in rumbling trucks and gleaming black cars, their gazes menacing. Between the commune of Ormes and the outskirts of Reims, she hadn't seen a single French civilian.

Still, she made it to the Brasserie Moulin, set on the corner of the rue de Thillois and the rue des Poissonniers, without incident just before the last rays of daylight disappeared. She easily found a parking spot behind the brasserie, for the streets were already all but deserted, the curtains above the storefronts and apartments drawn tight, many of them abandoned. She shouldn't be here, not with darkness approaching, but once she was inside, she knew Edith and Edouard would vouch for her.

As she pushed the front door open, she was already feeling a bit lighter, a bit more like herself. But the instant she looked up, she stopped abruptly.

She had expected the brasserie to be all but empty as the curfew neared, but instead, it was crowded, bustling, and filled with raucous laughter. It took Inès a second more to register that nearly every man in the room was wearing a German uniform. The four soldiers at the table closest to the door stopped in midsentence and stared as she entered, and she could feel her cheeks heating up.

Had she walked into the wrong place? She ran her fingernails up her left arm and scanned the room quickly, reassuring herself that this was indeed Edouard's brasserie, but what had become of it? A knot twisted in the pit of her stomach.

"Inès?" Edith hurried toward her from across the room, her hair done up in voluminous pin curls, her red lipstick perfect, her pale green dress unmistakably new. "Why are you here?" Edith hissed, grabbing her friend's arm and steering her away from the door, toward the back of the restaurant. "And would you smile, please? Pretend you're having a gay time."

"What? Why?" As Edith hustled her across the room, Inès locked gazes with a German officer, who winked at her despite the fact that he currently had his arm thrown around the shoulders of a big-bosomed woman in a tight dress.

"Because right now you have the look of a rabbit in the headlights, my friend," Edith said, her nails digging into Inès's arm. "*Guten Abend!*" She paused at the table of decorated officers to flash a broad, fake smile before dragging Inès the rest of the way into the kitchen, through the back hall, and up the stairs into the apartment above.

Edith waited until she'd closed the door behind them before she turned to Inès, her eyes wide and her face white. "What on earth are you doing here, Inès?"

Inès was still shaken, but she'd recovered enough to feel a wave of indignation. "What am *I* doing here? I should be asking *you* what *you're* doing! You're entertaining *Germans*? You're even *speaking* in German?"

A muscle in Edith's jaw twitched. "We can't afford to turn away business in these times, Inès."

"Good God." Inès shook her head. "Are you and Edouard . . . *collaborators*?" She whispered the last word. She couldn't have imagined such a thing, but what other explanation could there be?

"No!" Edith grabbed Inès's hand. "But what choice do we have, Inès? You must see that."

"I see you serving the enemy."

"Yes, well, the best way to beat an enemy is to become a friend, *non*?"

"What are you saying?"

"Inès, why have you come?"

The words wounded Inès. There'd been a time not so long ago that she'd been welcome without question. "To see you, Edith."

Edith squeezed Inès's hand. "Please, Inès, stay here until the dinner service is over. Edouard and I will explain."

Inès settled onto Edith's worn blue sofa to wait, but soon she found her eyelids growing heavy. She didn't realize she had dozed off until Edith shook her awake sometime after eleven, long after the restaurant should have closed for the curfew.

As Inès came to, she saw Edith sitting beside her on the couch and Edouard frowning at her from an armchair across the room. "Did someone send you, Inès?" Edouard asked before she'd had a chance to get her bearings.

"Send me?" Inès laughed in disbelief. "My own husband won't even trust me to help with the bottles. I'm too clumsy, too careless. I'm unreliable. He doesn't say it, but I know he thinks it. So no, Edouard. No one sent me."

"Then what are you doing here?" Edouard's mouth was set in a narrow line beneath his mustache, which was thinner than it had been the last time Inès had seen him. Come to think of it, he looked different in other ways, too, with slicked-back hair, a pallid cast to his skin, and a sharp black suit. He was almost a caricature of a French maître d'.

"I—I needed my friend." Inès glanced at Edith, who seemed different to her now, too. Edith was paler, her hair shorter, her fingernails bitten to the quick. "But I didn't expect to find the two of you in a room full of Nazis."

Edouard and Edith exchanged glances. "I need to tell her," Edith said softly.

"I disagree." Edouard glanced once more at Inès, his gaze hard.

"Tell me what?" Inès asked, but it was as if she hadn't spoken.

"We can trust her," Edith said to Edouard. "I'm sure of it. She would never betray me. She's my dearest friend."

Edouard frowned at Inès for a long time before finally turning to Edith. "Very well." He stood and nodded to Inès. "It has been a long day. I'm going to bed." He didn't glance in her direction again as he left the room.

Silence descended, and slowly, Edith turned to Inès. They looked at each other for a long time, and Inès told herself she wouldn't be the one to speak first.

"You have heard of Jacques Bonsergent?" Edith asked abruptly, breaking the laden stillness.

Inès frowned. "Was he in school with us in Lille?"

"No." Edith glanced down at her hands. "In November he was with some friends in Paris when a German officer, very drunk, staggered out and grabbed one of the women in his group, a new bride who had married just the day before. The new husband defended his wife by hitting the German officer, and then he ran. Bonsergent stayed and tried to help the German up."

"Goodness! You know this Monsieur Bonsergent?"

"I never met him. Please, just listen. Though Bonsergent denied being the one to strike the officer, he refused to give up the name of his friend. Just a few weeks later, he was sentenced to death."

"Just to frighten him, yes?"

"No. He was executed by a firing squad two days before Christmas."

Inès swallowed hard. Why was Edith telling her such things? "But . . . that's horrible."

"It was a turning point for many of us who had stayed quiet, who had tried not to become involved." Edith met Inès's gaze at last. "Can I trust you, Inès?"

"Edith, we're like sisters."

"I know. I know." Edith examined her hands again. "You see, Edouard and I knew that we could not stand by and do nothing. And it has gotten worse, Inès. Did you hear of the German officer who was killed in the Paris Métro last month? They didn't catch the man who committed the assassination, and so the Germans simply chose three men at random to be executed instead."

"What?"

"You do not listen to the BBC, I see."

"It's forbidden." The truth was that Inès didn't even follow the news that the Germans distributed; it was all too depressing. What else had she missed?

Edith's smile was sad. " 'A nation is beaten only when it has accepted that it is beaten.' A quote from Marshal Foch. If we accept the things the Germans are doing to us, Inès, it is the beginning of the end. We must fight back."

"Fight back? But what can we do? The Germans are in control now. It's better to just keep our heads down and—"

"And what?" Edith interrupted. "Let them murder innocent people?"

"But those are isolated incidents."

"No, they aren't. Nor are the Jewish regulations coming down from Vichy. Do you understand what is at stake?"

"Of course I do." But the truth was, Inès felt lost. What could she or Edith—or even Edouard—do to stop a war?

"So then you understand why we felt we had to do something." Edith leaned forward and grasped Inès's hands. "If you breathe a word of this—to *anyone*—Edouard and I will be arrested, probably even killed."

"A word of *what*? Edith you're frightening me."

Edith waited until Inès looked into her eyes, then she spoke slowly and clearly. "We are resisting, my dear friend. We are fighting for France."

Inès blinked at her. "But you're serving Germans in your brasserie! How is that resisting?"

"Because alcohol loosens lips." Edith released Inès and leaned back. "And loose lips mean that secrets sometimes spill out. We smile, and we cater to their every need, and always—always, Inès—we are listening."

"But who do you tell the secrets to?"

Edith sat back and regarded Inès for a moment. "The less you know about the specifics, the better," she said, and Inès felt a stab of frustration. Like Michel, it seemed her friend only trusted her to a point. Edith stood and yawned. "It has been a long day, Inès. Shall we head to bed now? I'm sure you're tired, too. You'll find your old bedroom just as you left it. I'll see you in the morning."

"But—"

"We can talk then." And with that, Edith was gone.

That night, Inès lay in the small bed that had been hers before she married Michel, and as she stared at the ceiling, she felt more alone than ever. Inès had come here to tell Edith she wasn't sure she was happy with Michel anymore, to ask her friend's advice. Instead, she had stumbled upon the fact that Edith was involved in something much more important, with consequences that ran far deeper than she could have imagined. It made Inès's problems seem silly, juvenile.

As she finally drifted off into a troubled sleep, she wondered what it meant that Edith had decided to resist, while Inès only wanted to keep life as it was before the war. Was Edith making a mistake? Or was Inès a fool for believing that she bore no responsibility to protect France? But one thing she was sure of: she would keep Edith's confidence. Otherwise, what kind of friend would she be?

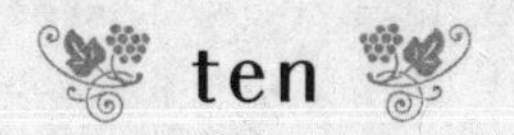

ten

SEPTEMBER 1941

CÉLINE

With Inès still in Reims early the next morning, Theo and Michel had to rely on Henri Beauvais, an ancient vigneron and Great War veteran who'd been friends with Michel's father, to give them a ride to Clos Vannier, in the nearby village of Écueil, to observe the first few hours of the harvest. Céline had wanted to accompany them, but Theo had been indifferent, and Michel had urged her to stay home for her own safety, something he'd been saying a lot lately. Though she knew he meant well, Céline was growing frustrated with being trapped on the grounds of the Maison Chauveau. It had been nearly a year since the first statut des Juifs had been announced, and three months since the second round of regulations had come down, barring Jews from professions ranging from banking to real estate, and giving local authorities the right to place them in internment camps should they violate any of the new restrictions. Céline was still considered Christian for the purposes of German record keeping, but they were all aware that the noose was being pulled tighter.

"I feel useless here," she had argued before they left.

"I know," Michel had said gently. "But there are German sympathizers all around us, and people who are jealous of our success here at Chauveau. Please, I realize it's a lot to ask, but I want to keep you safe."

Theo had grunted in agreement, and they had gone off without waiting for an answer.

And so Céline was missing the harvest, which felt like a punishment in itself. And then there was Inès, able-bodied and unimpeachably Catholic, off having a grand old time with her friend in Reims, not caring about the work she was missing or the way she was inconveniencing Michel and Theo. Céline had tried to have some sympathy for the other woman, but how could she be so selfish?

After an hour of straightening their cottage to keep herself occupied, Céline finally gave up and wandered out to the cellar entrance. She knew she would find some solace in the familiar caves beneath the earth.

As she descended the steps with a lamp, the cold air wrapped itself around her like an embrace, and she shuddered. Down here, the silence was a salve. She could be alone with her thoughts, which right now were all focused on her family.

She had finally received a letter from her father the day before, courtesy of Michel's mysterious friend, who apparently traveled all over the *zone occupée* delivering and collecting messages. She'd been greatly relieved to hear that her father and his parents hadn't been arrested or moved by the Germans, but the letter had also confirmed some of her fears. Her father was no longer allowed to work at the winery he'd overseen for thirty years, and he'd had to register—along with his parents—as a Jew.

Your grand-mère and grand-père are in the greatest danger, I fear, her father had written. *Because they were born in Poland, we do not believe the French government considers them French any longer. Right now, they are safe, but for how long? I am worried for all of us, but I know Theo will look after you, my dear, and that brings me some comfort. These are terrible times, and I pray that the darkness will soon lift.*

In the letter Céline had sent back with Michel's friend, she had spoken brightly, cheerfully about life in Champagne, saying it hadn't changed much, so her father wouldn't worry. To tell the truth—that she was afraid about the future—would be to place a burden on him he shouldn't have to bear. To tell him she had seen the signs posted around town—caricatures of Jews with hook noses, drawn to look like monsters—would be to frighten him. She was the one who had taken her father's advice to leave home with Theo. She feared now she would regret it for the rest of her life.

Her steps echoed as she moved deeper into the cool, chalky caves. There were the 1939s and the 1940s, still aging on the lees, the first two vintages since war had been declared. There were gaps where the older wines—the thirty-sixes, the blanc de blanc Theo had experimented with in 1938—should have been, but they'd been hidden or requisitioned by the Germans long ago. Céline knew the winding, twisting, mysterious cellars like the back of her own hand, but sometimes these days, all the empty spots made her feel as if she had lost her way.

"*Bonjour!*" An unfamiliar man's voice boomed down into the cellars from the direction of the stairs, and Céline froze. His accent was unmistakably German. "Hello, who is down there?"

Her blood ran cold. She quickly extinguished her lamp, her heart thudding.

"Do you think I'm a fool?" The man's deep voice echoed in the caverns. "You've just put your light out. I can see exactly where you are." His voice was smooth, even with the guttural consonants, his tone too casual.

Céline's mind raced. The cellars went on forever, twisting deeper into the earth beneath Ville-Dommange, but if he wanted to, he could follow the sound of her footsteps, the flash of the light she would eventually need to relight to find her way. There was nowhere to hide now that he knew she was here. But what did he want?

"I am going to give you sixty seconds," the German said. "And if you don't come up, I will begin shooting."

"No, wait, don't!" Céline called, hating the way the cave walls magnified the fear in her voice. She was trapped. "Please. I'm coming. I'm not doing anything wrong."

She didn't relight the lamp for fear that it would make her an easier target. In the darkness, she hurried toward the stairs, stumbling twice, and ascended into the bright morning.

"Well, well," the German said with a chuckle. "It's you."

When they finally stood face-to-face, Céline realized she recognized him, too. It was the officer who had supervised the younger men on the first day the Germans had pillaged Ville-Dommange, the one with the broad shoulders, narrow mustache, and dark, beady eyes. But she barely glanced at his face; she couldn't tear her gaze away from his pistol, which he held casually in his right hand, the barrel even with her heart. She had never had a gun pointed directly at her before.

"Aren't you going to say something?" the man asked, venom spiking the amusement in his tone. "I thought the French were supposed to be polite. Don't you say 'bonjour' even when you meet a stranger on the street? And we are not even strangers, are we? We are old friends."

"B-bonjour," Céline stammered, still staring at the gun.

"Céline, is that right?" he asked smoothly. "Or would it be more proper to call you Madame Laurent?"

"Yes," she said, her voice small. "I mean, yes, that is me. Madame Laurent."

"You're a nervous little thing, aren't you?"

"You—you are holding a gun on me."

He laughed, but there was no mirth in the sound; it was ominous, threatening. Nonetheless, he lowered the weapon, but he didn't holster it. "Now," he said, the facade of mirth disappearing as abruptly as it had arrived. "What were you doing? It is suspicious enough that a woman would be in the cellars by herself with the men away, but you extinguished your light as soon as you heard me call out. Why? What are you up to? You are hiding something?"

"No, nothing." Céline clasped her hands. "I promise. I just—you startled me."

"I didn't ask for an apology. I asked what you were doing in the caves."

"I—I was lonely."

"Lonely?"

"Yes."

"Yes, *sir*," he corrected. "You will address me with the proper respect."

"Yes, sir," she said quickly.

"Now. Explain yourself. You were lonely? What does that have to do with anything?"

She could only tell the truth. "I was missing my family, you see. My father, he has worked at a vineyard in Burgundy my whole life. He makes—made—wine, and sometimes, when I'm feeling most alone—"

"What is your point?" The German cut her off, and she realized she'd been babbling.

"I feel close to him in the caves. They remind me of where I come from, and I'm not sure I'll ever see that home again."

The German studied her, his eyes dark with something unsettling. At last he holstered his pistol, and she felt her shoulders sag in relief. "Being alone in the cellars, especially for a woman, is suspicious. Do you know there are people doing things down there, things to undermine the führer? Just last week, we came upon a man printing leaflets in his cellar in Aÿ. Do you know what happened to him?"

Céline shook her head, too afraid to guess.

When the German grinned, his teeth looked too sharp for a mere man; they belonged on a predator in the wild. He held her gaze as he raised the thumb and index finger of his right hand, mimicking a gun as he pointed at her. "We shot him dead, madame. If I ever catch you alone in the cellars—"

"I understand. Sir."

He didn't move, didn't break the oppressive eye contact between them. Instead, he continued to stare as his lips curled. "You mentioned your father," he said. "He's a Jew, yes?"

Céline's stomach pitched and rolled, and it took every ounce of self-control to keep standing there, acting as if his words didn't faze her. "Yes." There was no point in denying it; he clearly already knew. She had heard how meticulous the Germans were with their record keeping.

"I wouldn't have guessed," he said. "Not that first day, anyhow, though I see it now. You're attractive for a Jewess."

Céline could feel her cheeks heating up, and she didn't know whether it was fear or embarrassment. She didn't say anything, and the officer's eyes narrowed.

"I've just paid you a compliment," he said. "The proper response would be to thank me."

She swallowed. "Thank you."

"Very good. I don't believe we were ever properly introduced. You should know me, Madame Laurent, don't you think? Especially if we are to be friends."

"Friends?"

The officer laughed, and it was the same calculated, mirthless sound as before. "Oh, I think you'll find in times like these, it's helpful to have a friend like me. You should be honored that I'd even consider a friendship with a *Jew*." He nearly spat the last word.

Céline couldn't think of anything to say, so she merely nodded.

"Now, then. My name is Richter. *Hauptmann* Richter, which would be *Capitaine* Richter in your inferior language." He narrowed his eyes again. "Aren't you going to tell me how nice it is to meet me?"

"It—it's nice to meet you, Hauptmann Richter."

"There, there. You're learning." He moved closer, near enough now that she could feel the heat of his breath. "Now, Madame Laurent, I know I will never catch you doing anything you shouldn't be, because I hate to think of you in a labor camp. The conditions are not so nice. You understand?"

"Yes, sir."

"Good." He reached out with his left hand and fingered the lock of her hair that curled over her right shoulder. She stood frozen, his touch repulsive, dangerous. "I have my eye on you, Madame Laurent," he said, finally raising his gaze to hers. "*Céline.*" And then, without breaking eye contact, he let his hand drift from her hair to the swell of her right breast, over the thin layer of cotton. As she held her breath and tried not to retch, he traced a lazy ring around her nipple and smiled. "Oh yes, I have my eye on you indeed."

And then he was gone, withdrawing to his shiny black automobile while Céline stood as frozen as a grapevine in winter, trembling in the cold.

Céline didn't tell Theo about the encounter with Richter right away, because she knew he would chastise her for being in the cellars alone, and she couldn't handle the criticism heaped atop everything else. He would tell her that she didn't belong there, that of course a woman wandering the caves by herself would look suspicious, and that she'd brought the scrutiny on herself. So when he and Michel returned from the harvest in rare good moods, their words spilling over each other's as they told her about the surprising bounty from the first day of labor, she nodded along, trying to find some comfort in their optimism. If Mother Nature was finally smiling upon them, maybe the tide of the war would change soon, too, sending Richter and his men drifting east like jetsam.

"Things are turning around, Céline, they really are," Theo said, grinning at his wife. "Don't you think so, Michel? Bright times ahead, yes?"

"God willing," Michel replied, glancing skyward. "I think this year should get us back on track."

Inès returned home in Michel's Citroën, which had been fitted to run on *gazogen*, or ersatz fuel, just after the men did, pulling up in a cloud of dust and smoke and alighting from the car with an expression of unmistakable guilt. "Hello, everyone," she said without meeting anyone's eyes. "I'm sorry I'm a little late. How did the harvest go today?"

"Where have you been?" Michel asked, his voice low and cold.

"I left you a note. Didn't you get it?"

Without replying, Michel took Inès firmly by the arm and led her inside, slamming the door behind them.

"What excuse could she possibly have?" Theo muttered. From inside the main house, they could hear raised voices, Inès's an aggrieved staccato.

Céline shook her head, but she couldn't muster a reply.

"You're quiet today," Theo said as they turned and began to walk toward their cottage.

He reached for her hand, but she pulled away instantly, an instinctual reaction that she immediately regretted. She still felt dirty from Richter's touch.

"You're angry that we didn't bring you to the vineyard," Theo guessed when she didn't reply. "Céline, you know it's for your own safety and protection."

"And you think I was safer here?"

"Well, weren't you?" Theo gave her a pointed look, then turned away to open the door. He went in first, leaving Céline to trail after him.

"No," she said, her voice thick as she closed the door behind them.

"What do you mean?"

"A German officer came while you were out." It was some comfort that Theo's eyes widened in surprise. "Hauptmann Richter, the same man who came to raid our cellars after the invasion began."

"That's impossible. Those men all moved on as the Germans swept south and west. He would have had to go over someone's head in order to remain, and why would he do such a thing?"

"I can't explain why he was still here," Céline said, glaring at him. "But you're missing the point. He—he knows my father is Jewish. And he . . ." She hesitated. "He touched me, Theo."

Theo blinked at her. "Touched you how?"

"He ran his hand down my breast."

Theo frowned at her, his expression puzzled. "I'm sure it was accidental."

"It wasn't. I think I know the difference."

He raked a hand through his hair. "Well, what do you expect me to do? March down to the German headquarters and lodge a complaint?"

"I had hoped that you might have a bit of sympathy for me. And some concern."

"Of course I'm concerned." He hesitated. "Where did this take place? He knocked on the door?"

For an instant, Céline considered lying. "No. I—I was in the cellars."

The room went so still that in the sudden silence, Céline could hear the scampering of a small creature, probably a mouse, somewhere beneath the floorboards.

"In the cellars." Theo's voice was flat.

"Just for a moment. I needed to think."

"And you can't think here?"

"I am stifled by this place! Don't you understand that? By our home and by you and by the restrictions, and by all the ways our lives have changed. I just needed to find some peace."

"You're a woman, and you were here by yourself, with no one else around." Theo frowned. "You can't just put the Maison Chauveau in that sort of peril. What if he had suspected we were hiding something in the caves? Then where would we be? After everything that Michel has done for us!"

Céline swatted angrily at the tears that had pooled in her eyes. "This isn't about Michel."

"But you can't—"

"It's about me!" she interrupted. "Your *wife*, Theo!"

Theo hesitated before his expression softened a bit. He stepped forward and pulled her into his arms. "I'm sorry," he said into her hair as she stood stiff against him. "Of course. I'm sorry."

"I know." Céline's voice was muffled against his muscular chest, and she was glad, for he couldn't hear it trembling.

Theo was loading up the Citroën near the garage the next morning just before dawn when Michel came to the door. He knocked, and before Céline answered, he called, "If you're not dressed yet, Céline, I can have a word with you later."

Céline pulled the door open and smiled shakily at him. The fact was, she didn't put much time anymore into making herself presentable, which she knew bothered Theo. But she had scrubbed herself clean in the bath the night before, trying to forget Richter's hand on her body, and now her hair hung in waves, and her freshly scrubbed face shone. She was wearing an old, loose dress with work boots, as she had planned to spend the morning tending to their small vegetable garden. "No, I'm dressed, Michel. I couldn't sleep."

"Neither could I. Theo told me what happened."

"I'm so sorry." Céline hung her head. "I shouldn't have done anything to endanger the champagne house."

"Céline, I don't care about the champagne house. It's you I'm concerned about, and I wanted to say that I'm sorry."

"What for?"

"For taking Theo away with me and leaving you alone. I thought I was doing the right thing, keeping you safe, but I see now that I only put you in peril. I hope you can accept my apology."

"Michel, you have nothing to apologize for. I should never have been in the cellars. Believe me, Theo made that clear."

"And I wish he hadn't." Michel frowned and glanced over his shoulder. The hood of the car was open now, and Theo was inspecting something inside. "This is your home. I just don't want you in any sort of danger. I give you my word, Céline, that I will do all I can to make sure you're protected."

It was exactly what she had wanted to hear from Theo the day before. "Thank you," she managed to reply.

"Inès will be here with you today. Perhaps that will make you feel a bit safer." The tightness in his voice was unmistakable as he added, "She understands now that I need the car."

"Thank you, Michel," Céline whispered as he started to walk away. "For being concerned about me."

Michel turned back and smiled sadly. "All will be well, Céline. I promise. We're in this together."

Late that evening, with the lights out and Theo's weight on top of her in bed, Céline closed her eyes and tried to drift away, to find herself in another place and time. But as Theo grunted and pushed himself inside her, covering her jaw in dry, hungry kisses, it was Michel's face she saw in her mind, Michel's voice she heard in her ear, making promises he couldn't possibly keep.

Startled and embarrassed, she forced her eyes open and clung to Theo's back, trying in vain to hold on.

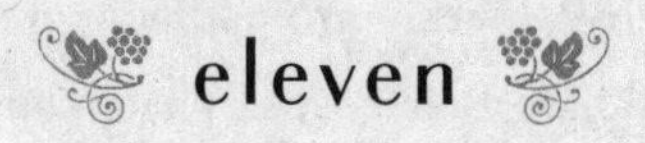

eleven

JUNE 2019

LIV

Liv woke at midnight to the sound of strangers' laughter in the hall outside the hotel suite and realized she had fallen asleep on the couch in the parlor. She sat up with a start and fumbled her way in a panic to Grandma Edith's door, which was closed. She quietly cracked it open and breathed an audible sigh of relief when she saw her grandmother sleeping soundly there among a pile of fluffy white pillows. The older woman had obviously come back while Liv slept and hadn't bothered to wake her. Liv closed the door and crept into her own bedroom, but after she had washed her face and changed into pajamas, it took a long time to fall back asleep, her annoyance at her grandmother's mysteriousness simmering just beneath the surface.

"Where were you last night?" Liv asked when Grandma Edith finally emerged into the parlor, already fully dressed, just before ten the next morning.

Grandma Edith hesitated before dropping her gaze. "Watch

your tone, Olivia," she said mildly. "Perhaps you forget that I'm a grown woman who has the right to come and go when and where she pleases."

"I never said you didn't," Olivia shot back, aware that she sounded like a sullen teenager. "I was just worried about you. You said you didn't feel well, and then you vanished."

"Yes, well, here in France we believe in the benefit of a walk from time to time."

"But you didn't tell me you were going out."

Her grandmother opened the suite's small refrigerator. "I assumed you would piece that together when you noticed I was no longer here. I see you didn't use any of your time alone to go to the market. That would have been nice."

"You wanted me to go grocery shopping?"

"First of all, no one calls them grocery stores here." Grandma Edith closed the refrigerator door. "Secondly, are you telling me you did not leave the hotel? In a city you've never been to before?"

"I wanted to be here when you came back." She glared at her grandmother. "By the way, your attorney dropped by with some paperwork."

Grandma Edith's head snapped up. "My attorney?"

"Ah, finally a reaction," Liv muttered. "Yes. Julien Cohn. You've been with his family's law firm for seventy years? In

Reims, a city you've never once mentioned? Do you want to tell me what this is all about?"

"Not particularly." Grandma Edith scratched her arm and gazed out the window. "But I suppose I'll have to at some point. That's the reason we're here, isn't it?"

"*What's* the reason we're here?"

Grandma Edith didn't answer. Instead, she strode toward her room. "Get dressed, Olivia. I have a call to make, and then we're going out."

"He's handsome, isn't he?"

They were the first words Grandma Edith had uttered since leading Liv out of the hotel and onto the bustling street. Liv glanced around but saw no one particularly notable, except perhaps for a silver-haired man sipping coffee at a table outside a blue-awninged café to their right. "Him?" she asked.

"What? No!" Her grandmother looked scandalized. "I was talking about Julien Cohn. Obviously. I hoped you had not lost all sense of good taste after your divorce."

Liv narrowed her eyes, but Grandma Edith just smiled innocently.

"Well?"

"Does it matter?" Liv thought of Julien's wedding ring. "So is that it? You've dragged me to Reims to look at unavailable, handsome men for the purpose of evaluating my sanity?"

"So you admit he is handsome, then?"

Liv shrugged. "Well . . . yes, of course. My divorce just made me single—not blind."

"Then there is hope for you yet. Now, here we are."

Grandma Edith stopped abruptly in front of a brasserie on a side street, and Liv looked up. " 'Brasserie Moulin,' " Liv read aloud, and her grandmother nodded, but she didn't go in. Instead, she stood frozen on the sidewalk, her eyes suddenly glassy. Though it was still early, the tables outside were already packed with people talking, laughing, enjoying their coffees and their glasses of champagne. Liv's mouth watered as a waiter bustled by with a steaming basket of *pommes frites*.

"It has hardly changed," Grandma Edith murmured, more to herself than to Liv. She took a small, tentative step forward, but her knees buckled, and Liv grabbed her elbow just in time to keep her from falling.

"Grandma Edith! Are you all right?"

Grandma Edith regained her balance and yanked her arm away. "Of course. Perfectly fine. Well, what are we waiting for?"

Liv followed her grandmother inside, staying close in case the older woman faltered again. As Grandma Edith asked a young, dark-haired waiter for a table in her elegant, clipped French, Liv gazed around.

The brasserie was dark with wood paneling, an expansive bar area, and droplights overhead spilling narrow pools of light into the aisles. The tables matched the wood of the bar, and each was lit with its own small lamp. Though the windows in the front opened to the modern street outside, there was something timeless about the furnishing of the interior, something that made Liv think this place had probably looked the same fifty years ago, maybe even one hundred years ago, as it did today.

"Voilà," said the waiter as he led them to a table and pulled out chairs for them both with a flourish. He handed each of them a double-sided laminated menu as they sat down, then whisked away, back to the front of the restaurant to help the young couple that had just entered.

"Have you been here before?" Liv asked, scanning the list of appetizers.

"*Oui.*" Her grandmother didn't elaborate, but the color had drained from her face, and her hands were trembling.

"Are you sure you're all right, Grandma Edith?"

She finally made eye contact. "Would you stop asking me that? I'm not about to keel over, if that's what you're concerned about."

"You just seem"—Liv hesitated—"shaken. I'm worried about you."

"Well, do not be." Her grandmother returned to studying her menu.

"Okay," Liv said slowly. "So, um, is there anything you recommend?"

"Don't be foolish. I'm quite certain the menu has changed since I was here last."

"Well, when was that?"

"Oh, seventy-five years ago, give or take."

"Seventy-five—" Liv began to repeat, but she was interrupted by the arrival of another young waiter, clad in all black, who ran down a list of specials in rapid French that Liv couldn't entirely follow, mostly because she was too busy trying to puzzle out what her grandmother had just said. *Seventy-five years?*

Grandma Edith ordered a coupe de champagne for each of them without consulting Liv and then excused herself to *les toilettes* as soon as the waiter hurried away. Liv watched her go before shaking her head and returning to the menu. She scanned the front—a list of tartares, a few salad options, a potato cream soup, a house terrine—and then turned the menu over. The back featured several main courses—seared tuna with sesame seeds, sea bream in pistachio oil, a burger with fries—and a specialty cocktail list. At the bottom of the page was an italicized paragraph titled *Histoire de la Brasserie.*

Liv began to skim the restaurant's history, translating the French as she went. She was impressed to read that it had been here since

1888, and as she read on, she learned that the original owner, Gilles Moulin, had passed the brasserie on to his son, Pierre Moulin, who had no children of his own and thus passed the brasserie on to his sister's eldest son, Edouard Thierry, in 1936.

Liv stopped reading and looked up in the direction her grandmother had disappeared. Thierry was, of course, Grandma Edith's last name and Liv's maiden name. Grandma Edith still hadn't emerged from the bathroom, so Liv turned her attention back to the menu, her curiosity piqued. Surely it wasn't a coincidence that the older woman had chosen a restaurant whose past owner shared their family name, was it? She read on.

Soon after Champagne was occupied by the Nazis in the summer of 1940, Edouard and his wife became active in the French Résistance. Along with a local network, they helped disrupt Nazi movements in and around the Marne, and ultimately provided Allied troops with information that proved crucial in battle. Edouard and his wife moved away at the end of the war, and the brasserie was passed to Edouard's younger brother, Guillaume, who sold it to Humbert Bouchet, a young World War II veteran, in 1950. The Brasserie Moulin is today owned by Humbert's grandson, Edouard Bouchet, who was named in honor of the proprietor who showed so much courage in the face of the Nazi Occupation.

When Liv looked up again, Grandma Edith was finally on her way back to the table, shuffling slowly and gazing around as if she'd seen a ghost.

"Have you decided on something to eat?" she asked once she'd settled, with some difficulty, back into her chair. The waiter arrived with two tulip glasses of champagne, and Grandma Edith held hers up and clinked it against Liv's without missing a beat. She took a small sip and said, "I might be in the mood for a salade Niçoise. Or perhaps an omelette."

"Are we related to the Thierrys who used to own this brasserie?" Liv asked instead of replying.

Grandma Edith set down her champagne and put a shaking hand to her forehead. "*Pardon?*"

Liv held up the menu and pointed. "It says that a man named Edouard Thierry owned this place during World War II."

Grandma Edith glanced at the menu, and for an instant, her features melted into something soft, mournful, almost open. "Why, yes, Edouard," she whispered.

"Grandma Edith, was he your husband?" Liv knew only that her own dad had never known his father. Grandma Edith never spoke of him. "Were *you* involved in the Resistance like Edouard was? Is that why you've never told me that you had a connection to Reims?"

Grandma Edith blinked at Liv. "It says that? That Edouard was involved with the Résistance?"

"Yes, but you haven't answered my—"

"My God," Grandma Edith murmured. "If he had lived to see his secret printed up on his own brasserie's menus like—" She stopped abruptly, and Liv leaned forward, sure that her grandmother was about to reveal something.

But before she could continue, they were interrupted by the arrival of their waiter. "*Bonjour mesdames, avez-vous fait votre choix?*" he asked, utterly oblivious to his terrible timing.

Grandma Edith looked confused, and then she frowned and gestured to her champagne glass. "*Je ne veux pas de cette coupe de champagne. Je veux un martini. Du Gordon's, s'il vous plaît, avec une olive.*"

The waiter glanced at Liv and then nodded, whisking the champagne away and hurrying toward the bar.

"Well?" Liv asked.

"This was an important place in many lives," Grandma Edith said after a long pause. "Lives that were saved. Lives that were lost."

"Edouard, you mean? Did he die after the war?"

The waiter arrived again, silently setting down a martini with a single green olive on a spear and then hurrying away. The older woman took a sip. "The war was a long time ago, Olivia. We all made our choices."

"Grandma Edith, please! What are you talking about?"

"I—I want to tell you. But it's very hard, you understand."

"You want to tell me *what*? Is that why you brought me here? Were you here during World War II?"

Grandma Edith didn't answer. Instead, she swirled her olive around before popping it into her mouth and then draining the remainder of her martini in one long swallow. She opened her handbag, withdrew two twenty-euro notes, and placed them on the table. "It seems I've lost my appetite. I'm sorry. Please feel free to stay and enjoy lunch without me." She rose, and not waiting for an acknowledgment, began to hurry toward the exit.

"Grandma Edith, wait!" Liv grabbed her own purse and rushed after her grandmother, but the older woman was moving surprisingly quickly and was already out the door by the time Liv reached it. Just before Liv followed her outside, though, she noticed something on the wall to the right of the entryway, an old framed black-and-white photo with a plaque beneath it. She hesitated, the words engraved there catching her eye: *Edouard et Edith Thierry, 1939.*

Her heart thudding, Liv looked to the grainy image of a tall, handsome man with thinning black hair, and his small, dark-haired wife, both of whom were posing in front of the Brasserie Moulin with proud smiles on their faces. The woman was Grandma Edith, Liv was sure of it. The photograph was eighty years old, and not terribly focused, but her diminutive size was just right, and her slightly mischievous smile matched Grandma Edith's exactly. Liv stared in awe, reaching up to touch the young Edith Thierry's face, before reminding herself that it was the older Edith Thierry, the one who was ninety-nine and stubborn as a mule, who needed her now.

She pushed out the door, scanning the street for her grandmother, who had nearly been swallowed up by the crowd on the sidewalks. But Liv could still see her, a block down to the left. "Grandma Edith!" she called. "Wait!"

But her grandmother didn't slow, and after pushing through a cluster of tourists, Liv reached the door to their hotel at the same time Grandma Edith did. "Grandma Edith!" Liv cried, and finally the older woman turned as Liv opened the hotel door for her.

"Olivia? What are you doing here? I thought you were going to stay and have some lunch."

"It was you, wasn't it? You *were* Edouard's wife! What happened, Grandma Edith?"

She sighed and walked into the hotel lobby. Liv hurried after her.

"Grandma Edith? I saw the picture. You and Edouard, outside the brasserie in 1939."

"What picture?" Grandma Edith stepped into the open elevator and held the door for Liv, but she avoided eye contact.

"It was just beside the front entrance. The plaque said 'Edouard and Edith Thierry.'"

"Well then, it seems you already have your answer."

The elevator doors slid open on the sixth floor, and Grandma

Edith got out. Liv scrambled after her but stopped short as she rounded the corner toward their suite and saw Grandma Edith's attorney standing in front of their door, clutching the same manila envelope he'd had yesterday.

"Madame Thierry!" he said, his face brightening. "Just the woman I was looking for." He held up the envelope, but his smile fell as Grandma Edith snapped it from his hands, bustled past him without a word, and breezed into the hotel room, slamming the door behind her. He turned to Liv. "Is she all right?"

"I have absolutely no idea." When Julien gave her a puzzled look, Liv added, "We just came from the Brasserie Moulin, which was apparently owned during World War II by my grandmother and my long-lost grandfather. But she won't tell me a thing."

"Ah." Julien glanced at the closed door once more and then back at Liv.

"Do *you* know her story? About whatever happened at Brasserie Moulin?"

Julien hesitated. "Some of it."

"And?"

"And . . . Liv, I cannot tell you, I'm afraid. But, ah, I would just remind you that things are not always what they seem."

"Oh good, more cryptic statements," Liv muttered. She dug through her purse, searching for her own key. "It's not just her story, you know. It's mine, too. My father died when I was just a little girl, and my grandmother refuses to talk about the past. She's ninety-nine. If I don't start putting the pieces together, they'll be lost forever."

"And I think that is why she brought you here."

"To dance circles around the truth while drowning herself in gin?"

Julien laughed. "Perhaps." His expression softened, and he added, "She hasn't spoken of the past in many, many years. It must be painful."

"But—"

Julien held up a hand. "But you're right. You deserve to know. And so I suppose there is no harm in telling you at least that your grandmother did live for a time here in Champagne. In fact, she met my grandfather here many years ago, during the war."

"So your grandfather knows about her past, too?"

"The pieces she chose to share, yes, and the pieces he witnessed himself. But I'm sure there's more to the story." Julien reached out and squeezed Liv's hand. "Give her time."

She was struck by the warmth and strength of his fingers against hers, and she quickly pulled away. "Thanks."

"*Pas de quoi.* And remember, Liv, the best things in life are worth waiting for." And then, with a murmured *au revoir,* he was gone.

twelve

FEBRUARY 1942

INÈS

After the harvest ended, autumn turned to winter, the days shortening, the nights turning frigid as ice crusted the vines. Michel had grown colder, too, bit by bit. Inès had tried to make him understand why she'd needed to see Edith, but it had been months now, and he hadn't forgiven her. Not that she needed his absolution, but it felt as if he'd closed himself off to her since September, and that was a long time—in the midst of a war, no less—to continue feeling as if you'd made an enemy of the person who was supposed to love you most. Then again, she'd been losing him long before that.

"It is not that I'm angry at you," Michel said wearily late one night in early February as he climbed quietly into bed beside Inès and found her awake, shivering beneath the thin blankets. Outside, snow fell lightly. "It is that my trust in you is shaken."

"All because I took the car for a night, many months ago?" Inès asked, hating how desperate she sounded. "Michel, I've apologized a hundred times. But I feel so stifled here."

"Don't you think we all do?" He sat up, and even in the darkness, even without seeing his face, she knew he was vibrating with principled anger. "You can't just run away when things get difficult!"

"I wasn't running away! I just needed to breathe."

"Breathe?" Michel choked on a laugh. "Do you know how lucky we are? How lucky *you* are? All of France is starving, and because we live near farmland—and because the Germans want to keep us happy in order to keep the champagne flowing—we have enough to eat, enough to heat our home. We still have a way to make money, to make it through the war. There are people in the cities who would kill for that, Inès. Do you understand?"

"Of course." And she did; on her return from Reims, in the light of day, she had seen living skeletons clutching ration tickets and standing in lines that snaked for blocks. "It's just that you still have a purpose, Michel. You still get to be *you*. Who have I become?"

He looked away. "These are trying times for all of us."

"You don't understand. I'm—I'm not happy."

"For God's sake, Inès!" Michel shoved the blankets aside and climbed out of bed. "Is that all you think about? Your happiness?"

He stormed out of the bedroom, slamming the door behind him, before she had a chance to reply. In his absence, the tears came, and she angrily wiped them away. Didn't she know better than to let his words hurt her?

Now, in the deep darkness of the night, with Michel's criticism washing over her, something stirred in Inès, something angry and righteous, and she threw the covers off, shivering as she groped around for the cardigan Céline had knit for her, a gift for the holidays that had embarrassed her, for all she'd gotten Céline in return was a tube of lipstick, purchased on the black market through a local vigneron's young son. It had seemed at the time a great luxury, for many women were resorting to using beetroot to stain their lips. But Céline had merely given her a pinched smile and a murmured merci before turning away in unspoken judgment.

Inès was sick of feeling useless, shallow, and unprincipled. She knew she wasn't as knowledgeable as Michel, Céline, and Theo were about what was happening with the war, but that didn't mean she didn't care. And though she wasn't particularly good at anything having to do with champagne production, she was tired, too, of Michel making her feel as if she no longer had a place here. She was going to go tell him that before she lost her courage.

She lit a lamp and shoved her feet into her decaying boots. They had once been warm and solid, but they'd been worn so many times the soles had mostly disintegrated, and there were holes in the toes. Still, they were all she had, and they would provide some measure against the wet freeze outside. She slid into her fraying overcoat, pulled on a wool cap, and slipped out the back door into the deep, bleak evening.

Even with the lamp lighting her way, it was almost impossible to see through the inky night. Still, up ahead, from the entrance to the cellars, she could see a faint wash of light, and she knew Michel was belowground. It was time to confront him face-to-face after months—no, years—of being made to feel useless.

As she descended from the silent, snow-swept world above, her footsteps landed dully against the stone. They were loud enough that Michel should have heard her coming, so she was puzzled when the light drifting out from one of the winding tunnels far ahead to the right didn't waver. Didn't he hear her? She almost called out, to let him know it was only her, but a small, vindictive part of her took some comfort in the idea that he might think she was a German soldier approaching. He deserved to feel ill at ease on his own turf, as she so often did.

But when she rounded the corner into the dimly lit cave, she gasped, for it wasn't just Michel standing there; there was another man, tall and swarthy, and they were both scowling and pointing pistols at her. Inès gave a little scream and turned to run.

"Inès, wait!" Michel barked, taking two quick steps toward her. He grabbed her arm and wrenched her back into the cave, where the other man, whose black overcoat was swept with snowflakes and whose left cheek was marked from eyebrow to chin with a deep scar, still stood with his gun leveled at her head.

Inès screamed again, and Michel tightened his grip. "For

God's sake, Inès, shut up!" He turned to the other man and said, "It's okay. This is my wife."

"Your wife," the man repeated flatly, but it took another moment for him to lower his weapon. When he finally did, he continued to glare at Inès, his small black eyes slits of suspicion. "What is she doing here?"

But Inès was no longer listening, for she had seen what was behind the men. Three wine barrels, the kind that were used to age the single-vineyard wines before they were blended, sat with their heads pried off. It wasn't wine inside the barrels, though; it was rifles, dozens of them. "Michel?" she breathed, unable to pry her eyes away.

"Now she's seen us!" barked the man. "She knows. This wasn't part of the deal."

"Go," Michel said. "I'll take care of it."

"You'll take care of it?" Now the man's fury was aimed at her husband. "You know Fernand doesn't tolerate mistakes."

"I'll fix it." Michel's tone was stiff, controlled, and his nails dug into Inès's arm so hard that she winced. "Now go."

"Fernand will hear about this." The man cast one more look of seething fury at Inès, then slipped from the cave, his footsteps somehow silent in the night, as if he were a ghost, someone who had never really been there at all. But when she finally dared to glance at Michel, she knew from his expression that she'd imagined none of it.

"Do you want to tell me what you're doing?" he hissed.

"Do you want to let me go?"

Michel instantly released her, as if surprised to realize he'd still been holding on. Inès rubbed at the spot where his fingers had been, and an expression of guilt flitted over Michel's face before it hardened into something colder.

"Inès, why are you here?"

"You're going to act like *I'm* the one doing something wrong? What *is* this?"

"What is what?" His attempt to move in front of her, blocking her view of the rifle-loaded barrels, might have been laughable if the stakes didn't feel so high.

"The guns, Michel. The barrels full of guns."

His expression changed then, anger cracking into guilt, and then fear. "You can't tell anyone, Inès."

"Do you really think I would?"

"I don't think you would betray me on purpose, but—"

"But what?" She cut him off, her frustration bubbling over. "But *what*, Michel? You don't think *this* is a betrayal?"

"What are you talking about?"

"How could you put us in danger this way?"

"Ah, so you're worried about yourself." Michel's voice had taken on a familiar frigid, superior edge, and it made Inès furious.

"How dare you act like I'm being selfish? If the Germans found these weapons, they'd arrest all of us, Michel, not just you.

We'd be put to death, Theo and Céline, too! Do you understand the danger you're putting us all in?"

"I'm not the one putting you in danger! Can't you see that? It's the damned Germans!"

"But we're safe if we play by their rules!"

"Play by their rules? There are no rules! We have to fight back, and—"

"We just have to keep our heads down! You said so yourself!"

"*Non!*" Michel's shout echoed through the caves, and he glanced around, suddenly conscious of the racket they were making. "*Non,*" he said more quietly. "We have tried that. For nearly two years now, Inès, we've played along. But I'm done."

"So you're doing what? Smuggling weapons? For whom?"

He ignored her questions. "Maybe we're safe, but what about the ones we can't protect? There are rumors, Inès. They're coming for the Jews soon, just like they did in Germany. How can we stand by and let our friends and neighbors be taken away for nothing? For the mere fact of their birth?"

Something shifted in Inès as Michel averted his eyes. "Are you talking about Céline? You're doing this to protect *her*?"

"I mean *all* the Jewish people in our community. Does it matter that I wish to protect Céline, too?"

She stared at the cache of weapons for a long time, trying to form the words her heart wanted to say. "Yes, it matters, Michel. It matters very much. Why is it more important to you to protect Céline than to protect me?"

"How can you ask that? You're relatively safe because you're Christian. She is increasingly defenseless."

"And what if the Germans came looking for me because of what you're doing here?"

Michel didn't answer. As she glowered back, something flickered in his eyes, and in that instant, Inès found herself wondering whether he loved her anymore. There was no warmth in his expression now, no forgiveness. He saw her as the enemy, a threat. She hadn't been a perfect wife to him, but she deserved more than this.

"Why didn't you tell me what you were doing?" she asked.

"Inès, it doesn't concern you."

"Of course it does," she said softly. "You don't trust me, do you?"

"I . . ." Michel hesitated. "It's not that. It's just—I can't involve you in this."

She took one last look at the rifles, and felt a strange sensation of pieces slipping into place, the future being locked in. "Well then, good night," she said, then she turned away and retraced her steps into the blank, frigid night. Somewhere in the distance, a lone dog howled, and as the wind picked up, Inès could feel tears freezing on her cheeks.

In the morning, Inès slept late without meaning to. Now that they were in the dead of winter, the sun didn't rise until around eight. Most days, Inès was up much earlier, stoking the fire, readying the house for the day ahead, brewing ersatz coffee made from malt and acorn for Michel, scrounging up what she could for a small breakfast. But last night's discovery had left her drained, and since Michel never returned to bed, there was no one to wake her.

She went to the window and peered out into the cold morning, but the footprints in the snow were long gone, all traces of the shadowy visitor and Inès's argument with Michel already erased. She quickly dressed for the day, piling her hair into a bun and pulling on the sweater Céline had made for her. But it quickly felt itchy and oppressive, so she took it off and shoved it back into a drawer.

When she finally made it downstairs, she could hear sounds outside the window as she began to put away the dishes stacked on the counter. She recognized Michel's voice, and then Céline's high-pitched laughter. Something shifted in Inès, and she gripped the counter to steady herself. Michel was laughing now, too, the deep sound of it drifting in through the windowpane. Anger dug its spikes into Inès's skin. *She* was the one who knew her husband's secrets, who had agreed to bear the risks of his decisions, and he was outside entertaining Céline?

She pulled aside the curtain slightly. Michel stood just centimeters from Céline as he leaned in close to murmur something. Was Inès imagining something romantic between them? That was crazy, though, right? Inès thought she knew her husband well enough to say that he would never betray the vows of their marriage, but last night had proven that she didn't really know him at all.

Céline laughed again at something Michel said and they stood staring at each other for a long moment. It was the kind of look lovers shared before they kissed. But then Céline pulled back, and Michel turned to go toward the caves. Still, Inès had seen enough.

She wouldn't be made a fool of. She wasn't going to sit here in sleepy Ville-Dommange, playing the role of the submissive wife, while he made dangerous decisions about their future and flirted with the wife of his *chef de cave*. She smashed the plate she had been drying against the floor, and out the window, she could see Michel's head snap in her direction. He started toward the house, but she was already turning away, heading for the stairs to pack a small suitcase.

She didn't care anymore that Michel needed the car; let him catch a ride with one of his shadowy friends if he had to. If Michel had decided that Inès wasn't enough for him, and that he needed to risk her life in order to protect Céline, then so be it. She was going to Reims.

thirteen

FEBRUARY 1942

CÉLINE

After Michel disappeared into the main house, Céline wondered whether Inès had seen her talking to him and had misinterpreted the conversation. Had she been laughing too hard with him? Had her body language betrayed the increasing closeness she felt to him? Certainly she'd been feeling things she shouldn't, but she hadn't acted on them, of course. She would never do that.

In reality, Michel had only asked her whether she was quite well. "You look a bit under the weather," he'd said, and she'd laughed, explaining that Theo had recruited her last night to taste a few different vintages of Chauveau, to make sure his 1938 was developing consistently, and that perhaps she'd had too much. Michel had still seemed concerned, though. "I don't mean to pry," he had said, "but if there is something weighing on your mind, you can always come to me."

"I'm fine, thank you," she had replied. After all, what would she say—that his concern meant a great deal to her, because her own husband seemed not to care at all? That she felt lonelier than she ever had, and that sleeping next to Theo now felt like sleeping with a stranger? That she couldn't bring herself to speak her fears about her father aloud to Theo anymore, because she knew he would react with a shrug and then change the subject to fermentation or the health of the vines? All of those things would be a betrayal of her husband, and so she merely shook her head and said, "I—I should begin work."

That's when she'd heard the sound of something breaking inside, and Michel had rushed off, cursing Inès under his breath.

Twenty minutes later, Céline and Theo were working side by side in the cellars, riddling bottles in silence, when there was the sound of a car engine roaring to life overhead.

"Is Michel going somewhere?" Theo asked without breaking his rhythm. With both hands, he continued to turn two bottles at a time an eighth of a revolution to the right, barely disturbing them in their *pupitres*, their wooden A-frame racks.

"I don't think so."

"Would you go check?" Theo didn't look at her as he continued to turn bottles at lightning speed. She envied his effortless skill—though she tried to keep up, she felt like a novice in comparison.

Céline brushed her hands off on her pants as she rose. She grabbed her overcoat and hat from the bench by the door and hurried down the main passageway of the cellar toward the stairs, emerging aboveground just in time to see the Citroën pulling down the drive, its taillights reflecting off the narrow patches of snow that hadn't yet melted. Michel was staring after it, his fingers laced behind his neck.

"She's leaving again," Michel said. They watched the car until it disappeared around the bend. "Merde," he muttered. "After last night . . . Christ."

Michel's jaw was set in anger, and for once, Céline didn't know what to say to him. She wondered what had happened between Inès and Michel the night before, but it wasn't her place to ask. "I'm sorry," she said, knowing it wasn't enough.

"I just—I thought she was different." Michel said the words quietly, almost as if talking to himself.

Céline understood exactly what he meant, for it was how she felt about Theo these days, too. "War has a way of revealing who we really are."

He looked at her, surprise in his eyes. "Yes. It does."

They held each other's gaze until they were interrupted by the sound of an approaching engine in the distance. Had Inès's conscience kicked in? But it wasn't her; there was a dirt-streaked farm truck turning from the main road through their front gates. It rattled noisily toward them, sputtering from its makeshift fuel.

"It's Louis," said Michel, starting down the drive.

As the man parked beside Michel and got out of the truck, slamming the door behind him, Céline recognized him as the son of one of the vignerons they had been buying grapes from for years. He glanced at Céline, and without exchanging pleasantries, he began to speak to Michel in low tones. It was clear that she had no part in the conversation. She had just turned to retreat back to the cellar when Michel called out for her. "Céline, could you please come here?"

She looked back and saw both men watching her. Something about their impassive expressions made her stomach twist in fear. "Is something wrong?" They didn't answer, so she walked over to them hesitantly.

Michel put a hand on the small of her back, his touch so light she could barely feel it. Still, it comforted her. "Céline, do you know Louis Parvais?"

The other man, a bit younger than Michel with thick black eyebrows and an impressive beard, nodded at her, his dark eyes somber.

She nodded back. "I believe we've met briefly. Bonjour, monsieur."

"Bonjour." He seemed to be waiting for Michel to say something.

"Céline," Michel said. "Louis has brought news. He, ah, delivers messages from time to time."

Céline glanced quickly at Michel and then at Louis. Was he the messenger Michel had told her about? "What is it?" she asked.

"It's news from Burgundy," he said, glancing at Michel once more before his gaze settled on her. "I'm afraid your father and his parents have been arrested."

Céline's knees felt suddenly weak, and she swayed on her feet. Michel steadied her, his hand firm on her back now. "It will be okay," he murmured, but she knew it wouldn't be.

"What happened?" she managed to say.

"Your father was picked up along with a few other men—all Jewish—on suspicion of conspiring to undermine the Germans."

Céline could feel her eyes widen. "But—"

"Obviously false charges," Louis said quickly. "But nevertheless, your father has been taken to prison. His parents—your grandparents—were taken a day later."

"No," Céline whispered. "None of them were involved in anything. I know they weren't."

"I'm sure you're right. The Germans have begun arresting Jews on flimsy accusations. There's someone from the local council making inquiries, and it's our hope that your father and grandparents will be released."

"And if they're not?"

Louis exchanged looks with Michel. "They are sending Jewish prisoners east on transports to Germany and Poland, madame.

But we will do our best to ensure that your family is not removed from France."

"You can't give up hope, Céline," Michel said. "If Louis says there is a chance, it is true."

"Please, tell no one what I've told you today," Louis warned. "I will bring more news when I have it." He climbed back into his farm truck and rumbled away before Céline could say another word.

"Are you all right?" Michel asked once Louis's vehicle had vanished around the bend. His hand hadn't moved from her back.

"No." She tried not to imagine her father and her elderly grandparents behind bars. "I must go home to Nuits-Saint-Georges, Michel. There must be some way I can help, and—"

"No." Michel cut her off, his tone both gentle and firm at the same time. "You can't. If your father is already known to the authorities, they would waste no time in ascribing meaning to your reappearance. The best way to keep safe is to stay here."

"But—"

"There's nothing you can do."

"I have to tell Theo."

Michel reached out and grasped her hands. "You mustn't, Céline. Please, it would be too difficult to explain how you received word. Trust me, my contacts are doing all they can to secure your father's release."

"Your contacts? What have you become involved in, Michel?" The surge of fear she felt over his well-being surprised her.

He studied her for a long time. "You would never betray me." It wasn't a question as much as it was a statement of fact.

"Of course not."

"Meet me in the cellars after sunset tonight."

"What will I tell Theo?"

"Tell him nothing." Michel's eyes bore into her as he let go of her hands. She felt suddenly unmoored. "You are the only one I trust."

For the rest of the day, Céline tried her best to act normal. When she'd returned to the caves after her encounter with Louis and Michel, she had assumed she would have to concoct a story to explain her absence, but Theo merely grunted to acknowledge her.

She tried to turn bottles with him for a while, but her hands were trembling now, and when Theo noticed, he told her to leave. "You're shaking the wine, Céline," he'd said, as if she couldn't hear the glass clattering against the wood. "Get ahold of yourself, would you? Perhaps you can begin sorting through the corks that have come in."

Céline hadn't managed more than a nod, but she'd been grateful to leave the caves—and Theo—behind. Aboveground, Michel was nowhere to be seen, and as Céline headed to the barn, where they kept crates upon crates of corks, she thought about Michel and the risk he was clearly taking to help her. What favors had he called in with Louis to get news of her father? The thought made her feel sick to her stomach, but she couldn't decline his help.

The sun slipped below the horizon around six thirty, and after Céline trudged back to her cottage, shared a small dinner with Theo, and quickly washed the dishes, she told him she needed to see if Inès had some yarn she could borrow to mend a few pairs of socks.

"Is she back?" Theo asked without glancing up from the book he had just begun reading, something about vinification.

"If she's not, perhaps Michel will know where she keeps her mending supplies."

"Right."

Céline watched him for a moment. His face was lit by lamplight, his expression serious. "Theo, I'm very worried about my father," she said quickly. She couldn't say more without betraying Michel's confidence, but she needed to share at least this, to give him the chance to comfort her.

"I'm sure he is fine."

"But the Germans are coming for Jews. It's beginning."

Theo scanned her face, then returned his attention to his book. "Céline, you mustn't believe the rumors. Your father will be perfectly all right. Now go see Inès before it gets much later. Take a lamp."

She stared at him, her eyes watering, before grabbing her overcoat and hat and slipping out the back door into the cold night. When she reached Michel's door, she glanced at her own cottage. All the curtains were drawn tight; Theo wasn't watching her. He probably hadn't given her a second thought since returning to his book.

She took a sharp right and headed for the entrance to the cellars. Once she was belowground, she lit her lamp, cleared her throat, and called out, "Michel?"

There was no reply at first, but then another light came to life from deep in the caves, and she heard footsteps. Soon after, she saw Michel round the corner ahead and gesture to her. "Come, Céline," he called.

She hurried toward his light, conscious of the inelegant slap of her wooden soles against the stone floor. Michel was in a storage cave deep in the cellars to the right, and by the time she reached it, he had retreated back inside.

"What did you tell Theo?" he asked instead of greeting her as she entered the cave and saw him standing behind several wine barrels.

"That I needed to borrow something from Inès. I don't think he listens much to me these days anyhow."

Michel frowned, and Céline feared she had gone too far. He and Theo had once been quite close, and Céline knew they still considered each other friends, even if their perspectives about the war differed. Besides, it certainly wasn't Céline's place to be criticizing her husband in front of the man who was technically his boss. But then Michel beckoned her deeper into the cave. "I know just how you feel," he said. "There's something I would like to show you."

Céline moved closer, her curiosity piqued as Michel set to work prying the head from one of the barrels. Surely he hadn't called her down here to discuss wine. Perhaps she had done something wrong when she'd last cleaned the barrels, but she couldn't imagine Michel summoning her to the cellars late in the evening to chastise her, either.

Still, nothing could have prepared her for what she saw when Michel finally set the barrel head aside and beckoned her closer. She peered into the barrel, then stumbled backward when she realized it was full of long guns.

"Michel!" She pressed a palm to her chest in a desperate attempt to slow her suddenly racing heart. "What on earth is this?"

"This is how we will win the war," he said calmly, still watching her closely.

"No," she protested. "No, no, no. This is too dangerous, too—"

"It's something I must do." His voice was low, confident.

"There are many of us, people who live by the rules in plain sight, but work to undermine the German authorities."

"How long have you been doing this?"

"I've been wanting to do *something* since the day the Germans first arrived in Ville-Dommange. But it was difficult to find a network to work with at first. Few people around here know me well, which is proving an asset, but early on it presented a challenge. I needed to earn their trust." He paused and glanced back at the guns. "I've been involved for the past few months, since one of the organizers admitted how helpful it would be to move supplies in and out of the caves."

She swallowed hard. "Why are you showing me this?"

He set the head back on the barrel, and the air seemed to return to the room. "Because, Céline, I want you to understand that there are people fighting against the Germans. That there's hope for your father and those like him."

"But why you?"

"Because I cannot sit idly by while innocent people suffer." He took a step toward her, and then another. His breath was soft and warm on her cheek. "Because this war is destroying us. Because if we do not stand up to injustice now, who do we become? We are French, Céline, and that means we fight for liberty. For equality. For brotherhood. It is in my blood. I cannot do things differently."

Céline stared at him, rooted to the spot. "But if the Germans find you—"

"They will not."

"But if they do—"

"It is a risk I take." He reached for her hand. "I just wanted you to know that you are not alone."

Tears stung her eyes. "Does Inès know?"

"Yes." He hesitated. "That's one of the reasons I wanted you to know, too. She found me last night. I had to tell her the truth."

"My God, and she left this morning for Reims . . ."

"She will not betray me." Michel's tone was firm.

She wondered how he could be so sure. "And Theo?"

Michel frowned. "I know I have already asked you to keep the news about your father from him. And I must ask that you keep this from him, too. This isn't an area of the cellars he frequents, and I know he leaves the care of the barrels mostly to you and Inès. I don't think he will stumble across this. I'm sorry. I know that puts you in a difficult position."

"But why tell me, then?"

Michel studied her. "Because I trust you. Theo, he is a great winemaker, but sometimes I fear he cares more about prestige than he does about morals. We're in the midst of a war, and honestly, Céline, I don't give a damn about how our champagne tastes right now, or what kind of a profit we turn. I care about people surviving."

"I do, too."

"Then trust me."

This time, it was Céline who took a step closer. "I do," she whispered. "I always have."

Time seemed to slow as they leaned closer to each other. But just before their lips could meet, Céline pulled back, blinking. "I—" she began.

"I'm sorry." Michel moved quickly away. "I should—I should get back to this. And you should return to Theo before he becomes concerned."

"Yes, right." Céline hesitated. "Michel?"

"Yes?"

She was still shaken by the step she had very nearly taken across a line, a point of no return. But she was sure of one thing: that she couldn't let Michel do this alone. "I want to help," she said.

"Absolutely not." His answer was instantaneous. "It is too dangerous. Especially for you, Céline."

"You don't understand," she said. "That is exactly why I must do this. If the Germans have taken my family, I no longer have anything to lose."

"But I do," Michel said. "And I cannot lose you."

fourteen

JUNE 2019

LIV

By her third day in Reims, Liv had scoured the Internet for any references to Edouard Thierry and the Brasserie Moulin, but she'd found little, save for a website that had reprinted the same historical information that appeared on the menu. She had even called the restaurant that morning and muddled her way through asking the manager about Edouard and his role in the Resistance.

"I know only the things you've already read," the manager replied in English, apparently recognizing Liv's accent. "I'm sorry I can't be more help."

So when Grandma Edith swept out of her bedroom at eleven thirty in a cloud of perfume, her eyes twinkling as she suggested a lunch out, Liv was relieved. Perhaps this meant her grandmother was ready to reveal what had compelled her to bring Liv here. Liv was increasingly sure that it had to do with the mysterious Edouard Thierry.

"I have to make just one stop before we eat," Grandma Edith

said as they headed out of the hotel into the late morning sunshine. "I hope you don't mind. It's just a short walk."

They strolled in companionable silence for a while, passing the enormous church that Liv could see from her window, which looked just like Notre-Dame in Paris. "When I first came to Reims," her grandmother said, stopping to let a group of schoolchildren pass, "the cathedral hadn't yet been entirely rebuilt. It was decimated during the First World War. It's incredible to see it now in such wonderful shape."

Liv looked up at the massive building in confusion. Its soaring twin towers filtered the sunlight, while hundreds of statues looked down on them from high overhead. A carving of Jesus hanging from the cross above the entrance to the left looked like it had been there for hundreds of years. "What do you mean it was decimated?"

Grandma Edith pursed her lips. "They don't teach any of this in your American schools, do they? You see, this was one of the hardest hit areas in all of Europe during the Great War. The front line was just a few kilometers outside town, and Reims might as well have had a target painted on it; the city was bombed so often and so severely that the people who lived here moved their schools, their hospitals, their whole *lives*, into the crayères—the old chalk quarries, which are used for champagne storage—beneath the earth. More than eighty percent of the city was completely destroyed, and the cathedral itself suffered very heavy damage."

"Really? You'd never know from looking at it."

"Yes, well, we don't all wear our scars on the outside," Grandma Edith said. "But if you look closely, you can see the chips in the stone from the shelling. This whole city was a different place then. Do you notice all the art deco buildings? The ones that look a bit like they belong in Miami Beach rather than rural France?"

Liv nodded. The juxtaposition of the old and new had struck her from the start.

"That's because so much of what is here today was constructed just after the war, in the 1920s. That was the style at the time."

"Were you here in the twenties, then?" Liv asked.

"Don't be daft. I was just a small child then."

"Well, I never knew until yesterday that you'd spent any time in Reims at all, so forgive me for not having your mysterious time line straight," Liv grumbled.

"If you have a question, just come out and ask it."

"Fine. Let's start with something simple. You lived here for a while, right? How old were you when you got to Reims?"

Grandma Edith narrowed her eyes, and Liv was sure she wasn't going to answer, but then she said softly, "Eighteen. It was 1938."

"So did you come here with Edouard?" Liv pressed. "Or did you meet him when you got here?"

"Don't pretend you understand the past." Grandma Edith picked up the pace, turning right onto the rue du Trésor.

"I'm not," Liv protested. "I understand none of this. That's the point. I'm just trying to figure out what happened to you."

"And I am trying to tell you," Grandma Edith countered. "It is what I brought you here for, Olivia. But you have to let me do it in my own time." Before Liv could reply, her grandmother stopped abruptly in front of a squat brown building and pushed the intercom button to the right of the entryway. A buzzer sounded, unlocking the door, and Grandma Edith pushed it open. "Wait here. I just have to deliver something upstairs."

Liv glanced at the small plaque to the right of the front door: *Cohn Société d'Avocats.* It was, Liv realized, Julien Cohn's law firm. "I'll come with you," she said.

"No. This is a private matter." Grandma Edith hurried inside, letting the heavy door swing closed behind her.

Liv tried the door, but it was locked, so she buzzed upstairs, hoping she would be granted entrance as easily as her grandmother had been.

"Your grandmother says she'll be down shortly," said the tinny female voice that came through the intercom.

"Oh. Merci," Liv replied, feeling foolish.

When Grandma Edith reappeared a few minutes later, Liv was surprised to see Julien a few paces behind her. "Well, hello," he said with a smile.

"Hi." She could feel her cheeks suddenly flaming, and she turned away, embarrassed. What was wrong with her?

"Your grandmother mentioned you two were going to lunch," he said, "and she invited me along."

"Um, okay."

"Manners, Olivia," Grandma Edith said sharply. She turned and began walking before adding over her shoulder, "Julien is our guest."

"Of course. I'm sorry." It wasn't that Liv minded the charming, perfect-haired lawyer joining them; it was just that if Julien came along, it was unlikely Grandma Edith would be spilling any secrets. Liv gave Julien a small, polite smile as they fell into step behind Grandma Edith, who was bulldozing through the pedestrians clogging the crowded sidewalk.

"I hope I'm not interrupting anything," Julien said as he kept pace.

"I was just hoping my grandmother would be ready to talk about Edouard and the Brasserie Moulin today."

He smiled. "And you think your grandmother is a woman who can be rushed?"

"I'm delusional, I know."

Julien laughed, and some of Liv's frustration melted away. She gave him another smile, this time a real one.

"Here we are!" Grandma Edith announced from up ahead,

waiting for Liv and Julien to catch up. She had stopped outside a tiny brasserie with a few empty tables outside, overlooking the edge of the Place d'Erlon. "I have read wonderful things about this place on Facebook."

"Your grandmother is on Facebook?" Julien murmured.

"I had no idea she even knew how to email," Liv replied.

Julien opened the door for Grandma Edith, who flashed him a flirtatious smile as she slipped inside. Liv rolled her eyes as she followed her in. She waited with Julien just inside the entryway as the older woman exchanged a few words with a waiter, who gestured outside and grabbed three menus.

Once they were seated and Grandma Edith had ordered a bottle of Bergeronneau-Marion champagne, she closed her menu with a definitive snap and stood up. "Well, if you two will excuse me, I just realized that I am very tired. I think I'll go back to the hotel and take a nap."

Liv stood, instantly worried about her grandmother. "I'll come with you."

"Nonsense." Grandma Edith deposited several bills on the table. "The champagne is on me. Stay. Enjoy. I'll see you when I wake up, Olivia."

She walked away before Liv could say another word. Liv sank slowly back down into her seat just as the waiter reappeared with their bottle of champagne, expertly popped the cork, and poured two tulip glasses. He looked at Grandma Edith's empty chair and then at Julien, who shrugged and said, "*Elle est partie.*" The waiter nodded and whisked her empty glass away before hurrying off.

"I'm sorry about that," Liv said. "If you want to leave, too . . ."

"And leave you to drink an entire bottle of champagne by yourself?" Julien asked. "Besides, I love Bergeronneau-Marion. Your grandmother has good taste."

Liv smiled. "Do you think she'll be okay?"

"I feel certain of it." He raised an eyebrow and then his glass. "To your grandmother."

"To my grandmother," Liv grumbled, clinking glasses with Julien and then taking a long sip. The champagne was crisp and full, and its bubbles tickled her tongue. "May she one day learn to act like a normal human being."

Julien laughed and then fell quiet. In the silence between them, with butterflies fluttering in her stomach again, Liv had the strangest feeling that she'd just been set up on a date. But that was ridiculous; he was married, and she wasn't the kind of person who flirted with other people's husbands, even when they were as attractive as Julien.

They were interrupted by the reappearance of their waiter, who filled their water glasses from a carafe and took their order: beef tartare with a green salad for Liv, and filet of beef for Julien.

"So, tell me about your wife," Liv finally blurted out when

the waiter vanished. She needed to remind herself that the butterflies in her stomach had no business there. "How did you meet?"

Julien looked confused, but he answered politely. "Well, Delphine and I were in school together years ago. We began to date when we were both fifteen."

Liv forced a smile. "Did you know right away that you'd marry her someday?"

"Well, I thought she was very beautiful at first. But it was only once I got to know her that I knew I would fall in love with her." He paused to take a sip of his champagne. "What about you? You are involved with someone? Your grandmother mentioned you divorced recently."

"Of course she did," Liv muttered. "I'm pretty sure the day I signed the papers qualified as one of my grandmother's favorite 'I told you so' moments."

Julien smiled. "Oh, I don't think so. Of course, your grandmother, she loves to be right, *oui*? But she has mentioned many times how concerned she is about you."

Liv groaned. "Great. So you must think I'm completely pathetic."

"No, not at all! I think it must be very difficult when someone you believe in becomes someone you don't recognize anymore."

Liv half laughed. "So I see she's gone into great detail about my failed marriage."

"Oh no, I'm sorry. She really hasn't." Julien turned a bit pink. "I just—I can imagine how hard that must have been on you."

"Right, so, uh, I'm going to change the subject before I feel like even more of an idiot, okay?"

"Liv, I didn't mean—"

She held up her hand to stop him. "Really, it's fine. So, Julien, do you and Delphine have any kids?"

When Julien smiled again, his whole face lit up. "A daughter, Mathilde. She's about to turn six. She is looking forward to the end of her *école maternelle*, which I think you call preschool? Prekindergarten? Next year, she will be with the bigger children in *une école primaire*, which of course feels impossible to me. The time goes by so quickly. Every day, she reminds me more of her mother."

"Well," Liv said. "Mathilde is very lucky to have you."

"Thank you," Julien said. "I try very hard, but sometimes, I know I fall short. But enough about me. Your grandmother, she has not told me much about your life. Do you have any children?"

The question hit Liv in the gut. "No, I don't. Sometimes life doesn't work out exactly the way you want it to, you know?"

"You want children, then?"

Liv examined her lap. "I did," she mumbled.

"But certainly it's not too late, right?"

Liv opened her mouth to reply, but Julien waved his hands to stop her.

"I'm sorry, Liv. That's a very personal question."

"I don't mind. As long as I won't bore you with the answer."

"Not at all."

Liv met his gaze and looked quickly away. "I—*we*, my husband and I—had trouble conceiving. We actually tried for years to get pregnant, and I think that was why our marriage began to fall apart. I—I couldn't give him what he wanted."

"What *he* wanted? What about what you wanted?"

"We both wanted to have a family. It felt like a failure when I couldn't make that happen. My ex, he was someone who was used to having a perfect life. All the fertility treatments, all the specialists we had to see, all the times we got our hopes up—it was just too much." Liv stopped abruptly and put her hand over her mouth. "I'm so sorry. That was way more information than you needed. Talk about oversharing." She closed her eyes.

"No. I asked you, Liv. And I'm glad you told me, because it gives me the chance to say to you that I'm sorry that happened." He hesitated. "When you are married, you are supposed to be partners above all else, to be there for each other through thick and thin, in sickness and in health, whatever comes your way."

Liv's eyes felt damp. "That's how things are with you and your wife?"

Julien looked down at his hands and then back at Liv, a shadow across his face. "Liv, you do know that my wife is—"

Liv waved her hands to stop. "Oh God, sorry, it's totally not my business to be asking about your marriage, is it? Seriously, it's been so long since I've been alone with an attractive man that I—" She stopped and shook her head, her cheeks on fire. Had she really just called him *attractive*? This was mortifying. "Great, and now it sounds like I'm hitting on you. I'm so sorry."

Julien laughed, the dark expression gone. "Well, being called attractive by a smart, beautiful woman isn't the worst thing that has happened to me today. There's certainly no need to apologize."

Liv groaned. "Can we change the subject again, forget I said anything?"

He grinned. "But what if I don't want to forget?"

The words sounded almost flirtatious, and Liv looked away before she could read into them. "So, um, Mathilde, huh?" she said. "Do you like being a father?"

"Liv, it's the most incredible thing I've ever done in my life." The light that came on in his eyes made Liv want to cry. Would Eric have felt that way if they had succeeded in getting pregnant? Liv knew immediately the answer was no, and that made her wonder why she'd been so eager to build a family with a man like that. Maybe it was because she'd never really believed that men like Julien existed. "And what about you, Liv?" Julien asked after a pause. "Do you still want to be a mother?"

Liv sighed. "Honestly? I'm forty-one, and I have no idea what

I'm doing with my life right now. I don't think I know what I want anymore. I just—I feel lost." It was the first time she'd admitted it aloud.

"Liv," he said, and he waited until she looked up. "I don't think you are lost. I think your future is open. You're ready for whatever magic comes along."

"Yeah, but who's to say there's any magic coming?"

"I am," he said slowly. "You just have to believe."

But later, after she'd parted ways with Julien outside the restaurant, she let herself imagine, just for a moment, what it would be like to have a life in which she had a family to care about and a partner who loved her the way Julien evidently loved his wife. But the thought was so far from reality that it only made her feel worse.

Julien was wrong. Maybe his life was magical, but hers was a mess, and she had no idea how to fix what was broken.

fifteen

FEBRUARY 1942

INÈS

Inès spent her drive to Reims stewing about Michel—the fact that he didn't trust her, the revelation that he was hiding munitions without telling her, and the way he seemed determined to make her feel small and insignificant. She was tired of feeling as if she didn't matter, though it was certainly nothing new.

But then she'd seen the way he'd looked at Céline outside the kitchen window, and something had shifted within her. She recognized the expression on his face, because it was the way he once looked at her. What if her husband hadn't just lost interest in her, but had fallen in love with Céline? But that was ridiculous, wasn't it? Though Inès knew he was frustrated with her ineptitude around the champagne house, her disinterest in politics, surely he knew she was trying. In any case, Edith would talk some sense into her.

But when she arrived at the brasserie late in the morning, it was closed up tight, and no one answered when she pounded on the door. She went around back to Edith's apartment, but there was no answer there, either. Hugging herself tightly and turning into the fierce, frigid wind whipping through the streets of Reims, Inès finally walked away in a daze.

Where could Edith be? It was a Wednesday morning, a time when Edith and Edouard should have been preparing to open for lunch. She imagined Edith at a clandestine meeting somewhere, delivering information to a shadowy contact like the one Inès had stumbled upon in the cellars of the Maison Chauveau, and the more she thought about it, the more irritable she felt. How was it that everyone seemed to be walking around in possession of precious secrets, while Inès was coasting through a life that hadn't changed at all, a life that meant nothing in the grand scheme of things?

Perhaps she could persuade Edith that she could have some value as a worker for the underground, too. She would make Edith see that she was trustworthy, and she would finally be able to show Michel she was someone he could respect.

But the longer she walked around Reims, keeping her head down to avoid eye contact with any of the German soldiers strolling by, the colder and more abandoned she felt. By the time she passed by the Brasserie Moulin for the sixth time that day and finally found it open, her mood had darkened again. She went in and spotted Edith immediately.

"Where have you been?" she asked Edith as she approached the bar.

Her friend looked up from drying glassware. "Inès? What are you doing here?"

"I've come to see you. I've been in Reims all day, Edith, but you were out."

"Yes, well, Edouard and I had somewhere to be." Edith's eyes slid away. "I didn't know you were coming." She gave her a small smile. "Are you all right, then?"

Inès could feel her shoulders relax a little. "Where were you?"

Edith blinked. "Just at a friend's apartment for a bit."

"Which friend?" Inès didn't know why she was pressing; she likely didn't know all of Edith's friends anyhow, which made her feel sad. Life had moved on here without her, just as it had at the Maison Chauveau.

"Someone you don't know." Edith hesitated and then crossed from behind the bar to take Inès's hand. "My dear, you don't look like yourself. Would you like to go upstairs to our apartment, perhaps take a nap for a bit?"

Inès shook her head. "Perhaps I can help you out in the restaurant tonight."

Edith glanced over her shoulder, where a bartender was drying glasses, three waiters were chatting, and two Germans were deep in conversation at a table in the corner. "Oh no, Inès, we have plenty of help."

"Are they in on it, too?" Inès nodded to the waiters. "Do they . . . listen to conversations?"

Edith's eyes widened and flashed as she released Inès's hands. "I'm sure I don't know what you mean, Inès," she whispered.

"I'm sure you do."

When Edith spoke again, her tone was frosty. "Be careful, my friend."

Inès closed her eyes. This wasn't going how she'd imagined it. "I'm sorry, Edith. I didn't mean—" She stopped and took a deep breath. "I need you, Edith. Nothing is working out the way I thought it would. I'm useless at the Maison Chauveau, and Michel has grown to despise me."

"I'm sure that's not true," Edith said, her eyes darting quickly to the Germans in the corner again before returning her divided attention to Inès. "You're the love of his life."

"You've barely seen us these past two years, Edith. Things are different now."

"I'm so very sorry you're feeling that way. But I'm not sure what you think I can do."

"You can help me, Edith. You can let me have a role in whatever it is you're doing here. Please. I want to show Michel that he can trust me. I want him to look at me the way he . . . the way he looks at Céline." And there it was, the raw truth, the thing Inès most feared.

"What are you saying?" Edith asked softly. "You think he's having an affair with Céline?"

"I—I don't think so." Inès hesitated. "But the way he feels about me has changed. Maybe if I work with you . . ."

"No, Inès." Edith's tone was firm. "There is nothing you can do. You are welcome here anytime, but only as my dear friend." She leaned in closer. "The work we are doing here is dangerous."

"And you think I cannot handle it."

"It's not that."

"Then what is it?"

Edith sighed. Edouard emerged from the kitchen and frowned at her, his eyes darting to the Germans in the corner. Edith nodded slightly, unspoken words passing between them. She turned back to Inès. "I'm sorry, but I really must deliver some beers. But stay as long as you like. Come sit at the bar, and I'll have the bartender fetch you a glass of wine, all right? You are always welcome here. But don't think that you can casually become involved in something you don't understand just because you want to win your husband back. That's not how things work."

As Edith walked away without turning back, Inès watched her go. She had the strange sensation that she had fallen off a ship and her best friend had just walked away with the only life preserver.

Three hours later, the dinner service was in full swing, the brasserie was crowded with Germans, and Edith had vanished into the crowd, leaving Inès alone. She had been installed at the bar since Edith had dismissed her that afternoon, and the bartender had steadily refilled her glass, his expression gradually changing from one of disengaged politeness to one of pity as the room around her grew blurrier and blurrier. By the time a clean-shaven man with slick silver hair and a perfectly tailored gray suit sat down beside her and said *bonsoir*, the world was fuzzy, and Inès was finally at ease.

"And what is a beautiful woman like you doing out alone on a night like this?" the man asked, gesturing for the bartender. He ordered her a glass of champagne without waiting for her answer and then turned his gray eyes back to her. "Surely there is a gentleman somewhere wondering where you are."

Inès flushed at the compliment. "Yes, well, my husband is too busy thinking about business and war," she muttered before she could stop herself. "He probably hasn't even noticed that I'm gone."

"I would notice," the man said, lowering his voice until it was almost a purr. "I would feel your absence deeply, were I the one you had chosen."

That got her attention, the idea that she had *chosen* anything at all. She felt so constrained by the decisions she had already made that she had lost any sense of control over her own life. It made her feel like nothing, but looking into the eyes of the man at the bar, she felt something she'd almost forgotten. This man clearly found her attractive, and with that realization, she regained something she thought had been lost.

She didn't say anything, for she had nearly forgotten how to flirt, and besides, that wasn't what she had come here for. Her champagne arrived then, little bubbles racing to the surface, and the man raised his glass. "To you," he said, watching her closely.

"And you." She took a small taste. It was surprisingly refreshing to have a glass of champagne that hadn't been made by her husband, to enjoy it without sitting across from someone who was analyzing every sip.

"I suppose I should introduce myself," the man said. "My name is Antoine. Antoine Picard."

Inès let him take her hand. "Inès Chauveau."

"Chauveau, as in the Maison Chauveau?"

"It is owned by my husband."

"Ah. Well, it is a pleasure." He brought her hand to his lips and kissed the back of it softly. "A true pleasure, madame. But it is a shame for me that you are someone else's wife, I think."

"And perhaps it is a shame for me that I have a husband who doesn't seem to care whether he has a wife at all." When Inès saw something spark in the older man's eyes, she knew she had crossed a line. She could have taken it back, forced a laugh, softened the words by adding something about how Michel was just busy, but she held her tongue and watched as the man's gaze locked on hers.

"Your husband does not sound like a very wise man," Antoine said, watching her carefully.

"He is very educated," Inès said. "Far more than I."

"It sounds as if he has reminded you of this more than once. He does not put much stock in your opinion?"

"Well . . . yes." Inès blinked. How did the man know? "He treats me as if I'm a child."

"Well, that is a mistake," Antoine said, leaning in closer. "Because it's clear to me that you are very much a woman."

Inès saw Edith across the room watching her, and she turned away before she could be branded by her friend's judgment. If Edith didn't trust Inès to be a part of her world, why should Inès care what she thought? Still, Inès could see the scene through Edith's eyes, and she knew it looked damning. Antoine Picard was nearly old enough to be Inès's father, and yet it was quite clear from the way he had moved in possessively that his intentions were anything but paternal, even after she had mentioned her marriage. *Especially* after she had mentioned her marriage. She knew she should be careful.

"I should go," Inès said reluctantly.

"Stay a little longer," Antoine said, angling his body closer to hers. She could smell his cologne, musky and powerful. "Finish your champagne, at least. Perhaps you'll tell me a bit about yourself."

"Oh, well, I'm not very interesting."

He leaned in. "I doubt that very much."

And so, after a bit of encouragement, Inès had found herself unspooling the tale of her life, from Lille to Michel, and listening intently as Antoine explained that he had worked for the regional government for years but had taken on a new role now that the Germans were in power. "It is important to get along, so that everything goes as smoothly as possible," he'd said, lowering his voice. "Of course I'm still one hundred percent on the side of France, but the Germans are here for now, aren't they? It's in everyone's best interest to work with them, I think."

"That's just what I've been telling my husband!" Inès blurted out.

"Have you? And does he not agree?"

Inès hesitated. It felt disloyal to be criticizing her husband's position on the Occupation, but at home, she wasn't allowed to have an opinion. Here, this virtual stranger seemed interested to hear what she had to say. The feeling that he cared about her thoughts was more exhilarating than she would have imagined. And it wasn't as if she was going to say anything about Michel's hidden guns. "He seems to be getting angrier and angrier as the months go by," she said. "But I think that kind of anger is dangerous. Stay off the Germans' radar, and we'll be safe, that's what I say."

"You're a wise woman, Inès," Antoine said, and as he stared at her with respect shining in his eyes, she felt herself flushing with power.

As he began to talk again, telling her about his large apartment in the center of Reims, and his corner office with a view of the cathedral, Inès was so impressed that she hardly noticed when another drink arrived. They stayed there, sharing the details of their lives, until the brasserie closed. He kissed her gently on both cheeks, his lips lingering longer than they should have, before he bid her goodbye.

"Be careful there," Edith warned later that night as Inès stumbled toward the bedroom that had been hers before she left to marry Michel. "Remember that a dalliance in wartime comes with stakes."

"How could you suggest that I would do such a thing?" Inès demanded, outraged, although she had been considering exactly that. Before Antoine had departed that night, he had leaned in and whispered into Inès's ear, asking if she'd consider meeting him again the following evening. She had hesitated, but now, with Edith already assuming she could be so easily unfaithful, something in her snapped. Edith and Michel were too virtuous and important for her, apparently. But with Antoine Picard, she'd finally felt she had some value. And it wasn't as if she were planning to sleep with him.

And yet she had. The very next night, after another day during which she'd been left alone while Edith and Edouard disappeared on secret errands, she met Antoine at the bar of the Brasserie Moulin and agreed against her better judgment when he suggested finding somewhere else to have a meal. "I know the owner of a very nice place just around the corner from the cathedral," he whispered in her ear. "Would you like to accompany me? It might be nice to escape your friend's watchful gaze." He nodded to Edith, who was across the room, glaring at him, her arms crossed over her chest.

Inès locked eyes with Edith and then looked away. Edith could never understand what it meant to be discarded, for the war had only drawn her and Edouard closer. "A meal would be lovely," she murmured. And so they departed without another glance, though Inès could feel Edith's eyes burning into her back.

That night, Inès ate better than she had since the war had begun—four sumptuous courses at a small, dimly lit bistro called Arnaud's—and when she'd asked Antoine how he managed to get around the ration restrictions, he'd merely laughed and said that life was too short not to break a few rules. "Besides," he'd added with a smile, "who could blame me for wanting to impress such a beautiful woman?"

Antoine was effusive where Michel was reserved, practiced where Michel seemed like an amateur, loquacious where Michel preferred to silently brood. Instead of acting as if he were above Inès, he genuinely wanted to know what she thought of the Occupation, of the news coming from the battlefields, of the situation in which the Champenois currently found themselves. And though she knew she wasn't as educated about current affairs as she perhaps should have been, she liked the way he listened to her when she tried to explain why she felt that people like her husband were overreacting. "You are," he said as their coffee—*real* coffee—arrived, "a breath of fresh air."

How lovely to be thought of that way, instead of as an insubstantial twig. Perhaps that was why, after a few glasses of wine and an evening of being listened to carefully, Inès finally agreed to accompany Antoine back to his apartment nearby, though she knew better. "After all," he had said quite reasonably, "it is after curfew, and I don't want any German soldiers harassing you. And what if you return to the brasserie and your friend is not awake to let you in? Come, you will be safe with me."

And she had indeed felt protected as he took her arm and gently steered her toward his building on the rue Jeanne d'Arc. She'd felt sheltered as he guided her up the stairs with his hand at her elbow. And she had felt valued as he opened the door to his apartment and said, "I hope very much that you like it here, Inès."

And then, as he closed the door behind them, his lips fell upon hers for the first time, and whether it was because of the alcohol coursing through her or the loneliness that had become her constant companion, it didn't feel wrong. It felt exactly how it was supposed to feel with Michel, though it hadn't in some time. Antoine was gentle at first, but then his kisses grew hungrier, and as he drank her in, pressing his body against hers, she felt *desired*. It was intoxicating, almost enough so to make her forget that what she was doing was so terribly wrong.

Although Michel still dutifully took her to bed once or twice a month, Inès had never felt this sort of desire from him. Even at the beginning of their marriage, their lovemaking had felt careful, cordial. Now it felt perfunctory at best, a man occasionally servicing his wife in the polite manner that was expected. He was the only man she'd ever been with, and until that very moment, she'd felt a dismayed kind of certainty that intimacy would always feel like that.

But Antoine, he *wanted* her. It wasn't obligatory, and his mind wasn't elsewhere. He wasn't thinking to himself that he had more important things to do, or that she was not his intellectual equal. No, Inès could sense it in the deliberate way he unfastened her dress, his long, manicured fingers working their way carefully over each button. She could see it in his eyes when he turned his gaze to hers, could feel it in his touch as he peeled her slip away from her body and stroked her shoulders gently, could taste it in his mouth as he covered hers once again. It was wrong, and she knew it, but for the first time in her life, she could feel her body screaming at her that this was what she'd been missing.

So when at last her dress lay in a puddle on the floor, and he pulled away to ask, "Inès, may I take you to bed?" she only hesitated for a moment before saying yes. She thought of Michel just once, with a quick stab of guilt, as Antoine led her gently to the bedroom, but then she pushed her husband from her mind and focused instead on the man before her, who made love to her with finesse, and then fell asleep holding her tightly in his arms, like she was something to be cherished.

sixteen

JULY 1942

CÉLINE

Since the morning in February when Inès had broken a plate and driven off in a rage, she had been increasingly absent from Ville-Dommange, visiting her friend Edith once every two weeks, which suited Céline just fine. Céline could breathe when Inès was gone; she didn't have to worry that an innocent laugh shared with Michel would be taken the wrong way, or that Inès's anger at something insignificant would overshadow a whole day of work.

Inès had been more pleasant, too, her mood sunnier, which made everyone a bit more relaxed.

"Each time she goes to Reims, she comes back a new person," Céline marveled to Michel in the caves one day. "It's like magic."

"Time with Edith is good for her, I think," Michel replied with a small smile. "They've been friends since they were girls. Edith is the closest thing she has to a family."

"Except for you," Céline reminded him.

Michel looked startled. "Well, yes, of course."

But Céline wondered whether the thought had actually crossed Michel's mind before she pointed it out. After all, the gulf between Michel and Inès seemed to have widened. In contrast, the polite distance that had existed between Michel and Céline had long since vanished, and she felt closer to him than ever—close enough by mid-July to finally work up the courage to ask again to become involved in his work against the Nazis.

"No," Michel said immediately. "Absolutely not. If there were to be any suspicion of illicit activity here, there's at least the chance that the Germans would accept an explanation from me—or from Inès or Theo. But you . . ."

She bit her lip. "I'm half Jewish, so they would be all too happy to deport me."

"We cannot take that risk."

"But don't you see? That's just why I can't sit idly by. Besides, they haven't been deporting Jews from the rural regions yet, have they?"

But the next Monday, the Germans swept through Champagne and arrested forty-three foreign-born Jews, simply for the crime of being Jewish. The roundups came on the heels of mass arrests in Paris just three days earlier, in which more than thirteen thousand Jews were taken—including more than four thousand children.

It was almost too terrible to be believed, but by the end of the week, more horrific news had trickled in. According to Michel's sources, seven thousand Jews had already been quietly removed from France and sent to concentration camps somewhere in the east. She'd received no further word about her father and grandparents from Michel's friend Louis, and she was terrified that they were among the deportees.

"I don't think you are in any danger," Theo said the night after the arrests in Champagne, as he and Céline lay in bed, both of them wide-awake. "It was just foreign-born Jews."

"Foreign-born Jews," she repeated flatly. "Like my family."

"We don't know that anything has happened to them," Theo said.

But Céline knew, with a certainty she couldn't explain. There was no chance the Germans would have allowed them to remain in prison in France when they were clearly stepping up deportations. The question now was what would become of them. Her father was relatively hearty and could probably bear the backbreaking work that would be required of him in a labor camp. But what about her aging grandparents? Especially her grandmother? "No one is safe anymore," she said.

Theo was silent for a while. "I won't let anything happen to you."

Céline was glad for the darkness, glad that he couldn't see the expression on her face. "It wouldn't be up to you, Theo, if they came for me."

"I would put up a fight."

"And wind up dead? There would be no point."

In the silence where his reply should have been, she closed her eyes and tried to imagine Theo standing up to a handful of French policemen, or maybe a few uniformed Germans. She couldn't visualize it, but she could see Michel there in her mind's eye, one of his contraband rifles trained on the officers. "*Run*," he would urge her in that low, confident voice. It was enough to make a tear slip down her cheek, for as sure as she was that he would defend her, she was equally sure he would be executed for it. She could never live with herself if she let that happen.

"Céline?" Theo eventually broke the silence. "When did you stop believing in me?"

She opened her eyes. "Pardon?" But she'd heard him.

"I'm your husband. You should trust me to fight for you."

"I know." But how could she explain it? There hadn't been a single moment that her feelings toward him had changed. It had been a slow, steady slide. "It's not that I don't believe in you, Theo. It's that I fear you don't really understand what we're fighting for."

"What? Of course I do."

"But you've been so immersed in your job that you've barely looked up to see the world crumbling around you."

"You would fault me for working diligently?"

"No," Céline replied. "It is just that in times like these, champagne production is not the most important thing."

"So we should all just stop working? Let society collapse?"

"Hasn't it already?"

"But if we just keep holding on a little longer . . ."

"Then what?" Céline demanded, sitting up in bed. She suddenly felt furious. "What happens if we hold on, Theo? No one is coming to rescue France. And what happens when the Germans have finally purged all the foreign-born Jews? Who do you think will be next? You've seen the signs around town. They're not going to stop! How can you suggest that holding on will be an answer to anything?"

"You are too emotional." Theo sat up beside her and grasped her hand. "Céline, I know you're worried about your father and grandparents, but—"

"But *what*?" She pulled away from him. "Don't you understand that with every day that passes with no word from them, I imagine the worst?" She felt powerless, frightened, and angry at people like Theo—people who were willing to sit back and let it all happen, because it wasn't happening to *them*.

"You are worried, Céline, and that's reasonable. But let's not get ahead of ourselves."

"Oh, Theo." Céline threw the sheets off and got out of bed.

"Don't you see? You'll never be ahead of anything, for you're content merely to follow."

The next day, Theo had disappeared by the time Céline awoke on the couch. He'd left a short note asking her to get started with the riddling while he inspected a vineyard with Michel. *We will be back before noon*, he'd added. The words were as cold and detached as he himself had become.

Céline dressed quickly in a cotton dress and her wooden-soled shoes and headed for the cellars, longing for their chill. The July day was already shimmering with heat, the air oppressive. As she descended the stone steps, she exhaled and then filled her lungs with the subterranean coolness, tinged with the sweet, familiar scent of minerals married to yeast.

"Céline? Is that you?" Inès's voice came from somewhere deep in the cellars, shattering Céline's sense of calm.

"Hello, Inès!" Céline called back, her voice full of as much faux friendliness as she could muster.

"Oh good! I could use your help!"

Inès emerged from one of the caves ahead and waved cheerfully as she waited for Céline to approach. "Hello," Inès said brightly. "You're looking well this morning."

"Um, thank you," Céline said, confused by Inès's good cheer.

"You look well, too." It was true, Céline realized; Inès appeared reinvigorated; her cheeks were pink, her smile broad. "What are you doing?"

"Michel asked before he left if I could pull ten or twelve barrels so we can begin scrubbing them out this afternoon. But I can't quite reach them, and I was wondering if you could possibly support me as I climb up, just so I don't fall."

"Yes, of course."

Céline grasped Inès's arm and helped her up onto a large overturned barrel so she could reach a bit higher. Inès stood on tiptoe and pulled an empty barrel down from the shelf, grunting with the effort. "Here," Céline said, reaching for the barrel, "give it to me."

In fifteen minutes, they had pulled down the dozen barrels Michel had requested, stacking them at the entrance to the cave. "Thank you," Inès said, her cheeks flushed. "I couldn't have done that alone."

Céline smiled. "You're stronger than I realized."

"I think that living here has forced me to develop muscles I did not know I had." Inès held up a narrow arm and flexed a nearly nonexistent bicep. "Heavyweight champion of the world!"

The two women giggled, and Céline felt a rare sense of camaraderie between them. Where had this version of Inès been hiding?

"Céline?" Inès asked after they had sobered. "Are you worried?"

"Worried about what?"

"Michel." The mirth was gone from Inès's face now, replaced by something unfamiliar. Was it sadness? Fear? Inès appeared suddenly vulnerable, almost childlike.

"What do you mean?" Céline asked carefully.

"He said that he told you about the guns. Whatever he's doing, Céline"—she gestured into the depths of the tunnels—"it's dangerous, isn't it? I think he's making a mistake, don't you?"

Céline opened her mouth to reply, but a faint sound from overhead stopped her. It was an approaching vehicle, and as she and Inès both looked toward the ceiling of the cellars, a bad feeling formed in the pit of her stomach. "It's too early for Michel and Theo to be returning," Céline said.

"You're right." They exchanged glances and, without another word, headed for the stairs.

They were aboveground by the time an unfamiliar black coupe stopped in front of the main house. A broad-shouldered man in a spotless German officer's uniform, his jackboots gleaming in the sunshine, unfolded himself from the car. Shading his face with his right hand, he peered around until he spotted them. He smiled thinly, his mouth twisting beneath his narrow mustache, and Céline felt ill when she recognized him as Hauptmann

Richter, the German who had threatened her—and pawed her through her blouse—the previous September.

"Ah," he said, his smile broadening but not quite reaching his small, dark eyes. He slammed the door of his car shut and strode over to the women. "Just who I was looking for."

Céline tried to arrange her features into a pleasant expression. "Hello, Hauptmann Richter."

"So you remember me. Very good." He stopped in front of her, glancing once at Inès and then turning his full attention back to Céline. "Where are your husbands?"

Céline hesitated, but there was no point in lying. It was clear the men weren't there. "Out," she said. "Inspecting a vineyard."

"They'll be back at any moment," Inès added quickly, and Céline felt a small surge of relief as Inès moved closer to her, until their arms were touching.

"Then it appears we are alone for now." Richter was only looking at Céline.

"What can we do for you?" Inès asked loudly.

He kept his eyes focused on Céline. "I just wanted to make sure you'd heard the news."

Just then, there was a noise in the distance, followed a few seconds later by the appearance of Michel's trusty old Citroën chugging down the drive toward the house, enveloped as usual in a cloud of exhaust. Céline's sigh of relief must have been audible, for Richter's eyes narrowed. "Oh, how fortunate," he said. "Your men have returned. I'll be able to speak with all of you."

Céline's heart lurched as the Citroën screeched to a halt just two meters from them. Michel jumped out of the driver's seat, while Theo alighted from the passenger side. "What can we do for you, Hauptmann Richter?" Michel said, his tone even. But his eyes were wild and worried.

"Ah, Monsieur Chauveau, we meet again." He turned his gaze to Theo. "And you? You are the husband of this Jewess?"

Theo frowned and nodded. Céline wrapped her arms around herself, feeling suddenly cold, even in the thick summer heat.

"And you are a Jew, too?" Richter continued.

"No, of course not." Theo's reply was too fast, too adamant, and though it was true, it felt like a slap across Céline's face. "Besides, she's only half Jewish," Theo added quickly, and Richter chuckled.

"Is that how you justified marrying a *mischling*?" He licked his lips and turned his gaze back to Céline. "Well. I have come to make sure you had heard about the Jews we took away from Champagne this week."

Céline couldn't trust herself to speak. She glanced at Michel, whose eyes were trained on Richter. She couldn't read his expression, but his stillness scared her.

"Of course, but it was only foreign-born Jews," Theo said into the uncomfortable silence.

Richter's gaze didn't move from Céline. "For now."

"I was born in France," Céline said, her voice shaking, and Richter chuckled again.

"And that is why your name was not on our list. This time." Finally, he turned his attention to the men and nodded slightly. "I just wanted to make sure you were aware. I'll leave you to it."

He turned without another word, climbed back into his little car, and roared away.

It was Theo who spoke first. "What in the hell was the meaning of that?" Theo glared at her as if Richter's unsettling behavior had been her fault.

"Enough," Michel said quietly. He glanced at Céline. "The best thing we can do now is to not show the Germans our fear or our anger."

"But—" Theo began.

Michel held up his hand. "It is clear that this Richter fellow is aware of Céline. We must keep our ears to the ground about any movement against French-born Jews, all right?"

Céline and Inès nodded. Theo was still angry. "Come, Céline," he said. "Let's go home." He took her arm and steered her toward their house before she could respond. Céline looked over her shoulder as they went and saw Michel watching them with a frown.

Theo started in on her as soon as they were out of Michel's

and Inès's earshot. "Why did the German seem so interested in you?" he demanded.

"What are you implying?" Céline stared at him in disbelief.

Theo didn't answer. His face was red, his eyes wide and angry. "I've been thinking about it, and I think you should go south. Michel has contacts in the *zone libre*."

"What? No." Céline was startled; where had Theo come up with this idea? He had never mentioned it before. "I'm not leaving."

"That's foolish. You'd be safer there."

"There's danger everywhere," Céline shot back as they reached their front door.

"Just because Michel thinks you're safe here doesn't mean you are. It's not his place to be making decisions about my wife, you know."

"Nor is it yours!" Céline cried. "It's *my* life we're talking about."

"But it's not just your life, is it? It's all our lives! You being here, it puts us all in danger! You could ruin everything!"

"Ah, so is that what this is about? Not protecting me, but protecting the business?"

"I didn't say that. But you would so easily ruin the Maison Chauveau, just to prove a point?"

"She stays." Michel's voice came from behind them, firm and

low, and Céline whirled around. How long had he been there? What had he heard?

"But—" Theo began, his palms outstretched.

"She stays if she wants to," Michel said, cutting him off. "She will always have a place here, where we can look after her. Do you understand?"

"I understand perfectly." Theo's jaw flexed. "Excuse me." He went into the house, slamming the door behind him and leaving Céline and Michel alone.

"Michel, I—" Céline began, but he shook his head, and she stopped.

"You will be safe here, Céline," he said, holding her gaze. "I swear, I'll protect you with my life."

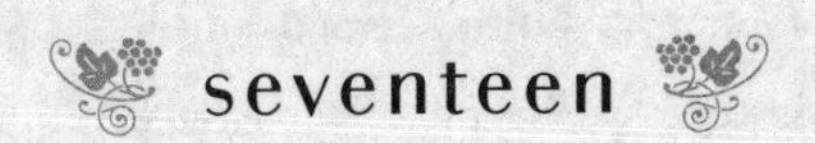

seventeen

JUNE 2019

LIV

For three days after Liv's conversation with Julien, she thought about his words—and the way she'd blurted out that he was attractive and then barreled on to ask him personal questions about his life—and felt more foolish with each passing day.

"I didn't bring you here to mope," Grandma Edith said over breakfast one morning. "And if you tell me you're thinking about Eric, I will have to disown you."

Liv forced a smile as she systematically dismantled the croissant that she'd plucked from their room service tray. She was still in her pajamas, while Grandma Edith was already in chic black pants, a white blouse, and red flats that matched her lipstick. "No, I wasn't thinking about Eric."

"Then who? I know that look. It's the look of a woman mooning over a man."

"What? No. I'm thinking about your attorney, actually. But not in the way you're implying."

"Julien?" Grandma Edith seemed amused. "And why not? He's very handsome, yes? And would you stop picking at your croissant? Honestly, Olivia, did your mother raise you in a barn?"

Liv rolled her eyes, but she obediently set the croissant down and brushed the crumbs from her fingers, feeling like a chastised child. She picked up her cup of coffee and lifted it to her lips.

"So why is Julien Cohn on your mind, then, if not for those perfect buttocks of his?" her grandmother asked innocently.

Liv choked on the sip she had just taken. "Grandma Edith!"

"What? I'm not dead yet. Now, are you going to answer my question?"

Liv sighed. "Julien just made some good points, that's all."

"Do be more specific, dear. I don't have all day."

"He just—he asked me some questions about my life. About what I want for myself. And it made me think about how maybe . . ." She paused. "Maybe I need to pull myself together and figure out what kind of life I actually want before it's too late. You know?"

"Ah." Grandma Edith took a small, satisfied sip of her coffee. "It seems Julien is as wise as his buttocks are perfect."

Liv gave her grandmother a look. "I think maybe I said too much, though. He was just being polite, and I started babbling about Eric and babies and leaving my job. I probably sounded like a lunatic. I think I scared him away."

Grandma Edith raised an eyebrow. "Olivia, dear, a true lady should never air her dirty laundry to the first gentleman who happens by. But you're in luck. You didn't frighten Julien, at least not that I'm aware of. He just had to go to Paris for a few days on business."

"And you know this because . . . ?"

"Because the business was on my behalf." Grandma Edith checked her watch. "In fact, he'll be here any minute. I'm not sure how you do things in America, but here in France, we prefer to be dressed with at least some makeup on when guests drop by."

Liv stood abruptly and headed for her bedroom. "Why didn't you tell me he was coming?"

"I wasn't aware you cared so much. Oh, and you have croissant crumbs in your hair!" Grandma Edith added helpfully as Liv slammed the bedroom door.

Fifteen minutes later, with a black cotton dress thrown on and her hair purged of pastry, Liv emerged into an empty parlor. It took her a few seconds to realize that her grandmother and Julien were on the balcony, deep in conversation. She took a few steps toward the French doors and was just about to join them outside when she heard her name. Surprised, she stopped to listen.

"I do not want to overstep," Julien was saying in French. "But I think you need to tell Liv the truth. It would change her life for the better."

"What do you know?" Grandma Edith's tone was much softer than her words were as she added, "What are you, twelve?"

"I'm forty-four, actually," Julien said with a small smile, not missing a beat. "And maybe having a better understanding of who she is will help Liv right now."

"I know you're right. But I must do this in my own time," Grandma Edith said at last, turning abruptly and heading back into the hotel room. She stopped short when she saw Liv in the parlor. "How long have you been standing there, Olivia?"

"Um, I just came out of my room," Liv lied. "Why?"

Grandma Edith narrowed her eyes. "No reason. Would you please see Julien out?" She disappeared into her own room without another word, slamming the door behind her. Liv turned back to the balcony and locked eyes with Julien, who was studying her intently. She hesitated before heading out through the doors to join him.

"Hi," she said.

"Bonjour, Liv," Julien said with a smile.

"Are you okay? It looked like my grandmother was laying into you."

He shrugged. "It's exactly how my grandfather talks to me. The trick, I've discovered, is to just not take their bait."

"Well, you must be better at that than I am." Liv smiled at him and then averted her eyes. "Listen, about the other day, I'm really sorry. I don't know what came over me."

"What do you mean?"

"The conversation we had—I unloaded on you like you were my therapist or something. I'm sorry. You're just—well, you're easy to talk to."

"You are easy to talk with, as well," Julien said. He took a step closer. "And there is no reason to apologize. I enjoyed getting to know you a bit better."

The silence that hung between them felt laden with something it shouldn't have, so Liv hurried to fill it. "Um, my grandmother asked me to walk you out."

He checked his watch. "Liv, perhaps this is a bit too forward of me, but I don't have to pick Mathilde up from my mother's house for another hour and a half, and your grandmother happened to mention you still haven't seen much of Reims. Would you fancy a quick walk around the city center before I have to leave?"

"I—" Liv didn't know what to say. "I don't want you to feel obligated."

He looked surprised. "Obligated? But this is something I'd like to do. Unless you do not."

The problem was that all Liv wanted to do in that moment was to walk out the door with Julien and never come back. But Grandma Edith probably wouldn't appreciate that, nor would

Julien's wife. Still, there was nothing wrong with accepting a quick tour from him, was there?

"Well?" Julien asked.

Liv smiled. "Sure, I'm in."

Ten minutes later, Liv was strolling east with Julien, toward the cathedral Grandma Edith had pointed out just days before. As they walked, Julien gestured to buildings here and there, explaining that the town had been almost completely rebuilt after the First World War. He led them past the Subé Fountain in the Place d'Erlon, the town's central square, and explained that the woman on the top, representing victory, was taken by the Germans in 1941 for her bronze wings. She wasn't replaced, he said, until 1989. Closer to the cathedral, they walked by the Carnegie Library, a beautiful art deco building built after World War I with money donated by American steel magnate Andrew Carnegie. It replaced the town's city hall, which had previously housed the library and had been destroyed in 1917.

"So what were you talking about with my grandmother?" Liv asked after he had pointed out a few more notable buildings and they had lapsed into a companionable silence. "I didn't mean to eavesdrop, but I heard you say my name when you were out on the balcony."

Julien blinked a few times. "How much did you hear?"

"Enough." It was vague enough to be the truth.

"Well then, you know it is a conversation you must have with her. For what it's worth, I think your grandmother is trying to do what's right. I'm afraid I might have offended her, though, by giving her my opinion. I have a habit of *me mettre le doigt dans l'oeil*—um, putting my foot in my mouth sometimes."

"I doubt that," Liv said as they turned onto the rue Cardinal de Lorraine and the cathedral soared into view just ahead. "I think you're probably pretty good at saying exactly what you intend."

"Why does it feel as if you know me so well, Liv?" His fingers brushed against hers.

"It feels like you know me, too." The air between them felt electrified, so Liv quickly changed the subject, taking a giant step away from Julien and almost falling off a curb as they finally stopped in front of the enormous church. "The cathedral looks just like Notre-Dame did before the fire," she said. A shiver ran through her as she regained her balance.

"Notre-Dame de Paris?" Julien smiled sadly. "Yes, what a tragedy that was. But you know this is Notre-Dame, too, yes?"

Liv looked at him blankly.

"Notre-Dame de Reims, that is," he clarified. "Of course the world is far more familiar with the cathedral in Paris—I blame Victor Hugo—but ours has always rivaled it in importance."

Liv raised an eyebrow.

"I see you doubt me, but let me lay out my case."

"You *do* sound like a lawyer."

Julien tilted his head back and laughed. "Okay, yes, true. But I am only a part-time lawyer, so maybe this story will only be partly dull. You tell me." He gestured to the church's grand facade. "Ground was broken on this church on the sixth of May in the year 1211, which admittedly was forty-eight years after the Parisians began building *their* Notre-Dame. A point to the Parisians! But ours sits on the site of a church that dates back to the fifth century, which I think is a point to us, yes? And it is where Clovis, king of the Franks, was baptized by Saint Remi." He looked at Liv expectantly.

"Um, who?"

Julien feigned horror. "Well, of course, Clovis was the first king of what would become France. His baptism here in the year 496 by Saint Remi, the bishop of Reims at the time, was the beginning of converting all the Franks to Christianity, which was a huge turning point in our history. That act began to unify France for the first time, and it happened right here. The original church was burned to the ground, but as you can see, the church built in its place in the thirteenth century was quite adequate."

"Exactly the adjective I was thinking of," Liv said with a smile, looking up at the Gothic towers, the beautiful rosette windows, the thousands of intricate statues. "*Adequate*."

Julien laughed. "Yes, well, I was being modest on behalf of the church. But in fact, it was also the place in which for many, many years, French kings were crowned. Thirty-three of them, to be exact, including the ill-fated Louis XVI." Julien checked his watch. "Well, we have a lot to get to in your mini tour of Reims, so I'll finish with this: the cathedral holds more than twenty-three hundred statues, it is a UNESCO World Heritage site, *and* it features a famous stained-glass window set by Marc Chagall. But perhaps most important, it was nearly destroyed during the First World War—first by an enormous fire, not unlike the one that happened this spring at Notre-Dame de Paris—and then by years of shelling. But it was rebuilt."

"My grandmother mentioned something about that," Liv said softly, surprised to feel tears in her eyes.

"Notre-Dame de Paris will be rebuilt, too, Liv," Julien said, his tone gentle as he looked at her closely. "It will survive."

Liv nodded and cleared her throat. "How do you know so much about the history of this place, anyhow?"

"The summer before I went away to university, I was a guide for a company that does walking tours of Reims in English. It's funny what sticks. I could probably tell you a thousand random dates and facts about this city, but I routinely forget where I've left my keys."

Liv fell into step beside him as they turned away from the

cathedral and began walking in the opposite direction. "Okay, so what's your favorite Reims fact, then?"

"Well, I think perhaps I have three." He led her around a corner, and they turned right. "The first is that although this city was nearly destroyed a century ago, during the First World War, it was entirely rebuilt and restored to its earlier majesty. We are in a city that never bowed, never broke. That has always made me very proud to be a Remois. I think that's a spirit you can find among our winemakers, too. They have weathered Mother Nature's worst and survived."

They passed a courthouse and several cafés, and then Julien steered them right and left again as they walked by the town hall and a few stores. "Another thing I appreciate is that Reims is a place that protects its people," he continued. "My grandfather found shelter here because of the goodness of a few during the Second World War, when deportations were taking place. There are dozens in the city who were not so lucky, including his parents, but the tale of my grandfather's survival mirrors many others."

"What happened?"

"There was a time in World War II when Germans were taking away Jewish citizens, sending them to concentration camps. It is a stain on France's history."

They were walking through a sunlit park now, crossing to the other side, but still, Liv felt a chill. "Forgive my ignorance, but I thought deportations were more in places like Germany and Poland."

Julien shook his head. "In France alone, there were more than seventy-five thousand innocent people sent away to concentration camps, including many children. Only a very small number of those survived."

"That's horrible," Liv said.

"Yes, but all around the country, including here in Reims, there were people working for underground networks to fight the Nazis and help save innocent people. My grandfather was assisted by just such a network. He lived because of the courage of those who risked it all."

"That's incredible."

"It is." Julien steered her down another street, and then he stopped in front of a red brick building. "And for all the horror of the Second World War, there's another piece of beauty right here." He gestured to the building and Liv followed his gaze. "This is where the war in Europe ended, on May 7, at 2:41 in the morning."

"Wait, World War II ended here? In Reims?"

"You never knew that, did you?" He smiled at her. "There was a second treaty signed a day later in Berlin. That's why we think of the following day, May 8, as Victory in Europe Day. But the initial terms of surrender were agreed upon right here, while your General Eisenhower, who had his command center in Reims, was upstairs."

"You're kidding me."

"A man should never joke about love or war." He grinned at her and put a hand on her shoulder to steer her gently away from the unassuming building where the course of history had been altered. "Come. Let's head back toward your hotel, shall we? I hate to cut this short, but I do have to go get Mathilde."

They walked for a little while, weaving in and out of the crowd in the Place d'Erlon as they approached the fountain with the winged statue. "You mentioned back at the cathedral that you're only a part-time lawyer?" Liv asked.

"Oh, yes. Well, actually, it is a decision I made a long time ago so that I could spend a bit more time with Mathilde. I have the feeling that I am going to blink, and her childhood will be over. And in the end, would I prefer to have spent more moments with her, or would I prefer to have a bit more money?" He shrugged. "I am lucky to be in a position to be able to make such a choice. I have plenty to get by on, and since it's my family's firm, I'm able to be a bit more flexible with my hours."

"Mathilde is really lucky to have you, Julien."

He shrugged. "I'm the lucky one, I think."

They turned onto the rue Buirette, and Liv was disappointed to see her hotel looming ahead of them. The whirlwind tour of

Reims had gone by far too quickly. "Thank you so much for showing me around," Liv said as they stopped outside the hotel. "You're an amazing tour guide."

"It was my pleasure, Liv, truly." He moved closer, until they were just inches apart, and though propriety told Liv she should step back, she didn't want to. "I know I don't know you well yet, but I think you're extraordinary. I hope that's all right to say."

"Julien," she said softly. She meant to say more, to disrupt whatever was happening between them, but she couldn't make her mouth cooperate with her brain.

"I really enjoyed spending time together today," he murmured. "I hope you did, too." And then, in what seemed like slow motion, he put his hand on her cheek, leaned in, and after a brief hesitation, brushed his lips softly, gently, against hers.

She kissed back for only a second before pulling away with a gasp. "What are we doing?" She swiped her hand across her mouth.

His eyes widened. "I'm so sorry. I thought—I mean, it seemed like . . ." He trailed off as he collected his thoughts. "I'm very sorry. I—I haven't kissed anyone other than my wife since I married her, and I just thought . . ." He didn't finish his sentence.

"No!" she said. "I can't believe . . . I would never . . ." She was stammering, and she didn't know how to complete her thought.

"I—I should go," Julien said. "I must have misread the situation,

Liv. Again, I'm very sorry." He turned his back and hurried away, walking briskly toward the corner and turning left around a building without a glance back. And though she was appalled with herself, there was a part of her that missed him as soon as he was gone.

Back in the hotel suite twenty minutes later, Liv was sitting alone on the couch in a daze, her index finger pressed against her lips, when Grandma Edith emerged from her room in a cloud of Chanel No. 5, her lipstick freshly applied. "I'm going out for a little while," she chirped, and then stopped abruptly when she saw Liv's face. "What is it, dear?" she asked.

Liv shook her head. "Nothing."

Grandma Edith studied her briefly and then smiled knowingly. "Ah. You have feelings for young Julien, don't you?"

Liv opened her mouth to deny it, but she couldn't say the words. "Why does life have to be so complicated?"

"But I think perhaps he has feelings for you, too, my dear. I have seen the way he looks at you. What is so complicated about that? You both deserve to be happy."

"Are you kidding? I could never do that to his wife!"

"Olivia—" Grandma Edith began.

"No. There's nothing you can say!" Liv wiped her eyes. "How could you think I'd be okay with that?"

"Olivia!" her grandmother said again, her voice sharper.

"Seriously, just stop, Grandma Edith! You can't justify this. I know that having affairs is very French and all, but I could never live with myself. How could anyone? What kind of a person does that?"

Grandma Edith looked like Liv had slapped her. "Well, you'd be surprised, Olivia, what one can learn to live with."

And then, without another word, she strode out of the hotel room, leaving Liv alone in a cloud of silent shame.

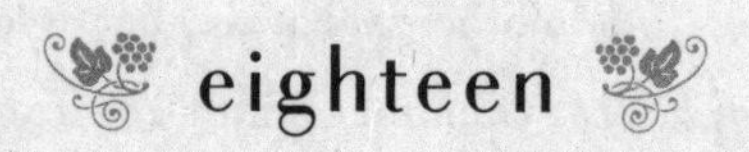

eighteen

AUGUST 1942

INÈS

For six months after that first night with Antoine, Inès had been seeing the older man once or twice a month on brief visits to Reims. She always told Michel that she was with Edith, and although he'd made it clear that he didn't appreciate being without an automobile, he'd been surprisingly open to the idea of letting her go without argument. It kept the peace between them, but Inès suspected that more than that, it kept her away from the property, one less liability to worry about as Michel continued his illicit activities. He had moved the weapons, or perhaps had sent them on their way, but either way, they hadn't been there when she'd gone back to check a week after discovering them. Still, there were many nights when Michel slipped from their bed while Inès feigned sleep. She knew he was up to something, and that he would never trust her enough to include her in it.

Inès knew also that Edith was aware of her affair and was appalled by it, but her friend had agreed to keep her confidence.

Edith's discretion wasn't purely out of friendship, but out of a need to keep her own secrets, too, though it didn't matter. She would cover for Inès if Michel ever wondered where she was, and in return, Inès would keep quiet about Edith's and Edouard's work spying on the Germans. Of course, Inès wouldn't dream of betraying her friend, but it was better this way, this bartering of hidden things, this trading of lies. It kept them all safe.

"I know you are not asking my opinion," Edith had said late one May evening when she ran into Inès just off the Place d'Erlon. Edith was hurrying toward the Brasserie Moulin, probably from another clandestine meeting, from the wild-eyed look of her. Inès was headed to Antoine's apartment and hadn't even told Edith she was in Reims. "But you are making a grave mistake, Inès."

"You wouldn't understand," Inès replied, unable to meet Edith's gaze. "You have a husband who loves you."

"Michel loves you, too!"

"He doesn't, Edith. You must understand that. He thinks I'm a fool."

"And the best way to deal with that is to *become* a fool?"

The words cut deep. "Is that what you think I am?"

Edith hesitated before reaching for Inès's hands. "No, my dear friend. I think you're sad. And I think you're searching for purpose. But becoming someone's mistress is not the way to find yourself."

"You don't know anything about it," Inès protested, pulling away.

"Please," said Edith as Inès turned to go. "Just think of what you're doing. Think of where it could lead. I'm begging you."

But Inès wouldn't look back. She knew that there was no excuse for her behavior. But how could Edith grasp what this felt like? Antoine made Inès feel alive for the first time in years. He was genuinely interested in her opinion, which was nearly as titillating as the way he seemed to know every inch of her body. He didn't judge her when she was uninformed about something the way Michel did; he took the time to explain things so she could understand. Sometimes, as they lay in bed smoking real cigarettes Antoine had somehow procured, he would even mention someone he knew socially—the mayor of Reims, the Vichy ambassador to the United States, even the former French prime minister—and confide something that one of those important men had told him. Antoine was powerful, well connected, worldly—and of all the women he could have chosen, he wanted *her.*

It had all felt very dreamlike and uncomplicated until the afternoon in August she arrived at his apartment an hour ahead of schedule and found him entertaining two Nazi officers. A Wagner opera was oozing from the phonograph in the corner, the room was filled with cigar smoke, and there were two empty bottles of brandy on the table when Inès entered using the key Antoine had given her two weeks before.

"You're early," he said tersely, jumping to his feet. There was none of the usual warmth in his eyes when he looked at her.

"It was just that I couldn't wait to see you," she said in a small voice.

"And what have we here?" one of the Nazis asked, attempting—and failing—to rise from his seat on Antoine's couch. His eyes were glazed over, his uniform jacket unbuttoned to reveal a sliver of his hairy potbelly, and Inès felt a wave of revulsion. "Is this the entertainment? Picard, you sly dog, you!"

"No, no." Antoine's smile was large and fake as he steered Inès toward the bedroom. He practically threw her inside and shut the door behind her. His voice was muffled as he added, "Just a friend of mine, dropping by for a visit."

"A friend!" The German-accented reply filtered through the door, followed by a loud burp. "Is that what you French call your prostitutes these days?"

Inès leaned into the door, but she didn't hear Antoine defend her honor. Instead, he guffawed and then told the men it was perhaps best if they went on their way; he would call on them tomorrow.

Inès emerged after silence had descended in the apartment. She found Antoine standing by the couch, aggressively smoking a cigarette, with one of the empty bottles of brandy clutched in his other hand like a weapon. When he looked at her, his eyes were wild, angry.

"What are you doing here so early?" he demanded. "You can't just show up whenever you please."

"You gave me a key." Inès stared at him in disbelief. "I thought you'd be happy to see me."

"Inès—"

"You let them call me a prostitute?"

"What was I to do, Inès?" He stormed into the kitchen and threw the bottle into the sink.

"Defend me!" she cried, following him.

"Do you know who those men were? That was Erhard Krüger, one of the highest-ranking Nazi officers in the Marne, and Franz Rudin, who knows Hitler personally."

A chill ran through Inès. "But what were they doing here? In your apartment?"

Antoine slammed his fist onto the kitchen counter. "Damn it, Inès, do I need to spell it out for you? They're friends."

"But . . . you're a collaborator?" She knew he worked with the Germans as part of his job, and she had let herself believe that he had access to contraband items and sumptuous meals because he had money and friends in high places. She just hadn't entirely grasped that those friends might be part of the German high command. "Antoine, how could you?"

"Oh, Inès." He stubbed out his cigarette in the sink and crossed the kitchen, taking her into his arms. "Please, my darling, you must let me explain."

"What could you possibly explain?" But some of the anger had leached out of her, replaced by a desperation to have this whole encounter justified, for what would it say about her if she'd spent the past several months as the *maîtresse* of someone who was working for the Nazis? "Please, you *can* explain, can't you?"

Antoine kissed her gently, and she let him. "Oh, sweet Inès," he said. "I know it is popular to hate the Germans now, but you must understand. They have a great vision for our country. All those who think the German Occupation will harm us in the end don't have a clear view of history. It is our own fault that the Germans were able to take us over so quickly. They are stronger than we are, and they have a better plan for economic stability in the future."

"But—"

"I thought you smarter than this, Inès," Antoine said, his voice an octave deeper now. "I thought you were the sort of woman who couldn't be fooled by false propaganda. Was I wrong?"

She could feel herself blushing. "No, of course not."

"At the end, Inès, only those of us who choose the right side will survive. I only want what is best for France. How can you fault me for that?"

In the silence, with his imploring gray eyes piercing her

defenses, she could almost see his point. Besides, who was to say that Michel and Edith were right? Still, there was one thing that bothered her. "But the deportation of Jews last month . . ."

He shook his head. "Inès, do you really think the Germans would remove people who weren't causing any harm? The Jews who were taken away were all guilty of working for the Resistance in some way."

A lump lodged itself in Inès's throat as she thought of Michel's clandestine work. "But—"

"Inès, you must understand. The Germans had no choice."

"But didn't they take children, too? Certainly the children hadn't done anything!"

"The people who were arrested are merely being sent east to work camps, where they can atone for their crimes. It's a kindness on the part of the Germans to allow them not to be separated from their families. It's mad to believe that the inclusion of children was anything but a favor to these people."

"But the German signs around town saying that all Jews are criminals and thieves . . ."

Antoine sighed. "Oh, Inès, certainly no one's mind will be changed by a few posters. The posters are foolish, but they mean nothing in the grand scheme of things."

Inès thought of Céline. Certainly the propaganda wasn't

meaningless to her. "But *you* don't believe what they're saying about Jews, do you?" she asked in a small voice.

"Inès! Of course not!" Antoine looked horrified. "Please, you must believe me. But I also understand why those who are trying to harm the Third Reich must be sent out of the country. Inès, think about it. What would the Germans have to gain by sending innocent people away, anyhow?"

Inès looked at him for a long time, wondering why her stomach was still in knots when she wanted so much to trust him. "I suppose."

"I knew you would understand, my darling." He reached for her again and kissed her softly. "Now, shall we go have dinner? I've booked us a table at Arnaud's."

Inès hesitated, but when she looked into Antoine's eyes, there was no danger there, no malice. "Yes," Inès said, and she knew that with that single word, she'd chosen a side, even if she hadn't quite intended to. So she did her best to put their argument behind her and let him lead her out of the apartment and down to the street below. At Arnaud's, they found an intimate table waiting for them, along with a chilled bottle of champagne, which was enough, for now, to quiet the voices of doubt in Inès's head.

By October, another successful harvest had come and gone, and with the new *vins clairs* fermenting in their barrels, and the days growing shorter as winter approached, Inès should have felt more relaxed. After all, the Maison Chauveau was surviving the war. Of course, Céline still trudged around with a somber expression, the weight of the world on her shoulders because she had yet to hear from her family.

Though things should have been looking up, Inès felt more unsettled by the day, because her conscience was finally screaming at her about Antoine. While he talked easily, knowledgeably, about German strategy and the inevitability of Nazi world domination, Inès was finding it more and more difficult to agree with him. He was so confident that German victory throughout Europe was only a matter of time. But what if Hitler's military wasn't infallible? And perhaps more troublingly, what if being on the side of victory didn't necessarily mean you could sleep at night?

And Inès could not, not anymore. At home, while Michel snored beside her, she lay awake, trying to bat away the voices in her head that asked questions she didn't want to answer. The explanation Antoine had given her about the first round of Jewish deportations in July no longer made sense to her, given the Germans' increasingly aggressive anti-Semitism. And what about the fact that all the Nazis seemed to be living *la belle vie*, while the French were going hungry, freezing to death in the cold? With another winter approaching, how could Antoine so calmly look the other way?

On a rainy Friday night in early October, Inès was lying in Antoine's arms after another sumptuous meal when she heard the roar of several trucks outside, the screeching of brakes on the street below. Antoine was snoring, and at first he didn't stir when she tried to wake him.

"Antoine!" she hissed again, shaking him, and he opened his eyes at last.

"Marie?" he called out, and Inès tensed, for it was a name he'd said before, in those foggy first seconds of consciousness.

"No, it's me," she said, trying to keep the hurt out of her tone. "Inès." She didn't know who Marie was, but Inès had long understood that she might not be Antoine's only lover.

"Yes, yes, of course, that's what I said." There was a perturbed note to Antoine's voice as he sat up and reached for his trousers, which were hanging from the edge of the bed. "Well, what is it?"

"I think something is going on outside."

Antoine climbed out of bed and moved to the window. "Yes. It's happening," he said.

"What is?" She joined him, wrapping a blanket around her naked body, and she gasped when she realized what he was looking at.

On the street below, in blackness lit only by the moon overhead and a few flashlights, uniformed Germans were dragging children from the building across the way toward French police vehicles. There were four of them, all boys, ranging from perhaps seven to fourteen. The smallest was tiny, scrawny, with a thick shock of black hair, and as he kicked and screamed and tried to shake his captor off, one of the Germans backhanded him across the face. Inès gasped as his little body went limp. He was thrown into the car with the others.

"What is this, Antoine?" Inès finally managed to whisper past the lump in her throat, but she already knew, even before he answered her.

"Jews," he said without looking at her.

"Where are they taking them?"

"Drancy, probably." His tone was flat. "An internment camp just northeast of Paris."

"But what about their parents?"

"Already deported, most likely. There are situations like this all over, children who shouldn't have been allowed to remain unattended when their parents were arrested. The authorities are finally remedying the problem."

"But . . . they're just boys."

Antoine finally turned to her. "It's not a perfect system. But with winter coming, they'll be safer with their mothers and fathers."

"But—"

"It's not for us to worry about, dear." His jaw was set, his eyebrows drawn together. "It's not just children tonight, anyhow. It's another roundup, like the one in July."

"Another roundup?" Inès felt breathless.

"Yes, my dear. Standard procedure. Now, shall we return to bed?"

But Inès couldn't imagine sleeping, not now. What would happen to those poor children? And what if the arrests were broader this time, encompassing more than just foreign Jews suspected of wrongdoing? What if Céline was in danger? "I—I have to get home," she said.

"In the middle of the night? Are you mad?"

"No. I—I just have to get back, that's all."

Antoine studied her. "Ah. Is this about the Jewish woman who lives on your husband's property?"

Inès was suddenly light-headed. "I—I've never mentioned that there's a Jewish woman there. How would you know that?"

"There aren't so many Jews who live in the Marne, Inès. Certain people who have seen us together have made me aware. To be honest, it's been somewhat problematic for me. I've had to explain that you have nothing to do with harboring her."

Inès gripped the window frame for support. She didn't know where to begin. She felt sick to her stomach. "Antoine, Céline has done absolutely nothing wrong. Anyhow, I'm not *harboring* anyone. She has every right to be here."

"Don't worry, *ma chère*. Like the last deportation, this one is just for foreign Jews, and she was born in France, yes?"

Her head spun. "So you knew about it all along? The arrests tonight?"

Antoine shrugged. "I know about a lot of things. See, Inès, didn't I tell you how helpful it is to be on the right side? With me?"

Outside the window, the police cars were pulling away. "And Céline? Is she safe for now? Or are your friends coming for her, too?"

Something in Antoine's expression changed, and Inès realized too late she had misstepped. When his smile reappeared, it was cold. "Oh, my *friends* might come for her at some point, but not tonight." He put a hand on her upper arm. "Now, I will ask you again: Shall we return to bed?"

Inès could only shake her head. Her stomach churned with guilt, anger, revulsion, powerlessness.

Antoine shrugged and turned away, but Inès couldn't pull herself from the window, even though the poor little boys were long gone. As she heard Antoine begin to snore peacefully in the bed behind her, she closed her eyes and tried not to think about the choices she had made and where they might lead. It took her only a few more minutes to hastily dress, grab her car keys, and head for the door.

By the time Inès made it home to Ville-Dommange in the pitch darkness of a blackout night, she had worked herself into a panic thinking of Céline's safety. What if Antoine had been lying? What if the authorities were coming tonight after all?

She pulled the Citroën to a halt outside Céline and Theo's cottage and jumped out without even bothering to cut the ignition. Theo came to the door holding a lantern, Céline just behind him in a dressing gown wrapped hastily around her. "What is it?" Theo demanded, shining the light in her eyes. "Inès, what's the matter?"

"I—" Now that Inès was here, she realized she was at a loss for words. What was she to say, that her lover had made her believe that Céline might be in danger? "There's—there's been another roundup," she said.

"Oh dear God." Céline pulled her gown tighter and clutched her belly as if she'd had a sudden, sharp pain. "Where? Who?"

"In Reims." Inès found that she could not meet Céline's eye. "Perhaps elsewhere, too. I—I was concerned about you."

"Oh, thank you, Inès." Céline reached out to squeeze Inès's hands in hers. Her palms were warm and strong, and somehow the contact made Inès feel even more ashamed. "You drove back from Reims in the middle of the night to warn me?"

"I—I was worried." Inès was too embarrassed to keep meeting Céline's gaze. What would Céline say if she knew that for months, Inès had been enjoying the high life while things grew more perilous for the Jews of the Marne?

"I can't tell you how much I appreciate it." Céline's eyes were filled with tears.

"Céline," Theo cut in, "we should get you somewhere safe, just in case."

Céline nodded, turning to her husband. "Yes. Let's go see Michel. He'll know what to do."

She brushed past Inès, already heading outside, and as Theo's gaze met Inès's in the lamplight, she thought she recognized something familiar there, an expression of being overlooked, bypassed for something better, just as she had been. But then he turned away, and the look was gone. "Let's go," he grunted, and Inès followed him into the dark night.

Michel had been startled to hear Inès's news, but he'd wasted no time in bringing Céline down to the caves and settling her behind the hidden wall, guarded by the silent Madonna. She stayed there for two days, with Inès bringing her meals and making awkward conversation every few hours. But by the third day, they all felt confident that the roundups were over, and Céline hadn't been on the list. She had emerged from the cellars, and life had gone on as usual.

Except that for Inès, it hadn't. The fear she'd felt for Céline had been real and deep, and the more she thought about it, the more she wondered how Antoine could possibly be right. He had so easily justified the Jewish deportations months earlier, and in the moment, his words had made sense. But what if Inès was the fool Michel seemed to believe her to be after all? Had she made a huge mistake by taking Antoine at his word? The questions settled in the pit of her belly, heavy as rocks.

Six days after Inès had fled Reims in the middle of the night, Michel and Theo left early in the afternoon to check on some vines in nearby Sacy, leaving Inès and Céline alone in the cellars, where they were tasked with sorting through the bottles they'd received from their supplier earlier in the week. The quality of the glass had gone sharply downhill, yet another result of the Occupation, and before they could be filled with wine over the winter, they all had to be hand inspected to make sure they weren't broken, weak, or otherwise compromised.

"Inès," Céline said after a while, breaking the silence between them. "I haven't thanked you properly yet for what you did last week, driving from Reims after dark just to warn me. I owe you very much."

Inès put her hand over her mouth and shook her head. "No, Céline. It is I who owe you."

Céline blinked a few times. "Surely not."

"No. I—I fear I have misjudged you." Inès hesitated, her eyes sliding away. "I'm ashamed to say that for the past few months, I've been jealous. It sounds crazy to say, I know, but I thought that perhaps there was something between you and Michel."

"Michel?" Céline turned red. "How could you think such a thing?"

"I know. I'm terribly sorry. I realize I imagined it, probably because I . . . well, I feel as if I am losing my hold on my marriage."

"Inès—"

"I have to do something, Céline. I keep making the wrong choices, and I—" Inès stopped abruptly before she could say something she'd regret. She wiped away a tear. "I need to become someone better, that's all. I know that now. Anyhow, I apologize. I'm sorry for doubting you, and I'm sorry for burdening you with this now. My marriage isn't your problem."

"Inès, I'm so sorry," Céline whispered. The concern etched on her face was so deep that Inès began to sob again. After an awkward pause, Céline put an arm around her. Inès cried into the other woman's shoulder briefly before gathering herself and stepping back.

"Thank you," Inès said, "for being so kind. I don't deserve it."

By the time Michel arrived home that evening, his hands and face streaked with vineyard dirt, Inès had made herself a promise. Things would be different from now on. She would break things off with Antoine the next time she saw him. It was the only thing to do. Antoine might have given her attention, but good men didn't choose the wrong side in a war like this, and Inès was horrified that it had taken so long for her to realize that. She needed to give Michel—and their marriage—another chance.

"Welcome home, my love," Inès said as Michel hung his coat by the door.

He turned to her with a frown. "Hello." He bent to untie his boots, and when he straightened and found her still standing there, his eyebrows drew together in confusion. "Is there something else, Inès?"

"Yes. I—I want to apologize. I want to be a better wife to you. You're a good man, and I don't think I've given you enough credit for that."

"Oh." He stood and eyed her. "Well, thank you." He hesitated. "You are a good woman, too."

The exchange felt awkward, like they were two near strangers. The distance between them gaped wide. "I—I love you," Inès said, stepping closer, and as she said the words, she felt certain they could be true again. She had loved him when she'd married him. She tried hard to remember what that had felt like, the electric feeling that had coursed through her each time he looked her way.

"Well. I love you, too."

"Come to bed, Michel," she murmured, standing on tiptoe to press her lips against his. She moved into the familiar arc of his body, which now felt foreign to her. Where Antoine was sinewy and narrow, Michel was solid and strong.

"Inès—" he began, but she cut him off with a kiss.

"Make love to me, Michel," she whispered. "*Please.* I am your wife." She knew she sounded desperate, but she was. She needed this, something to pull her back from the edge, something to redeem her.

"Inès—"

She kissed him again, and this time, he kissed back. When he finally pulled her into his arms, she sighed with relief.

She led him to the bedroom and slipped out of her dress, tugging at his belt before he could change his mind. As they fell into bed, it felt as if they were doing a well-rehearsed dance, and when Michel's touch felt mechanical, Inès told herself that it had merely been a long time since they'd made love.

When it was over, he held her briefly before pulling away. "I need to inspect some things in the caves. You'll be all right?"

It wasn't quite the pillow talk she'd been expecting, and she tried not to compare his abruptness to the gentle care Antoine always took with her after they'd been together.

"What about dinner?"

"I'm not hungry, Inès. Thank you."

"Will you stay for a little while, Michel? Here? With me?"

He was already pulling his clothing back on, reaching for his boots. "I need to get to the bottles."

"Bottles?" she couldn't resist asking. "Or guns?"

Something flickered in Michel's eyes, and when he spoke again, his tone was cold, terse. "Bottles. Like I said. Get some rest, Inès."

Inès was still awake when Michel returned to bed hours later, smelling of chalk and night. She closed her eyes and pretended to be asleep as he slipped beneath the covers beside her, his back turned, as far away from her as he could possibly be.

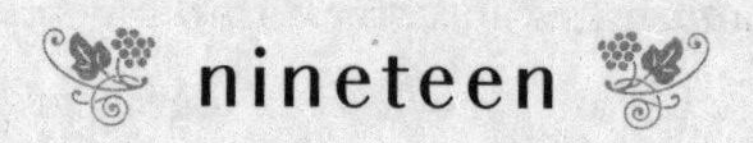

nineteen

OCTOBER 1942

CÉLINE

After the troubling conversation Céline had with Inès about the other woman's marriage, her stomach fluttered with guilt for the rest of the day. Inès was a better person than Céline gave her credit for, wasn't she? Some of their conversations earlier in the war had made Céline believe that Inès didn't grasp the plight of the Jews, but last week had proven otherwise.

Céline wondered if she had been too eager to join Michel in treating Inès as if she were a naive simpleton. If she had taken the time to be kinder to Michel's wife, to talk to her, would Inès have gotten things so wrong all those months ago? Inès wasn't stupid. She was young, and she'd turned her back on most news of the war.

Michel had been frustrated about that, angry that Inès didn't understand the stakes, and he'd stopped talking to her about anything serious because of it. But he'd been wrong to assume it was because Inès was incapable of grasping the situation. No, like

Theo, Inès had closed her eyes to something terrifying, finding comfort in easy explanations. It was what so many people were doing, and Céline understood that now. She wished that she, too, could pretend that none of this was happening. What if she lived in a world in which her biggest problem was that she was feeling things for Michel that she shouldn't have been—not that she was terrified every day that her father and grandparents were being carted off to their deaths, and that she would be next? It was all too much.

She supposed that was why, when she had crossed paths with Michel alone in the cellars one evening nearly three months earlier, fueled by loneliness and despair, she had silenced the doubts in her head for a few seconds and reached up to steal a single forbidden kiss. Electricity had shot through her whole body, her lips tingling with the taste of him. She'd known it was wrong, of course, but Michel was as alone as she was, and she had seen the hunger in his eyes when he looked at her lately, the desire. Still, what had she done? "I'm so sorry," she had begun, mortified as she backed away. "I should never have—"

But Michel had pulled her to him immediately, lacing his fingers through her hair and kissing her deeply. "My God, Céline," he'd murmured. "I've been waiting so long to do that."

"But Theo and Inès . . ."

"Are not the people we thought they were," he said firmly.

"Céline, don't you feel it? This connection between us? I've known for so long that I love you. Don't you feel the same?"

She'd felt breathless, buoyed with hope for the first time in years. Tears in her eyes, she whispered, "Yes." A week later, they'd made love for the first time, alone in the cellars, and Céline had known there was no turning back.

Now, her heart full of things she knew she'd regret, she waited until Theo fell asleep before slipping out of bed and out the back door with a lamp.

The coolness of the cellars enveloped her as she quietly descended the winding stone steps and made her way toward one of the caves in the back, down the long hall, right, left and then right again down a narrow passage. In the back of the cave was a room partially obscured by a brick wall, a room no one would notice if they weren't looking for it. There was a blanket on the floor there, hidden between two enormous rows of racked bottles, and she sat down, pulled it around her, and waited.

She sat there for almost an hour, and had just begun to panic when she heard footfalls on the stone floor leading toward her hiding space. She stood and squinted into the darkness as a shadowy figure appeared at the entrance to the cave, lamplight surrounding him like a halo.

"Michel." Relief flowed through her. "Thank God. I was worried about you."

"I'm so sorry I'm late." He made his way into the room, kissed her on both cheeks. "Inès wanted to talk, and—"

"It's okay. You don't have to explain." In fact, Céline did not want him to. Just thinking of Inès, hearing her name on Michel's tongue, made her feel terrible. When Inès had tearfully apologized earlier for suspecting Céline of having an affair with Michel, it had been all she could do to stop from throwing herself at Inès's feet and telling her everything: the fact that they had already begun their affair, the fact that she had been helping Michel with his underground work for two months now. The fact that she was painfully, irreversibly in love with him.

"Céline," Michel breathed, and this time, he kissed her on the mouth, long and deep. "I must tell you something."

She realized for the first time that his clothes were rumpled, his expression heavy with guilt. "Michel, has something happened with the network? Please tell me it's not Madame Gaudin." Céline had grown fond of the tough middle-aged woman who had become their point of contact in the past few months. By day, she was the stout, hearty housewife of an unsuspecting vigneron. By night, she was a crusader who slipped from hiding place to hiding place with rifles concealed beneath the folds of her dress. Just a few weeks ago, she had been stopped by a German sentry while hiding six long guns, and the man hadn't suspected a thing, had merely waved her on in disgust when she began babbling about pig manure and fertilization. She had laughed about it for twenty minutes that night as she'd helped hide the guns in a Maison Chauveau barrel bound for the north.

"No, no, it's nothing like that," Michel said. He raked a hand through his hair. "It's Inès. Céline, I'm sorry, but I had . . . I had *relations* with her tonight. I had to."

"Oh." Céline took a step back and her breath caught for a moment. But she had no right to be hurt, did she? He was *married* to Inès, for goodness' sake. And perhaps the other woman was turning over a new leaf. Maybe this was a sign that Céline should put a stop to their affair. But she couldn't.

"Céline—" Michel began.

"No, you don't have to explain," Céline said. "You did nothing wrong."

"But you are the one I love."

"And she is the one you married." Céline smiled through her tears. "And that puts you and me on the wrong side of things, doesn't it?"

They stared at each other for a few moments, and just as Céline had finally summoned the courage to say the words she needed to say, Michel spoke. "It's time, Céline."

"Time?"

"For the drop." Michel studied her face. "Are you sure you want to help with this? I'm still reluctant to put you in danger."

Céline hesitated for only a second before nodding, her heart racing. Since Michel had finally agreed to let her help him with his underground activities in August, she had worked only in the caves, receiving arms shipments brought in by Madame Gaudin and a man known only as *Le Renard*, the Fox. Michel said it was safer that way, that if anything went wrong, she could claim she'd merely been working with the wine in the cellars. But she had been begging to do more for the cause, and finally, the night before, Michel had agreed, saying that he might need a hand with something. He hadn't told her what they'd be involved in, though.

"Come," Michel said. He laced his fingers through hers, and together they hurried out of the cave and made their way aboveground.

The sky was clear, the moon half full, casting just enough light over the rolling hills that Céline could see the skeletal outlines of the naked, resting vines in the darkness. "What's happening?" she whispered. "Where are we going?"

"Trust me," he said. In silence, he led her into the vineyards, where they made their way along a neat row, their footsteps crunching on the cold earth and fallen leaves in the darkness. Surely they were being too conspicuous, their footfalls too loud, their movements too obvious, but she believed in Michel, and so she followed.

A moment later, they reached the road, and at first, Céline couldn't understand why they'd come. There was no one here, and it would be crazy for someone to be driving around at night doing anything illegal; noise on the empty roads could be heard from kilometers away. Simply standing there seemed foolhardy; what if a German truck rumbled by and a soldier spotted them? "Michel?" she began tentatively.

But then, from the shadows near the curve of the road just fifty meters away, two men dressed in all black emerged in silence, both of them pulling some sort of cart. "You're late," one of them growled in the darkness. "And *this* is the help you bring? She's a woman!"

"She's strong and capable," Michel said firmly.

"And you trust her?"

"With my life," Michel said, his voice soft.

Céline could barely make out the man who had spoken; he wore the darkness like a cloak, and only the whites of his eyes glinted in the half moonlight.

"Well, I suppose you'd have to," the man said at last, "since if she gets you caught, they won't hesitate to shoot you in the head." He snorted, a sound that was somewhere between amusement and annoyance, but he beckoned to the man with him, and together they pulled their cart toward Michel and Céline, both of them grunting with the effort. The second man was slightly smaller and thinner, and as he drew closer, Céline saw something that looked like kindness in his eyes. He nodded to her, and she nodded back.

"Don't say I didn't warn you," said the larger man to Michel, utterly ignoring Céline, and then both men slipped back into the shadows and were gone.

"Come, we mustn't delay," Michel said, moving forward and grabbing one of the cart's two arms. "Just do your best. I'll handle as much of the weight as I can, but I'll need your help to make sure we don't tip it on the uneven ground. The shipment's larger than I expected it to be."

Céline hesitated as she looked at the cart, the wooden kind that mules pulled across farmland. The bed was full of something heavy, concealed beneath a layer of straw. "Guns?"

"And explosives." He gestured to the second arm of the cart, and Céline bent to slide under it, propping it on her shoulder. Michel grunted, and Céline felt the cart jerk forward. She joined him in pulling, and they began to wheel the cart across the dark vineyard, back toward the entrance to the cellars.

"But where do the weapons come from?" she asked several silent minutes later as she struggled to catch her breath. They were nearly halfway home.

"I don't ask. The British, maybe? The Dutch? Hell, maybe America or Canada. All I know is that the bend in the road is the perfect place for drops to happen. From here, the arms can be stored in our cellars until our contacts can come pick them up."

She stumbled on an exposed root, nearly overturning the cart, but Michel reached out to catch her before she hit the ground, and she quickly regained her balance. "I'm sorry," she whispered.

"No, I'm the one who's sorry," he said. He grunted as they heaved the cart over an uneven patch of ground. "This is too much for you. I should have figured out how to do this myself."

"No, Michel, please. I want to be a part of this."

"But why, my love? Why not let me keep you safe?"

Céline looked up at the tiny pinpricks of light overhead and wondered if somewhere out there, her father was seeing the same sky. What about the people working for Resistance networks all over France? Or the soldiers in trenches all across the Continent, trying to beat back the Nazis? Out here in the star-dusted darkness, she was tiny and insignificant, a mere speck of light on the earth. But doing this made her feel, at least for a moment, that she was more than that, as if the decisions she was making might play a role in changing the world. "Because," she said at last, "I want to be part of something bigger, Michel."

"You are. We all are, those of us who work in the shadows," Michel said. The main house was in sight now, and Céline imagined Inès inside, fast asleep and oblivious to the danger outside her door. "We are soldiers in an army that the Germans will never see coming," he added. "We are the ones who will win back France."

Céline could feel tears burning her eyes as she turned her attention from the stars to the man beside her, the one who had changed her life in ways he couldn't yet understand. "We are the ones," she said softly, "who will reclaim the future."

Madame Gaudin arrived sometime after midnight, a cloak drawn tight around her. She was built like an ox, but there was something feminine about her yet the same. Her voice was sweet, her mannerisms rough, and as always, Céline was fascinated by all the contrasts that seemed to exist within the same woman. Then again, Céline knew better than anyone that people had multiple sides. Who would have thought, even six months earlier, that she could have betrayed her husband, loved a man who belonged to someone else, and fought for France, all while pretending to be the same industrious, proper wife she'd always been?

"You have the guns?" Madame Gaudin singsonged as she descended into the cellars, her eyes darting around nervously, as always.

"They're just in there," Michel replied. "Explosives this time, too."

"Good," Madame Gaudin said. "Good." She glanced at Céline. "And you? I understand you helped?"

"Yes, madame." Céline didn't know why she felt suddenly nervous.

Madame Gaudin studied her for a moment, and Céline had the uneasy sense that the older woman was reading her like a book. Could she see all of Céline's secrets? "Good," Madame Gaudin said again after a long pause. She turned back to Michel. "The boys are upstairs with a cart. Why don't you go get them? Céline and I will ready the barrels for transport."

Michel nodded and headed for the stairs. Madame Gaudin gestured to Céline.

"What you're doing is dangerous, you know," Madame Gaudin said as soon as Michel was gone. "You should be careful."

Céline took a deep breath. "But it's the same work you've been doing all along, madame," she said. "I want to be useful, too."

Madame Gaudin's eyes bore into hers. "I wasn't talking about your work with the Resistance. I was talking about the romance between you and Monsieur Chauveau."

Céline could feel herself turning red. "How did you—"

Madame Gaudin held up a hand to stop her. "I remember what it was like to be young, and I know that the heart wants what it wants. But there's danger in betraying those close to us, especially in times like these."

Céline swallowed hard, guilt coursing through her like a river. "I know."

"I know you love him. I can see it in your eyes. He loves you, too, I think." She sighed. "But you're on treacherous ground."

She turned away before Céline could reply. Céline took a few deep breaths to steady herself before following Madame Gaudin into the cave where the arms were hidden. Madame Gaudin gestured to a barrel and began to roll a second one into the hall.

"Where do the guns go from here?" Céline asked abruptly after the silence between them had grown uncomfortable. "Who do you give them to?"

Madame Gaudin stopped and looked at Céline, her hands on her hips. "Questions are even more dangerous than falling in love with the wrong people." She paused, staring at her, before adding, "You've never asked before."

"I'm asking now. Please. I want to know that I'm doing some good."

"It's better that we only know our own role on the line," Madame Gaudin said. "That is risk enough." She brushed her hands off and strode out of the cave before Céline could ask another question, and by the time Céline finished pushing her own barrel into the hall, the older woman had disappeared. For the next twenty minutes, Michel and two other men came up and down the stairs, lifting barrels between them and making their way back up into the inky night.

"What did you say to Madame Gaudin?" Michel asked once the arms-laden barrels were all gone and he had descended back into the caves to get her. "She seemed upset."

"I—I asked her what the guns were for."

Michel raised an eyebrow. "That wasn't wise."

"I know." Céline hesitated. "Is she gone?"

"Yes." Michel beckoned Céline to a stone bench in the hall. They sat together in silence. "Céline, you must know that at some point, these guns might be used to kill the enemy. The Germans, they will not listen to reason. The only conversation they understand is one that takes place at gunpoint."

Céline nodded and closed her eyes. "I understand." And she did. But there had to be a cost for taking a life. What did it mean for her soul that she was putting weapons into the hands of people who might use them to kill?

"What is it, Céline?" Michel asked, putting a hand on her cheek.

She opened her eyes to look at him. "Madame Gaudin knows about us."

Michel studied her, his expression impassible. "She doesn't miss a thing, does she?"

Céline shook her head, and as silence fell, she tried again to force the words she needed to say to the surface, the ones that would change everything. She took a deep breath. "There's something else I need to tell you, Michel. Something important."

He took her hand, and she wondered if he could feel how clammy it was. "What is it, my darling?"

Céline steeled herself to say the sentence she'd been rehearsing for two weeks now, ever since she had missed her time of the month for the second time. "Michel, I am pregnant."

She held her breath as Michel stared at her, his mouth slightly agape. In the silence, she imagined that he might be regretting this complication, hating her for letting it happen. "Oh, Céline," he said at last. "It is Theo's?"

"No, no!" She reached for his hands. "Michel, it is yours."

He squeezed her fingers tightly, his eyes widening. "You are certain?"

"Yes." She didn't explain, but she knew she was right. She hadn't had relations with Theo in months, although as soon as she had realized, she had rushed to lie with him, which she knew made her the worst person in the world. It was the only answer, though, wasn't it? What else would happen if her belly began to swell without his involvement? Certainly he would understand immediately who the father was, and who knew what kind of revenge he might take? No, there were too many deadly secrets at the Maison Chauveau to risk it. "Are you angry?" she asked when Michel still hadn't said anything.

"Oh no, Céline, of course not." He blinked, and she could see his eyes glistening. "I'm so very, very happy."

"You are?"

He wiped away his tears. "Céline, I love you. There's nothing in the world that will change that."

"But a baby will complicate things."

"Things are already complicated. And yes, we will have to keep this a secret for now, but Céline, we will have a *child*. Together. The best pieces of you and me. It's—well, it's glorious."

She threw herself into his arms and he held her more tightly than ever. She didn't realize she was sobbing until he pulled back slightly and reached down to wipe her cheeks with his thumb. "What is it, my love?" he asked.

"I'm so very frightened." Céline put her hands on her belly. "For you, for me, and now for this baby. And what happens once the child is here? We won't be able to keep the truth from Theo and Inès forever."

"We will figure it out."

"I just imagined this happening so differently one day."

"But it's happening *this* way. And a life conceived in love is always a blessing, no matter the complications."

"I know." But it was difficult to feel the joy she wanted to, for the baby's arrival into the world would always be cloaked in wrongdoing. The joyous news also drove home the reality that her child would probably never meet his or her grandfather, and that would be a burden Céline would have to bear. So much had been taken from her, but she recognized that by claiming Michel as her own, she was guilty of taking something, too.

"Céline," Michel said, grasping her hands. "I think it would be best if you end your involvement with our little group now."

Céline had already thought about it, the idea that stopping her work with the underground would help keep her—and more important, the baby—safer. But she couldn't, not with so much still at stake. "No. If I don't fight for a better future, I have already failed our child."

"But if you don't survive . . ."

"I am already dead if I stop being who I am." Céline's tone was firm, though she had no idea whether she was making the right choice. "All of us have personal reasons to step back, don't we? But nothing great happens without great risk. I'm certain, Michel. There's more to fight for than ever before."

"But—"

"*Please.*"

He looked at her for a long time. "All right."

As he took her hand and led her deeper into the cellars, she imagined that she could feel the baby stirring within her, though she knew it was far too soon.

twenty

JUNE 2019

LIV

Liv knew she'd been rude to snap at Grandma Edith the day before, but she was tired of walking on eggshells, of fumbling her way through the dark while Grandma Edith held all the cards. Besides, what was so wrong with expressing disgust over the possibility of an affair? She still couldn't believe Julien had kissed her—and that she hadn't immediately stopped it. The thought had kept her awake all night, and she was up before dawn, ready to apologize to her grandmother, at least. But Grandma Edith spent the morning holed up in her own bedroom, refusing to talk to Liv beyond barking through the closed door that she was perfectly all right.

After a while, Liv got dressed and set out from the hotel headed south, away from the Place d'Erlon, not sure where her feet would carry her. Why was it that the first man to make her laugh in months—the first man who'd made her feel valued in ages—belonged to someone else? She wiped at her lips angrily, furious at herself. Had she led Julien on by confiding in him about her own troubles and giggling at his jokes?

But even now, even with guilt sweeping through her, she felt a strange, shameful sense of emptiness. She had liked bantering with him. She had been at home with him. And when he'd kissed her, it had felt right. What did that say about her? She was apparently no different from Eric's new girlfriend—except she was a decade and a half older and knew all too well the kind of despair and damage infidelity could bring.

She slowed to let a group of tourists pass in front of her on the corner of the rue de Thillois, and as she did, she looked up and saw that she had paused just across the street from the Brasserie Moulin. She stood there, wondering if she had subconsciously come this way or whether it was a sign. But it didn't matter. She was here, and she wanted the truth. She crossed the road and headed inside.

"*Bonjour, une table pour une personne, s'il vous plaît,*" Liv said to the waiter up front, glancing again at the framed photo of her grandmother by the door. The waiter smiled, grabbed a menu, and began to lead Liv to a table, but she called out, "Wait!"

He turned, surprised. "*Oui*, madame?"

"Do you speak English?"

He hesitated. "A little. What can I do?"

"I just—I had a question about this photograph." She pointed to the picture, and he returned to look at it.

"Yes?"

"This is going to sound strange, but I think the people in it might be my grandparents."

The man frowned. "These people, the Thierrys, they owned this brasserie many years ago."

"Yes." Liv tapped the photo. "My grandmother is Edith Thierry. She brought me here to Reims."

"But the woman in the picture, she couldn't possibly be alive, madame. She'd be well over one hundred years old, I think."

"Ninety-nine, actually, which would have made her nineteen in this photo. I'm just—I'm looking for answers. I was hoping I might find them here."

He still looked doubtful, but he nodded. "Let me show you to a table, and I will see if I can find Jean-Pierre Rousseau. He has been here for many years. Perhaps he knows some history. I will check."

"Thank you so much."

The waiter smiled as he led her to a seat. "De rien. I hope you find what you are looking for."

Ten minutes later, Liv was sipping a glass of Moët & Chandon brut and rereading the story of the brasserie's history on the menu when an older man, perhaps in his late seventies, with gray hair, dressed in a shirt and tie, approached. "Excuse me," he said in perfect English. "You are the young woman looking to speak to someone about the history of the brasserie?"

"Yes, that's right." Liv rose to her feet, but he gestured for her to sit back down.

"Please, I will join you, if that is all right." He pulled out a chair. "I am Jean-Pierre Rousseau. I manage the dining room."

"It's a pleasure to meet you, Monsieur Rousseau. I'm Liv Thierry Kent," Liv said, extending her hand.

"Ah, so you *are* a Thierry. That is what Jean-Marc thought you'd said. And you have some family connection to the Brasserie Moulin?"

"I think my grandmother, Edith Thierry, is the one who owned the brasserie during the Second World War along with her husband, Edouard. Is there any chance you knew them?"

He shook his head. "I've been here only since the 1960s. But my father was here during the forties. He worked for the Thierrys."

"Your father?" Liv leaned forward. "Is he still around? Could I speak with him?"

Monsieur Rousseau shook his head. "Oh, how I wish. My father died of a heart attack many years ago, when he was just fifty. But when I was young, he used to tell me some stories of the war, of his time here."

"Like what? Did he talk of the Thierrys?"

"Yes, of course. He liked them very much. I see you reading

the menu, and so you must know they were involved with the Resistance. But do you know how vital they were? The German officers who came here would drink very much—the bartenders were always pouring them free drinks—and they would say things they shouldn't have. The Thierrys and their staff eavesdropped. In fact, my father once overheard a German lieutenant speaking of the imminent arrests of the leaders of a small Resistance cell operating here in Champagne, and he was able to get word, through the Thierrys, to Count Robert-Jean de Vogüé, who warned them. They disappeared before the Germans could get them."

"Who was Count Robert-Jean de Vogüé?"

Monsieur Rousseau chuckled. "You are familiar with the Moët & Chandon champagne house?"

Liv glanced at her glass. "Of course."

"Well, de Vogüé was the head of that house, the largest one at the time. A very important man, you understand, and one whom the Germans treated with respect when they first arrived here, because he was so influential with the other houses." Monsieur Rousseau leaned forward conspiratorially, his eyes twinkling. "He also was one of the people in charge of the Resistance in the eastern part of France."

"Wait, the head of Moët & Chandon was in charge of the Resistance?"

"No one was who they appeared to be in those days, madame. The Thierrys seemed to be collaborators, for example, so who would have thought that they were actually working with de Vogüé to undermine the Germans? At Piper-Heidsieck, the owners were hiding guns. At Krug, they were hiding pilots." He tapped the base of Liv's glass and added, "This champagne represents history, my dear. Heroism. Bravery. The people behind these wines helped save France."

Liv stared at the hundreds of tiny bubbles racing from the bottom of her glass to the surface. "And the Thierrys? They were part of this?"

"*Mais oui.* They were at the center of it."

"What happened to them? Do you know?"

Monsieur Rousseau shrugged. "Perhaps if your grandmother is indeed the same Edith Thierry, you know more than I do. You see, after the war, people in town did not immediately understand that the Thierrys had been working with the Resistance. Many still thought they had allied with the Germans, and they were hated for it. I understand that Madame Thierry left while the war was still ongoing, and Monsieur Thierry left town soon after the liberation. The brasserie was closed for a while before it was purchased by the Bouchert family, and by then the town knew the Thierrys had been heroes. But they never returned."

"They survived the war, though?" Liv asked. "I mean, obviously my grandmother did, but my dad never knew his father. I always thought perhaps he had died during the war."

"No, they survived. But many around them did not. I do remember my father saying that Madame Thierry's dearest friend was shot by the Germans for being a *résistante*. My father thought it strange because she'd had a paramour who was allied with the Germans, but who knows? Perhaps she was stealing information from him, too. As I said, no one was who they appeared to be in those days. It was around that time that Madame Thierry left, I think. My father always assumed Monsieur Thierry had eventually gone to join her. In any case, isn't it extraordinary to think of all the everyday people who risked their lives for France? If you are right about who your grandmother is, madame, she is one of those heroes."

Liv swallowed hard. How had Grandma Edith never spoken of such tragedy? Was that why she kept everyone at arm's length now? "Thank you, Monsieur Rousseau," she said.

"It was my pleasure to speak with you. Young people today are not often very interested in the past. I hope you find what you are looking for." He beckoned to Liv's waiter and added, "I will ask your waiter to bring you a glass of Chauveau, on the house, as you say in America. I don't think our story would be complete without it."

"Chauveau?" Liv asked.

"Why, yes." Monsieur Rousseau turned to her waiter and ordered in French. Then he turned back to her. "You see, Edith Thierry's best friend, the one who was shot by the Germans, was a woman named Inès Chauveau. She and her husband owned the Maison Chauveau, one of the finest houses in all of Champagne."

After finishing the glass of Moët and then the glass of Chauveau, Liv's head was spinning. Monsieur Rousseau's story had only complicated things further. Liv still couldn't understand why her grandmother had dragged her across an ocean to Champagne, only to sit in a hotel room and sulk in between darting out for mysterious errands, but if she had been involved in the Resistance—and had lost her best friend because of it—her caginess at least made a bit of sense. Perhaps Grandma Edith, who had never worn her heart on her sleeve, was still in mourning. Maybe that was why she was having so much trouble telling Liv whatever it was she had brought her here to say.

When Liv let herself back into the hotel room, Grandma Edith was reading a newspaper at the table, a glass of champagne beside her, a bottle chilling in a bucket. She glanced up as Liv entered. "Where have you been, dear?" she asked.

"Out." Liv still wasn't sure how to address what she'd just learned.

"I've just opened some champagne. Would you care for a glass? I'd like to talk with you."

"I just had nearly half a bottle, actually," Liv said, and Grandma Edith raised her eyebrows. "I'd better not."

"Don't be such a stick-in-the-mud," her grandmother said. When Liv hesitated, Grandma Edith rolled her eyes. "It's rude to let someone drink alone, dear. There's a glass right there for you. Come now, pour yourself some."

Liv reached for the bottle and pulled it halfway out of the ice before stopping abruptly. "You're drinking Chauveau?"

"Yes," Grandma Edith said evenly, but she didn't meet Liv's gaze. Liv felt a surge of pity for her grandmother and the best friend she had apparently lost more than seven decades earlier.

"You knew the people who owned that champagne house, didn't you?" Liv asked carefully.

Grandma Edith blinked a few times. "Yes."

"Is that what you want to talk to me about?"

"No. Now, are you going to pour yourself some or not?"

Liv filled her glass halfway, took a small sip, and sat down opposite the older woman. Bringing up the Maison Chauveau hadn't elicited much of a reaction, but she wasn't sure that mentioning Grandma Edith's old friend Inès Chauveau would work, either. So instead she took another sip and told herself to be patient. Grandma Edith seemed to be searching for the right words, and

Liv had the feeling she was about to reveal something important.

"Olivia, dear, I was hoping to clear something up," she said at last.

"Good," Liv said. "Is it about the brasserie? And your involvement with the Resistance?"

"What? No." Grandma Edith looked startled. "It's about Julien."

"Oh. That."

"Olivia, wherever did you get the idea that he was married?"

Liv stared at her grandmother in disbelief. "Well, from him! He told me all about his wife, Delphine, and his daughter, Mathilde. He was honest about that, at least." Liv could feel herself getting angry. "And you know what? After the first time I met him, I actually felt *better* about my future, because I thought it was clear how much he loved them. It made me feel hopeful, like maybe I could meet someone like that one day, too. And then he tried to cheat on his wife! With *me*! I mean, is that it? Are there even any good guys out there anymore? Or are they all dogs? Is that the lesson here?"

"Are you quite done?"

Liv glared at her grandmother, who was coolly sipping her champagne. "What could you possibly say to justify any of this?"

"Delphine is dead, Olivia. She died six years ago."

Liv's breath caught in her throat. "Wait, what?"

"In childbirth. There was a complication while she was delivering Mathilde, and the doctors couldn't save her. It was devastating for poor Julien, but he has soldiered on, because he had to."

"No, that can't be right." Liv spun through their conversations, all the mentions of Delphine, the wedding ring on Julien's finger. "He told me so much about her, and . . ." But he had only spoken of her in the past tense, hadn't he? "Oh my God, Delphine is dead," she whispered.

"That's what I was trying to tell you yesterday," Grandma Edith said. "And according to his grandfather, he hasn't gone on a single date in the past six years. You, it seems, are the first woman he has had an interest in. And clearly that has worked out quite well for him."

"Oh God." Liv put her head in her hands. This changed everything. Or did it? What could come out of a flirtation with a man who lived some four thousand miles away from her, especially one who hadn't dated at all after the loss of his wife?

Still, she owed him an apology. "Would you excuse me for a minute?" Liv asked weakly. "I think I have to call Julien."

Grandma Edith checked her watch. "His business card is on your nightstand, in case you need his number."

Liv nodded and hurried into her room, where she dialed the cell number listed. But the call went to voice mail after a single ring, and she felt like an idiot.

When the beep came at the end of his outgoing message, she plunged in. "Julien, it's Liv. Liv Thierry Kent. My grandmother just told me about Delphine, and I'm so, so sorry. I don't even know where to begin. I—I'm obviously a total idiot, but I thought from the way you'd talked about her that she was still alive, and well, you can imagine what I must have thought when you kissed me. But obviously I was wrong, and now I owe you a huge—"

The phone beeped again and disconnected before she could finish her sentence. "Apology," she muttered to herself. She stared at her phone, willing it to ring, but it stayed stubbornly silent. After five minutes, when it was clear that Julien wasn't going to call back, she got up and returned to the parlor.

"Did you reach him?" Grandma Edith asked.

"I left a message." Liv sighed. "A stupid, convoluted message that—" She was interrupted by the ringing of their hotel room phone, and for an instant, as her grandmother reached for it, Liv let herself hope that it was Julien.

"*Oui, nous allons descendre tout de suite,*" Grandma Edith said, and as she hung up, Liv looked at her hopefully. She had said they'd be right down; was it possible Julien was here? But Grandma Edith merely shook her head and said, "Come now, there's no time to mope. We must get going or we'll miss the last tour of the day."

"The last tour? What? Where?"

"The Maison Chauveau."

"The Maison *Chauveau*?"

"Well, you asked me about it, did you not? So I've just booked us a tour. Don't tell me now that you're *not* interested."

"No, of course I am." Did this mean that Grandma Edith was finally about to reveal the reason she'd brought Liv to Reims?

"Well, then, let's go. We don't have all day." And with that, her grandmother whisked out of the room, leaving Liv no choice but to follow, a thousand unanswered questions swirling in her wake.

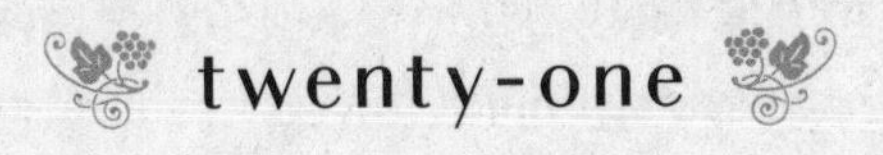

twenty-one

JANUARY 1943

INÈS

After the cold October night that Inès had come home to Michel, things had been different. Inès had recommitted herself to their marriage, and promised herself that she would make love to her husband at least once a week until she could feel him returning to her. One day, his responses might even be filled with passion rather than just dutiful obligation. In the meantime, she deserved his coldness.

But she hadn't been able to bring herself to return to Reims to tell Antoine it was over, and she knew that was cowardice on her part. She suspected he wouldn't take the news well, and that he'd be angry, which felt dangerous given his connections. Perhaps if she just avoided Reims altogether, Antoine would simply forget about her. Surely he had other women who held his attention, too, like the Marie whose name he sometimes called out. Maybe he wouldn't give Inès a second thought.

But then, one afternoon in early January, just after the snow had started to fall, Edith showed up at the Maison Chauveau while Inès was preparing dinner. Michel was holed up in the cellars with Theo, tasting small sips of vins clairs and jotting down notes about the quality and flavors they found in the young wines from each of the different vineyards. Their notebooks were filled with words like *tart berries*, *bread dough*, *gravel*, *smoke*. It was beyond Inès how they managed to taste such nuance when she could only taste fermented grapes.

"Edith! What are you doing here?" Inès had cried, throwing her arms around her best friend. "I've missed you so much." She regretted now that she'd made so many trips to Reims only to see Antoine, avoiding Edith on purpose because she knew Edith was judging her. Now it felt foolish, a waste of time. How had she allowed the pursuit of a man's affection to get in the way of a dear friendship?

"I've missed you, too," Edith said, disentangling herself from Inès's embrace.

"Is everything all right?"

"Not exactly. I come bearing a message from a *friend*." Edith sounded as if she might choke on the last word. "One of our best customers, a Monsieur Picard, has been wondering where you've been and would like to arrange a meeting."

"Oh." Inès could feel the heat on her face as she pulled Edith inside the house and drew her over to the hearth so that they could warm themselves. "Edith, I know what you must think of me, and—"

"It is not my business," Edith interrupted. "But Monsieur Picard, he has allied himself with some very powerful men." She hesitated. "They are not good people."

Inès didn't trust herself to speak, for what could she say? That she already knew of Antoine's allegiance to the Nazis? That she had somehow managed to reconcile it in her mind? Edith would hate her.

"I don't think you realize the stakes here," Edith said, her voice soft with concern. "My dear friend, it won't happen today or tomorrow, but rest assured, there will be a reckoning. You don't want to be on the wrong side, do you?"

Inès felt a surge of fear. Was Edith warning her of something the underground had planned for Antoine? Or was it Antoine himself that Inès should be frightened of? "Yes, I know. I'm trying to make it right."

"Then come with me to Reims. Talk to him. Tell him that you cannot do this anymore. I'm sorry, Inès, but he knows you're my best friend, and I just can't have someone like him angry with us, not with the work we're doing. You have to fix this, put it behind all of us. I told him I would do my best to ensure you'd be at the bar tonight."

Inès hesitated. "Yes, all right." She pulled Edith down to the cellars with her, and together they told Michel that Edith had dropped by to surprise Inès and was hoping Inès might be able to come spend an evening with her in town.

"Of course," Michel said, and Inès tried not to feel hurt by the relief on his face. "Inès is always so much happier after she returns from a night with you."

Edith glanced at Inès. "Wonderful. I'll drive her back tomorrow myself."

"Say hello to Edouard for me," Michel said cheerfully, and then he resumed his work.

As Edith and Inès ascended the stone steps and headed for the house, Edith reached for Inès's hand, and for a moment, it felt just like old times. In the schoolyard in Lille, when they were both little girls, before the Germans had torn the Continent apart for the second time in a century, Edith used to fold her hand around Inès's to tell her silently that everything would be all right.

"Do you still love him?" Edith asked a few minutes later as she watched Inès pack a small overnight bag.

"I don't think I ever did, Edith. He was a distraction, something to make me forget how useless I am."

"You're not useless. But I wasn't talking about Antoine. I was talking about Michel."

"Oh," Inès said. "Yes. Of course I love him. But I don't think it's the way a wife is supposed to love her husband. And I'm not sure he loves me at all."

For once, Edith didn't try to offer false comfort. "This war has put us all backward," she said at last. "I think things will be better when the Germans go. I hope so, at least."

"But will that ever happen?" Inès asked.

"For the sake of all that is right in the world," Edith replied, "we have to believe it will."

As they walked out of the house a few minutes later, Inès spotted Céline heading from her cottage toward the cellars. The other woman turned and waved, her growing belly on full display, and Edith gasped. "Inès! You didn't tell me Céline was expecting a baby!" She didn't wait for an answer before striding out to meet Céline halfway down the drive.

Inès had to force a smile as she hurried after Edith. "Yes, yes, we're very happy for her and Theo." Of course, the words were true, but she was ashamed to admit that the good news also made her feel a bit envious. Inès and Michel had not yet talked of having children, and though Inès imagined that they would one day, it felt like part of a far-off future she couldn't imagine.

"Céline, congratulations!" Edith exclaimed, embracing the other woman as they met in the garden. Edith knew Céline only in passing, through Michel and Inès. "I had no idea!"

"Thank you," Céline said, her cheeks turning a bit pink.

Céline seemed to glow now, her happiness overriding the despair of the war. She shot Inès a small smile as Edith pulled away.

"When do you expect the baby to arrive?" Edith asked.

"Sometime in June, I think," Céline said, her eyes darting quickly to Inès again.

"How wonderful," Edith said softly. "Edouard and I have talked of having a baby, but in these times . . ." She trailed off.

"To be honest, I'm very afraid," Céline said. "But if this is what God intended . . ."

"It's joyous news," Edith said firmly. "And you have been well?"

Céline nodded and smiled slightly. "My biggest problem is that I'm hungry all the time, and there's never enough food."

"I'll see what I can do about getting you some extra rations."

"Oh no, I didn't mean that!"

"I know. But let's make sure this baby is as healthy as possible, shall we? There will be enough challenges awaiting when he or she is out of the womb."

Céline hesitated. "Thank you. You are very kind."

Inès clapped her hands. "All right, shall we go now to Reims, Edith?"

"Yes, yes, of course," Edith said. She smiled once more at Céline. "Congratulations again."

"Thank you," Céline said. She turned and continued on toward the entrance to the cellars as Inès and Edith got into Edith's car.

"You don't seem to like her," Edith said as she pulled the car carefully down the drive, which was slick with ice.

Why was it that Edith could always see through her? She supposed it was because they'd been like sisters for so long, but she'd never had the same ability to discern what Edith was thinking. Lately, her friend had become even more of a mystery to her.

"I do like her," Inès said. "It is just that she has always seemed to belong here more than I do."

"Certainly that's not true." Edith gave Inès a look of concern as she pulled to a stop before turning onto the main road.

"I've been married to Michel for three and a half years now, and I still feel like a guest at the Maison Chauveau sometimes. But Céline, well, Céline is at ease here in a way that I am not. And I suppose that bothers me."

"Is that why you began your affair?" Edith asked quietly. "Because you feel as if you don't belong?"

"I don't know." Inès stared out the window at the vineyards that rolled by. The bare vines were like skeletons lined up in formation, a silent army against the gray sky. "I'm ashamed, Edith. I know you're judging me harshly, and I deserve that. I've made a big mistake."

Edith didn't say anything for a moment. "We all make mistakes. But life goes on, and we can always become better. It's not the decisions in your past that matter, but the choices you make about your future."

Inès watched as a convoy of German vehicles passed, one of them skidding slightly on an icy patch before the driver regained control. When the trucks had disappeared behind them, Inès looked at Edith. "Are we still friends? Or have I lost you, too?"

Edith glanced at Inès and then turned her attention back to the road. "You will never lose me, Inès. I will always be here."

It was perhaps Edith's words of solidarity that gave Inès the courage she needed to face Antoine that evening when he appeared at the Brasserie Moulin.

"Hello, my dear," he said, leaning in to kiss her on the cheek near the front door where she'd been standing, waiting for him to show up. "It has been far too long. I've missed you very much."

She pulled away. "And I, you."

"We should make up for lost time, then." His hand closed around her forearm like a vise. "Shall we go to my apartment?"

"No," she said quickly. "I think we should stay here for now. Shall we have a drink?"

Across the brasserie, Edith was watching her and gave her a slight nod when their eyes met over the crowd of Germans. Antoine looked put out, but he didn't refuse as Inès led them to two seats at the end of the bar. He pulled her chair out for her and then slid into his own. "You have been absent for a long time," he said as Inès studied the bottles behind the bartender. "I don't like having to summon you."

"Things at the champagne house have been busy," she said without meeting his gaze.

"Is that all it is?"

She turned to him. "No." She drew a deep breath, steeling herself. "Antoine, I can't do this anymore. I was wrong to betray my husband and I . . ." She hesitated. "I am trying to be a better person."

Antoine's eyes narrowed almost imperceptibly. "It's far too late to change who we are, my dear."

Inès blinked a few times. "But I *am* a good person."

"Good people don't betray those they have made promises to." He went on before she could protest, leaning closer until he was breathing his words right into her ear. "In any case, you should understand, Inès, that it is not so easy to disentangle oneself from a liaison in the midst of a war."

To anyone observing them, they must have looked like two lovers having an intimate conversation, but Inès could feel a chill settling over her. "What are you saying?"

"Oh, my dear." His tone was ice-cold as his dry lips brushed her earlobe. "As you know, I have friends in high places. And there's a cost for betrayal."

She blinked a few times, trying to steady herself. "I am not betraying you, Antoine. I—I care for you. It is just that I cannot continue this way."

"And you think that it is your decision to make?" His eyes were hard as he leaned back to study her.

"I do think that if you consider what I'm saying, you will agree."

"No, I do not think I agree at all. In fact, I think perhaps I will mention you and your husband to one of my friends. Perhaps Hauptmann Müller over there." He nodded across the room to a rotund officer with a Hitler-like mustache. "Or the weinführer, Otto Klaebisch. He's a dear friend. I'd hate to see your husband's business suffer as a result."

"Are you threatening me?"

"Inès, I'm insulted. I'm a gentleman." He smiled coldly, and she felt a surge of anger alongside her fear.

"Yes, well, you're not the only one with friends," she snapped back. "Perhaps there are members of the underground who would like to hear about your friendship with the Germans."

All at once, Antoine went very still, and Inès knew instantly she'd made a mistake. "Ah, so you know people in the underground?"

"No, of course not." She backtracked quickly. "I was just saying that I'm not the only one with much to lose."

"It sounds as if *you* are threatening *me*." His calm felt eerie, dangerous to Inès.

"No, I—"

"I would hope not," he interrupted. "It would be foolish. As I have explained to you, I am not ashamed of what I'm doing. I'm merely being practical. And what are the foolish *résistants* going to do anyhow, Inès? Write my name on a wall? Publish my name in a secret tract that only a dozen people will read? Who cares, Inès? They will all be executed soon enough for their treason."

"Antoine—" she began to say, but again, he cut her off.

"Go home, Inès." He pushed his chair back abruptly and stood. "Go home and stop playing city girl. I was a fool to become involved with you from the start, to think that you could be anything more than an insignificant whore." He put a few coins on the bar, gave her one last hard look, and strode away, his posture rigid and angry.

Inès watched him until he walked out the door and then turned back to the bar slowly, only to realize that there were at least a dozen other patrons, half of them German officers, all of them watching her. She swallowed hard and scanned the room for Edith, but her friend was nowhere to be seen. So she summoned the bartender and ordered a dry martini. She was determined to pretend that nothing was wrong, and to linger here long enough that the men eyeing her would go back to their own conversations, their own lives, and forget all about her.

It was nearly an hour—and two cocktails—later that Edith

reappeared at the back of the restaurant and beckoned to Inès. Inès quickly paid and headed toward Edith, a bit unsteady on her feet. She hadn't realized she'd had so much to drink, but then she hadn't eaten yet, either. The gin had gone straight to her head.

"Oh, Edith, it's over, I think." She leaned into her friend, and Edith grasped her upper arms, steadying her.

"Was he angry?"

Inès nodded miserably.

"You did the right thing." But Edith looked concerned, exhausted. "Listen, something has happened. I know you need to stay with us tonight, but we have other visitors in our apartment, too."

"Visitors? But who?"

"Come," Edith said, something strange in her tone. "I will introduce you."

They ascended the stairs behind the kitchen, and when Edith unlocked the door to the apartment, she didn't turn on the light. She pulled Inès inside and shut the door. "I'm back," she said into the room.

A flame flickered in the darkness, illuminating a man and a woman sitting on the floor. Their clothes were scuffed with dirt, their faces wan and hollowed. "Hello," said the man. He was, Inès guessed, around her age.

"Hello," she replied, and then looked to Edith for an explanation.

"Inès, I'd like you to meet Samuel Cohn, and his sister, Rachel. Samuel, Rachel, this is my dearest friend, Inès, who will also be staying with us tonight. You can trust her."

"It is a pleasure to meet you, madame," Samuel Cohn said while his sister continued to study her suspiciously.

"Nice to meet you, too." She glanced helplessly at Edith, trying to understand what was going on.

"Inès," Edith said slowly. "Samuel and Rachel are traveling and needed a place to stay."

Samuel cleared his throat. "To be frank, madame, we are Jews. We had word that the Germans were coming for us tonight, and we didn't know where else to go."

"Inès, we have helped others like the Cohns before," Edith said. "They were told to come to us, but only in case of an emergency."

"I am sorry it has come to this, Madame Thierry," Samuel said. "You are very generous to take us in."

"It is not a problem," Edith said kindly, though Inès could see the tension creasing her friend's forehead. "Unfortunately, with Inès staying with us tonight, too, things will be a bit cramped. I think perhaps you two can share the bedroom, and Inès can take the couch, if that's amenable. It will be safer for them to be behind closed doors," Edith added.

"I'm sorry, madame," Samuel said, looking at Inès. "If there was somewhere else for my sister and me to go, rest assured we would."

"No," Inès said. "Please don't worry. And call me Inès. If we are sharing quarters tonight, we shouldn't be so formal."

Samuel smiled. "All right. Inès, then."

"Inès, may I have a word?" Edith asked, and Inès followed her into the bedroom Edith shared with Edouard, whom Inès hadn't seen all evening. "I'm very sorry about these circumstances," Edith whispered once she had closed the door behind them. "Especially because this puts you in some danger."

"You don't need to apologize," Inès said. "I told you I want to help."

"I must ask you, is there any chance at all that Antoine will return tonight and try to find you in my apartment? If there is, I must look for some other arrangement for the Cohns."

"No," Inès mumbled. "He's gone."

Edith studied her. "All right. Edouard should be here soon. He is trying to find a place to hide the Cohns tomorrow. Obviously they are not safe here for long with so many Germans walking around beneath our feet."

"What about our cellars?" Inès asked suddenly. "We could hide them. It would be perfect, Edith. The Germans would never think to search for them there, and even if they did, they'd never find them. You remember when I first moved to

Ville-Dommange and got lost down there myself? It's a labyrinth."

Edith frowned. "No, Inès. I don't think it's a good idea."

"But I want to help. I want to be a better person."

"Inès, your entanglement with Antoine makes you a risk." Edith softened a bit as she added, "I'm sorry. I don't mean to hurt you. But how could anyone in our network trust you after seeing you with him?"

Inès felt as if her friend had slapped her across the face. "Do *you* trust me?"

Edith hesitated. "Yes, of course." But she didn't meet Inès's gaze, and the real answer to Inès's question was painfully obvious.

Inès forced a smile. "I understand." But she wondered, as Edith walked her back into the parlor with a blanket and a pillow, whether she would be permanently marked by the choice she'd made with Antoine. Was it possible that one sin could stain your soul forever? Or could one do enough good that a mistake of such magnitude could eventually be erased?

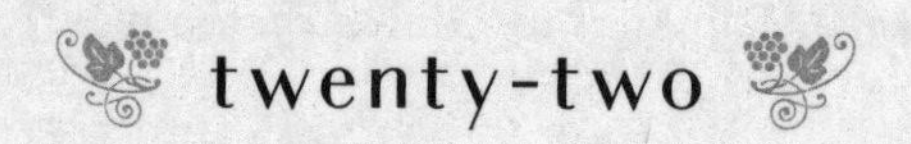

twenty-two

JANUARY 1943

CÉLINE

With Inès in Reims with her friend Edith for the night, Céline waited until Theo was snoring beside her before sliding out of bed, pulling on her coat, and slipping into the darkness outside as a light snow fell.

Michel was waiting in the cave where they usually met. He opened his arms, and Céline fell into them, wordless, her swollen belly between them.

"How are you feeling?" Michel asked when she finally pulled away and sat on the stone bench.

"Better," Céline said with a small smile. "It is extraordinary to feel the baby beginning to move."

Céline had actually felt the baby's first kick two weeks earlier, but she'd been careful not to say anything, for she had misled Theo about the baby's expected arrival date. The baby would be born sometime in May if she went full term, but she had told Theo the arrival date was in June, just in case he stopped to do the math. He had been placing his hand on her belly lately, asking when he might be able to feel the baby, and she had just shrugged, keeping the magical moments to herself for now. The whole pregnancy had felt to her like she was in possession of a special secret, something more beautiful than she could have imagined, but also something potentially ruinous.

Then there was the fact that each time Theo touched her belly, each time he gazed at her with love in his eyes, she felt a surge of guilt so powerful it nearly knocked her off her feet. He was trying to protect her, take care of her, because as far as he knew, she was carrying his child. How would he feel when he found out the truth? His renewed affection made the situation so much worse. He had become again, in many ways, the man she had married nearly eight years earlier, but of course it was too late to turn back the clock.

"Is the baby moving now?" Michel asked. She nodded, and he smiled, his whole face lighting up, as he reached tentatively for her belly.

"Sweet baby," she murmured, "that's your papa. Can you feel him?"

Michel leaned in and whispered to her womb, "I love you already, and I have not even met you yet, my child."

When the baby kicked once, sharply, hard enough that Michel could surely feel it, the rush of love Céline felt was enormous. Michel was smiling in disbelief at her belly, his hand still cradling it, his lips still centimeters away, and she had a fleeting, beautiful vision of a future for the three of them—Michel, the baby, and her. Though the circumstances were terrible, this was what was meant to be.

When Michel finally pulled away, his expression was serious. "Darling, I have news."

All at once, the clear image of the future seemed to disappear. "What is it?"

"I must go tonight to Épernay."

"But it's already two in the morning."

"Yes. There is something planned for dawn. I will not be back until late tomorrow morning, and I need you to keep Theo away from the caves so he is not aware of my absence. I don't think Inès will be home until much later, so she should not be a problem."

"What are you doing, Michel?" Fear rippled through her as the baby went still, perhaps sensing her apprehension.

"It is better that you do not know."

"But you've always trusted me to help."

"This is not about trust, my love." He hesitated. "In case things go wrong, I want you to be able to deny knowing anything."

"Michel, please, don't do this." She knew what she was asking was unfair, but the closer she got to the baby's arrival, the more she selfishly wanted to keep them all safe. Of course they both continued to work with Madame Gaudin, but moving arms on their own property felt somehow different than venturing out in the dead of night, looking for trouble. "Please, think of me. Think of the baby."

"But I am. There is word that the authorities are planning another round of Jewish arrests. You're not in danger yet—it's foreign-born Jews again, the ones they missed last time. We are hoping that by creating a, er, problem for them, we will distract them long enough to get a few more people to safety."

"What are you planning?" Céline asked. She thought of the rifles that he had delivered to Madame Gaudin just last week. "Please, Michel, don't do anything that you'll regret."

His smile was exhausted. "You know it is too late for that."

Céline looked away. "Then just come home to me safely."

Michel leaned in and kissed her then, slowly, tenderly. "My Céline," he said. "All I want is the chance to come home to you for the rest of my life."

Céline couldn't sleep after bidding Michel goodbye, and she was in the kitchen before dawn, boiling water for ersatz coffee. The sun had just come up when she saw through the kitchen window a vehicle at the end of the lane, driving toward the main house. Her heart leapt to her throat before she recognized Edith's car. She glanced at the clock. It was barely eight.

She watched as the car pulled up, but Edith didn't drive

away when Inès went inside the house. After a few minutes, Inès reemerged, glanced around, and hurried down the drive toward Céline's cottage. Céline's mind spun. Should she claim ignorance about Michel's absence? Or try to come up with an excuse to explain it?

By the time Inès knocked on her front door, Céline had pasted on a smile. "Good morning!" she chirped, perhaps too cheerfully. "What brings you back so early?"

"Oh. I just wanted to get home." Inès avoided her gaze. "Is Theo around? I can't find Michel."

"Actually, Theo is still asleep."

Inès checked her watch. "My goodness, I'm sorry. I didn't realize the time."

"Are you okay?"

"Yes, yes. But it seems strange that Michel is not home."

"He had to go meet with a vigneron," Céline blurted out.

"So early? And in January?"

Of course it had been a silly excuse; very little happened in the vineyards when the vines were under a veil of ice. "I'm not sure what it was about, but it seemed important."

Inès's eyebrows drew together. "Well, which vigneron was he going to meet? Do you know when he'll be back?"

"No, I don't know." Céline expected Inès to shrug and return to her own house then, but the woman lingered in her doorway, biting her lip, and finally, Céline said, "Are you sure you're all right?"

Inès didn't answer right away. "Can I trust you, Céline? I mean, really, really trust you?"

"Why yes, of course," Céline answered before she could think of the obvious response: that she wasn't trustworthy at all; she was a monster who slept with other people's husbands.

"I know you are aware, too, of Michel's, um, work in the cellars," Inès said.

Céline swallowed hard. "Yes," she said carefully. "But Theo is not."

"I know. That's why I am hoping *you* can help me," Inès said, and for the first time, Céline realized the other woman was nervous, jittery.

"What is it, Inès? Has something happened?"

"I need help hiding something."

"What do you mean?"

Inès looked at her for a long time. "Please, come with me."

Puzzled, Céline followed Inès to Edith's car, which still sat idling in front of the main house. As they drew closer, Céline was surprised to see two people sitting in the back seat, their heads ducked low. Edith was staring at Céline with the expression of a rabbit caught in the headlights. She rolled down her window.

"Inès," Edith said, her voice tight, "you said you were going to get Michel."

"He is not here," Inès said, and Edith's eyes flicked once more to Céline. "But Céline will help us. Michel trusts her, and so do I."

This time, Céline could not resist flinching, but she kept her eyes evenly on Edith's face. "Yes. You can trust me." She glanced once more at the two figures in the back, a dark-haired man and a dark-haired woman, both with their heads still bent as if avoiding her gaze could make them invisible. Whatever this was, it was dangerous.

Edith's expression softened, and she glanced at Céline's belly. "It is just that I do not want to get you involved."

"I'm already involved," Céline said pointedly, and though she hadn't explicitly admitted to working with Michel, Edith seemed to understand.

"Samuel, Rachel, it is all right," Edith said, and Céline watched as the two figures in the back seat finally straightened. They were younger than she expected, maybe in their early twenties, and the woman looked frightened, while the man looked exhausted.

"Hello," said the man.

"Hello." Then, remembering that Theo could awaken at any time, Céline glanced back at Edith. "I'm sorry, but my husband will awaken soon, and it's better that he doesn't see you. How can I help?"

All at once, Edith looked worried again. "This is Samuel Cohn, and his sister, Rachel. They're Jewish, and the Germans are after them. They just need a place to hide for a night or two before we can connect them with an escape line. I tried desperately to find another place, but it seems we are entirely out of options. This is absolutely our last resort." She cast a look at Inès, her mouth set in a thin line, and Céline wondered what had happened between the two friends. Edith looked back at Céline as Inès turned away, blushing. "If your husband can't be trusted, though . . ."

"Don't worry about that," Céline said. "There are many things here he has no idea about." She felt a surge of guilt. "It is just that we need to move quickly."

Edith considered this. "All right. Where shall we put them?"

"There's a room in our cellars that's nearly impossible to find."

"The cave where we've hidden the wine?" Inès asked.

"No, not that one. Theo knows about it, remember? We can't hide the Cohns anywhere that he might stumble upon them. There's another hidden cave, too, farther back."

Inès looked confused, and Céline realized too late that she was about to give away one of Michel's secrets, the small room within a cave down several twisting halls where he sometimes met with other résistants—and where he even occasionally rendezvoused with Céline. But there was no time to worry about that; they needed to get the Cohns belowground before Theo saw what they were doing.

"Very well. There's an entrance to the cellars through our house," Inès said. "We'll just need to move the armoire. Come on."

Edith and the Cohns tumbled out of the car. "Thank you," Rachel whispered, touching Céline's hand briefly as they all headed inside, and Céline forced a smile at the other woman. She glanced once more down the drive to her own cottage, but there were no lights on inside, no sign that Theo had seen anything.

Inside the house, Edith helped Inès push the armoire aside while Céline grabbed a lamp, and then the five of them made their way quickly down the narrow stone steps. Céline led them through the maze of chalky tunnels in silence until they reached the cave that concealed the small room behind the brick wall.

"How did you know about this place?" Inès asked her as the Cohns and Edith ducked inside, and Céline averted her gaze before shrugging.

"I have helped Michel hide some things here," she said.

"I wish he had trusted me," Inès muttered.

"He *does* trust you," Céline said quickly, but as she and Inès stared at each other in silence, she had the feeling they both knew the words were a lie.

"This place is incredible," Edith said.

"Michel put it in before the Occupation," Céline said. "Just in case."

"But when?" Inès asked, an edge to her voice. "We were all here with him, helping him to prepare."

"I don't know," Céline lied, aware that this wasn't the time to point out that Inès had spent much of the first half of 1940 working on her hair and makeup, rather than readying the Maison Chauveau for what to Céline had seemed inevitable.

"Well," Inès said, turning to the Cohns, "as you can see, you will be safe here until Edith can move you."

"Thank you," Samuel said, looking Inès in the eye before turning to nod at Edith, and then, finally, Céline. "Truly. I don't know how to tell you how much this means. I know you're all putting yourselves in harm's way for us. I promise, we will repay you someday."

"That's not necessary," Edith said.

"We must stand up to the Germans," Inès said with a confidence Céline had never heard before from her.

On the way out of the caves, after promising the Cohns they would be back later in the day to bring them some food, Inès took Céline's hand and squeezed it once. Edith walked ahead of them, and Céline had the strangest sense that she seemed angry.

"Thank you," Inès whispered to Céline. "I didn't mean to involve you. I had assumed Michel would be here."

"It's no problem." Céline pulled her hand away. "I wanted to help. But tell me, how have *you* suddenly become involved with hiding people?" She knew the words sounded accusatory, but she couldn't reconcile the Inès she'd always known with this new woman who had arrived today with a show of impassioned heroics. It made her uneasy.

"The Cohns came to Edith while I was visiting her. Edith didn't want to send them here, but she had no other options." Inès cleared her throat. "I persuaded her it would be all right."

"Oh." Céline was still confused. Since when was Edith assisting fleeing Jews? It all made Céline feel disoriented, and despite herself, she wondered at Inès's motives. Of course, it was clear Inès really wanted to help the Cohns, but why? So she could feel involved in something important? So she could prove to Michel that she was on his side after so many months of flitting to and from Reims like she didn't have a care in the world?

But maybe that wasn't it at all. Céline felt a surge of guilt for her rush to judgment. Maybe the war had really made Inès a better person, and Céline hadn't noticed the transformation.

"Céline," Edith said a few minutes later, after Inès and Céline had walked her to her car. "I'm very sorry to bring this situation to your door. It isn't fair of us to put you at additional risk. We simply didn't have another option."

"Edith, I'm very grateful to you for helping people like the

Cohns," she said carefully. "And I want to help, too. I know Michel will feel the same way."

Edith gave her a strange look, and Céline realized that the last line should have been Inès's—not hers. But Edith kissed her on both cheeks anyhow and bid her adieu before embracing Inès with a whispered, worried thank-you. And then she was gone, leaving Céline alone with Inès, wrapped in a web of secrets that grew more complicated by the day.

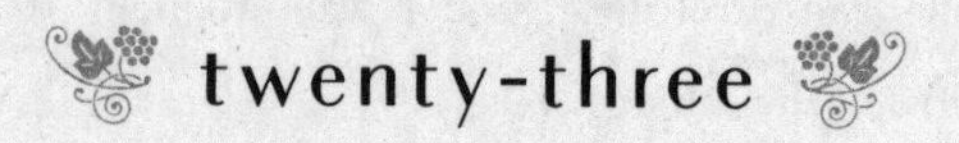

twenty-three

JUNE 2019

LIV

The ride to the Maison Chauveau took twenty-five minutes, first on a motorway out of Reims, and then on a narrow country road that led through small towns dotted with vineyards.

The champagne house itself sat on a small hill at the edge of Ville-Dommange, a tiny village whose sign welcomed visitors to a "premier cru" winemaking region. The narrow streets were peppered with cozy cottages and tiny gardens, and the town itself was surrounded by long, neat rows of vines that seemed to disappear into the horizon. At the gates of the Maison Chauveau, which featured the letter *C* forged in ironwork script, Grandma Edith took care of paying the driver, while Liv glanced around. Though there were houses in sight far down the lane, the Maison Chauveau was isolated, surrounded in front by a small, neatly tended vineyard plot, and in back by a much larger vineyard that stretched all the way down the hill.

"Well, come on, then," Grandma Edith said, gesturing to Liv as the car drove away. "I suppose we should get this over with."

Liv followed her up the stone drive to a pair of dark, glossy double doors, which her grandmother pushed open like she'd been there a thousand times before. Inside, there was a small gift shop with a tasting bar attached. A young couple sat sipping champagne, their heads bent close together as they whispered to each other.

"Are you okay?" she asked Grandma Edith. The older woman had begun wandering around the room as if in a trance, and Liv wondered what she was thinking about, what she was seeing in the past. Had she spent time here with her friend Inès, the one who had died during the war?

"What did you say?" Grandma Edith asked, finally turning to Liv and blinking a few times, as if she hardly recognized her granddaughter.

"I was just asking if you're all right. Maybe we should sit down for a little while."

"No, no, I'm fine." Grandma Edith glided away, toward an old stone fireplace in the corner, and Liv watched with concern as she reached out, her hand shaking, to touch the mantel. "This used to be . . ." she whispered, her voice trailing off.

Liv started after her, but then she felt her cell phone vibrating in her purse. She pulled it out, checked the screen, and felt her heartbeat accelerate. With one last concerned glance at Grandma Edith, Liv answered. "Julien?"

"Liv." His voice was deep, certain. "I'm sorry I missed your earlier call. I was in a meeting."

"I thought you were ignoring me."

"No, Liv, never. I would not do that."

Of course he wouldn't. She realized that now, that he wouldn't leave her hanging. "Julien, I wanted to apologize. I thought that your wife was still alive, and—"

"Liv," he interrupted, and she closed her eyes, bracing herself for a dismissal. "The misunderstanding was my fault. I assumed your grandmother had mentioned it, but I should have known that I can never count on her to say or do the things I expect."

Liv glanced at Grandma Edith, who now appeared to be whispering to the fireplace. "That might be the understatement of the year."

Julien chuckled. "Liv," he said, sobering. "I thought I felt something between us, but—"

"You did," Liv cut in. "I felt it, too, but I thought I was betraying your wife, and then when you kissed me—"

"You must have thought I was the worst man in the world."

"No. I think I was so upset because I *wanted* you to kiss me. I was angry at myself."

"You wanted me to kiss you?"

She took a deep breath. "Yes. And that's why I was kind of hoping you'd do it again. Unless I totally scared you off."

Julien's silence made her stomach swim until he spoke again. "I'm on my way back to Reims now, actually. Could I take you to dinner tonight?"

"Actually, I'm not in Reims. My grandmother, in typical mysterious fashion, just announced an hour ago that she wanted to tour the Maison Chauveau in Ville-Dommange, so we're here now."

"Chauveau?" Julien asked instantly. "Is she okay?"

Liv looked at Grandma Edith again. She was clutching a window frame with white knuckles, staring out toward the vineyards. "Honestly? I'm not sure."

"I'm just in Tinqueux. I can be there in ten minutes. Would it be all right if I join you? I promised my grandfather that I'd do my best to look after her while she's in town."

"Of course." After hanging up, Liv looked for Grandma Edith, but she had vanished. "Crap," she muttered, scanning the room once more before heading through the double doors leading out toward the vineyard behind the building.

She was relieved to see her grandmother standing just beyond the back door, gazing into the distance.

"Was that Julien?" Grandma Edith asked as Liv walked up beside her.

"Yes. He's going to come do the tour with us."

"Yes, of course he is."

"Are you okay?"

Grandma Edith didn't answer. In the distance, a flock of black birds took flight from beyond the slope of the hill, and Liv watched them go. It wasn't until she lost sight of them that Grandma Edith finally spoke. "Do you ever think that the ghosts of the past are still with us? And that perhaps they've been here all along, to remind us of all we have lost?"

Liv followed the older woman's eyes back out to the long rows of vines, and for a moment, she thought of her own father, whom she'd barely had a chance to know. She'd been just a baby when he died, but sometimes, especially in times of darkness or doubt, she felt a presence with her, and she wondered if it was him. She could almost believe it, for how could a parent ever fully leave a child without knowing whether he or she would be all right?

As a car made its way down the narrow lane in the distance, heading toward the main house, Liv watched as a large white bird lifted off, startled by the passing vehicle, and she thought of Delphine, Julien's wife, who'd never known her daughter at all. Perhaps she was still here, too, watching over all of them.

Liv felt tears in her eyes. "Yes, I believe that very much."

"I wonder sometimes why I am the one still alive after all this time," Grandma Edith said, her voice a whisper. "I was never supposed to be here at all."

"Well, I'm glad you are," Liv said. "You've been the one constant in my life all these years."

Liv slipped an arm around her grandmother, who didn't resist, and the two of them stood there for a long time, each of them communing with their own ghosts as they gazed out over the vines toward an infinite horizon.

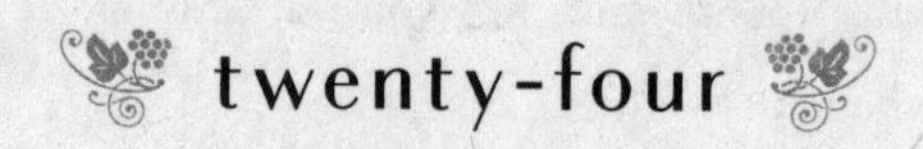

twenty-four

JANUARY 1943

INÈS

Perhaps she could be redeemed after all.

That was what Inès was thinking when Michel came home late on the morning of the Cohns' arrival at the Maison Chauveau, his Citroën bumping over the frozen drive. Céline was inside her own cottage with Theo, having begged him to repair their broken stove as a distraction, leaving Inès to give Michel the news about their new guests.

"You are telling me that in the hours I have been gone, you have agreed to harbor two refugees?" he asked when she was done telling him the story of the Cohns' escape from Reims.

"Please don't be angry. It was no longer safe for them above the brasserie, and—"

"I'm not angry, Inès," Michel interrupted. "I'm just surprised. I had no idea you were involved with such things." He was looking at her like perhaps he'd never really known her at all.

"Well, yes," she said, turning away. She didn't want to tell him that she'd merely stumbled upon the Cohns, and that in fact she had come very close to being on the other end of this fight. But she was on the correct side now, and surely that was what mattered. "I just want to do what is right," she said demurely.

"Well." Michel seemed at a temporary loss for words. "I'll go meet them now. Would you prepare them something to eat? They must be hungry after their travels."

"I've already packed them a lunch," Inès said, picking up the small bundle of cheese and bread she'd put together while she waited for Michel's return.

"Does Céline know?" Michel asked suddenly.

Inès hesitated. "Yes. She was here when Edith and I arrived with the Cohns. I needed her help."

"And Theo?"

"No. Céline was not sure whether to trust him."

"Good." As they walked outside to the main entrance to the cellars, Michel added, "Where exactly are they?"

"In the secret room. The one Céline knew about, but I did not." She couldn't keep the sting out of her voice. "You were keeping it from me?"

Michel sighed as they reached the bottom of the winding steps. "I'm sorry, Inès."

But what was he sorry for, exactly? For shutting her out of

her own life, her own marriage? "I would have kept your secret, you know."

He hesitated. "I know." But he didn't look at her again as she followed him wordlessly deeper into the twisting darkness, their way lit only by the lamp he carried.

They found the Cohns hunched where Inès had left them, partially hidden behind barrels. "Samuel? Rachel?" Inès called out. "It is Inès. I have brought my husband, Michel."

Slowly, the Cohn siblings emerged, Rachel looking worried, and Samuel sheepish. "*Désolé*," Samuel said, coming forward to greet Michel and Inès. "We heard footsteps, and we weren't sure what to do."

"You did the right thing," Michel assured them. "Welcome to the Maison Chauveau."

"I'm very sorry for the inconvenience," Samuel said.

"Nonsense." Michel's smile was tense but genuine. "It is the two of you who are owed the apology, for the way France has treated you. We will try to keep you safe until our country comes to its senses. It seems the world has gone mad, does it not?"

"Indeed."

"Now, I must ask something of you."

"Yes, anything," Samuel said instantly.

"My head winemaker, Theo Laurent, is a good man, but he knows nothing of the activities I carry on here. It would be better if he does not know of you and your sister. I feel that we could trust him if it came down to it, but I do not want to put him in the position of having to weigh the laws against his conscience."

"We understand," Samuel said, glancing at Rachel, who nodded. "We will stay out of sight."

"Good," Michel said. "And we will make every effort to move you as soon as possible. We'll just need some time to obtain false papers."

"Yes, of course," Samuel said. "And I promise, we will repay you and your family one day, just as soon as we are able."

"There is no need," Michel said.

"But we must."

The two men shared a moment of silent understanding. "Well," Michel said, glancing at Inès once more. "I should begin making arrangements. Inès, would you like to stay and make sure the Cohns are comfortable?"

"Of course."

"I'll leave you to it, then." Michel gave her a perfunctory kiss on the cheek before nodding to the Cohns and leaving the cave.

"Here, I have brought you some food. I don't know when you last ate," Inès said once Michel's footfalls had faded. From the way they ravenously attacked the small spread she placed on the stone bench, she guessed that it had been a long while. "Is there anything else you need?" she asked as Samuel and Rachel polished off the last of the minuscule meal. "We don't have much, but—"

"No, no, we are grateful for every kindness." Samuel hesitated. "I meant what I said to your husband. We will owe you after this, all of you, Madame Thierry and Madame Laurent, too."

"You owe us nothing."

"But you are risking your lives to save ours. Before I was barred from university, I was studying the law. And when the war is over, I will finish my final exams and become a lawyer. I very much hope that I am one day in a position to help you, and to make sure that the law is always on the side of those who are virtuous."

"I'm not so sure that's what I am." The words were out of Inès's mouth before she could consider them. "I've done things I regret very much."

"Whatever has happened, I will tell you this: a person who has lost her way would never risk her life to help people in need. You're a good person, madame."

Inès pressed her lips together. If he realized what she'd been doing behind her husband's back, he would feel differently. "May I ask you something?"

"Of course."

"Why were the Germans after you?"

"Why indeed," he muttered. "Well, I suppose it's because we were born in Poland. My whole family came here when Rachel and

I were just small children, so France is the only home we have ever known. We are as French as you are, I think. But to the Germans, it doesn't matter. Rachel and I were on our way home from visiting a friend in October when we saw the vehicles in front of our house. We hid and watched them take our parents away. I did nothing to stop it, and that is something I will have to live with forever."

"But surely you'll be reunited after the war. They're only sending Jews to work camps."

"Is that really what you believe?" Samuel's tone wasn't unkind. "Madame Chauveau, the camps are a facade. Most people—especially those the Germans don't deem fit for labor—are disappearing upon arrival."

"But that can't be true. The French police wouldn't be complicit in something like that."

Samuel sighed. "I think many of them might not have understood at first what they were involved in, just as many French civilians do not understand it now."

Inès just looked at him.

"The police know now, though. I believe they do, anyhow. Did you know that during the roundups in Reims in July, there was a French policeman who killed himself instead of making an arrest?" Samuel asked after a moment.

"What?"

"I saw it with my own eyes. He was dragging a child out from her home, a little girl who couldn't have been more than five or six. He turned to his commander and cried out, 'You know where they're going! How can we send a child to that fate?' His commander replied in a low voice, something I didn't hear, and gestured angrily to the truck where the girl's family waited. The French officer bent and whispered something to the girl—I imagine he told her to run, because she did—and then he took his pistol to his own head and fired without a second of hesitation."

"He shot himself in the head? Just like that?" Inès felt suddenly cold all over.

"I think he could not live with himself. Or maybe he just knew that taking his own life would give the girl a chance to get away in the chaos."

"And did she?"

Samuel smiled slightly. "Last I heard, she was living safely with a family in the countryside. And as for the French policeman, well, maybe now he has found some peace. Perhaps in dying to give someone else the life that was always meant to be hers, he was redeemed."

It took three days for Michel to connect with someone capable of moving the Cohns along an established escape line. Inès held her breath, as did Michel and Céline, each day as Theo descended into the cellars. Of course Inès had walked the underground halls thousands of times without noticing the hidden room, but what if Samuel or Rachel coughed or knocked against something with Theo in earshot?

On the fourth day, Inès was surprised to see a dark car she didn't recognize pull down their drive just after dusk. "It is time," Michel said, and after he and Inès moved the armoire in the kitchen, he made his way down to the caves without another word. In Céline and Theo's cottage, Inès could see a light on, the shadows of Céline and Theo at the table, and she prayed that Céline would keep her husband's attention away from the windows.

Michel emerged ten minutes later with Samuel and Rachel, both of whom exchanged kisses with Inès.

"We will not forget the kindness you have shown," Samuel said as Michel hurried them toward the door. "May God keep you safe."

"And you," Inès replied, feeling a strange sense of emptiness as soon as they were gone. By the time Michel came back into the house, she was crying.

"You hardly knew them," Michel said, eyeing her warily and then glancing out the window toward the Laurents' cottage, where Theo's shadow was still visible at the table.

"But I feel responsible, Michel. I couldn't live with myself if they didn't make it safely to freedom."

"All we can do is perform our own duties as effectively as

possible and hope that luck is with us. Come, help me move the armoire back in place."

"So have you hidden people here before?" Inès asked carefully as she wiped her eyes and crossed the room to help Michel push the large piece of furniture back over the cellar's entrance. "Helped them escape? Has this been going on beneath my feet all along?"

Michel seemed to be considering his words as he stepped back. "Inès, I want very much to keep you out of this, for your own safety."

"I think it's too late for that, don't you? You owe me the truth."

Michel just looked at her, and in his gaze, she saw suspicion, uncertainty.

"You owe me *trust*," she said quietly, her tears coming again, and finally, he moved toward her and wrapped her in his arms. She couldn't remember the last time he had held her this way, like she was something of value, something that deserved protection, and it only made her cry harder.

"Shhhh," he murmured, stroking her back until her tears ceased.

"Michel?" For a moment, she was sure he would kiss her, but instead, he cleared his throat and stepped back. Out of his arms, she felt suddenly unmoored.

"To answer your question," he said, "no. The Cohns are the first people I have concealed."

"But yet you knew exactly where to send them when Edith and Edouard couldn't find them a way out."

He gazed at her for a long time. "There is a network that moves secrets across the Swiss border."

"Secrets?"

"Information. From within our country."

"What kind of information?"

"Documents. Microfilms, sometimes. Whispers that help the Allies understand what is coming next. It's run by some Dutch people who have formed a community here in France."

Inès felt a shiver run down her spine. "And you are part of all this?"

He glanced at her. "This network doesn't go through Champagne. But from time to time, there are people here who have contact with the line. And I know that recently they've been moving refugees."

"But how?"

"There are false documents. Cover stories. Handshakes with authorities who are secretly on our side. It is all very dangerous, Inès, and that is why I don't want you involved."

But she was already involved, and they both knew it. "Where will the Cohns go from here?"

"Paris. And then, I believe, south to Lyon, and then Annecy, near the Swiss border."

Inès stared at her hands for a long time in silence. They were hands that had betrayed her husband, but they were also hands that were capable of saving lives, and there was power in that. She reached across the divide and touched Michel lightly on the arm. He jumped as if she'd burned him, and she withdrew. "I want to help more people."

"It is not possible."

"*Anything* is possible."

Michel shook his head. "Theo has no idea what we're doing, and to do this again, right under his nose, would be to flirt with disaster."

"Then tell him."

Michel blinked. "I cannot."

"Why? Céline knows, doesn't she? I'm sure he would do anything to protect her, with a child on the way. He would not put the mother of his child in danger by betraying any of us."

Michel looked away. "You must understand, Theo is much more rigid in the way he thinks about right and wrong. It is what makes him a good winemaker, but perhaps not a great contributor to our cause."

"I thought he was your friend."

Michel frowned. "He was. But we think of things differently now. And though I believe he would do anything to protect Céline, I'm not so sure he has the same allegiance to you or me."

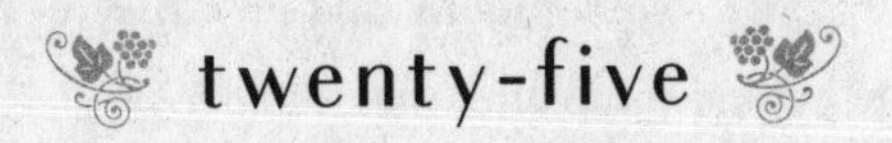

twenty-five

MARCH 1943

CÉLINE

After they'd gotten word in February that the Cohns had made it safely to Switzerland, Céline had suggested to Michel that they should volunteer to hide more refugees, since they had the perfect spot to do such a thing. But he had vehemently disagreed, telling her it would put her—and the baby—in too much danger. "It is perilous enough that we are still working to move arms across the region," he said without meeting her eye. "To do more than that, Céline, would be far too dangerous."

By March, though, the demand for safe houses was greater than ever, and the cold German officer, Hauptmann Richter, hadn't reappeared with any more threats, so Céline begged Michel to reconsider. "We have the means—and the location—to help people," she said. "Michel, we are very careful. We must do this."

Earlier that morning, Theo had said he needed to go into Reims for some supplies, and Inès had asked if she could go along in order to see Edith. It was the first time Céline and Michel had been alone in more than a month, and now they were lying side by side in the hidden room after making love on a pile of threadbare blankets. Michel's hand rested gently on Céline's growing belly.

"My love, think of the risk," Michel murmured, tracing circles around her navel. She felt the baby stir.

"The risk in not helping is far greater," Céline replied, her eyes half closed as she moved to lay her head on Michel's chest. He laced his fingers gently through her hair, stroking her head so tenderly that she thought she might fall asleep. "It is very possible that I myself will need to avail myself of an escape line. And don't forget that this child will have Jewish blood, too. Who knows how far the Germans will go? Better that we become part of the way out, so we can escape if need be."

Michel didn't say anything right away, but his hands traveled with more agitation across the crown of her head, his fingers tangling in her waves. "A way out won't do us any good if we are already dead," he said.

"Then we will do our best to stay alive."

"And you think we can trust Inès?"

Michel's mention of his wife jolted Céline out of her dreamlike reverie, and she sat up abruptly. "Look at us, Michel, sneaking into the caves as soon as our spouses disappear. She is more trustworthy than we are."

Michel sat, too, then rose to his feet. He offered a hand to Céline. Her arms and legs were swollen, the weight of her belly making her unsteady. "I suppose you are right," Michel said. "But if she finds out about us now . . ."

Céline swallowed hard, because a revelation was inevitable at some point, wasn't it? She could hardly think of it without feeling ill. There would be so much pain, so much upheaval, and it would be her fault. But it could not happen while the war was still being waged, for betrayal made people do terrible things. "She will not find out anytime soon, Michel."

"If we are going to take in more refugees, we need to tell Theo about our work with the underground, too. It is only a matter of time, otherwise, until he stumbles upon the truth."

"I know." Céline had already thought of this, of the risk they would take in including her husband. But they had no choice, not if they were going to save lives. Not if they were going to save their own souls.

Céline had expected Theo's initial reaction to be negative, but she hadn't expected the vehemence of his opposition.

"No." He sat at the table, his hands folded, his soup growing cold, as Céline clasped her hands in front of him in a fervent plea. "No, Céline. Absolutely not. It is not our concern."

"Of course it is! How can you say that?"

He shrugged. "We are living away from the city. No one is bothering us, and we are bothering no one. This is the way we will survive the war, with our heads down."

"Do you really believe that keeping my head down will save *me*?" Céline demanded.

"They are only taking away foreign Jews, not—"

"Stop!" She jumped to her feet and nearly lost her balance. Placing one hand on her belly and the other on the table for balance, she repeated, "Stop. You are merely regurgitating the things the Germans want you to say."

"And what you're saying is just propaganda from those who oppose the Germans. None of it has anything to do with us. The only way to ensure our safety is to do nothing!"

"Doing nothing is for cowards!" she cried.

"No!" Theo's face turned red, and he stood, slamming his hands onto the table. "Feeling as if you have the ability to effect change is for *fools*!"

"But if not us, then who?" Céline demanded. "If everyone thinks only of their own fate, who will save us? Who will save France?"

"Save France?" His laugh was bitter. "It is too late for that, Céline. And look, look at the situation we find ourselves in." He gestured to her belly. "You are pregnant! How did we make such a mistake? I will love our child, of course, but he or she is another Jew to protect, a liability! The only way to do that is to stay out of the Germans' way."

"You think this baby is a *liability*?"

"I didn't mean it that way. Just that the baby makes things all the more dangerous. We must think about our child."

"I *am* thinking of the child! I am trying to preserve a future!"

"And I am trying to save your life!" Theo shouted.

"You think you have the power to do that, but you do not. You are nothing, *nothing*, to the Germans. No, you are less than nothing, for you married a Jew. So you are already in danger, Theo. You just don't see it."

He shook his head. "No. My answer is no. I do not agree to helping refugees. I do not agree to sheltering illegal Jews. And I do not give you permission to put yourself—or my child—at risk."

"Theo," Céline said, her tone desperate, pleading.

"No. And that is final." He gave her one last look before striding out of the room. A few seconds later, she heard the front door slam.

Slowly, Céline sank back down into her seat at the table, her hand on her belly. "Baby," she whispered in the silence, wondering if her unborn child could hear her voice, could feel her resolve. "We do not need his permission to be who we must be.

Do you understand that?" Within her, the baby stirred, kicking once, in exactly the spot where her hand rested. "I will protect you, whatever it takes."

On the day before March's first full moon, late in the month, the cellars filled with a dozen workers—most of them children between twelve and fifteen who were grateful for the small fee Michel would pay them at day's end—and despite her growing exhaustion, and the way her whole swollen body ached, Céline made her way belowground to help. It was tradition to begin bottling the wines the day the springtime moon rose in the sky; for hundreds of years, winemakers in Champagne had believed that the power of the lunar cycle drew the bubbles into the bottles.

Céline worked beside Inès, who seemed extra solicitous. "Are you all right?" Inès asked her repeatedly, glancing with concern at Céline's belly, which had grown enormous. The baby would arrive within seven weeks, in the first half of May, according to Céline's math, but to Inès, the sheer size of Céline's belly must have been confusing; like Theo, she had been told that the baby would come in June.

"I'm fine," Céline reassured her. Though her belly was huge and her limbs swollen, Céline also knew there was something radiant about her, too. She could feel it, and she could see the glow every time she looked in a mirror. Despite everything, she was the happiest she'd ever been.

"You should rest. Why don't you sit, Céline? There are plenty of people to help us today. You don't want to exhaust yourself."

Céline blinked back sudden tears. She didn't deserve Inès's kindness. "Don't worry about me," she said. "Besides, this baby will have to learn to make wine one day, too. Might as well begin the lessons early."

She'd meant it as a lighthearted deflection of her discomfort, but Inès gave her a strange look. "You've already decided the baby will be a winemaker like Theo?"

Céline realized too late that she'd been thinking, instead, that the baby would perhaps inherit Michel's business one day. Certainly Michel would leave Inès after the war and legitimize his relationship with Céline. But of course she couldn't say that. "I think winemaking will be in his blood."

"*His* blood?" Inès smiled. "You are so sure it will be a boy?"

"I think so." Now that the baby was moving with regularity, Céline was getting used to thinking of the person he would be when he emerged from the womb—and she was almost certain of his gender. At night, when she dreamed of a life with her child, it was always a little chubby-cheeked boy she saw, his eyes blue like his father's, his hair dark and thick like hers. The best of both of them.

"How wonderful. I'm sure Theo would be thrilled to welcome a son."

Céline could feel her breath catch in her throat. "Yes."

"You're looking very pale," Inès said, putting a hand on Céline's arm. "Let's walk upstairs for a little while, take a rest in the house." When Céline began to protest, Inès cut her off firmly, adding, "Please. I'm exhausted. You would be doing me a favor."

Céline finally nodded and let Inès lead the way. They ascended into a bright, crisp morning, and Céline had just closed her eyes and inhaled the fresh air when the peace was shattered by the rumbling of an engine. She blinked a few times before her eyes adjusted enough to the sunshine to see a shiny black Mercedes rumbling down their drive, a Nazi flag flapping in the breeze.

"God help us," Inès said behind her. She took Céline's hand, and together they stood still as the car approached and drew to a halt.

Céline recognized the man who alighted from the passenger seat as the tall and broad-nosed Otto Klaebisch, the weinführer, for whom Michel and Theo had developed a grudging respect. The driver, she did not know, and she had just begun to relax, to believe that this was merely a routine inspection, when Hauptmann Richter unfolded himself from the back seat.

His eyes fell on Céline immediately. "Good day, Madame Laurent," he said as he stroked his thin mustache, his eyes pointedly fixed on the generous swell of her breasts beneath her cotton dress. She pulled her ragged sweater around her, and it was only then that he raised his gaze to hers, smirking at her discomfort.

"Good day, ladies," Herr Klaebisch said. "Forgive the intrusion, but we are traveling all over Ville-Dommange today, inspecting cellars. If you will excuse us, we will head belowground to find your husbands."

"Yes, of course," Inès said, as if Klaebisch had actually been asking her permission. Céline found that she could not speak; she was frozen under Richter's unwavering gaze.

Klaebisch and his driver headed for the stairs to the cellars, but Richter, who was still eyeing Céline, called after them, "I will stay here with the women and make sure everything is in order."

Klaebisch turned and assessed Richter. "Very well." And then they were gone, swallowed by the earth, while Richter continued to pin Céline with his gaze.

"Hauptmann Richter," Inès said loudly, moving closer to Céline. "Perhaps you'd like to come into the house. I can make you some coffee."

"Your French coffee is swill."

"Then perhaps some bread?" Inès asked.

"No," Richter said. "But you go. I'd like to have a word alone with Madame Laurent."

"Oh, I'm not hungry," Inès said quickly. "I think I will stay here."

Richter finally turned his attention to her, his glare hot with anger. "I asked you to go."

"Oh, but you couldn't possibly have meant it that way," Inès chirped, and Céline allowed herself to admire the other woman's show of faux-ignorance. "Besides, if there's something you need to say to Madame Laurent, it would be helpful for me to hear it, too."

Richter glowered at her before eyeing Céline again. "Very well. I did not realize you were expecting a child, Madame Laurent."

"Yes."

"Might I say that you look quite well?" When he smiled, she thought of a fox preparing to pounce on its prey. "Pregnancy agrees with you."

Céline fought her urge to flinch under his gaze. "Thank you."

"Of course the baby will be a Jew, too. Such a shame."

Céline swallowed hard and didn't say anything.

"But I could protect you," Richter continued, his tone even as he watched Céline's face. "Both you and your child. If you ask me to."

He seemed to be waiting for something, so Céline managed to say, "Please, do not hurt us."

"Oh, I am not the one you should worry about. I am only telling you that in times like these, a friendship like ours could be useful to you. Am I right in thinking you would do anything to save your child?"

Céline's heart thudded. "Of course," she whispered.

His smile was cold, vicious. "Good. Very good."

"Hauptmann Richter?" They were interrupted by a deep voice behind them, and Céline spun around to see the driver of the car ascending from the cellars. "Herr Klaebisch would like to have a word."

Richter turned back to Céline as the driver waited for him. "I will be back," he said in a low tone, and then he strode away, toward the cellars.

Céline didn't breathe again until Richter was belowground.

"Are you all right?" Inès's voice sounded very distant, and the world swam before Céline's eyes as she struggled to remain upright. She felt Inès's hands grip her elbows, steadying her, and then the world righted itself. "Céline? You are all right?"

"Yes, I think so," Céline finally replied, gripping Inès for support.

Without another word, Inès helped her into the house and settled her gently into a chair. She set about boiling water, and by the time she returned with a cup of ersatz coffee, Céline was feeling a bit better.

"You mustn't put too much stock in what Richter said," Inès said soothingly. "He is just trying to intimidate you."

"But he's not wrong. My baby will be in danger."

"Michel and I won't let anything happen to either of you."

Céline shook her head. "Thank you." Within her, the baby had gone still, as if waiting to see what would happen next. She wondered whether Inès really believed her own words—that she and Michel would have any power of protection—or whether the statement was simply a kindness, offered because there was nothing else to give.

Céline knew that Richter wasn't done with her, but she hadn't expected his return quite so soon.

That evening, with Michel and Theo gone to a meeting of vignerons in Sacy, and Inès safely unaware within her own house, he appeared at her door in silence, his eyes burning holes in her. He had ridden a bicycle there, Céline realized, instead of arriving in a car, so Inès wouldn't have heard his approach. "Madame Laurent," he said, "there are some things I must follow up on in your cellars. You will show me belowground?"

"I—I don't think it's appropriate," she stammered, her hands protectively on her belly. "My husband should be back soon, and I—"

"No, he won't." Richter smiled coldly. "I know he's with Monsieur Chauveau at a meeting of winemakers. I feel certain they will be quite delayed."

"But surely Madame Chauveau—"

"Will be completely unaware of my presence." He finished her sentence for her, and then grabbed her arm. "Come, Madame Laurent. You do wish to protect your child, don't you? But my friendship isn't free. I thought I made that clear."

"Please, I can't—"

But Richter was no longer listening. He tugged her from her house, ignoring her protests. As he pulled her across the garden and toward the stone steps that led beneath the earth, she understood both what he wanted and that she would have no power to say no. She whimpered in the darkness, which only made him chuckle. "Is something wrong, madame?" he asked.

"Please don't make me do this."

"I am not making you do anything." He picked up his pace, finally releasing her as he thrust her toward the entrance to the cellars and paused to illuminate his crank flashlight. "I am offering you a chance to save your child. Surely any mother would want that." He didn't wait for a response before shoving her toward the stairs. She stumbled on the first step, nearly falling, and he caught her roughly by the arm, laughing as she gasped. "*Hoppla!* You're no good to me if you're dead at the bottom of these steps, *du Schlampe*!"

She pulled away and gripped the rail, descending as slowly as possible, her mind spinning as she tried to buy a bit of time. "My husband will report you," she said as they reached the bottom of the stairs and he pushed her toward the first cave on the right, which was lined with resting bottles.

"Oh, I do not believe you will tell your husband. Because if you do, I would have no choice but to denounce you as a lying Jew. And lying Jews are sent east." He chuckled. "In the camps, there is not much use for pregnant Jews. And certainly not for their babies."

They were in the cave now, and he set the flashlight down beside him and let her go. For a second, she considered running, but then he pulled a small knife from his pocket and flipped it open. It glinted in the slanted glare of the flashlight as he brandished it casually. "I hope I won't need to use this to convince you."

"N-no." She couldn't tear her eyes from the knife, and this time, when he grabbed her around the waist, she forced herself not to flinch.

He pushed her against the wall, face-first, and once she was pinned, he reached under her skirt with his free hand, his sweaty fingers cold against her flesh. "There, there," he murmured as she whimpered in fear, and then his fist closed around her underwear and he pulled hard, ripping the fabric as he tore it loose.

She gasped and gritted her teeth to keep from crying out.

"No, please," she begged, forgetting the knife momentarily, but as soon as she tried to pull away again, she found the blade pressed up against her right cheek.

"Stupid, worthless cow," he grunted in German as he unfastened his trousers, the sound of the belt buckle like a bell tolling in the darkness. "I told you to stay still."

"Please, please don't. What if you hurt the baby?" That's when she felt him shift slightly. For an instant, she thought that her words had given him pause, but then he pulled her back and slammed her head against the wall, hard enough that she lost consciousness for a few seconds.

"You think I give a shit about your Jew-child?" he barked as her world swam back into focus.

She was slumped on the cold ground, her head throbbing. "Please, I—"

"Get up!" he screamed at her.

She strained to rise to her feet, but her limbs were useless, uncooperative. "I—"

"*Steh jetzt auf!*"

She moaned and tried to speak, to tell him she was trying, but her tongue wouldn't cooperate.

He cursed at her in German, then pulled her roughly to her feet and slammed her against the cold, wet wall again. "This is what happens when you refuse to follow orders," he growled, and then a wave of excruciating pain washed over her as he dragged the knife down her right cheek, splitting her skin into a jagged river of blood. She screamed in agony, and instantly, the knife clattered to the ground and his thick hand was around her mouth and nose, suffocating her. "Shut the hell up, *du Hure*!" he hissed in her ear. "You asked for this."

When he finally took his hand away, she gulped the air greedily as pain coursed through her. She could smell her own blood, could feel it trickling down her shoulder. Then he was against her again, naked below the waist, nearly inside her. He grunted, the sound inhuman, animal-like. "You're a filthy Jewish whore. You're lucky a man like me wants you."

She closed her eyes and braced herself, reciting a silent prayer to God in her head that her baby would be protected and that it would all be over soon. But instead of the horrific violation she knew was coming, there was only a muffled cracking sound that reverberated through the cave, and then Richter's body went slack against hers. She heard him hit the ground with a thud. Clutching her shredded, oozing face, she whirled around.

Inès was standing there in the light of the tilted flashlight, clutching a champagne bottle with both hands. Its base was stained crimson, and between them lay the still form of the German officer, blood pooling under the back of his head, his pants twisted around his knees. His eyes were closed, a sneer still pasted across his ugly features. "Is—is he dead?" Céline asked.

But Inès wasn't looking at the still form of Richter; she was staring in horror at Céline. "My God! You're covered in blood. What did he do to you? Did he . . . ?"

"You got here before he did what he came to do."

"So the baby . . . ?"

Céline closed her eyes and placed her hand on her belly. She could feel the familiar wingbeat of motion in her womb as the baby shifted within her. "The baby is safe, thank God. But Inès, we have to move quickly. We have to make sure he can't come after us." Céline tugged her skirt back down and squatted at Richter's side, her hands supporting her belly. She glanced at Inès, who still had the bottle hoisted high, a weapon if they needed it. With shaking, blood-slicked hands, Céline reached for Richter's neck, moving her fingers around until she felt a faint pulse. "He's still alive," she said, backing up quickly, as if he might awaken at any time and finish what he'd started. She looked up at Inès. "You—you saved me. How did you know?"

Inès finally turned her attention to Richter. "I saw him from the window, dragging you toward the cellars. I knew you were in trouble."

"Thank you." The words were woefully inadequate. "But what now?"

Inès was still focused on the crumpled German officer. "If he wakes up, we'll all be executed."

"Yes," Céline whispered.

"So we cannot let him wake up. That is all there is to it."

"But what do we do?"

"We wait," Inès said. She bent beside Richter and carefully pulled his handgun from his holster, then she stood again, the gun trained directly on him. "We wait for Michel to come home. He will know what to do."

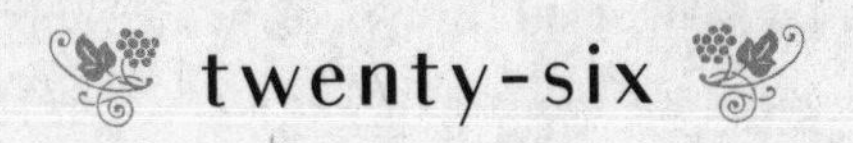

twenty-six

JUNE 2019

LIV

Julien arrived at the Maison Chauveau just before the five o'clock tour began, leaving barely enough time for him to kiss both Liv and Grandma Edith on their cheeks before disappearing to purchase a ticket.

"I had forgotten," Grandma Edith said as she regarded Liv with amusement, "just how silly people act when they are in love."

Liv realized that she was still touching the spot on her face where Julien's lips had been, and she hurried to put her hands behind her back. "I'm not in *love*, Grandma Edith," she protested, aware that her face was probably flaming. "It's just a crush."

"Crushes are for children," her grandmother said, raising an eyebrow. "And you are most certainly not a child."

Julien rejoined them just as a college-aged man moved to the front of the waiting area and called out, "Everyone for the English-language tour, please assemble here! We're about to get started."

Grandma Edith herded Liv toward the tour guide, and Julien followed. "English, can you believe it?" Grandma Edith said to Julien. "The sacrifices I make for my granddaughter."

"I heard that," Liv said.

The older woman rolled her eyes at Julien, who laughed.

"Welcome, everyone, to *La Maison Chauveau*, the House of Chauveau, a world-famous champagne house here in Ville-Dommange, France," the tour guide began as the group—two middle-aged couples in addition to Liv, Julien, and Grandma Edith—edged closer. "My name is René, and I grew up not far from here. In fact, when I was a boy, my father worked in the cellars here at Maison Chauveau, so you could say I grew up with the legends of this place. I will begin by telling you a bit about the history, and then we will visit the cellars."

Liv's mind wandered as René began to talk about the Chauveau family founding the house just after the French Revolution, and growing it in the middle of the nineteenth century along with their pioneering neighbors to the south, the widow Clicquot and Jean-Remy Moët.

Liv glanced at Grandma Edith, who had a stricken expression on her face. "What's wrong with her?" Liv whispered to Julien, who frowned and shook his head. "Is this because she was friends with the woman who owned this place? The one who died?" Liv continued, earning her a glare from one of the tourists in their group, a middle-aged woman wearing too-tight leggings and running shoes.

"Shhhhh," the woman hissed, and Liv narrowed her eyes.

"I think your grandmother is okay," Julien said in a low voice, and Liv turned her attention back to the tour guide.

"Along with the rest of the Marne, Ville-Dommange was nearly destroyed during the First World War, and the Chauveau family, along with many others in the region, lost almost everything," René was saying. "The Marne suffered more damage than most other French departments. As for the grapes, forty percent of the vineyards of Champagne were ruined during the war, and it took many years for the region to recover. The Chauveaus were one of the families hardest hit, and it is said that this strain contributed to the early death of the house's owner, Maurice Chauveau, in 1935. His wife, Jacqueline, died the same year, and the *maison* was taken over by their only son, Michel Chauveau, who was then just twenty-one years old."

Grandma Edith made a choking sound, and then she began to cough violently, doubling over as Liv rushed to her side. René stopped speaking, his forehead creased in concern, and while the legginged tourist continued to glare at them, Grandma Edith finally straightened and held a shaking hand up.

"I'm all right," she said. "I apologize."

"Grandma Edith, do you need to leave?" Liv whispered. "We can go outside, or—"

"No!" Grandma Edith's rebuke was sharp, and she glanced at Julien before softening. "No. I need to hear this." She pointed to René. "*Vous pouvez continuer*, young man."

"Merci, d'accord," René replied before turning back to the group. "So, Michel Chauveau took over the house after that. Now, I will continue my story in the cellars, if you will follow me."

René turned and began to walk away, and Liv moved again to Grandma Edith's side to support her as they followed him. The older woman was shaking, and Liv exchanged concerned glances with Julien. "Are you sure you're all right, Grandma Edith?" she asked.

"Stop treating me like a child," she snapped. "I'm perfectly fine."

René led the group to a door against the back wall of the main room. "Just before the Nazis came to Champagne during World War II, Michel Chauveau had the foresight to conceal this entrance with an enormous armoire. That way, Monsieur Chauveau was able to come and go unobserved if he needed to, simply by moving the furniture. Today we have widened the entrance to make it more accessible. The stairs are still a bit tricky, though, so if anyone needs assistance . . ." His gaze drifted to Grandma Edith.

"I am perfectly comfortable on my own, thank you very much," she said icily.

René shrugged and led the group down a set of winding stone steps into what looked like a vast network of halls underneath the earth. As they descended, the air grew colder. "Because these cellars are dug into the chalk beneath the earth, the temperature down here is very constant. Here in these caves, regardless of the season, they are a steady ten degrees Celsius, which is about fifty degrees Fahrenheit for you Americans. They were installed over the course of three decades during the second half of the nineteenth century, because the owner at the time, Pierre Chauveau, was obsessed with the success of the larger champagne houses in the nearby city of Reims. Many of those houses stored their wines in underground *crayères*, which is a French term for chalk quarries. These quarries had been constructed by the Romans beginning around AD 300, but not for winemaking; they only wanted to take the chalk from the earth to use it for buildings, which left Reims with many, many cold tunnels beneath the earth. In Ville-Dommange, there were no such *crayères*, so Pierre Chauveau—fixated on competing with the larger houses—endeavored to make his own. Thankfully, he died before he could completely bankrupt the family, and his son, Charles Chauveau, who took over upon his father's death in 1902, was able to salvage the champagne house and begin making it into something extraordinary."

All around, unlabeled bottles rested on their sides on giant wooden scaffolding, and in one of the caves, barrels sat in neat, silent stacks. "Unlike some of the larger houses, most of our work is still done by hand, including the riddling of our bottles," René said as they walked. "Three or four months before the wine is to be released, there is a worker, a master riddler, who comes down here to turn the bottles, just an eighth of a turn each day, to dislodge the sediment that has collected as the wine ages. Here, on the bottles tilted downward, you can see the yeast cells and particles collecting in the neck. Soon these bottles will all be positioned fully neck down, and then comes disgorgement, when the bottles will be immersed in a very cold solution to freeze the sediment, opened by a machine, the sediment popped out, and the remainder filled with a mixture called *dosage*, a blend of sugar and reserve wine. This is the stage that determines how sweet the champagne will be. At Chauveau, we tend toward wines that are less sweet, so the flavor really shines through. Most of our portfolio is brut or extra brut, which means that it contains less than twelve grams per liter of residual sugar, or less than a half teaspoon per five-ounce glass."

René led them deeper into the ancient tunnels, which were illuminated by overhead lights and lamps at five-yard intervals, and Liv found herself thinking about the secrets these chalk walls must hold. The scent of the air reminded her of the basement of the house she'd lived in with her mother just outside Boston when she was twelve; it smelled like stone, dirt, and cold.

Finally, at the end of a twisting hall, René took a sharp right into a small cave that was completely empty. He waited for the group to filter in. Grandma Edith was the last to round the corner, and as she did, she inhaled sharply.

"What is it?" Liv whispered, and Grandma Edith shook her head, but Liv could see that the color had drained from her face.

"This is a very interesting place," René said, putting a hand on one of the stone walls. "It looks like just an ordinary cave, right? But during the war, this cave contained a small room that was hidden behind a brick wall, built by Michel Chauveau."

"What'd he use it for?" asked the tourist in the leggings as her husband pulled out his iPhone and began snapping pictures.

René's eyes twinkled. "*Résistance*."

"I thought this was supposed to be an English tour," the woman grumbled. "What's that mean?"

René cleared his throat. "Resistance," he said, making the word sound as American as possible, and the tourist nodded, apparently satisfied. "In other words, he was one of the résistants—ordinary people fighting against the Nazis—who operated here in the Champagne region. Now we don't know anything definitively, but it is said that not only did Michel Chauveau hide munitions here, he hid refugees."

"Only two," Grandma Edith said suddenly. "He planned to hide more people, but it was not safe."

Liv turned to stare at her grandmother, as did everyone else.

"Er, yes," René said, giving Grandma Edith a confused look. "It sounds as if you have taken this tour before."

"No," Grandma Edith said. She glanced at Julien, who was staring straight ahead.

"What is she talking about?" Liv whispered as René resumed speaking.

Julien just shook his head and pressed his lips together.

René gave Grandma Edith a few nervous glances as he told the group that Michel Chauveau was part of an organization that printed a Resistance tract, blew up train tracks, and even reportedly killed a German officer. "So you see," René concluded triumphantly, "when you drink a glass of Chauveau, you are really tasting heroism in all those bubbles. The Maison Chauveau helped save France."

"So what happened to him anyways?" asked the tourist in the leggings. "Michel Chauveau?"

"Well," said René, leaning in conspiratorially. "He died in 1943, leaving his champagne house to his wife, Inès Chauveau, but then she vanished, too. Since then, the Maison Chauveau has been run by a trust set up just after the war by a law firm in Reims."

"How'd Michel Chauveau die?" asked the tourist in the leggings.

The tour guide cleared his throat. "He was arrested by the Germans, and no one knows quite what happened after that."

"Well, that's simply an incomplete answer, young man," Grandma Edith said, and René turned to her, confusion etched across his face.

"But that's what's in the tour guide notes, madame," he said.

"Grandma Edith," Liv said, placing her hand on her grandmother's arm, but the old woman shook her off.

"Michel Chauveau was executed by the Germans in the center of Reims," Grandma Edith said, her voice shaking. "On the rue Jeanne d'Arc, to be exact, at Gestapo headquarters. He was betrayed, you see, by someone he once thought he loved. Someone who never deserved that love in the first place, I think."

The cave was silent as everyone looked at Grandma Edith.

"How do you know that, Grandma Edith?" Liv finally asked, her voice low. "You knew him?" She must have, Liv realized. If what the man from the restaurant had told her was true, Michel Chauveau was the husband of Grandma Edith's best friend.

Grandma Edith's eyes were full of tears as she looked up at her granddaughter. "Yes, Olivia. Yes. I knew him well." She turned and strode out of the cave before Liv could reply.

"Madame! You'll get lost!" René called, starting after her, but Julien put his hand up.

"Let her go," he said. "She knows these caves."

René opened and closed his mouth, but there must have been something in Julien's tone that stopped him.

"I have to make sure she's okay," Liv said to Julien, but he just shook his head.

"Let her have a few minutes to herself," he said. "This is the first time she has been back here in many years. I think she needs to be alone."

"But . . ." Liv's mind raced.

Julien glanced at René and then back at Liv. "Let's take a walk, shall we?" He turned once more to René. "We'll see ourselves out. I apologize for the interruption." He steered Liv out of the cave, and as they walked back to the stone steps, she looked for Grandma Edith, but she had seemingly disappeared.

Aboveground, Julien led Liv quickly through the gift shop and out the front door. Once they were standing outside the main house, she turned to face him. "What is *happening* here? Why did my grandmother freak out like that?"

"Oh, Liv." Julien sighed. "I wish I could tell you, but as I've said, it is her story, not mine."

"Then why won't she tell it?" But the question was rhetorical, and they both knew it.

"Come," Julien said, taking her hand, "let's look at the view, shall we?" He led her a few hundred yards from the main house, toward a smaller cottage that appeared well tended. They passed it and stopped at the edge of a hill overlooking the valley. "Grapes," Julien said, "as far as the eye can see. One day, they will be part of great champagnes that find their way all over the world. It's incredible when you think of it, isn't it?"

"You're changing the subject."

He smiled. "I'm merely pointing out the beauty of this place. It's a place your grandmother once loved."

"And yet she has never in her life mentioned it," Liv muttered. "You're sure you can't tell me what's going on?"

"I wish I could."

Liv shook her head, frustrated. "Fine. So what about you?"

"Me?"

"If you can't tell me my grandmother's story, what about yours?"

He looked down at her. "My story isn't so interesting."

"Will you tell me about Delphine?"

He sighed. "Someday, if you'd like, I will tell you all about her. She was the mother of my child, Liv. I was very much in love with her. There were no problems in her pregnancy, no reason to think she would not be completely fine. But there was a complication in the hospital, and . . ." He trailed off and shook his head. "Well, you know, of course, that she died, and Mathilde lost her mother. I have tried to keep her memory alive for my daughter all these years, and of course she will always be a part of my life. I will always love her.

"But," he continued, "I've been realizing lately that perhaps living in the past means you don't give yourself a chance to move into the future. When we talked that day at the brasserie about your life, it made me think of my own, too, and how I've been stopping myself from going forward. My possibilities are wide open, just like yours, and I think I needed to remember that. You, Liv, reminded me."

"I'm so sorry about your wife," Liv said as Julien took a step closer. "It's the kind of loss I can't even imagine."

"Thank you. We all suffer losses. But it is how we choose to move ahead that matters, isn't it? We must honor the past without turning our backs on the future." He brushed a strand of her hair from her cheek, his hand lingering there against her face. "I hope that now that you know the truth, you do not think I was terribly out of line to kiss you."

"No." And then, summoning her courage, she closed the final inches between them and pressed her lips gently to his. His hands tangled instantly in her hair, and he tugged her toward him.

"Better later than never?" she asked, finally pulling away with a smile.

"I agree." He laughed and stroked her cheek with his thumb. "As long as we can do it again." He leaned in and kissed her, with more passion this time, his lips parting hers.

She kissed back, lost in the moment, until the sound of someone approaching snapped her out of it. She pulled back as she realized it was Grandma Edith standing there, blinking at them. Liv covered her mouth, embarrassed. "Grandma Edith, I—"

"If you're done making out like a couple of teenagers, I'd like to go now, please," her grandmother said.

Liv could feel her face flaming as Julien chuckled. "I'm afraid I'm to blame, Madame Thierry," he said. "But I promise, I'm being a perfect gentleman."

"Well then," Grandma Edith said, "we should probably depart before the two of you get any more amorous."

She turned and walked back toward the hired car, without bothering to wait for them.

"I should, uh—" Liv gestured awkwardly after her grandmother.

Julien smiled. "Of course. May I call you later? Or should I let you get your grandmother settled first?"

"I'll call you once she heads to bed for the night, if that's all right."

Julien leaned in and gave her a light kiss on the lips, lingering there for a few extra seconds. "Do you need me to follow you back now?" he asked as he stepped back. "Or do you think she'll be all right?"

"I think she'll be okay," Liv said, touched by his concern. "At least she's acting like herself again." But by the time she climbed into the back seat beside Grandma Edith, the indignant energy seemed to have drained from the older woman. Now she sat slumped against the window, her eyes closed, her breathing rapid and shallow. "Are you—" Liv began to say.

"Please," Grandma Edith said, her voice hoarse. "Don't speak, Olivia. I'm perfectly fine. I'd just like some peace."

Liv nodded, and as the driver started the car and pulled away, she watched out the window as Julien, and the Maison Chauveau, faded into the distance.

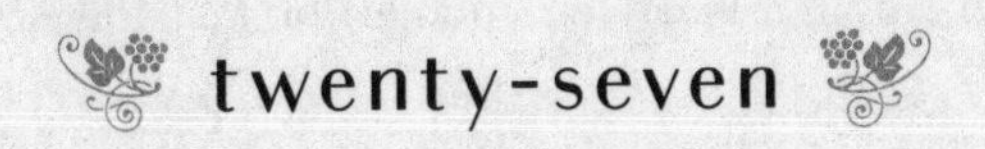

twenty-seven

MARCH 1943

INÈS

Inès and Céline stood guard over Richter's large, crumpled body for nearly ninety minutes, waiting for Michel and Theo to return. They couldn't leave him alone, and they couldn't move him, either—he was too heavy, and where would they put him anyhow?—but staying there beside him was torture. At least a dozen times, Inès tried to convince Céline to go aboveground to press a clean cloth to her tattered cheek, to rest in case the baby was in danger, but she had refused, saying that she couldn't take the risk of leaving Inès alone with such a monster. "What if he wakes up?" she fretted aloud again and again.

Finally they heard the growl of an approaching car overhead. As brakes squealed and the engine cut off above them, the women exchanged worried glances. "Will you go up and make sure it's Michel?" Inès asked.

Céline shook her head. "No, you go. I will watch Richter."

"But—"

"You have already risked enough for me, Inès. I—I don't deserve it."

Inès hesitated before handing Richter's pistol to Céline and heading for the stairs. Carefully, she emerged aboveground, and as her eyes adjusted to the moonlight, she recognized Michel's car and exhaled in relief. He got out of the driver's seat as Theo climbed from the passenger seat. "Michel!" Inès hissed.

He spun around, searching the darkness. "Inès? What are you doing out here?"

"Come quickly. There's an emergency."

When Theo followed, Inès didn't try to stop him, though she wondered if she should. He hadn't been involved until now in anything illegal taking place in the cellars. But there was no way Céline would be able to explain away the giant wound on her cheek, nor could Inès come up with a reason why Michel was needed in the cellars so urgently. So she stood silently aside as Michel and Theo rushed belowground. She took a deep swallow of the crisp evening air before following.

By the time Inès made her way back into the cave where Richter lay, Theo was squatting with his arm around Céline, who had finally crumpled to the ground, and Michel was gaping at them, Richter's gun in his hand and an expression of anguish on his face. "What in God's name happened?" he asked, turning to Inès.

"I—I saw them from the window," Inès said, and Michel's

eyes flashed to Céline, who was sobbing now, her head down, as Theo tried to stop the blood flowing from her face with his scarf. "He was dragging Céline."

"Was she . . . ?" Michel asked.

"I came down the stairs behind them. He was—he was hurting her. You can see her face." Inès couldn't imagine how much pain Céline was in. "But I stopped him before he did what he had come here to do. And the baby is okay, too."

Michel's tormented gaze flickered around the room and landed on the bloodstained champagne bottle. "You hit him with that?"

"Yes," Inès said.

"And he was alone?"

"Yes."

"Thank you," Michel said. "My God, Inès, thank you for being so brave."

"Of course." But something about his gratitude struck her as odd. She shook off her misgivings. "What do we do now? If he wakes up . . ."

"Yes, I know," Michel said.

Theo looked up, finally paying attention. "But what do you suggest? We can't just murder the man."

"Don't fool yourself," Michel said. "He would have killed Céline without a shred of remorse. And the baby—" He stopped and shook his head. "He has left us no choice."

"Michel," Céline said, and then stopped, pressing her lips together.

"Don't worry," Michel said gently. Then he turned to Inès. "Céline likely needs a doctor, but I think we cannot afford to call one, for there will be too many questions. Can you do your best to care for her?"

"I will do what I can," Inès said.

"Michel—" Theo said.

Michel turned to him. "And you, Theo? Are you with us or against us? I will not hold it against you if you choose not to help, but I do require your silence. It is your wife whose life has been saved."

Theo glanced at Céline and then back at Michel. He looked angry, frightened. "I will help," Theo said, "but we will never speak of this again."

"Fine," Michel said. "Inès, take Céline upstairs. Don't make a sound."

Inès hesitated. The decisions they were making here would affect them forever.

"Inès," Michel said urgently, handing her Richter's gun. "Go. Now. I don't know how much time we'll have before the Germans come looking."

His words snapped her out of it, and she pulled Céline into her arms and led her gently out of the cave, a trail of blood falling behind them as they went.

Inès cleaned Céline's wound and helped slow the bleeding, and though she knew Céline needed medical attention, she agreed with Michel: it was too risky. If Richter had told anyone he was going to the Maison Chauveau that evening, their property would be crawling with Germans as soon as it became clear he was missing. Their best hope of appearing innocent was to involve as few people as possible.

Céline's bleeding eventually stopped, and she fell asleep atop the covers in Inès and Michel's bed, her hands curled under her belly, as they waited for the men to return. Inès stroked her hair, thinking about the future. They were all in peril, and not just because of the events that had passed that night. Would any of them survive?

Eventually, Inès dozed off beside Céline and was jarred awake sometime before dawn by the slam of the front door below. She sat up with a gasp and fumbled for Richter's gun on the bedside table. She was clutching it when Michel entered the bedroom, his clothing stained with blood and dirt.

"How is she?" he asked as Inès set the gun down, got out of bed, and put a hand on Céline's forehead.

"Okay for now, I think." Inès crossed the room and wrapped her arms around him, but his body was stiff, unresponsive, and when she withdrew, she realized he was still watching Céline.

"We should bring her to her own house," he said.

"Yes."

Michel changed his shirt quickly, leaving the bloodied one crumpled on the floor, and then he scooped the sleeping Céline gently into his arms. "I'll return in a moment," he said without looking at Inès.

"Wait," Inès said. "Theo. Is he—"

"He is bound by his complicity in this," Michel said stiffly.

"And Richter?"

"He's dead, Inès. It is best you know no more than that."

"You got rid of his bicycle, too?"

He nodded. "We left it two towns over, by the side of the road. That should throw the Germans off for a little while."

He left carrying Céline, and Inès sat rigid on the bed for a long time before forcing herself to get up and grab his shirt. It all felt surreal, terrifying. Was there any possibility they could get away with this, or had they all signed their own death warrants tonight? She boiled water, and she was just about to begin washing the garment, when Michel reentered through the back door, took one look at her, and snatched the shirt away.

"The blood will never come out," he said. "We must burn it. Your clothing, too."

"But we have so little . . ."

His eyes flashed. "We will have *nothing* if the Germans come. Come on, Inès, you know better."

His tone stung, but she turned anyhow and stoked the fire smoldering in the hearth. She thrust his soiled shirt in, watching as the flames licked greedily at the cotton, reducing it to ashes.

Michel returned a few minutes later. "Come. We must wipe the cellars clean of blood before the sun is up. You can burn your clothes when you're done."

Inès nodded, and together they filled buckets and hurried out back and down the stairs to the cellars. They worked on their knees in silence, scrubbing as hard as they could with old rags until the blood on the floors, and the crimson streaks on the walls, faded into the forgiving stone. When they were done, Inès was so exhausted that she could barely stand, but Michel helped her to her feet, and supported her as they walked upstairs in silence.

"Rest," he said when they reached the back door of the house. "Just give me your clothes, and I will take care of things."

"But you must be very tired, too."

"Inès, you saved Céline. You saved the baby."

When Inès didn't move, Michel whispered, "Go," and she was surprised to see his eyes filled with tears. It was only later, after she had left her bloodied clothing in a pile at the door and fallen naked into bed, that she realized it hadn't even occurred to her to comfort her husband, to ease his pain, to wrap him in her arms and promise everything would be okay.

Was it because she knew that it wouldn't be, that her words

would be meaningless? Or was it because she herself was empty, drained of everything that made her who she was? The questions gnawed at her as she finally drifted into a deep, dreamless sleep.

For three days and two nights, they waited, hardly acknowledging each other, jumping each time they heard the distant hum of vehicles passing by on the main road, flinching each time a flash of motion cut through the dusk. It seemed inconceivable that there wouldn't be a price to pay for Richter's life, but as the minutes ticked by, Inès let herself begin to believe that perhaps Richter hadn't told a soul where he was going, that maybe no one would think to follow his trail to the Maison Chauveau. Maybe there were other women Richter had leered at, threatened, attempted to violate. There was a chance Richter's colleagues didn't even know about Céline and the way her curves and forbiddenness had become bait for a cruel animal.

Céline's wound began to heal, the ragged edges knitting themselves together into something dark and hard, but it didn't appear infected. Inès knew the scar would always remind Céline of the terrible night, but within her, the baby continued to move. And though she walked around with a blank expression, dark circles swelling under her bloodshot eyes, Céline seemed to draw solace from the fact that her baby would be all right. Inès was proud of having preserved one innocent life, at least, but even that feeling couldn't erase the growing sense that a storm was coming.

And then, on the third night, Inès woke with a start from a deep, dreamless sleep to find Michel's side of the bed empty and cold. She sat up, her heart thudding. It was nearly midnight.

She slipped from the bed, lit a lamp, pulled on a coat and a pair of boots, and made her way outside. The moonlit property was still and silent, no sign of any German officers. But if Michel wasn't dealing with questions from the occupying authorities, where was he? He had promised to hold back on his work with the underground until the Richter storm blew over, but had he lied? Inès scanned the vineyards, the drive, until finally her eyes came to rest on the entrance to the cellars. The slightest bit of light slipped out from underneath the closed doors, and Inès knew in an instant that her husband was belowground. Anger swept through her; how could he make the decision to put any of them at additional risk at a time like this? Especially Céline?

She considered going back to bed, confronting him in the morning, but she knew she'd never be able to sleep. So she wrapped her coat more tightly around herself, an armor of indignation, and hurried toward the entrance to the caves, ready to berate him for his disregard for their safety.

Then again, what if it was just that he couldn't sleep and had retreated under the earth to find some solace? She softened slightly as she made her way down the winding stairs. She had done the same more than once, and what would it prove other than the fact that her husband was human? Perhaps she shouldn't bother him. But she was already belowground, and there was movement in one of the caves far ahead to the right. If nothing else, she could comfort Michel. If this was his hour of darkness, maybe she could be his light.

She crept along quietly, not wanting to startle him, and as she turned the final corner into the cave with the hidden room where Céline had helped her hide Samuel and Rachel Cohn not that long ago, the words were in her throat. *We will handle this together*, she would tell him. *I am by your side, my love.*

But Michel wasn't in the cave thinking or weeping or even storing arms. He was on the floor, amid a mound of blankets, on top of someone he was kissing passionately.

Inès screamed, the sound splitting the silence, and he whipped his head around, his expression a mask of horror as he saw her. He scrambled to his feet, a blanket clutched in front of him, his face crimson as he groped around for his trousers. "Inès, please, I can explain," he began.

But Inès was no longer looking at Michel. She was looking at the woman who had been beneath him. "*Céline?*" she whispered in disbelief.

The other woman's naked breasts hung huge and tender, her

skin stretched pale and tight over her swollen belly as she groped around for blankets to cover herself. Inès could hardly believe what she was seeing. How could Michel betray her with someone she knew, someone who had pretended to be her friend? And all while Céline was carrying Theo's child in her womb! It was unimaginable.

But then, in a terrible flash of clarity, Inès understood the truth in front of her. How had she been so blind? "Your baby," she whispered to Céline, who looked stricken but still hadn't said a word. "It is Michel's, isn't it?"

Michel was speaking now, as he fastened his trousers, but his voice sounded far away. Inès was alone in a tunnel of grief. She knew the answer in her bones before Céline said the words.

"Yes," Céline whispered, tears coursing down her ruined face. "I'm so, so sorry, Inès!"

Inès couldn't find the words to reply. Instead, she slowly backed out of the cave, and then she turned and ran. Their pleas for forgiveness echoed behind her and then faded into nothing.

It wasn't until Inès was in the car, flying through Ville-Dommange in the moonlit darkness, that she began to cry. She had been in the house for ten minutes before climbing angrily into the Citroën with an overnight bag slung over her shoulder, and in that time—as she packed and threw clothing on—Michel hadn't come after her.

As far as she could tell, he hadn't emerged from the cellars at all, and neither had Céline. Even when caught, even when cornered, they had chosen each other. And in a strange way, that hurt more than anything.

As the shadows of Reims came into view—sooner than they should have, for Inès was driving far too quickly—her grief had begun to crystallize into something darker: fury. Cold, hard fury.

She swerved to avoid a dead animal in the road and nearly careened into a ditch, but she managed to right the car at the last minute, the tires protesting on the dirt. By the time she rolled into the dark center of Reims, she was vibrating with the force of her anger.

She parked a few blocks from the Brasserie Moulin and ran there, hugging the shadows, hoping beyond hope that the place was still open. It was; Edouard was tidying things behind the bar while Edith tended to the only customers in the place, a long table of laughing German officers, some of them so drunk they were flopped onto the table, half asleep. Edith was leaning in close, listening to something one of the Germans was saying, when the door banged closed behind Inès. Edith's head jerked up, and several of the Germans spun to stare at her.

Relief coursed through Inès—her best friend would know what to do—but the feeling was short-lived. Edith charged across the restaurant, her face frozen in anger, and grabbed Inès by the arm.

"Edith, I—" Inès said.

"What are you doing here?" Edith hissed, already dragging her toward the stairs in the back of the restaurant.

"I needed to see you, Edith, because—"

"Don't you see that I'm in the middle of something important?" Edith said, glancing over her shoulder and flashing a fake, sunny smile in the direction of the Germans she'd just been talking to. One of them waved pleasantly and returned to his conversation.

"Please, Edith." Inès was crying now. "Michel has betrayed me, and—"

"I want to talk with you, Inès, but I can't right now. Those officers over there were just discussing battle plans. I need to hear what they're saying. Go wait for me in the apartment."

"But—"

"Now, Inès!" Edith hurried away, and Inès glanced at Edouard, who was glaring at her from behind the bar as he filled beers. A few of the Germans were looking in her direction, but they returned their attention to their drinks as soon as Edith hustled back over with a fresh tray. Inès continued to weep as she hurried up the stairs, letting herself into the apartment.

No one wanted Inès. She was a fool in everyone's eyes, an unwelcome nuisance. She hated Michel right now, but she hated herself more. How had she been so blind? The minutes ticked by, and a hot ball of anger roiled in her stomach. Where was Edith? Hadn't she seen how distraught Inès was? Surely she had collected whatever information she needed by now. Was Inès really so insignificant to her? The longer she sat on the tufted sofa in the center of Edith's apartment, the more her frustration mounted until she was filled with it, inflated like a balloon ready to burst.

A half hour crawled by, and then another. From below, Inès could hear voices, laughter. The Germans were still drinking, still carousing, still spilling their secrets. It was becoming clear that Edith wouldn't be upstairs anytime soon, and the loneliness was closing in. Inès stood up, a snap decision made. Without giving herself time to reconsider, she let herself out the back entrance and hurried down the stairs. She couldn't go home, but if not to Edith, where else was she to turn?

There was just one person in the world who had actually wanted to be around her. And though he wasn't a good man, he was a man who had *seen* her, even coveted her. Despite her misgivings, she needed to be seen now, by *someone*, or she would go mad. She would go to Antoine, just for tonight, and worry about the consequences in the morning.

She hugged the shadows as she traced the familiar route to the rue Jeanne d'Arc, just two blocks away. She hadn't seen Antoine since January, two months ago, and she hoped he hadn't replaced her with a new maîtresse.

But his apartment was dark and silent, and when she knocked again and again, no one came to the door. He wasn't there. She sagged into herself and began to turn away when she realized something. She still had his key! Was it still tucked into the lining of her handbag, where she'd kept it hidden from Michel?

She fished around, tearing the fabric aside, until her fingers settled on something small and cold. She closed her eyes and exhaled in relief. She withdrew the key and turned it in the lock, letting herself into the apartment. Though she had hoped for some comfort from Antoine, she realized as soon as she closed the door behind her that she was grateful to instead find herself alone. In the dark loneliness, there would be no one to judge her, no one to ignore her, no one to reject her.

She lit a lamp she found near the door, and immediately the light glinted off the small collection of bottles Antoine kept in the corner for entertaining. She wondered with a surprising surge of jealousy whether he'd had other women drinking with him since she had departed. Pushing the voices in her head away, she headed for the bottles and poured herself a large snifter of cognac. She swallowed it down in one large gulp, the brown liquid burning her throat, searing warmth into her belly. A few minutes later, the magic had reached her brain, and all of a sudden, the things that had seemed so terrible a little while ago were more manageable. She poured herself another drink and, taking the bottle with her, went to sit on the sofa in the parlor. The more she drank, the more it felt like things might just be all right.

Inès awoke sometime later to the scratching sound of a key in the lock, laughter and voices outside the apartment, a creaking door, and then silence. "Who's there?" Antoine's voice cut through the darkness, and beneath it, the murmurs of a woman.

Inès struggled upright. Her head throbbed. She'd lost count of how many snifters of cognac she'd had, how long she'd been sitting in the dark. Now the room came slowly into focus, and Inès could see Antoine glaring at her from the doorway while the rail-thin, heavily made-up blond woman behind him—clad in towering heels and a silk dress—gaped at her.

"Inès?" Antoine said, breaking the heavy silence. "What are you doing here?"

"I'm sorry," Inès said. "I didn't know where else to go."

He cursed under his breath and stared at her for another minute. "Wait here," he barked, then slammed the door, shutting her in and taking the blonde with him. When he returned ten minutes later, he was alone, his expression furious.

"Who was that?" Inès asked in a small voice.

His face purpled with rage. "You can't possibly be serious. You have no right to ask that. You ended things between us two months ago, Inès. And now you stand here in my apartment, questioning me? How did you even get in?"

"I still had your key. I—I thought you'd be alone."

"What, you thought I was sitting around pining for you?" He sneered at her. "I forgot you the moment you left, Inès. What are you doing here? What is the meaning of this?"

She opened her mouth, ready to unload on him, but what came out instead was a single, exhausted sob. "I need you," she whispered, trying—and failing—to pull herself to her feet. "I didn't intend . . . I mean, I . . ."

"Are you *drunk*?" Antoine asked, recoiling in disgust. "What is wrong with you?"

"My husband," she mumbled. "He was sleeping with the wife of the winemaker, who's pregnant, but it turns out that the baby isn't her husband's, and that my husband got her pregnant, and I think he's actually in love with her, and . . ." She trailed off, no longer sure of where she was going with this.

Antoine stared at her, and she couldn't tell whether the look in his eyes was one of revulsion or pity. "Christ. Come to bed, Inès. You're a wreck. You can tell me in the morning."

"But in the morning, nobody will love me," Inès moaned, the words running together. A yawn swallowed the rest of what she wanted to say, and Antoine all at once looked very tired.

"You need to sleep," he said, but she was already drifting off into the blackness as he picked her up and carried her into the bedroom.

When she finally opened her eyes again, it was too bright. She squinted at the clock in the corner of the bedroom. *Noon?* She sat up abruptly, which made her head spin. How had she slept half the day? Michel must be worried sick. But then, in an instant, it all came rushing back—Céline, the baby, her midnight flight to Reims—and she sank back into the pillows, horrified. Had she really let herself into Antoine's apartment last night, poured cognac down her throat until she could hardly see, sobbed to him about Michel? Her head throbbed, reminding her that the answer was yes.

A key turned in the lock, and Inès heard footsteps in the apartment. The door to the bedroom cracked open, and Antoine stood there. He was dressed in a suit, and he looked dashing, victorious, his silver hair slicked back and his eyes gleaming. "Ah, she's finally awake," he singsonged. He strode into the bedroom and opened the drapes all the way, sending far too much sunshine pouring into the room. Inès put her hands over her eyes, but Antoine just laughed. "You had quite a lot to drink last night, my dear."

"I'm so sorry," Inès groaned, thrown by his cheerfulness. "I shouldn't have bothered you. I think I interrupted you on a date."

"Oh well, I would have been furious if not for two things," he said brightly. "First, the young lady I've been seeing is a nitwit, very easily convinced. I was able to explain to her that you were just a Nazi whore, come to deliver a message from the officer you were fucking."

The vile language made Inès recoil. "Antoine, I—"

He held up a hand, stopping her. "Second, you were *very* forthcoming last night about the events that have gone on at the Maison Chauveau as of late. And since my German friends have been quite concerned about the whereabouts of a certain Hauptmann Richter, I was very happy to be able to deliver them this morning the answers that they sought."

"Wh-what?" The room had gone very still.

"The news that such a prominent champagne house owner was involved in his disappearance?" Antoine chuckled. "I thought that Hauptmann Bouhler's head was going to explode when I gave him the news."

"Oh my God," Inès choked out. "Antoine, what have you done?"

"What have *I* done?" Antoine gave her an amused smile. "I have only done my duty. Can you say the same?"

Inès's mind crawled back to the previous evening, but her memories were sluggish, covered in sludge, and she couldn't undredge them. "Whatever I said, I didn't mean it! Please, take it back. You have to tell the Germans that I was wrong!"

"Oh, but we both know you weren't." He took a few steps forward and reached out to stroke her face. She pulled back as if she'd been burned. "Don't be so dramatic, Inès. Your husband and his mistress will get what they deserve."

"Oh God, no!" Inès tried to rise from the bed, but Antoine pushed her back down.

"Dear Inès, you had far too much to drink last night," he purred. "Stay, sleep it off for a little while."

She tried to shove past him, but he pinned her to the bed. "I have to go," she whimpered. "I have to warn them. I have to—"

"When I'm done with you," he said. "Didn't you come here for comfort?" He was already unzipping his trousers, keeping one hand firmly on Inès as she struggled to pull away.

Inès screamed, but Antoine covered her mouth, his cocky smile replaced instantly by a sneer.

"Think of it this way, Inès," he said, climbing atop her. "The sooner this is over, the sooner you can run back home to Ville-Dommange."

As he pulled up her skirt and thrust himself inside her, Inès bit her tongue, so hard that it drew blood. What had she done? Were Germans storming the Maison Chauveau? Were they hauling away Céline, Michel, Theo? Or were they executing them on sight?

When Antoine finally finished and shoved Inès out of bed, she staggered toward the door, clutching her torn clothes around her. As she slipped her shoes back on and ran out into the street, sobbing, she knew with a terrible certainty that she was already too late.

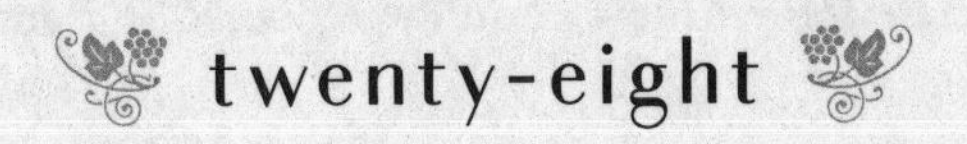

twenty-eight

MARCH 1943

CÉLINE

After Inès had stumbled upon them in the cellars, Céline had tried to run after her, to apologize, to explain. But Michel pulled her back, holding her gently by the arms. "What would you say?" he asked miserably.

"But, Michel, how can I just let her go without trying to make her see that this isn't just a fling? That I love you?"

"My darling, that would only make matters worse."

And so she had hidden her face in his shoulder and waited in the darkness, feeling the baby swim within her, until they heard an engine start up overhead, growling in the drive before fading into the distance.

Inès was gone, and with her, any chance Céline had of undoing the damage she had done.

They made their way back upstairs in silence, and in the shadows, Michel kissed her gently before they parted ways. "It will be all right," he promised. But she knew he was lying, for how could he know? How could he see anything but doom in the future?

In their bed, Theo slept soundly, with no clue that their lives had changed forever. Now it was only a matter of time before he knew the truth, too.

Céline tried to sleep, but she couldn't. Instead she listened to the sound of Theo's snores, wondering if this would be the last night she would lie beside her husband. Where was Inès right now? Céline imagined she had probably gone into Reims to seek comfort from Edith. But what if Inès's flight from Ville-Dommange had been fueled more by anger than pain? What if she did something rash? Céline shook the thought away and chided herself. How could she think such a thing? She was the one who had committed the unforgivable sins here, not Inès.

She closed her eyes and touched her right cheek. The wound was dry, jagged, peeling at the edges, an indelible reminder of what had happened only a few days ago. But it wasn't just Richter's face Céline saw imprinted on her eyelids when she flashed back to the horror that had passed in the cellars. It was the face of Inès, too. Inès, who had come to her rescue. Inès, who had risked everything to save Céline's life, the life of Céline's baby. Inès, whom Céline had so coldly betrayed. How had she managed to justify it to herself? She could hardly remember anymore, but she knew it was inexcusable.

In the morning, just as dawn began to bleed over the horizon to the east, there was a knock on their front door. Céline's whole body tensed. Had the Germans come after all? Theo yawned and stretched, oblivious to her terror. "Who could it be at this hour?" he asked, getting out of bed and heading for the door without waiting for an answer.

Céline opened and closed her mouth, but no sound came out. She heaved herself out of bed, cradling her heavy belly. Was this it? She slipped her feet into boots, a sweater over her shoulders, and tried to brace herself for the worst. But as she made her way out of the bedroom, it was only Michel's voice she heard, unnatural, strained. His eyes flicked to hers as she appeared behind Theo in the doorway.

"Céline, good morning," he said, nodding formally as if he hadn't just held her naked last night, as if he hadn't created the baby swimming in her womb, as if he didn't know her as well as any man had known any woman. "I was just telling Theo that Inès took the car."

Céline swallowed hard, but she found she couldn't speak.

"Any idea why?" Theo asked.

Michel hesitated. "No."

"She's going to get herself killed one of these days," Theo grumbled, and Céline and Michel exchanged a quick look of guilt.

"Well, yes, that's what I'm afraid of," Michel said. "So I'm going to go over to Monsieur Letellier's domaine and see if he will let me borrow his car so that I can try to find her."

"I'm sure she went into Reims," Theo said, "to see that friend of hers. You'll find her at their brasserie, surely."

"Yes, probably," Michel agreed. He shot another glance at Céline. "In any case, I just wanted to let you know where I was going."

"Good luck," Theo said, but Céline still couldn't speak past the hard lump of guilt lodged in her throat.

Later, with Theo gone down into the cellars to rearrange some of the newly filled bottles, Céline was moving around the house like a ghost, waiting for news from Michel, when there was a sharp twist in her belly, and then suddenly, liquid was gushing down the inside of her thighs, soaking her dress and shoes. She gripped the back of a chair for support and stared in horror at the puddle forming beneath her. It was too soon, wasn't it? The baby shouldn't be here for another month and a half. This couldn't be happening.

But it was. Her water had broken, and she needed to get help. Her hands under her belly, her heart thudding, she made her way to the entrance to the cellars as quickly as she could.

"Theo!" she called into the open door.

What if God was punishing her?

"Theo!" she cried.

What if her baby was in danger?

There was no answer from her husband, so Céline gripped the rail and made her way carefully into the caves. "Theo! I need you!"

What if Theo knew, just from looking at Céline, that she'd been lying all along?

"Theo!" she screamed, and then suddenly, there he was, emerging from a cave and wiping his hands on a small rag.

"Céline? What is it?"

"The baby!" she managed. "The baby is coming."

"Now? But it's too early!"

Her body was wracked by a sudden contraction, forcing her to double over in pain. "Please, Theo, help me."

His face was white with fear as he scooped her into his arms and began to carry her toward the stairs. "I'll have to go get help."

"Madame Foucault from the vineyard down the hill is a midwife," she said.

"But we don't have the car. Damn it!"

This, too, was Céline's fault. What if her baby died because she'd driven Inès away? "Can you go on foot to fetch her?"

"I can't leave you," Theo said as he carried her toward the house.

"You must, Theo. We need help. I'll be all right." Céline wasn't sure of this, but the baby would have a better chance if a midwife was here.

He nodded reluctantly. Inside the house, he gently placed her atop the bed and brought her another blanket, a glass of water. She tried to focus on inhaling and exhaling evenly as she rode out another contraction.

"I'll take Michel's bicycle. I'll be back as soon as I can, Céline. I promise."

Céline forced a smile at him through tears. This was all wrong. Michel was gone. Theo still believed the baby was his. Céline was a monster, and this was the beginning of her penance.

"I love you, Céline," Theo said before he left.

"Go, Theo," Céline replied, because she couldn't lie anymore, not now. She needed all the help she could get from God.

The baby arrived, tiny and purple, just past three o'clock that afternoon with Theo looking on as Madame Foucault, a gossipy woman with severe white hair and an enormous waistline, coached a screaming Céline through breathing and pushing. It was a boy, hardly longer than Céline's forearm, weighing around two kilos, less than a small bag of sugar. But Madame Foucault massaged his chest and pumped his lungs, and after a terrifying minute of silence, he finally cried out, the tiny sound like the mewl of a cat, and Céline wept with relief.

As the sun crept toward the horizon, Michel still hadn't reappeared, and the baby was shivering incessantly, even when wrapped in blankets, even when cradled in Céline's arms. She heard Madame Foucault whisper to Theo, "I'm not sure he'll survive."

But he had to. He had to live, or what did any of this matter? So Céline stroked his tiny head, which was covered in a dusting of black fuzz, and kissed his small cheeks, which were still too blue. "My baby, my baby," she whispered to him again and again. "You are a fighter, like your father. Please, my darling son, fight. Fight for me."

By the time the old woman's husband arrived to take her home, darkness had fallen, and the baby was finally breathing regularly. His tiny eyes—blue and clear—had opened as he gazed up at his mother in wonder, and his lips had even managed to find Céline's breast. He nursed for a little while, his swallows greedy.

"I will try to find a doctor in the morning," Madame Foucault promised. "Just keep him warm. It's a good sign that he's eating."

"How can I ever thank you enough?" Céline asked, never taking her eyes off her son.

Later she dozed while Theo kept watch over the baby breathing on her chest, and when she awoke, Theo kissed her gently and stroked the baby's forehead.

"He is a miracle," Theo whispered. "To arrive so early and to live . . ." He wiped his eyes. "A miracle."

Céline searched his face, but she saw no sign of suspicion, and she relaxed slightly. "A miracle."

"What should we name him?"

"I—I don't know yet." The truth was, she wanted Michel to have a say in the decision.

She had just fallen asleep again, cradling the baby, when there was a pounding on the front door. Theo tensed and gave Céline a worried look. "Who could it be at this hour?"

Céline could only shake her head. Her mind spun. How would she protect the baby if the Nazis had arrived? "I'll come with you," she whispered, and Theo helped her out of bed and handed the baby to her before they made their way across the parlor.

Theo swung open the door, and there stood Inès, her hair wild, her eyes glassy and red. "Oh, thank God. I've come to warn you that—" Inès began, but then her eyes slipped past Theo and landed on Céline and the sleeping bundle in her arms. She stopped abruptly. "You had the baby?"

"What is it, Inès?" Theo asked. "What's wrong? What did you come to tell us?"

But Inès didn't answer. She was frozen, and as the baby stirred slightly and turned his head toward Inès, she gasped. "The baby looks just like him," she whispered, and Céline's eyes filled with tears, for Inès was right. How had Theo not noticed it yet, the slope of the baby's nose, the point of his chin? He was the spitting image of Michel.

"Inès, I—" Céline said, her voice hollow, but Inès was shaking now, her hand over her mouth, and before Céline could say another word, Inès turned and ran, stumbling across the dark garden to her own empty house. Michel still hadn't returned.

"What was that all about?" Theo asked as he shut the door.

"Perhaps she was just worried that the baby is so early," Céline said without meeting Theo's gaze.

"Yes." He nodded. "She's very strange these days, isn't she?"

Despite her sheer exhaustion, Céline couldn't sleep. As the hours ticked by, her worry over Michel's absence slowly morphed into terror. Something had to be terribly wrong. And what had Inès been trying to warn them about? Céline's stomach swam with fear.

Just before midnight, she heard the sound of an engine approaching. She leapt up, still cradling her sleeping son, and pressed her face to the window. An unfamiliar car drew to a slow halt outside, and then, as she held her breath, Michel emerged from the driver's seat, shutting the door softly behind him. The car must have been the one he'd borrowed from the neighbor. As he glanced at Céline's cottage, he didn't seem to see her in the window. He turned and hurried into his own house, and Céline closed her eyes and backed away, thanking God that he was safe and wondering what came next. She knew Inès would tell him about the baby.

As if sensing Céline's tension, her son stirred and began to root around. She helped him find her nipple and sat down with a sigh as he suckled weakly, his tiny hands resting on either side of her breast. "*Dodo, l'enfant do,*" Céline sang in a whisper, the lullaby her own mother had used to soothe her to sleep two decades earlier. "*L'enfant dormira bien vite. Dodo, l'enfant do. L'enfant dormira bientôt.*"

When the baby was done eating and had fallen asleep again, Céline dozed a bit on the couch in the parlor, slipping in and out of consciousness. She dreamed that her father and grandparents were somewhere in the darkness, crying, but their sobs sounded just like her own new baby's tiny mewling: helpless, sad, hungry. She awoke with tears streaming down her face and realized that there was a faint knocking on her front door. She glanced at the clock. An hour had passed since Michel had returned home. Surely it was he.

When she opened the door, the baby still cradled against her, Michel looked exhausted, but the instant his eyes landed on his son, something changed in his face. Where there had been worry, there was now only joy. Where there had been fear, only hope.

"He's beautiful," he said softly. His eyes traveled up to Céline's. "My God, are you all right? You must have been so frightened."

Tears welled in Céline's eyes. "He's too early, Michel, but he's strong. I think he will survive."

"God willing," Michel whispered. "May I . . . may I hold him?"

Céline glanced over her shoulder. "If Theo wakes up . . ."

"Can we go down to the cellars? I will help you on the stairs."

Céline hesitated, then half smiled. "I suppose it is never too early to show our son his future." As soon as the words were out of her mouth, though, she wanted to take them back. Had she sounded greedy? Had she assumed something he hadn't offered? She had imagined a life stretching before them, after the war, in which she and Michel made a home here, taught their child to make bubbles, grew old together, found happiness. But what if that wasn't his dream, too?

But then Michel smiled. "One day, he will know the caves like the back of his hand." He reached out and touched his son's tiny fingers, and Céline's heart swelled.

"I will get him an extra blanket."

Michel helped her to wrap the baby tightly against the cold, and then they shut the door quietly behind them and made their way into the night. Michel guided her through the darkness by the light of his lamp, and then he supported her as they made their way slowly and carefully down the stairs to the cellars.

In the cave with the hidden room, they found the blankets just as they'd left them the night before, when Inès had discovered them and the world had tilted on its axis. Had it only been a day ago? As Michel helped ease her down gently into the pile of softness, Céline could almost pretend that it had all been a bad dream, that Inès didn't know the truth, that danger wasn't swirling around them like a cyclone.

Michel asked to hold the baby, and as Céline gently handed the sleeping bundle over and watched Michel stroke his son's face tenderly, joy filled her, buoying her, and she imagined all of them floating away on the strength of their happiness.

But then she remembered Inès, the wildness in her eyes, the pain that Céline had inflicted, and her bubble burst. "Michel, I'm worried," she said. "When Inès got home earlier, it seemed like there was something important she wanted to say, but then she saw the baby . . ."

Michel nodded, never taking his eyes off the infant. He touched his son's tiny face once again. "I was concerned, too, but I spoke with her. Everything is fine. She was just upset about yesterday, understandably so. She's resting now."

"She was coming to warn us about something, though." Céline couldn't rid herself of the uneasy feeling. "What if something is wrong, Michel? What if she told someone about what we did to Richter?"

"She wouldn't do that," he said firmly. "Remember, she was involved, too. And she's a better person than that. She wouldn't betray us."

Céline hung her head, well aware of her own betrayal. "I know."

"Besides, who would she have told but Edith? And certainly we can trust Edith."

This, at least, made Céline feel a bit better. "I suppose you're right." Céline was still uncertain, but she settled back beside Michel, and he handed her the baby, whose blue eyes had opened. He blinked up at Céline and cooed, and all thoughts of Inès were suddenly gone, because all that mattered was this, right here, right now. "What should we name him?" Céline asked.

"What does Theo say?"

"He is not Theo's child." When Michel didn't say anything, Céline added, "I was thinking perhaps David."

"He who stood up to Goliath," Michel whispered, "and came out alive. Céline, it's perfect. David. Our son, David."

"Our son, David," Céline echoed. And finally, as their tiny son fell back asleep, Céline did, too, exhaustion overtaking her at last. She knew that as long as Michel was by her side, she was safe.

Céline awoke some time later to the sound of doors banging open, heavy footsteps on stone stairs, distant screams overhead. "Michel!" she cried, scrambling to her feet as she pulled David closer. "Wake up!"

Michel had dozed off beside her, and now he woke abruptly, panic flashing across his face as he scrambled to his feet and moved in front of Céline, backing her into the cave, as if he could hide her with his body from whatever was coming. "What is it? What's happening?"

"I don't know!" Jarred awake by his parents' hasty movements, or perhaps by their fear, David stirred and began to cry. Céline hastily offered a breast, but he couldn't latch on, and his screeches grew louder.

"He has to be quiet," Michel said urgently. "They'll hear him. They'll find us!"

"I know," Céline said. She was crying now, her tears falling on David's tiny face. "Hush, sweet baby," she murmured, but her voice shook, and the tremor in it only made him cry harder.

There were shouts in German, heavy approaching footsteps, screams growing closer. It was Inès shrieking, calling out Céline's name. Céline pressed herself into Michel, the baby wailing between them, and he held her tightly and whispered in her ear, "I will love you forever. Never forget that. I don't regret a moment of this."

And then the Germans were there in the entrance to the cave, four of them, their guns drawn and pointed at Céline, Michel, and the baby between them. "*Runter, runter!*" one of the men barked in German. "*Bas, bas!* Down on the ground!"

"Please, don't hurt the baby!" Céline cried, but the men ignored her as they rushed in and pulled a screaming David from her arms. One of them disappeared with him, and another shoved Céline to the ground, his knee driving into her back as she screamed and sobbed.

"*Halt die Klappe!*" the soldier yelled in German. "Shut up!"

But Céline couldn't stop, because she couldn't see David, and his screams were fading, and all that mattered was protecting him, and if she couldn't do that, she had failed, and her life was worthless. Michel was on the ground beside her, his head being smashed repeatedly into the ground until he stopped yelling.

"Michel!" Céline cried, and he turned, his eyes blurry and unfocused, but he was alive.

"We are here to arrest Michel Chauveau for the murder of Hauptmann Karl Richter," barked one of the men, hauling Céline to her feet and shoving her into the hall. She looked around wildly for her son. One of the soldiers held him, tucked under his arm like a loaf of bread, but David was alive, his tiny legs windmilling loose from his blankets as he screeched.

Céline choked on her sobs. "Please, please, whatever you do, don't hurt the baby."

"Shut up, Jew. Were you involved, too?"

And then, in the chaos, somehow Inès was there, her face red, her eyes wild. She grabbed the baby from the German, who looked like he was about to protest, but Inès began to scream again, an almost inhuman, animal-like sound, low and keening, and the German backed away from her, holding his hands up.

"No, no, there's been a mistake!" Michel's voice, thick and muffled, came from beside Céline. "Céline had nothing to do with Richter. It was only me, me alone."

"No," Céline moaned. "No, no, no!"

"*Genug!*" one of the Germans, the one with the mustache, barked. "Enough of your lies! How could you think you would get away with it?"

"No, it wasn't them at all!" Inès wailed. "It was me! It was my fault! I killed him! I killed Richter!"

Céline looked at her in shock, this unfamiliar cyclone of wild hair and tears. In Inès's arms, David continued to cry, and Céline instinctively reached for him, which earned her a blow across the face with the butt of a German pistol. The world swam around her, and David's shrieking faded, swallowed by the high pitch of Inès's screams.

"Enough!" the mustached German roared. "You are Inès Chauveau? We know you weren't even here when Hauptmann Richter was murdered. Why would you tell such a lie?"

"But, I—"

"Get out!" the German bellowed. "Antoine Picard has vouched for you. You were with him. Now go, before we arrest you, too!"

Céline choked on a hysterical sob as her mind reeled. Who was this Picard who was protecting Inès? And why was Inès trying to take the fall? It was only then that she understood, with a sort of confused finality, that this arrest was happening because of something Inès had set in motion when she fled to Reims the night before, something that could never be undone.

"I'm so, so, so sorry!" Inès sobbed, backing away. Her eyes were on Céline. "I never meant—"

The mustached German officer interrupted. "Enough! Hand the baby back and go! Now, before I change my mind and arrest you, too!"

"No!" Céline whimpered, reaching out again for David, earning her another blow to the face. The caves spun as she blinked and tried to stay conscious.

"What could you possibly want with an innocent baby?" Inès demanded, her expression vicious as she stared down the officer.

He sneered at Inès. "What could *you* want with him? He's a Jew, isn't he?"

"Not by your Nazi definitions, and you Nazis love to play by your rules, don't you?" Inès shot back, her eyes blazing. "He has only one Jewish grandparent, and anyhow, he was born right here in France. Besides, do you want the murder of an innocent baby on your conscience? What kind of a monster are you?"

The German stared at her before grunting and waving his hand dismissively. "What do I care, anyhow? You want a mischling bastard, you take it. Now go! You're nothing but a worthless whore anyhow."

Inès flinched and turned to Céline. "I'm so, so sorry, Céline. I never meant—"

"Just protect David," Céline said. The soldier holding her jabbed his gun hard into her spine, sending pain shooting through her. She winced and managed to add, "Protect him, Inès. I'm begging you."

"But—"

"Go, Inès, before they change their minds! Please!"

Inès hesitated for only a second more before turning and running, the baby clutched in her arms. Céline watched them disappear, David's cries fading into the chalk walls like they had never been there at all, like he had been merely a dream. And in the silence that he left behind, Céline knew she would never see him again. She also knew, with equal certainty, that her own sins had brought them to this moment, a moment somehow inevitable from the first time she had kissed Michel, the first time she had pushed away her doubts and let herself fall in love with someone who was never meant to be hers.

As the Nazis led her out of the cave, up the stairs, and out of the cellars, shoving Michel along behind her, she caught a glimpse of Theo in their doorway, staring at her in the early morning light, anger carved into his features. He didn't move, didn't try to help her, and she realized that he knew.

Inès and David had vanished, and she could only pray that Inès would understand, would know that the price for her betrayal was that she would be forever responsible for keeping David safe. As the Nazis shoved her into one car, and Michel into another, Céline looked out the window one last time at the rolling vineyards, the land that had held all her dreams.

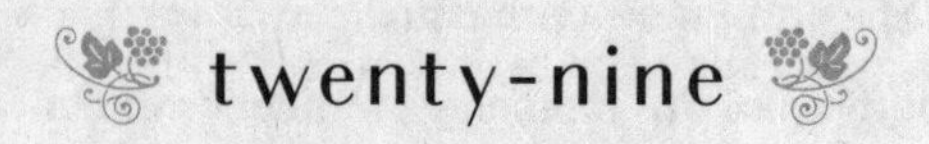

twenty-nine

JUNE 2019

LIV

Grandma Edith didn't speak again until the driver had deposited them in front of their hotel and she and Liv had made their way upstairs. In the suite, she sank into the tufted red couch. "Well," she said at last, "I see that you made up with Julien."

"Um, yes." Liv sat beside her uncertainly. "Is there anything you'd like to talk about?"

"What do you mean?"

"Back there, at the Maison Chauveau, you seemed very emotional."

"What is it with young people today needing to constantly state the obvious?" She sighed. "Besides, I could ask you the same question. One second you're moping, the next you're practically fornicating with young Julien. Do I need to be concerned about *you*?"

Liv could feel her cheeks flaming. "No."

"So you'll be all right, then?" Grandma Edith asked, and there was something softer about her tone now. "Because I won't be around forever to help you pick up the pieces, you realize."

"Is that what you call showing up at my door in New York and insisting that I accompany you on a harebrained trip to France?"

Grandma Edith shrugged. "Is it so terrible that I worry about you? I love you, Olivia, and I want to know that you're strong and happy. I want to know that Eric didn't break you."

"Are you just trying to change the subject so that I won't ask you about the Maison Chauveau?"

"Perhaps. But that doesn't mean I don't want an answer."

Liv stared at her grandmother before finally looking down at her lap. "Look, I think I needed to get away from Eric, miles away, to realize that I don't really miss him at all. I miss being *me*. Somehow along the way, I let myself be erased, and I don't ever want to do that again. I don't know what my life is going to bring now. But I like to think I'm finally headed in the right direction." She smiled as she recalled Julien's words of advice. "Let's just say I'm open to seeing where the tide takes me."

"But don't just let the tide carry you." Grandma Edith leaned forward and grasped Liv's hands, squeezing with surprising ferocity. "In life, my dear, you must actually go after what you want. You can't rewrite the past, but you can choose to live with your whole heart in the here and now."

"Grandma Edith—"

"No, let me say this. Please. I learned far too late that life is simply about being good and decent to others. It's as plain as that. But first, you must be good and decent to yourself. Find your own road. Find your own happiness. You must, my dear. You must, or you will wind up old and alone and full of regrets."

"Grandma Edith, why are you telling me all this?" Liv asked, her voice rising in frustration. "I appreciate all the words of wisdom, but why did you bring me here? What is it you really want to say? Or was this all just a crazy ruse to introduce me to the widowed grandson of your old friend? Because there are about a hundred other ways you could have gone about it. I mean, honestly, you could have just given me his email address and said, 'Hey, Liv, this guy is hot and single and lives in Champagne.' I probably would've bitten. I like hot guys. And champagne."

Grandma Edith finally cracked a smile. "I admit that I hoped you and Julien would get along. But no, that isn't why I brought you here. Nor did I expect you to be practically humping each other in public. Is that what you young people call it these days?"

Liv could feel herself blushing furiously. "Are you *trying* to mortify me?"

"Perhaps just a little." The older woman's mischievous smile was back, but it was quickly swept away by a wave of sadness. "Still, to see you with him there, at the Maison Chauveau . . . Sometimes I think God works in very strange and mysterious ways."

"Did whatever happened there have something to do with Julien's grandfather?"

"Not exactly."

"Then what? What are you so afraid to tell me?"

Grandma Edith looked down at her own hands, gnarled with age, swollen with arthritis. Liv wondered if she was mentally erasing the years, taking herself back to a time when her husband, Edouard, was still alive. "I'm not afraid, Olivia. It's just very difficult to revisit the past when you have tried so hard to forget it."

"What *happened*, Grandma Edith?"

"Beautiful things," she said softly. "And terrible things. Love between two people who were following their hearts, and betrayal by one who only cared about herself. And a baby. A beautiful baby who was born right there at the Maison Chauveau, which changed everything. These are the things I brought you here to tell you, my dear Olivia, but I am finding the truth harder than I expected."

"Tell me. Please. Whatever it is, it's okay."

"Is it?" Grandma Edith shook her head. "No, of course it is not. Still, bringing you to the Maison Chauveau today was the right thing, even if it was difficult. It's something I should have done a long time ago. I should have brought your father here, too, Olivia, but I wasn't strong enough."

"Why? What does the Maison Chauveau have to do with us?"

It took Grandma Edith a minute to speak. "My dear, your father was the baby born there, welcomed into the world by two people very much in love. His father—your real grandfather, a man named Michel Chauveau—owned the Maison Chauveau, you see."

"Wait, what? So my grandfather *wasn't* Edouard Thierry?" Liv's mind spun as she stared at Grandma Edith in confusion. "Did you have an affair with Michel Chauveau?"

"No, dear." She took a deep breath. "You see, by blood, I was never your father's mother. But I loved him as much as any mother could love a son. And I've loved you as much as a grandmother can love a grandchild. But I've always known it's not enough. That kind of love can never replace what was taken from you."

"I—I don't understand. What are you telling me?"

Grandma Edith stood and put a hand on Liv's arm. She was shaking. "I'm telling you I love you, Olivia, and I'm sorry that I've made all the wrong choices. Since your father was born, I've always tried to do my best. But it has never been enough."

And then, before Liv could ask another question, Grandma Edith was walking away. She went into her room, the lock clicking behind her, and Liv stared at the closed door, stunned and confused, as her grandmother's muffled sobs seeped out from underneath.

thirty

MARCH 1943

INÈS

Michel was executed at Gestapo headquarters on the rue Jeanne d'Arc in Reims, just blocks from the Brasserie Moulin, on the same day he was arrested. Theo, furious at being betrayed, had ridden his bicycle into town, planning to denounce him, but, he later told Inès, he had changed his mind along the way. Regardless of what Michel and Céline had done, he knew he did not have the right to take another man's life into his hands.

He had pulled up in time to see the soldiers drag Michel out of the building, already bloodied and bruised. They propped him against a wall, and before he could waver and fall, four Germans fired upon him simultaneously.

Theo told Inès this after he had packed up his belongings and asked her stiffly to drive him into Reims. "Where are you going?" she asked through her tears. Baby David pulled at the front of her dress with his tiny, cold hands, searching for her breast, but she had nothing to give him. How would she keep him alive?

"I am going south," he told her. "There are wineries in Burgundy that can use someone with my experience."

"When will you come back?" Inès asked.

"Never." He hesitated and gestured to David. "After you take me to the train station, go see Madame Foucault. She will know what to feed the child."

Inès nodded and wrapped another blanket around the baby to steel him against the cold. Theo held him while they rode in silence toward Reims, Inès's eyes blurring with tears each time she imagined Michel's lifeless body falling to the cold ground. *What had she done?*

"What will they do to Céline?" she asked as she wound the car through the narrow streets of Reims.

"I don't know." He gazed out the window in silence for a long minute. "They will probably send her east. They don't like to execute women in the squares unless their guilt is painfully obvious."

"And what will become of the Maison Chauveau?"

"It's yours now, I suppose." Theo shrugged. "But if I were you, I'd go far, far away. Not that you can run from the truth."

She glanced at him and saw fury burning in his eyes. As enraged as he was at Michel and Céline, he was angry at Inès, too. He knew what she had done, or at least he had guessed at portions of it. "I'm so sorry," she whispered. "I didn't mean for any of this to happen."

His only reply was a grunt, and when they reached the train station, he laid David gently in the front seat, closed the door, and left without looking back, his shoulders slumped, his bag slung across his back.

Inès watched him go, lingering there long after he'd disappeared, until a German officer bent and tapped on the window of her car. "Move along, madame," he said, his deep voice and thick accent making the words sound sepulchral.

Inès wiped away her tears and put a hand on the sleeping baby as she pulled away from the curb. She would go see Madame Foucault. She would focus all her energy on protecting David. With Michel dead and Céline gone, Inès was all David had.

Madame Foucault helped Inès procure a small amount of baby formula, suggesting that she needed to register David's arrival in order to receive the appropriate ration coupons, but Inès was terrified that if the authorities had an official record of who David's parents were, someone would come take him away, too. So she settled for dropping by Antoine's apartment one afternoon. Leaving David sleeping in the car, she stood at Antoine's door and refused to flinch as she threatened to invent a story for the Nazi command that he had been working for the underground as a spy unless he could arrange for regular deliveries of infant supplies.

Antoine had tried to laugh off her threats, but something in Inès's expression stilled him, and he ultimately agreed.

"But you'll owe me," he said darkly as she began to walk away.

"Oh, make no mistake," she said, turning back, fury burning a hole in her stomach. "You will get everything you deserve. I won't rest until you do."

He nodded, clearly taking her words as a promise and not a threat, and as he closed the door, she spat on his front step. As much responsibility as she had, as much guilt as she would always carry, at least her betrayal had been accidental, her tongue unwound by alcohol and sorrow. Antoine, on the other hand, might as well have murdered Michel with his own hands. She hated him nearly as much as she hated herself.

She drove next to the Brasserie Moulin and carried the baby inside. Edith was behind the bar, and when she saw Inès, her eyes widened. She gestured toward the back stairs, and Inès walked quickly across the restaurant, avoiding the stares of the Germans.

"My God, Inès, I heard about Michel," Edith said when they were alone in the apartment. She put her arms around her friend and then stroked the forehead of the baby. "I'm so sorry. Are you all right? What happened? Is this Céline's child?"

"Yes, this is David." Inès took a deep breath as Edith reached out to stroke the infant's arm. "And as it turns out, he's Michel's son, too."

Edith's head jerked up. "What?"

"Oh, Edith, what have I done?"

Through sobs, Inès told her friend the whole story, and as she did, she could feel Edith withdrawing, pulling away from her. She couldn't blame her friend, but Edith's physical recoil from Inès's sins only served to solidify Inès's own shame.

"I don't know what to do now," Inès said. David stirred, began to cry, and Inès pulled out the bottle she had prepared from the last of Madame Foucault's formula.

Edith took David gently from Inès's arms, then she took the bottle, too, offering it to him with such tenderness that Inès's heart ached. David gazed up at Edith with wide eyes while he gulped down the creamy liquid, and she cooed at him, tears filling her eyes, too. "It doesn't matter what you have done," she said. "All that matters now is keeping this baby safe."

"Of course it matters what I've done, Edith. Please, stop with the platitudes."

"Fine, have it your way." Edith rocked the baby gently, but her tone was firm, hard. "Michel was a good man. He did more for the cause than you will ever grasp. Was he a good husband to you? Perhaps not, but can you say you were a good wife?"

"No," Inès whispered. "I know I was not."

"Céline will die, too, you realize." Edith's tone had softened a bit.

Inès looked up, anguish twisting her heart. "What? No, I think they'll ship her east, to a work camp." But she knew she was fooling herself to hope that the camps were anything other than what Samuel Cohn had described, a place where most people disappeared upon arrival.

"She will almost certainly not survive," Edith said, her eyes glinting with tears.

Inès swallowed hard and stared down at her own hands as if there might be blood on them, visual evidence of the guilt she would always bear. But they were white, unmarred, and the lifelines on her palms disappeared inexplicably into infinity. "There's a chance, though," Inès said.

"Yes, there's a chance," Edith admitted. "But in the meantime, you must protect their child with your life."

"Yes, of course." But as she watched Edith soothing the baby, singing to him softly, rocking him gently until his tiny eyelids began to grow heavy, she had a sudden realization. "May I ask you something?"

Edith looked up from David, her small, peaceful smile disappearing. "Go ahead."

"Why have you and Edouard not had a baby?"

Edith sighed. "We tried before the war. And then we stopped, because it felt too dangerous to bring a child into a world like this. But after a while, we realized that life is too short." She turned her gaze back to David, stroking his face as he slept, and when she spoke again, her words were so soft that Inès had to strain to hear them. "So we began trying again, more than a year ago. But it seems God does not want us to be parents."

"Or perhaps you're destined to raise *this* baby," Inès said, and Edith's head snapped up.

"What?"

"Think about it, Edith. What do I have to offer David? I'm selfish, foolish. I'm responsible for stealing his parents from him. You were born to be a mother. I was born to be alone. I'm no good for anyone."

"That's not true."

"Isn't it?"

Inès could see the answer written in Edith's eyes, and as her friend turned away, Inès felt her own cheeks burning in shame.

"I could take over your work with the underground," Inès said. "You would be safe. You could keep David safe."

Edith looked back at her, her eyes wide. "You can't be serious, Inès. Do you really think anyone will trust you after what has happened?"

"But—"

Inès began to cry, and instead of coming closer, Edith backed away, still clutching David. "Inès, I love you, but you can't just snap your fingers and undo what you've done."

"I know. I know! That's why I have to do something. Anything! I have to redeem myself." This was what was meant to be. Inès knew it without a doubt. If Inès left the baby with Edith and simply vanished, Edith would have no choice but to become a surrogate mother to the child until Céline returned, and David would have the love he deserved, from someone who was good and kind and worthy of him. "I'm sorry, Edith. Will you watch David for just a little while? I—I just need to go to Ville-Dommange to pack a few things, and then I'll be back. After that, you won't have to worry about me again."

"Whatever you've done, whatever has happened, Inès, I will always worry about you. You will always be my friend. I will always love you like a sister."

Inès smiled sadly. "We both know I don't deserve that." She kissed David on the top of his head, inhaling the milky scent of him, and then she backed away.

When Inès pulled down the drive to the Maison Chauveau, the place where she'd built a half-life with a husband who was never coming back, she found a gray-haired man in a suit standing at the front door, jotting something in a notebook. At the sound of her approach, he turned and squinted at her, waiting as she got out of the car and approached tentatively.

"May I help you?" Inès asked.

"Madame Chauveau?" The man was wearing tiny round spectacles and a thin black tie.

"Yes."

"Ah, hello. I am Georges Godard, the Chauveau family lawyer. Perhaps you remember me from your wedding?"

She wouldn't have been able to pick him out of a crowd, but he was undoubtedly familiar. "Yes, of course, Monsieur Godard."

"Madame Chauveau, please allow me to say how sorry I am for your loss. I understand that Monsieur Chauveau is deceased." His expression was compassionate, though it looked a bit forced.

"Yes." She bowed her head. "Thank you."

"I've come by to see if I can offer my assistance."

"Your assistance?"

"You see, with Monsieur Chauveau deceased, the property will pass to you, his only living family." He swept his arm around, indicating the entire Maison Chauveau. "He saw to it. It will take some time for the paperwork to be completed, but I wanted to make myself available in case you need some assistance running things."

She blinked at him. "You've wasted no time in coming, have you?"

"Monsieur Chauveau asked me to help you, in case anything ever happened to him. But I trust that your winemaker will be able to assist you, too? A Monsieur Laurent, I believe?"

Inès shook her head. "He's gone. For good."

"I see. But you will be staying on, then?"

Inès hesitated. "No. I don't think I will. Not for now, anyhow."

"Well, perhaps I can help manage things until your return. For a small fee, of course."

So that's what this visit was about. Inès returned his thin smile. "Of course."

As he launched into a long-winded suggestion of a winemaker who currently worked for Ruinart in Reims, Inès found herself nodding along, her heart not in it. But here, on a silver platter, was a solution she hadn't even known she was looking for, someone to keep the Maison Chauveau from ruin, even if that came at a price. She would need to ensure that there was a future in this place so that one day, David could inherit his birthright.

Monsieur Godard handed her some papers that smelled of fresh ink. "I took the liberty of drawing these up in case you were interested in entering into an agreement with me to help manage the Maison Chauveau."

As she took them, she could see this meeting for what it clearly was—a shakedown. But she was too tired to care. She didn't need Michel's money. She didn't deserve it. Let Monsieur Godard profit while she was gone if he wanted to. "I will read them over and sign them tonight."

His smile faltered. "Wouldn't it be more convenient to sign them now?"

She ignored him. "You can pick them up tomorrow at the Brasserie Moulin, in Reims. Good day, Monsieur Godard."

"Wait," he said as she moved past him to let herself into the house. "My wife wanted me to ask you something." He hesitated. "There's some gossip in town that the winemaker's wife was arrested, too."

Inès swallowed. "Yes."

"And what of her baby? She was pregnant, yes? My wife heard that Madame Foucault delivered the baby just before Madame Laurent was taken by the German authorities?"

Inès's dislike of Monsieur Godard had now deepened into disgust, but she realized this was an opportunity. His eyes gleamed as he leaned forward, hungry for gossip, and Inès arranged her features into a mask of despondency. "Thank you for your concern, monsieur, but the baby died just yesterday. His lungs were not strong enough in the end."

"Oh, I'm very sorry to hear that." But Monsieur Godard didn't look sorry at all; he looked like the cat that had eaten the canary.

Inès knew that Monsieur Godard would take the lie and spread it all over Champagne. And that meant that David—whose mother's Jewish blood could otherwise put him in danger someday—might be able to safely disappear. Surely Edith and Edouard, with all their connections with the underground, could come up with a cover story to explain his arrival in Reims. "Yes. It is quite a tragedy."

"Well then, I will leave you to it," Monsieur Godard said, bowing slightly, obsequiously, as he began to back away. "I trust I will see you tomorrow at the Brasserie Moulin, then."

"Yes," Inès said, though she had no intention of seeing the smarmy lawyer until she had figured out a way to redeem herself. "See you then."

Inès brought two bags back to Edith's apartment—one full of her own belongings, one full of the baby clothes Céline had been sewing from repurposed garments for months, in anticipation of her baby's arrival.

She held David all afternoon, cooing to him, feeding him, trying to memorize his features. She could see Michel in him, as plain as day, and she could see Céline, too, in the fullness of his cheeks, the curve of his jaw. "I promise you," she told him as she rocked him gently, "I will do everything I can to make sure your life is a good one."

At the Brasserie Moulin, Edouard read over the lawyer's paperwork and suggested a few small changes to the proposed fee structure, but Inès waved his concerns away. "I only care that he keeps the Maison Chauveau alive," Inès said. "It will belong to David one day."

Edouard frowned. "But how will you accomplish that with no proof that he is Michel's son?"

"Because I own the Maison Chauveau now, and I can do with it what I wish," Inès said.

By candlelight, long after the others had gone to sleep, Inès carefully printed out a note willing the Maison Chauveau to Edith should anything happen to her. She knew that if she didn't return, Edith would find a way to make sure that David was legally her own, which would make him Edith's heir. Inès signed the note, leaving it for Edith, along with another more hastily scrawled message begging Edith to care for David while Inès was gone.

He is better off with you. You are good and kind, and I am not. I must make amends for what I have done, or I will never be the person I need to be. I understand now that fighting for France, fighting for goodness, is the only way I will find redemption. It is what Michel was trying to do, and I must carry on his work. If I do not return, and worse, if Céline does not survive, please do everything you can to ensure that David has a good life, and that he inherits the Maison Chauveau, which was never truly mine to give.

After signing that note, too, Inès left it on the desktop and returned to the parlor, where David slept peacefully, nestled in a pile of blankets on the floor. Inès watched his tiny eyelids flutter with the ghost of a dream, his little limbs twitching. Finally, after a very long time, she stood and slipped from the apartment, silent as a mouse, and disappeared into the dark night.

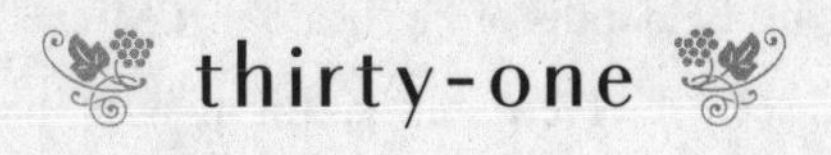

thirty-one

MAY 1945

CÉLINE

Céline was one of the lucky ones, they said, though that word—lucky, *chanceuse*—tasted false and ugly on her tongue, so much so that she could not bring herself to say it aloud, even when the nurses hovered over her, tended to her wounds, pinched her hollow cheeks, and called her survival a miracle.

But what if she was, in fact, one of the fortunate? What if she could return to the Maison Chauveau and find Michel there waiting for her, their David now a chubby-cheeked toddler running circles in the vineyards, his laughter floating like bubbles into the sky. It was that thought that sustained her through all the dark, terrible nights in Auschwitz, that place of ghosts and nightmares. In the nearly two years before the camp's liberation, she'd withered to thirty-five kilos, less than eighty pounds, skin stretched over bone. But she had survived because she had to. She had to come back to the love of her life, if there was even a chance he'd be there. She had to come back for their son.

She knew in the depths of her heart that Michel was probably dead. She had seen the Germans haul him away, had understood the price he would pay for his involvement in Richter's death. The fact that Richter was about to violate Céline, well, that would not mitigate Michel's fate, even if the Gestapo believed him. For two years now, she had made peace with the idea that he was gone, though the grief hadn't ebbed.

But David. There was a chance, wasn't there? Surely Inès had understood the stakes when she took him from Céline's aching arms. Had Inès understood that her penance for what she had done was to keep David safe? Céline had clung for two years to the belief that the answer had to be yes, that David was happy, healthy, alive.

But now, as she approached the Maison Chauveau on foot, after taking the train from Paris to Reims and hitching a ride with an American convoy into Ville-Dommange, doubt swept in, nearly paralyzing her. For up ahead, the sign that had once sat outside the property, announcing the Maison Chauveau to visitors, was gone, and beyond it, the caretaker's cottage, where Céline had lived a lifetime ago, was boarded up. She dropped her satchel—which contained only a bar of soap and a secondhand dress given to her by a sympathetic Red Cross worker—and ran the rest of the way to the main house, though her spindly legs—her muscles long since atrophied—shook and threatened to give out.

As she pounded on the door, her dread mounted. The rows of vines that Michel had once tended were withered, dead, black against the blue sky. The only sign that anyone had been there at all was a pair of tire tracks leading toward the barn on the back side of the property, the one where they'd once stored corks and empty bottles. When no one answered at the main house, Céline bit back her sob and ran toward the barn, flinging the doors open.

Inside, there was a black car she didn't recognize, as well as several barrels lying on their sides, clearly in various stages of being cleaned. Her heart leapt. There was someone here, seeing to the champagne production, even if the place appeared to have fallen into ruin. "Michel?" she cried, choking on the word. "Inès? Theo?"

But the man who finally emerged from a trapdoor in the floor—a new entrance to the cellars?—was a stranger. He was tall, thin, perhaps sixty years old, with a gray mustache and a thin nose. "Mademoiselle?" he ventured, blinking at Céline, who must have appeared to him to be hardly more than a child. Indeed, her hips had vanished, her breasts flattened into nothing; she was a stick with arms and legs, a spindly, withered vine.

"Who are you?" she asked, her voice hoarse with fear. "Where are Michel? Theo? Inès?"

He frowned, and there was compassion in his eyes as he said, "They are gone."

"Dead?"

"Who are you?" the man asked, his tone gentle.

"My name is Céline Laurent. My—my husband, Theo, was the winemaker here."

He stared at her. "Céline Laurent? But I thought you had died." He stepped forward and touched her arm awkwardly, as if he thought she might break from more contact than that. "I'm so sorry. Madame Laurent, my name is Alphonse Berthelot. I was hired as the winemaker here in 1943, but as you can see, I am working alone and am spread very thin. I've done my best to keep production going."

"Where is everyone?" she whispered.

"Your husband left before I arrived," he said. "The rumor is that he went south."

Of course Theo had fled. She had driven him away. She hoped he had survived, but in the end, it didn't matter, did it? She had barely thought of him at all in the past two years. "And Michel? Michel Chauveau?"

"You don't know?" Monsieur Berthelot frowned. "Madame, I'm very sorry to tell you that the Germans killed him, all the way back in the spring of 1943."

Céline's knees gave out, and she crumpled to the ground. She had known this was almost certainly the case, but having Michel's fate confirmed still shattered her. She was hardly aware of it when Monsieur Berthelot rushed to her side and tried to help her up, but it was useless. She was a rag doll. "You are certain?"

"I'm afraid so, madame."

"And the baby?" she whispered. "Where is the baby? David?"

For a second, the man looked confused. "Oh dear, I'd forgotten. Monsieur Godard, the attorney who hired me to oversee this place, said you gave birth just before you were taken."

From the deep well of pity in his eyes, she already knew the answer, but she had to hear him say the words. "Where is he? Where's my son?"

"Madame, I'm so very sorry. Monsieur Godard told me what happened. Your baby, he—he didn't survive."

"No," Céline whispered. "No, you must be wrong. I would have felt it if he had died." But the truth was, she could no longer feel anything. Survival at Auschwitz had depended on her ability to fool herself, to cling to hope, to live in her dreams rather than in the real world. She couldn't trust her own gut anymore, because her insides had been hollowed out long ago.

She wasn't aware that she had curled herself into a ball on the floor until the man vanished and returned sometime later with an old woman, a woman Céline didn't recognize at first. But then the woman said her name and helped her to a sitting position, and she realized that it was Madame Foucault, the white-haired midwife from the vineyard down the hill who had delivered David more than two years earlier.

"He's gone?" Céline whispered as Madame Foucault stroked her hair. "My David is gone?"

"You poor dear," the old woman murmured. "It will be all right."

"No, no it will not." Céline took a deep breath. "What happened to him?"

Madame Foucault hesitated. "I heard that it was his lungs, my dear. He was simply too early."

Céline began to cry again. The fault was hers, wasn't it? If she had only been able to keep him within her womb for more time, maybe he could have survived. But then again, if she hadn't borne him early, he would only have died in Auschwitz. He had been doomed, either way. "And Inès?" Céline asked. "Where is Inès?"

"Dead, too, I'm afraid."

"What? How?"

Madame Foucault's mouth stretched into a thin line of disapproval. "I heard she joined the underground, just like her husband. Foolish girl. She was in a safe house the Germans raided last July, just outside Reims."

"*Inès?* Are you sure?"

"It was the talk of the town, especially after what had happened to Monsieur Chauveau."

"I can't believe it." Now, when the sobs came again, they were for Inès, too, for another young life lost too soon. None of them deserved what had come their way.

Céline's father and grandparents were long dead—she knew now that they had been gassed upon arrival at Auschwitz in 1942—and any future she had dared dream of had been snatched from her trembling fingers. She looked down at her spindly arms, at the numbers inked just above her left wrist, numbers that were meant to take away her humanity, her name.

But without Michel and without David, she had no identity anyhow. How could she ever return to being Céline Laurent, the wife of a cold winemaker, the lover of a warm man who had never really been hers, the mother of a child whose death she had failed to prevent?

So she wiped away her tears, and with Madame Foucault's support, she struggled to her feet. She turned to Monsieur Berthelot, whose eyes were wet. Her story had moved him, and she knew he would help her. "I'm very sorry, monsieur, but would it be possible for you to drive me to Paris?"

"To Paris? Well, yes, of course, madame." He dashed off to get his keys.

"What will you do in Paris?" Madame Foucault asked.

Céline gazed out the barn door, where a sliver of the vineyards, of the rolling hills, of the magic of Champagne, was just visible. She wanted to remember this place, to fix it in her mind. "In Paris," she murmured, "I will disappear."

Life was no longer worth living as Céline Laurent. That woman—the woman who fell in love, the woman who still didn't regret it, the woman who had fallen asleep one night in her lover's arms and awoken to lose everything—didn't exist anymore.

If David was gone, then the last pieces of herself, the ones she had clung to in Auschwitz, had disappeared forever, too. And so she climbed into the passenger seat of the new winemaker's car and closed her eyes. When they arrived in Paris, and Monsieur Berthelot insisted on pressing some francs into her hand, she thanked him and said goodbye.

But the farewell wasn't for him, not really. It was for the life that would be forever behind her the moment he drove away. She would go as far from Reims as she could. She would blend in with all the other refugees returning from the grave. She would become someone new and hope that somewhere, there was a life ahead of her after all.

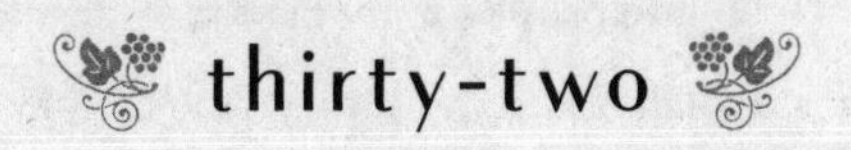

thirty-two

MAY 1945

INÈS

By the time the war in Europe ended, with the unconditional surrender of the Third Reich's armed forces signed right in the center of Reims on May 7, 1945, everything had long since changed for Inès.

After she had left Edith's apartment in 1943, she had gone first to Paris, but no one knew her there, and it was difficult to find her way into any sort of underground network. Desperate to help, she made her way south, finally arriving in the Auvergne, where she found a group of *maquisards* willing to let her join them in the Forest of Tronçais. She learned to shoot and became good at planting explosives under railway tracks to disrupt German transports. She thought sometimes that Michel might have been proud of her.

Inès was a dedicated, selfless soldier, and in return, she asked only one thing of the group's leader, a man named Tardivat, whom she'd grown to both respect and fear. "There is a man named Antoine Picard in Reims," she said as the war in France wound down in the summer of 1944. "I'm to blame for my husband's death, but Michel's blood is on Picard's hands, too. I want him to pay."

Tardivat had smiled wearily. "Consider it done. And try to forgive yourself, would you, Inès? We've all done things we regret."

Inès had looked away. "I don't deserve forgiveness, sir." The only way she would ever be able to live with herself was if she managed to reunite Céline with her son one day. It was a hope she had clung to over the long and painful months with the Maquis.

In the fall of 1944, two months after the liberation of Reims, Inès returned to Champagne and went straight to the Brasserie Moulin. But it was under new management, and all that the waiter at the front would tell her was that Edouard Thierry was still living in the apartment above the restaurant, rarely venturing out. "What about Edith?" Inès asked, bile rising in her throat. "What about the baby?" The man had only shaken his head and pointed upstairs.

Inès took the stairs two at a time and knocked on the door to the apartment, then pounded when no one came. She barely recognized the man who finally answered. Edouard had lost at least ten kilograms, his body concave now, and he had aged a decade since she'd last seen him a year and a half earlier. His hair had gone almost fully gray, his stubble white, and there were dark shadows under his eyes. "You're alive?" he rasped.

"Where is Edith?" Inès asked, grasping his hands. He seemed to rock with the weight of her touch. "Where's David?"

From within the apartment, she heard crying, the sound of a child, and Edouard looked over his shoulder and then back at Inès.

Inès pushed past him and found a toddler, nearly two years old now, standing up in a rickety crib, reaching out his chubby arms. He stopped crying when he saw her, and they stared at each other. In the time she'd been away, he had grown to look even more like his father. He had Michel's light hair now, his narrow nose, his crystal-blue eyes. But the shape of his face, the pitch of his chin, were all Céline. Inès bit back a sob and went to him. "Sweet David," she murmured, and as she lifted him up and held him to her, he babbled into her shoulder and buried his small fingers in her wild hair. "Oh, thank God."

"You will take him, yes?" Edouard spoke from the doorway, and Inès turned to find him watching her. "I cannot do this anymore."

"But where is Edith?"

"She's dead, Inès."

From the expression on Edouard's face, the shadows under his eyes, and the way he had avoided the question earlier, she had suspected as much. But hearing him say the words aloud still made her nearly double over with pain. She began to cry, and David frowned and reached out to touch the tears rolling down her cheeks. "How? What happened, Edouard?"

Edouard blinked a few times, his eyes wet, too. "It was just before the liberation. The Germans were going wild. They knew it was over. They came upon a meeting of résistants, and instead of arresting them, they broke down the door and just began firing."

Inès covered her face with her hands. "My God, Edouard. She was shot?"

"In the head," Edouard said, his voice flat as he touched the spot just above his brow. "She was unrecognizable. So when I was asked to identify her, I did not. I told the authorities she was you."

Inès froze. "What?"

"I thought you were dead already, Inès. We all did. You see, if the Germans had confirmed that they'd killed Edith Thierry, they would likely have arrested me, or worse, come to kill me. And then who would have looked after David?"

"But how did you explain Edith's absence, then?"

He shook his head. "Oh, I think everyone knew, including the Germans who used to frequent our brasserie. But it was all over by then anyhow, and in the chaos of the liberation, no one came looking. What mattered was that on paper, you, Inès, were the résistante, and Edith had simply vanished. You know the Germans and their adherence to their paperwork."

"Edouard, I'm so sorry," Inès said. "Maybe if I'd stayed . . ."

"It would not have mattered. Edith and I accepted our fate when we agreed to work with the Allies. And since Edith cared so much about protecting David, it was a responsibility I took seriously, too. As you can see, he is well fed, healthy." He nodded at the boy, who was watching him with round eyes. Edouard's tone was still strangely flat. "But I have nothing, Inès, nothing to give anymore. Edith was my world, and now she is gone. I cannot care for the boy any longer."

"I'm so sorry, Edouard. For everything." Inès wiped her tears away. "But what now? What do I do if everyone thinks I'm dead?"

He smiled slightly. "You become Edith. I quietly divorce you. And you go away and never come back."

"But—"

"Everyone here thought you were on the side of the Nazis," he went on without looking at her. "It was no secret here in Reims that you were the lover of Antoine Picard for a time. Just after the liberation, you know, he was executed for treason, based on a tip from a high-ranking maquisard."

Inès nodded, surprised to realize that she felt no pain, no regret, no guilt—only gratitude to Captain Tardivat for keeping his word. "I see."

"At best, Inès, you were thought to be a *collaboratrice horizontale.* At worst, an ally of the Nazis yourself, a traitor to France."

"But I never—"

Edouard held up a hand. "It doesn't matter, Inès. You are beyond redemption in this town."

"But you could tell people—"

"Don't you understand?" Edouard interrupted. "I was suspected for a long time of collaborating, too. People had seen the brasserie filled with Germans. I narrowly escaped execution myself, and only then because the Brits sent someone to vouch for me, to explain that Edith and I had been instrumental in delivering German secrets directly to the Allies, that we had risked our lives for France. I have no energy left, Inès, to prove myself again, or to go out on a limb for you. What have you done, anyhow, to deserve my help?"

Inès wanted to tell him about her months in the forests with the Maquis, the dozens of times she'd nearly lost her life, the German soldier she had been forced to kill with a pocketknife before he could arrest one of the leaders of the group. But what right did she have to compare her sacrifices to Edouard's? He had lost everything, while Inès had been responsible for every loss that had befallen her. Besides, to bring up her work with the Maquis would be to suggest that it had washed away her sins, and she knew it had not. So she bowed her head and let his anger and blame wash over her, because she deserved it, all of it. "You're right."

"So go, Inès." Edouard sounded exhausted. "Take Edith's identity papers. The two of you always looked like sisters anyhow. Become her. Honor her name. Try to make something of yourself. And whatever you do, take care of the boy."

Inès glanced at David, who was playing with her hair now, babbling to himself and paying them no mind. "I will," she whispered.

"Good." Edouard seemed as if he wanted to say something else, but after studying Inès intently, he simply shook his head and walked away, the apartment door slamming behind him. Inès knew she would never see him again.

A few weeks later, Inès had moved to Paris, taking David with her. She had chosen the city because it was the returning point for those who had been deported to concentration camps, and she was confident she would find Céline among the ghosts who were trickling back into the capital. It was her only hope of absolution.

For two and a half months, she went every day to the Hôtel Lutetia on the boulevard Raspail, searching for some sign that Céline had found a way to survive. But day after day, Inès walked home empty-handed to her small apartment on the rue Amélie. Some days she went east instead and strolled David through the Luxembourg gardens; other days, she walked him past the gold-domed building that housed Napoleon's tomb at Les Invalides. But always, always, she told the little boy stories of his mother and his father, brave heroes of France. His father, she said, had left on a journey and would not be coming back, but they were still waiting for his mother, who would surely return.

But the months passed, and in the third week of August, Inès finally found a hollow-eyed woman who said she had known Céline at Auschwitz. "Do you know if she has returned yet?" Inès asked, shifting David to the opposite hip and leaning forward eagerly. "We haven't been able to find her, though we've come here every day." The woman was emaciated, her fuzzy gray hair clinging to her head in patches, her body covered in rags.

"Madame," the woman croaked, "I'm afraid your friend is not coming back."

Inès had stopped breathing. She put David down, held his hand, and moved in front of him so that her body was blocking his. He understood nearly everything the adults around him were talking about these days. "What do you mean?" Inès whispered as David giggled and squirmed behind her legs.

The woman's eyes pooled with tears and she shook her head. "We were together in the barracks for a time. She came from a village near Reims, yes? Ville-something?"

"Yes, that's right. Ville-Dommange."

"My dear, she died in the winter, just before the camp was liberated. It was January, the second week, I think."

"Are you certain?" Inès swallowed hard, trying to fight the wave of guilt crashing over her. "Wh-what happened?"

"Tuberculosis," the woman said. "At least I believe so. It's not as if we could simply walk into a clinic to be diagnosed, you know." She laughed hoarsely and then sobered. "It was snowing outside the night she died, and she was coughing up blood. We all knew it was the end for her, and in the morning, she was gone."

"But she hasn't been on any of the lists of the deceased."

"The weeks just before liberation were chaos. I'm quite certain the Nazis were more concerned with covering their tracks than updating their records. Besides, to them, she was just a number, never a person. None of us were." She shook her head. "Sometimes I envy her, going before they marched us out into the wilderness. Besides, my whole family is dead. There's no one. Sometimes at night I ask God why he did not take me, too."

"I'm very sorry for you," Inès said. "But Céline wasn't alone. She had a child."

The woman's eyes flicked behind Inès and widened. "He is Céline's? Well, that is a tragedy indeed. She spoke of a son, but I never believed he had lived."

Inès glanced back at David, who was now pretending his hand was a truck and zooming it up and down her calf, making engine noises. He was completely oblivious to the woman's words, to the way they forever changed his world. "You're absolutely sure it was Céline? Céline Laurent from Ville-Dommange? There's not a chance you are wrong?"

"None," the woman said without hesitation. "She spoke sometimes of the champagne house she left behind, the man she had loved there."

Inès's heart lurched. "Yes."

"I'm sorry," the woman said. "But now it is time to rebuild, is it not? To try to make a future? You must make sure her child finds a good home, parents who love him."

Inès turned and bent to David, kissing him tenderly on the forehead before lifting him into her arms. "*Maman!*" he said excitedly, and the term of endearment made Inès begin to cry, for though she had tried to make him call her *Tante* Inès instead, to explain that his real mother was coming back for him, he still slipped from time to time.

"His home," Inès said, turning back to the woman, "is with me. And I'll love him with all my heart for the rest of my life."

"Well then," the woman said. "I suppose you are his mother now." And then she was gone, vanished back into the crowd before Inès could even ask her name.

Inès continued to take David back to the Hôtel Lutetia each day until the center for returning deportees finally closed, just in case the woman had been wrong, just in case there was a chance. But Inès knew she was living in denial. Finally, when Céline's picture was taken down from the board of the missing, Inès left the Lutetia with David for the last time, determined to begin a new life, a life in which the mother in the boy's fairy tales wasn't coming back, a life in which the woman left behind—a woman who didn't deserve to be the only one who lived—was all he had.

Inès returned to Reims just once, in 1946, and then only to ensure that the Maison Chauveau was not sold out from under her. She had intended to visit Monsieur Godard, the attorney who had initially presented her with the paperwork after Michel's death, but on her way from the train station, as a three-year-old David hurried behind her, clinging to her hand, she happened to see a plaque affixed to an unassuming door on the rue du Trésor. *Samuel Cohn Société d'Avocats*, it read. There was almost no chance it was the young lawyer she and Edith had helped shelter in 1943, was there? But what if fate had spared him the way it had spared her?

She picked David up and went inside. Just beyond the entrance sat a young secretary, who looked up expectantly. "May I help you, madame?"

"I am here to see Samuel Cohn," she said confidently.

"Whom should I tell him is here?"

Inès's heart fluttered. "An old friend," she said, and though the secretary pursed her lips at the vague response, she still slipped into the office behind a closed door, emerging a moment later to tell Inès that she could come in.

Inès didn't believe in miracles until she rounded the corner and saw a familiar figure—looking just as he had the last time she'd seen him—standing behind a grand desk. His eyes widened in recognition, and he hastily told his secretary that she could go.

"Inès Chauveau?" he asked, crossing from behind his desk to kiss her cheeks. He examined her in disbelief. "It can't be! I was told that you had died!"

"Well, I did, in a way. I am Edith Thierry now."

"But the real Madame Thierry—"

"Is dead," Inès finished softly, and then as Samuel's brow creased with confusion, she added, "And this is my son, David."

"Pleased to meet you, monsieur," David said politely, just as she had taught him to do, and then he tugged on her dress. "Maman, may I have my airplane now?"

"Of course, my dear." Inès handed David his toy, and he sat down on Samuel Cohn's floor and began to swoop it through the air, making engine sounds under his breath, while Inès told an astonished Samuel the whole story—from what had happened to Michel and Céline, to her adoption of Edith's name. He in turn told her about how he and his sister had been smuggled across the Swiss border with the help of a Dutch couple and had spent the remainder of the war safely in Geneva.

"You saved my life," Samuel concluded. "And my sister's. I owe you everything."

"You owe me nothing," Inès said quickly. "But I was hoping that nonetheless, you might be willing to help me with a situation that might prove a bit complicated."

"I am at your service, whatever you need."

And so Inès explained about how the Maison Chauveau had passed to her, and that she wanted to leave it to David, for it was his by right. "Perhaps it has been taken and sold already," she said. "Maybe I am too late. But if there's a chance of saving it, is there anything you can do so that ownership rests with me with David as my heir? It is, after all, his rightful inheritance."

"It will indeed be complicated," Samuel said with a sigh, "but I will do absolutely everything I can. Of course we'll need to establish a proper trail of paperwork officially making David your son, too. But considering the way so many records were lost or destroyed in the war, it shouldn't be difficult to plant a few *pieux mensonges*, white lies. So you plan to return to Ville-Dommange, then?"

"No. I cannot. I need to start over somewhere new. Maybe Paris, maybe even America. But there are too many memories for me here, and who knows what would happen if people realize that Inès Chauveau is alive? I cannot risk it, for I am all David has."

"I'm sorry," Samuel said, "that it has come to this."

Inès looked away. "It is my fault."

Samuel smiled sadly. "We all make mistakes. It is the war that turned those mistakes into losses that will last a lifetime. So we must keep moving forward, mustn't we? It is the only way."

Inès always intended to tell David about his past, but as the years went by, she lost the courage again and again. By the time they had relocated to New York, she had so fully become someone else—a French divorcée named Edith Thierry—that time only made the truth more difficult, more elusive. What would her son say when he learned that she was not really his mother? That she had indeed been responsible for his real parents' deaths? That she had taken him away from his ancestral home simply because she could not live with herself anymore?

Still, she knew she owed him honesty. Once, when he was seventeen, a senior in high school, she'd found a bottle of 1940 Champagne Chauveau in a specialty wine store on West Seventy-Second Street and bought it, though it had cost a small fortune. But it had been a sign; it had been the last vintage Michel and Theo had finished together before the world fell apart. All of them—Inès and Céline, too—had played a part in making the wine that year, and as Inès popped the cork in the living room with shaky hands, she felt as if she were holding something that belonged to another age, another reality.

She drank as she practiced telling David everything. Even though the 1940 harvest had been so terrible, the bubbles were fine and elegant, the wine itself buttery as brioche, with a crisp, lemony edge and just the faintest traces of caramel and chalk. It was perfect, a masterpiece, an ode to the land, to the cellars, to the winemakers. Céline had been right about this vintage; they had managed to make something beautiful from the chaos. Michel would have been so proud, and as she drank sip after perfect sip, she closed her eyes and imagined returning to Ville-Dommange, finding Michel there tending the cellars. His hair would be gray by now, his face lined, and he would embrace her and tell her that he knew it had all been a mistake, and that he forgave her.

By the time David came home from school, Inès was drunk, but still she had tried to tell him. "This is who you are," she had slurred, holding up the empty bottle, and he had stared at her, his expression somewhere in that soft place between concern and disdain. "Stop looking at me like that. I'm trying to tell you something important. Your father made this wine."

His eyes narrowed. "My father was a hero in the French Resistance in Paris." It was the story she'd told him a thousand times, exaggerating Michel's heroics and moving him to Paris, for she couldn't bear to tell David stories of Champagne. Of course it would have been easier to tell him about Edouard Thierry and pretend that Edith's real husband was his father, but she'd already told enough lies. "Now, all of a sudden, he's a winemaker, Mom?"

"But he *was*," Inès insisted, her words tangling together. "He always was, *mon ange*! He is your father, and your *real* mother was a woman named—"

"You're drunk, Mom."

She tried to stand and found she could not, so she sank back into the couch cushions. Her head hurt. "I'm just trying to tell you the truth."

"Just stop it," he snapped. Even in her drunken state, she could see the fury in his expression. "If you're not my mother, I don't have anyone, do I? So don't down a bottle of wine and try to change the whole story of who I am. If you have something to say to me, say it when you're sober."

"But—" Inès began, but David was already stomping away toward his room.

She hadn't had the nerve to try again, though she now realized how much easier it was to live with herself when she had a bit of alcohol in her system.

She told herself she'd tell him when he turned eighteen, for that's when he would officially come of age to inherit the champagne house according to the complex documents Samuel had drawn up after wresting control of the business from the attorney named Godard. He'd had a talented friend forge and backdate some documents establishing that Inès Chauveau had legally passed ownership of Champagne Chauveau to Edith Thierry before her tragic death. *I should feel guilty for committing a bit of fraud,* Samuel once told Inès with a shrug, *but for a long time, the legal system wasn't on my side or yours, was it? There should be no shame in reclaiming what is ours.*

Samuel had set up a trust to run the champagne house until Inès could bring herself to tell David the truth. But his eighteenth birthday came and went without her mustering the courage. Maybe she would tell him when he was twenty-one. Or thirty. Or thirty-five. Time and again, she tried and failed to bring herself to utter the words, and with each passing year, it became more difficult.

Samuel called her quarterly to check in, to see if there had been a change, to see if Inès was ready to bring David back to Ville-Dommange. But each time, she explained that she could not, and he told her he understood and would continue to run the champagne house's business operations for her, would continue to ensure the house employed one of Champagne's best winemakers, would continue to confirm that they were buying only the best grapes from the best vignerons. And, as he had done since 1946, Samuel would continue to put half of the profits in an account for David, and he would continue to send Inès the rest to make sure she and her son had everything they needed in the meantime.

It felt to Inès that she still had all the time in the world to come clean. But then, on February 13, 1980, a month and a half before David would have turned thirty-seven, his wife, Jeanne, called Inès in the middle of the night and told her the news: there had been a terrible car accident. David had not survived.

Inès knew she had lost her last chance at redemption, her final opportunity to try to make things right. She moved back to Paris soon after, for New York now held only the painful memories of raising a child whom she had somehow managed to outlive, just as she had outlived nearly everyone else who mattered in her life.

She would always regret failing to tell him, but one day, when the time was right, she would tell his daughter, Olivia. The Maison Chauveau belonged to her now, after all, and all Inès had to do was find the courage to speak the truth one last time. But how could she, after a lifetime of lies?

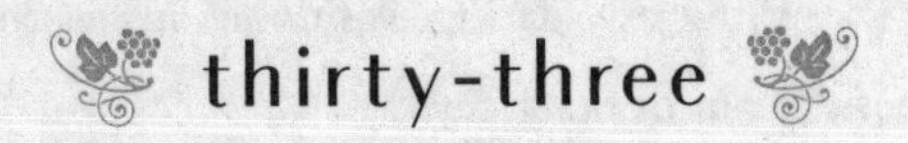

thirty-three

JUNE 2019

LIV

When it became clear that Grandma Edith wasn't going to reemerge from her room, Liv tried calling Julien, but when he didn't pick up, she finally took a shower, switched her phone to silent, and went to bed. It had been a long, confusing day, and she was exhausted.

She woke before dawn and smiled when she saw that she'd missed a call from Julien. "I'm sorry I didn't get to talk with you last night," he said in the message he'd left, his voice deep, his tone soft. "I didn't check my phone until after I'd gotten Mathilde to sleep. I'm probably calling too late now, actually. I'm sorry. But I just wanted you to know that I had a lovely time today, and, um, I very much look forward to seeing you again. Call me in the morning, Liv."

She dressed in a fog as she thought about whether to suggest to Julien that they meet for dinner that night. Was that too forward? Maybe that wasn't the way dating was done here. For that matter, maybe that wasn't the way dating was done *anywhere* this decade. She was woefully out of practice.

She was still smiling when she emerged from her room, but then she realized that Grandma Edith's door was open, and the suite was empty. She looked at her watch. It wasn't even seven in the morning yet. There was suddenly a knot in the pit of Liv's stomach. Where had Grandma Edith gone so early?

Then Liv's eyes landed on the coffee table in the middle of the room. On it sat two envelopes, one addressed to her, the other addressed to Julien, both in her grandmother's signature hand. She crossed the room quickly and tore open her note.

Dearest Olivia,

There are many things to say, but the truth is, I have never been as strong as I've wanted to be. I brought you here to tell you everything, to try to make things right in some small way, but it seems I lack the courage. Perhaps this, more than anything, is what defines my life.

Please summon Julien, and he will tell you the things that I cannot. The other note on the table is addressed to him; it gives him permission to break my confidence.

It is time you know who you are. I'm sorry I have failed you. But somehow, my Olivia, you summoned strength on your own, and I know now that whatever comes, you will find your happiness. Never forget how much I love you, even if I did not deserve to know you at all. Being your Grandma Edith has been one of the greatest gifts of my life.

All my love forever. xx

Liv reread the note, her hands shaking, and then she hurried back to her room to grab her phone. She dialed Julien.

"Liv." His voice was deep and warm when he answered. "Good morning."

"My grandmother's gone," she blurted out without returning his greeting. "She left a note."

"What? What did it say?"

"It sounded really final, Julien. She left one for you, too."

He cursed under his breath. "I'll be right over. Open my note in the meantime."

Liv hung up and slipped her finger under the flap of the envelope addressed to Julien. Inside, Grandma Edith had written:

Please tell Liv everything. It is time. Thank you for guarding my secrets for so long. You're a good man.

By the time Julien arrived fifteen minutes later, his dark hair a mess, his linen shirt wrinkled, Liv was pacing the hotel suite. She thrust both letters at him, and he read through them quickly, his lips moving with the words. When he was done, he looked up at Liv, the concern on his face mirroring hers. "What was the last thing she said to you? Did you see her this morning?"

Liv shook her head. "She was gone before I got up. But last night, she was saying all sorts of weird things—that my dad was actually the son of Michel Chauveau, who owned the Maison Chauveau, and that she was not actually my father's mother. It made no sense, and when I tried to get her to explain, she shut down. I thought she was just being dramatic, but now—" Liv pointed to the letters Julien was holding. "Now I'm really worried. Julien, it almost sounds like she's saying goodbye, doesn't it?"

"Okay." He set the letters down and pulled his phone from his pocket. "I am just going to call a friend of mine with the local police department. Don't worry, d'accord?"

Liv waited while Julien placed a call, explaining in rapid French that Edith Thierry wasn't exactly a missing person but that he was worried about her safety. He hung up and turned to Liv. "He will have the other officers keep an eye out. We will find her, Liv."

"We should go look, too," Liv said. She couldn't fight the feeling that something terrible had happened.

"We'll take my car."

As they left the hotel room, Julien squeezed Liv's hand, and he didn't let go. "Thank you," she said as they hurried down the stairs together.

In the car a few minutes later, Julien drove while Liv scanned the sidewalks for her grandmother. It was early, and the streets were quiet, so the old woman should have been easy to pick out. But there was no sign of her. In silence, Julien circled the block and then pulled to a stop in front of the Brasserie Moulin, which appeared to be closed. "Do you want to make sure she's not there?" he asked. "Just in case?"

Liv nodded and jumped out of the car. She raced to the door, but it was locked. She put her face to the glass and peered in, but the restaurant was empty. Back in the car, she turned to Julien. "Do you think there's any chance she called a taxi and went to the Maison Chauveau? She seemed so emotional about it yesterday."

"I was thinking the same thing. Yes, let's check." He merged back into traffic. "While you were looking in the brasserie, I called my grandfather and left a message. Maybe he'll have an idea of where to find her."

"Thank you." She was silent as she gazed out at the buildings of Reims blurring past the car. "Julien? What secrets did my grandmother want you to reveal?"

He didn't answer right away, but she could see his hands tighten on the steering wheel, his jaw flex. "I really do feel like it's a story that you should hear from her, Liv."

"But she's not here. And she asked you to tell me."

"I know." He sighed. "All right, where shall I begin? Well, to start, she is not really Edith Thierry. That is an identity she took on after the war, a name that once belonged to someone else."

Liv stared at him. "The wife of the owner of the Brasserie Moulin."

"*Oui.* The real Edith Thierry was your grandmother's best friend. As I understand it, she died helping the Resistance here in Reims. Shot by the Germans, I believe, toward the end of the Occupation."

Liv covered her mouth. "So who on earth is my grandmother, then?"

Julian glanced at her, his eyes full of concern. "Your grandmother's real name is Inès Chauveau. She was the wife of Michel Chauveau, who owned the Maison Chauveau." Julien paused as he took a right toward the edge of town.

Liv felt short of breath. "I—I don't understand. She told me yesterday that Michel Chauveau was my father's father, but she wasn't his mother."

"*Oui.* That's where it gets complicated. You see, Michel Chauveau had an affair with a woman named Céline Laurent, the wife of his *chef de cave*, his head winemaker. She was your father's real mother. But when Madame Laurent was taken away to Auschwitz, she left her newborn son with your grandmother."

"Oh my God, *Auschwitz*? What happened to her?"

"She never came back. Your grandmother, she always blamed herself for Madame Laurent's death, as well as her own husband's. But she knew she had to protect your father. There were people in Reims who believed she—Inès—had helped the Nazis."

"But she didn't, did she? Oh, God, please tell me she didn't."

"No, she didn't," Julien said quickly. "Actually, she helped save my grandfather's life. He was a Jewish refugee, and she sheltered him in the cellars beneath the Maison Chauveau until her husband could find him a safe way out of France." Julien turned onto Route D980, which would lead them to Ville-Dommange. "Whatever happened at the Maison Chauveau, Liv, your grandmother is a good woman. But she has never been able to forgive herself for the terrible mistakes she made seventy-five years ago."

"But what mistakes? Why did she blame herself for the death of my father's real parents?"

Julien was silent for a few seconds. "She may have betrayed them to the Germans just after finding out about their affair."

"No," Liv breathed. "How could she?"

"I don't believe it was intentional. But that doesn't change the outcome, does it? My grandfather says it's one of the greatest tragedies he has ever seen; your grandmother has lived her whole life defined by her guilt over what she did."

Liv let the words settle over her. Had Grandma Edith really caused the deaths of two innocent people, even if it was a mistake? "So is that what she brought me here to tell me?" she asked, her voice cracking. "That she has a terrible secret past? And that I'm not really her granddaughter?"

"But you are. Don't you see? Family is more than just blood. And I think she has spent a lifetime atoning for the things she did."

Liv looked at her hands but didn't say anything.

Julien pulled over on the side of the road and turned to her. "Liv, there was something else she brought you here to tell you, too."

She half laughed. "What else could there possibly be?"

"That the Maison Chauveau will be yours one day, Liv."

Liv opened and closed her mouth. "I—I don't understand."

"The house has been run by a trust administered by my family's law firm for seventy years. Since your father's death, it has always been meant to pass on to you. Your grandmother's primary stipulation was that she would tell you at the time of her choosing. The house is technically hers, since Michel Chauveau left it to her upon his death."

"You're telling me that *I* will inherit the Maison Chauveau?" Liv's voice had risen an octave.

"Upon your grandmother's passing, yes." The ringing of Julien's phone interrupted them, and he glanced at the caller ID, his eyebrows drawing together as he answered. "*Oui*," he said. "*Oui. Nous serons là rapidement.*"

"Who was that?" Liv asked.

"It was my grandfather." Julien's expression was grim as he pulled back onto the road and gunned the engine. "Your grandmother is at the Maison Chauveau. He is almost there. I told him we are on our way."

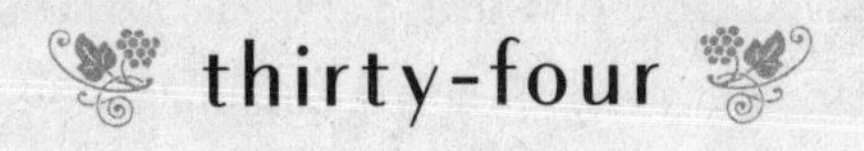

thirty-four

JUNE 2019

INÈS

Could the stain of what she had done ever be erased? Inès had played a courageous role in the Resistance, had brought her son to America for a new life, had always looked out for her granddaughter. She had donated millions to charity, had saved the lives of Samuel and his sister, had tried to bring honor to the name of Edith Thierry, her dear friend who had died trying to save France.

But it hadn't been enough.

David had still been robbed of his mother and father. Olivia had missed out on having a real grandmother and grandfather. And now, somehow, Inès was nearly a century old, still alive, still going, while Michel and Céline had never made it out of their twenties.

Inès knew she could live a hundred more years, do a thousand more good deeds, maybe even a million, and the scales would never be balanced.

She stood just outside the old entrance to the cellars at the

Maison Chauveau, the one that had been boarded up in favor of the new, larger entrance inside the main château. Samuel had done well; from the time she put the business in his hands in 1946, he had made the right decisions, hired the right people, transformed the Maison Chauveau into a profitable empire. Inès had hoped, when she left this place more than seven decades earlier, that one day it might be worth enough to help pay for David's college tuition, to help him get a start in life, perhaps buy a first house of his own. It had certainly done that—though he had never understood where the money had come from—but it had become so much more. By the time Samuel and his grandson sorted through the paperwork and passed it on to Olivia, she would be a millionaire many times over. And Olivia would have a home here forever, if she wanted it. This was what was meant to be, and it was Inès's fault that it was all coming together far too late. Perhaps her granddaughter could have been spared the pain of a bad marriage and a painful divorce if she had been living here in Ville-Dommange instead of New York, if she had understood who she was all along. Yet one more thing for Inès to regret.

Inès gazed out now at the rows and rows of Pinot Noir grapes that crawled toward the horizon. She wondered if the vines she could see now were descendants of the ones Michel had once cultivated so carefully. Even if they weren't, certainly they carried a piece of him. His blood had spilled here, seeped into the soil, become part of the earth itself before the Nazis had hauled him away. He had given all he had to this land. And now it would help sustain the granddaughter he never had a chance to know.

In the notebook she had left for Samuel to give to Olivia, Inès had written all the stories that she could remember about Michel and Céline. If Olivia took the time to read them, the words would breathe life into this place, and Olivia would understand that she was walking among the ghosts of the people she should have belonged to. Whatever happened, Inès knew now that Olivia would be okay. Inès had done all she could do, and now it was time. She was so very tired.

A car turned off the main road in the distance and pulled up the drive to the Maison Chauveau. Inès watched it approach, relief sweeping over her. Good, Samuel was here. It would be only a few minutes before the pills kicked in, and there were things she wanted to say.

The car drew to a halt, and the man who climbed out of the driver's seat did so with difficulty, slowly unfolding his long legs and then using his arms to launch himself awkwardly out of the vehicle. It was Samuel—stooped and slowing, but the same man she'd known since she was twenty-three. Her friend. The one person on earth who really knew her—knew everything she had done—and had remained by her side for all these years anyhow.

"Inès," he said, walking toward her with the support of a cane. "Are you all right?"

"Samuel," she said, smiling at him as he drew closer. They kissed on both cheeks, formally, but then he embraced her. They were both old as dirt, but being in his arms was as familiar as ever, and for a second, Inès could close her eyes and believe they were young again. She pulled away and gestured to a bench nearby.

"What is this about, dear friend?" Samuel asked, gazing into her eyes, after they sat down.

But he did not need an answer. She could see it written in his expression. He already knew. She looked away, over the rolling vineyards, toward the eastern horizon, where the sun was just beginning to warm the earth.

She hoped Olivia would choose this place. She thought maybe she would, at least for a while. She had seen the way Julien looked at her granddaughter, and the way she looked at him. That hadn't been Inès's intention when she'd first brought Olivia here, but the moment she had seen them together for the first time, she had known—and of course she'd had to meddle, just a bit, to help Olivia move past the fears that were holding her back.

Perhaps it was preordained, written in the stars, just like everything else. Long ago, Inès had helped save the life of Julien's grandfather. Now the boy was falling in love with Olivia—and Inès could see Olivia's heart opening again, too. That meant that

Inès could finally go in peace, knowing that her granddaughter would be all right—even if things didn't work out with young Julien. Olivia intuitively understood how to love in a way that Inès never had, and that meant that the girl would find her way to happiness, one way or another.

"Remember years ago, when you told me about that French policeman who killed himself on the street in front of your house during the roundups of 1942?" Inès asked Samuel now, leaning into her friend's shoulder for support. "I didn't understand it at the time, how a person could take his own life out of a sense of responsibility, but now I do."

Samuel's face crumpled in sad resignation. "Oh no, Inès, what have you done?"

She stared into the distance, watching as the edges blurred, the world began to slip away. She had run out of time. There would be no absolution.

"Perhaps what I should have done long ago," she said. "I never deserved all these years, Samuel. It isn't fair. I should not have been the one to live."

"But you were! You survived, Inès, and you did a lot of good in this world. You have to trust that God had the right plan for you!"

"But didn't I turn my back on God all those years ago? What if I made a deal with the devil, whether I intended to or not?" She could feel herself growing weaker, her muscles losing their hold on her bones, and so she gratefully accepted the support when Samuel put his arm around her. She could feel him shaking, but she didn't know whether it was from age or sadness.

"My dear friend," he said, "you didn't turn your back on God. You made mistakes, but you have spent a lifetime atoning. I'm proof of that, aren't I? I'm here because you risked your life to save me."

His voice sounded more distant now, though he was just beside her. She knew she was disappearing. She didn't have the strength to tell him he was wrong, that the saving of one life didn't counterbalance the losing of another. Nothing could.

"Inès, are you listening to me?" he said from somewhere far away. "You need to hear this. You are a good woman, Inès. You always have been, even if you never believed it."

She wished he wouldn't lie to her, not at the end, but she knew he meant well. "Please ask Julien to look out for my Olivia, whatever happens," she managed to say, but she wasn't sure he heard her, because she was already drifting, already rising up into the crisp Champagne sky, already watching the vineyards disappear beneath her, lines and lines of grapes and dreams running over the earth, fading into forever.

And then she was above the clouds, and Michel was there, looking just as he had on the day she married him all those years ago, when they still loved each other with innocent and open hearts, before the war and the world and the choices they made changed everything. "You're here at last," he said, coming toward her, washed in white light.

She was weightless, floating, but still, her heart was heavy with the guilt she had carried with her for decades. "Michel, I'm so sorry. For everything."

"Oh, Inès, we were young and foolish, all of us. I forgave you long ago."

Inès looked around for Céline, the woman who had replaced her, the woman who had always deserved the heart of Inès's husband. Inès had imagined they were spending eternity together, but it was only Michel here waiting for her. She felt a surge of grief, a knot twisting inside her. "Michel, where is Céline?"

But he only shook his head in silence as he took her hand. As they walked together toward the rising sun, toward the light that welcomed them home, Inès wept, for Céline's absence—the fact that she, too, wasn't waiting to greet Inès—could only mean that Inès would never be forgiven.

But then, in the center of the welcoming light, she saw David, and he was somehow both the child she had raised and the adult he had become all at the same time. "Mom!" he cried, and she forgot everything else—her sins, her guilt, the world she'd finally left behind—and ran to him. He had been reunited with his father, waiting for her all this time.

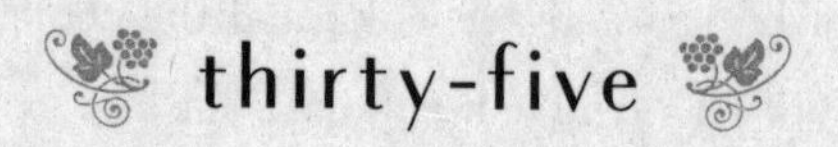

thirty-five

JUNE 2019

LIV

It took Julien and Liv twenty minutes to get to Ville-Dommange, and when they finally pulled the car up outside the main building of the Maison Chauveau, an hour before the place would open to visitors, Liv spotted her grandmother sitting on a bench overlooking the rolling vineyards to the right of the main house. She was leaning into an old man with wispy white hair, who must have been Julien's grandfather.

Liv and Julien jumped from the car at the same time and ran to the bench. Grandma Edith's eyes were closed, and when Julien's grandfather looked up, his eyes were red, his cheeks wet.

"She was a good woman," he said to Liv. "She never believed it, but she really was."

Liv looked from him to her grandmother, who was unnaturally still, a faint smile on her lips, and suddenly she understood what he was saying.

"No," Liv whispered, kneeling beside her grandmother and

grasping her hands, which were still so warm. "Grandma Edith, come back." She could feel tears rolling down her face, and she choked on the sob in her throat. "Oh God, no."

"My dear," Samuel said, reaching for Liv, his touch gentle and soothing. "Do not cry for her. After all these years, she has finally found her peace."

The following weeks went by in a blur. Grandma Edith was buried at a small cemetery on the south side of Ville-Dommange, just on the edge of the vineyards, with the name *Edith Thierry* engraved on her tombstone, the name *Inès Chauveau* beneath it just as prominently. Surely it would confuse a passerby or two, but after reading Grandma Edith's notebook of stories—confessions, really—Liv understood that her grandmother had never really stopped being the naive girl from Lille who had married a man she hoped would give her the world. For all her years of trying, she hadn't fully buried the ghost of Inès in the disguise of Edith.

Samuel spoke at her small memorial service, and in his words, Liv met a grandmother she had never known, a brave and sad woman who had sheltered refugees and fought Nazis in the forests of France, a woman who had found her way to America all alone to give her son a better life, a woman who had been nearly toppled by the force of her grief after her son's death.

"She was a hero, though she never saw herself that way," Samuel said to the crowd of a dozen mourners, most of them strangers to Liv. "But it is how I will always remember her, and I hope that all of you do, too. Especially you, her dear granddaughter, Olivia." He smiled at Liv, and she covered her face with her hands. "She loved you so very much, even if she sometimes had a rather difficult way of showing it."

A day after the funeral, Liv met with Samuel and Julien in their office and spent a day going over all the legal documents assigning ownership of the Maison Chauveau to her. There were accounts and investments she'd never known about that totaled more than twenty million dollars, and that was in addition to the millions tied up in the day-to-day operations of champagne production.

"You can do whatever you'd like, Liv," Julien said, handing her a batch of papers to sign. "You can stay here and have a hand in the business, or you can go home to New York, and the Maison Chauveau will continue to be run by a trust controlled by this law firm, which is what has happened for the past seventy years. Either way, it is yours."

"What do you think I should do?" she asked.

Julien held her gaze. "It is not my decision to make, Liv. But if you go, I hope you will allow me to visit you. I think I would miss you very much."

"And if I stay?"

His expression softened. "If you stay, I think you would make me the happiest man in France."

She smiled. "I'll take that under advisement, Counselor."

But she already knew she would remain in Champagne, at least for a while. It was as if it was what the universe had intended all along. Just when she had lost all sense of belonging in the city that had been hers, a new place had come along, a place that was always meant to be her home. It was like a gift from heaven—and perhaps it really was. Liv tried to imagine Michel, the grandfather she had never known, and Céline, the grandmother whose tiny infant had been ripped from her arms as she was carted off to an unspeakable fate. Were they looking down on her now? Did her return to the Maison Chauveau bring them some peace? What about her own father, who had never known this place at all?

The first thing Liv did when she came on board was to ask the Maison Chauveau's webmaster to update the champagne house's site with a short history of what had happened on this property, the abbreviated story of three lives—those of Michel, Céline, and a young woman named Inès who had lived to become an old woman named Edith. Liv hoped to one day honor all three of them in a much larger way, but beginning to speak the truth about the past felt like a start.

In the next few weeks, Liv met with the *chef de cave*, Jacques

Cazal, and the director of business operations, Sylvie Vaillant, and she decided to come on as a sort of apprentice to both of them so she could begin to learn the business. "I'm not sure I'll be any good at this," Liv said to Jacques, a sixty-something man with sparkling brown eyes who had been running the winemaking operations for more than thirty years. "Maybe I'm fooling myself."

"You know," said Jacques with a smile, "two hundred years ago, there was another woman not far from here by the name of Barbe-Nicole Ponsardin who was faced with a similar situation. Her husband had died, and suddenly, at the age of twenty-seven, she was faced with the question of whether she could follow in his footsteps and keep his champagne house alive."

"And did she?"

"Well, her husband was a man named François Clicquot. And when he died, she became known as the Widow Clicquot, or the *Veuve* Clicquot. She pioneered new practices in the champagne-making process, became one of the richest women of her time, and grew her company into one of the most well-known champagne brands in the world. You may have heard of it."

Liv laughed. "So she did all right for herself."

"I would say so. It took her many years, and there were ups and downs, but this land was in her blood, and she had the passion for it. There's no doubt that you, too, have the magic of this place coursing through your veins. I think that if you work hard and truly commit yourself to learning your heritage, perhaps you will be surprised at what you can accomplish here. And as long as you'll have us stay on, Sylvie and I will be happy to teach you everything we can. We love this place, too, and we all want it to continue being successful."

After Liv had gone to New York to pack up her apartment and returned to Champagne to move into the small caretaker's cottage on the Maison Chauveau property—which had been boarded up so long that it still contained some of Céline Laurent's belongings—there was a call one day to Julien's office, from a reporter at the French newspaper *Le Monde*, saying that a reader had tipped her off to the brief historical paragraph that had recently appeared on the Maison Chauveau's website and asking if she might come out for an interview. With the seventy-fifth anniversary of the liberation of Reims looming, she thought it would be the perfect time for a story about how the American grandchild of three heroes of the Resistance—Michel Chauveau, Céline Laurent, and Inès Chauveau—had come home to France to honor her family history.

Liv agreed, and when the piece was published a week later in the Sunday paper, it not only brought a rush of new business to the Maison Chauveau, it answered questions Liv hadn't even known she had. The reporter had dug deeper into the pasts of Michel, Céline, and Inès, and Liv learned that Michel had always lived on this land but had briefly considered leaving to become a scientist before his own father died. Inès had come from Lille with her best friend, Edith Thierry, who had married restaurateur Edouard Thierry, and they, in turn, had introduced her to Michel.

The reporter had tracked down details of Michel's death; he had been executed by a German firing squad in March 1943 without a trial after becoming a suspect in the murder of a German officer named Karl Richter. After the war, there had been rumors that Michel had been betrayed by a French collaborator named Antoine Picard, who was known to frequent the restaurant of Edith and Edouard Thierry. Picard had been tried and found guilty of collaboration and sentenced to death in the days after the liberation of Reims. He had died not far from where Michel's body had fallen.

Céline had been shipped to Auschwitz, where, probably unbeknownst to her, her father and grandparents had been sent, too. All of them perished there. Céline's husband, Theo, had gone south, ultimately settling in Burgundy, where he remarried soon after he learned that his first wife had died. He had one son and died in 1960 of cancer. The reporter found his son, who said that in his final days, all his father talked about was the Maison Chauveau.

But, the newspaper article had concluded, though their lives were lost, those who once walked the caves of the Maison Chauveau had been heroes whose sacrifices forever shaped the region, and, indeed, France. The story included the tale of Samuel's rescue, and recently declassified details about the way the Thierrys, Céline Laurent, and Michel Chauveau had helped the Allies, from hiding munitions in the cellars to passing information along to British spies. And Inès Chauveau, who eventually took on the name of Edith Thierry, had been a member of an armed group in central France that had helped liberate the country. She had, astonishingly, become a munitions expert, and a woman whose nickname in the forest was *La Beauté Intrépide*, the Intrepid Beauty, for her fearless, almost reckless pursuit of all Nazis. Even though she had lived to the age of ninety-nine, the reporter wrote, a piece of her had died with the others during the war, and in that way, she was a martyr of the Resistance, too.

Liv read and reread the article, her vision blurred by tears. How had she never known any of this? Her family's history was so tragically bittersweet, perhaps Grandma Edith's life most of all. Liv could hardly imagine the guilt and pain that had driven her into the woods of France in pursuit of redemption.

And though Liv had never wanted for anything, and though she had always understood that Grandma Edith loved her deeply, she couldn't help but wonder how different her life would be if Céline Laurent and Michel Chauveau had survived. But Liv couldn't imagine a life without her extraordinary grandmother, the woman who had given up everything—even her own name—to protect a little boy who wasn't hers. After all, if Grandma Edith hadn't brought David to America, he never would have met Liv's mother, and Liv herself would never have existed. And if Grandma Edith hadn't risked her life saving Samuel Cohn all those years before, there would be no Julien, either. It was incredible to think how deeply the decisions of the past had shaped the future.

That's what Liv was thinking about on the fourth Wednesday evening in August as she made her way up Julien's front walk. If Grandma Edith hadn't made the sacrifices she had, Liv wouldn't be here, wouldn't be standing on the doorstep of the man she had fallen in love with, waiting to meet his daughter for the first time. And so she looked heavenward to where the sunset was just beginning to streak the sky, and smiled. "Thank you, Grandma Edith," she said. "For everything."

Then, straightening the vintage Chanel scarf Grandma Edith had given her just before boarding the train that had brought Liv to Reims for the first time, she took a deep breath and knocked on the door.

epilogue

SEPTEMBER 2019

LIV

A month later, with the harvest about to begin, Liv sat in the main building of the Maison Chauveau going over some paperwork with Julien, Jacques, and Sylvie. She was trying to understand how they sourced the grapes from so many vineyards and managed to keep all the batches separate before blending. Jacques patiently explained the difference between the limestone-rich soil in the Aube and the chalkier earth in the Marne. Liv eventually signed off on the agreements with each individual vigneron, a formality that Samuel Cohn, and then Julien, had once been responsible for on behalf of the trust.

"I promise," Jacques said as he and Sylvie gathered their things and prepared to head out for one last meeting with the Comité Interprofessionnel du vin de Champagne before the workers descended on the vineyards. "Once this harvest is over, I'll start taking you to meet the vignerons. The grapes are as much a product of their expertise as they are a product of the land itself. You will find that when you come to know and trust the growers, you will usually trust their fruit, too."

After Jacques and Sylvie had gone, Julien helped Liv gather up all the papers. "You're really getting the hang of this," he said.

She groaned. "How is it that you understand it all so easily?"

He laughed. "Don't forget, I have a twenty-year jump on you. Since I joined my grandfather's firm, one of our main accounts has been the Maison Chauveau. I could probably tell you the soil composition of every single vineyard the champagne house works with."

"Vineyard soil, huh?" Liv asked, nudging him. "I love it when you talk dirty to me."

He stared at her for a long beat before he blinked in recognition of her joke and burst out laughing.

"I guess I'll have to work on my French flirtation." Liv grinned, loving the way her stomach still fluttered around him, even months after they had started dating.

"Oh, I think you're doing just fine." He leaned down to kiss her, and the butterflies in her belly beat faster now. She was in love with him, and she had fallen in love with his daughter, too. In a strange way, Julien and Mathilde already felt like her family, like perhaps they had been meant to be just that all along. And she knew all too well now that family was about more than just blood. She didn't know where this would lead, but as Julien had reminded her not so long ago, the future was wide open.

He took her hand and they strolled out into the main room where tourists circulated, picking up bottles and souvenirs to take home, reading the plaques on the wall, doing guided tastings at the bar. Since the article had appeared in *Le Monde*, they had been packed every day. Liv smiled across the room at René, the young tour guide who had shown her and Grandma Edith into the cellars just a few months earlier, and then her eyes roamed the crowd until they settled on an old woman who had just walked through the tasting room's front door with the help of a silver cane.

She was tall and white-haired, at least in her eighties or nineties, and she was leaning on the arm of a tall, broad-shouldered man in his sixties. There was something vaguely familiar about the man, but it was the woman Liv couldn't look away from. It wasn't the jagged scar running the length of her right cheek that captured Liv's attention, though; it was something about her eyes, something Liv recognized, though she was certain she had never seen her before. The woman's gaze locked on Liv from across the room, and it didn't waver as she and the man slowly approached.

"May I help you?" Liv asked when they reached her.

"You are Olivia?" She spoke English with a slight accent that wasn't entirely French.

"Yes, ma'am. It's Liv. I go by Liv."

"*Liv.* How fitting, for here you are, alive, which should be impossible. But God works in mysterious ways." The woman's eyes filled with tears, but she didn't blink. "Well, it is very nice to meet you, Liv. My name is—was—Céline Laurent. And I . . . I am your father's mother."

Later, with the sun casting a golden glow over the plump black grapes, Liv went for a walk with Céline through the vineyards while her son, Joël—who looked so much like Liv's father would have if he'd had the chance to grow older—stayed behind to talk with Julien.

"You see, my dear," said Céline, leaning into Liv for support as she used her cane to help her navigate the uneven ground, "I read *Le Monde* every morning online from my house outside Tel Aviv. The Internet is a wonderful thing, isn't it? Six weeks ago, I read the story about you and the Maison Chauveau, and at first, I could not believe it. But then Joël helped me to print out the photograph of you that accompanied the article, and when I saw your face, I knew. You look so much like your grandfather, Liv. It's your eyes. They're the same ones your father had, too.

"It took me a month to resolve to come," she continued. "I never thought I would return to this place, you see. When I left in 1945, after being told that both your grandfather and father were dead, I was sure I was leaving for the last time." She gazed off into the distance and then smiled slightly. "It took me another week to convince Joël that I was fit enough to travel at my age. But finally he understood how much I needed to see you in person. And here we are."

"My grandmother—I mean, Inès—always believed you died in Auschwitz," Liv said. "Her attorney Samuel told me that she searched for you for many months, going every day to the Hôtel Lutetia in Paris, but that she was told by an Auschwitz survivor that you had succumbed to tuberculosis just before the liberation of the camp."

Céline looked surprised. "My God. And I was told when I returned to the Maison Chauveau that Inès had perished, and, of course, David, too. But they both lived."

"I'm so sorry," Liv said, though the words felt terribly insufficient.

"You see, I was quite ill just before the liberation. And there was a time that I was very close to death. That is likely what the woman remembered. There was a lot of confusion at that time, and perhaps if she was sick, too, her memories were jumbled. But I fought death with every fiber of my being, because I believed your father was still alive. That is what kept me going, knowing that I had to return for my child.

"The fact is, I did not die in Auschwitz. I died *after* Auschwitz, when I came back here and learned that everyone was gone. I had nothing left to live for, so I spent a year simply drifting before I met a man named Paul Vogel. It was a long time before I loved him, for my heart was still with Michel. In fact, I suppose it always will be; when you love someone the way I loved him, that feeling never really fades, you see. In any case, Paul became my companion, and in 1950, when he asked me to marry him and move to Israel, I agreed, because there was nothing left for me in France."

Liv wiped a tear away as Céline paused to catch her breath.

"Joël was the second miracle of my life, for I never thought I would be able to have another child, not after what Auschwitz had done to me. It has been a mostly happy life, Liv, but I never forgot my firstborn, my first son."

"I—I don't know what to say. I'm so sorry." Liv cleared her throat. "My Grandma Edith—Inès—spent her whole life blaming herself for what happened to you. I know she would want me to tell you how terribly, terribly sorry she was."

"That makes me very sad, Liv, for you see, I don't blame Inès, not anymore. She was always careless when she was young, but never cruel. I know that she did not betray us on purpose. In a way, everything was my own fault. I stole her husband. I had a *baby* with her husband behind her back. Can you imagine the magnitude of that treachery? How must she have felt on the night she discovered us together and realized the truth?" Céline shook her head. "No, the fault was mine. But I couldn't have done it any differently. Michel was the love of my life, and if I had not loved him, my dear Liv, you would not be here today. So how can I regret a moment of it?"

Liv nodded, wiping away her tears. "But what about the fact that you missed a whole lifetime with my father and me, while Inès spent the past seventy years with a son—and then a granddaughter—who were really never meant to be hers?"

"But maybe you were. Maybe you were supposed to belong to Inès all along. Who can really know? I owe Inès more than I can say for saving your father, after everything I did to her. I will always regret that I never saw David again. But here I am, standing in the vineyard your grandfather once tended, with you, my granddaughter. Liv, I never imagined I would see the day. You are proof that miracles do happen." Céline leaned into Liv's shoulder. "Come, let's take a walk. I will tell you some things that I remember."

As Liv helped Céline stroll through the vineyards, listening raptly as she pointed out spots that had meant something to her and shared anecdotes about Michel and Inès, Liv felt as if she could see slivers of the past through Céline's eyes. So much had unfolded here, so many things that had shaped her own life, blessings and tragedies. Somehow, everything had come together to bring them to this moment.

"So what now?" Liv asked sometime later as the sun began to

set. They were making their way slowly back to the main house, where Joël and Julien were waiting. "Will you stay awhile?"

"Joël has been good enough to book our tickets with an open-ended departure," Céline said with a smile. "And I was hoping you and I might spend some time together, Liv, if you are willing. We've lost so many years."

Liv thought about Grandma Edith, whose life had been dictated by a terrible mistake, and about her own father, who was taken far too soon. "We have indeed," she said softly. "But as someone I loved very much once told me, you can't rewrite the past. But you can choose to live with your whole heart in the here and now."

"Your grandmother's words, I presume?" Céline smiled.

Liv bowed her head. "Yes."

"She was a wise woman, my dear, much more than I gave her credit for. I will always regret that." Céline sighed and looked into the distance for a moment, then turned her attention back to Liv. "Will you let me get to know you a bit, then? I want to know about your life, your family, your hopes and dreams. I want to know about the man your father grew to be. I want to know *you*, Liv, if that isn't too much to ask."

"I would like that." Liv reached out and took the hand of the woman who had lost everything to give her life. "I would like that very much."

author's note

Champagne.

What does the word conjure for you? If you're anything like me, you think of bubbles and celebration, France and fashion, good taste and a little bit of magic.

But did you know that the world-renowned sparkling wine comes from a region that has triumphed time and again over almost unimaginable odds? That war after war ravaged the vineyards of Champagne, each time threatening to wipe out the wine industry? That the central city of Reims, where many champagne houses have their headquarters, was almost entirely destroyed after more than a thousand consecutive days of shelling by the Germans beginning in 1914? Many of the region's most storied vineyards actually sat along the Western Front in the First World War, meaning that at war's end a century ago, the fields were filled with the blood of soldiers, plants ripped from the earth by constant explosions and gunfire, vines destroyed by poisonous gas. It's a wonder anything managed to survive at all.

I used to take champagne for granted. Somewhere far away, people were picking grapes and mysteriously turning them into something delicious that fizzed and sparkled. But now I know the fact that champagne still exists—nay, is flourishing—is nothing short of a miracle. Every time I sip a glass, I know the magic contained in the bubbles is more than just a trick of fermentation and carbonic gas; it's a testament to the blood, sweat, and tears of generation upon generation of winemakers. It's an ode to the perseverance of the human spirit.

The last major conflict to take place in Champagne was the Second World War, and local resident Stéphanie Venet, who lives near the vineyards of Ville-Dommange and whose grandparents were part of a small Resistance group during the war, sums up the attitude of the Champenois perfectly. "We were occupied, not destroyed," she told me. "So life goes on." Indeed it does, for the people and the vines.

It's important to note that *champagne* is not a catchall description for all wine that sparkles. To truly qualify as champagne, a wine must come from the Champagne growing area, less than a hundred miles from Paris in northeastern France. The region is unique; its location near the 49th parallel, close to the northernmost limits for effective grape growing, makes it a challenging place for grapes to survive. Beyond that, the ground itself—in some places containing a layer of chalk hundreds of feet thick—forces the roots of the vines to work harder to seek out moisture. But like the residents of Champagne, who have toiled for centuries to beat the odds, the vines themselves have found a way to thrive. This unlikely triumph is just one of the things that makes champagne—full of minerality and acidity, thanks in part to the chalky earth—so glorious, and so different from wines produced elsewhere.

When I first visited Champagne in 2014, on my honeymoon, I was captivated by its stories and its spirit. I have a deep interest in World War II—my previous novels *The Sweetness of Forgetting* and *The Room on Rue Amélie* are both set in France during that period—and as I researched the French Resistance for both books, I began to wonder whether the Resistance was active in Champagne, too. *Wouldn't it be poetic*, I thought, *if the same spirit of resilience that inspired winemakers to stand up to nature and circumstance also prompted them to stand up to the Nazis?*

And of course, if you've finished reading *The Winemaker's Wife*, you know that many winemakers in the region did exactly that. Much of their resistance was on a small scale—the mention in chapter 6 of winemakers using dirty bottles, bad corks, and second-rate cuvées in Germany-bound shipments is entirely true—but there was so much more at work in this region. Perhaps one of the most fascinating things I discovered at the outset of my research was that Count Robert-Jean de Vogüé, the managing director of the storied Moët & Chandon during the war, was also the leader of the Resistance movement in this area of France. He was arrested by the Gestapo in November 1943 and sentenced to death. In response, the winemakers of Champagne went on strike, and de Vogüé was instead sent to work in German labor camps, until he was liberated by the British in May 1945.

But de Vogüé's story is just the tip of the iceberg. Throughout the region, cellars and crayères were used to hide weapons, downed pilots, and refugees. Information was gleaned from the Germans and passed along to the Allies. At champagne houses including Krug, Piper-Heidsieck, Ruinart, and, of course, Moët & Chandon, people spent the war risking their lives for the cause.

The stories of the Chauveaus, the Laurents, and the Thierrys are fictional, but they are based on the reality of countless residents of the Champagne region who had the courage to stand up to injustice at the peril of their own lives. Sprinkled throughout the story are real characters—such as de Vogüé and the weinführer Otto Klaebisch—as well as plenty of historical tidbits and information about the process of making champagne.

Of course, writing a book like this requires lots of research, and I was fortunate to encounter many people along the way who were very generous with their time, knowledge, and resources.

I'd like to express my deepest gratitude to the lovely Virginie Bergeronneau, from Champagne F. Bergeronneau-Marion, a family-run champagne house in Ville-Dommange, where the fictional Maison Chauveau is located. Virginie took the time to answer many questions and host me at her family's champagne house when

I visited Ville-Dommange to research this book. Like many families in the area, hers has been in Champagne since the sixteenth century. Not only did I learn some new things about champagne production, but our visit gave me a better understanding of the deep roots that run through the community.

I also owe a great debt to Isabelle Pierre, the heritage manager for Veuve Clicquot, Krug, and Ruinart. We spent a lovely morning together in a private salon at Ruinart, where she shared many fascinating tales from all three houses. Afterward, I had the privilege of receiving a private tour of Ruinart's stunning crayères, where Madame Pierre pointed out many things that helped bring the spirit of this book to life. (She even showed me a picture of a Nazi soldier, hand-etched into the chalk walls of one of Ruinart's crayères, which was likely drawn by a cellar worker hiding beneath the earth during the Occupation.)

Historian Yves Tesson was beyond helpful, and I thoroughly enjoyed our lunch together at Brasserie L'Affaire in Reims. Not only did he introduce me to the magic of a proper *café gourmand*—espresso served with an array of miniature desserts—but he answered my many questions about the history of Reims and the surrounding area. He was very generous with his time and knowledge, and I'm so grateful.

I'd also like to thank Marie-Charlotte Wambergue, the international press and influence communications manager for Ruinart, and Julie Pertus, the planning and private client coordinator for the champagne brands under the Moët Hennessy umbrella (Dom Pérignon, Moët & Chandon, Ruinart, Krug, Veuve Clicquot, and Mercier), for helping put me in touch with Madame Pierre, and for helping to organize my visits. Brigitte Batonnet from the Comité Interprofessionnel du vin de Champagne (the CIVC) was also tremendously helpful in answering some questions of minute detail in regard to the history and production of champagne. And thanks also to Stéphanie Venet of ParisChampagneTour.com, who leads wonderful walking tours through Reims and helped me with some of my research.

I was unsuccessful in contacting historian Jean-Pierre Husson, who has done extensive research into the history of Reims, but I have to thank him anyhow for some of the wonderful scholarly articles of his that I found online, especially in regard to the Second World War.

The books *Champagne: How the World's Most Glamorous Wine Triumphed Over War and Hard Times* and *Wine and War: The French, the Nazis, and the Battle for France's Greatest Treasure*, both by Don and Petie Kladstrup, were thoroughly enjoyable and informative, as was Alan Tardi's richly detailed *Champagne, Uncorked: The House of Krug and the Timeless Allure of the World's Most Celebrated Drink.* Also helpful were *Le Champagne: Une Histoire Franco-Allemande* by Claire Desbois-Thibault, Werner Paravicini, and Jean-Pierre Poussou, and *Robert-Jean de Voguë: Le "quart d'heure d'avance" de Moët & Chandon* by Francine Rivaud and the aforementioned Yves Tesson, both of which I had translated from French. *Champagne: The Wine, the Land,*

and the People by Patrick Forbes, published in 1967, also provided an interesting glance into the recent history of Champagne and champagne production. *Fashion Under the Occupation* (Dominique Veillon), *The Escape Line: How the Ordinary Heroes of Dutch-Paris Resisted the Nazi Occupation of Western Europe* (Megan Koreman), and *Résistance: Memoirs of Occupied France* (Agnès Humbert) helped me fill in some of the details of wartime. The online resources available from the Union des Maisons de Champagne, especially their articles about the time line of champagne production, were also very helpful.

If you're looking for another novel set in French wine country during the Second World War, I recommend Ann Mah's *The Lost Vintage*, about a sommelier who unearths some dramatic history in Burgundy. And if you enjoyed *The Winemaker's Wife*, Tilar J. Mazzeo's nonfiction *The Widow Clicquot: The Story of a Champagne Empire and the Woman Who Ruled It* might interest you, too; it's also set in Champagne, during an earlier period (the nineteenth century).

Finally, to you, the reader: I hope that the next time you open a bottle of champagne—whether it's to celebrate a milestone or simply to enjoy on a weeknight—you'll think of the light and darkness, the tragedy and the triumph, that are part of every glass. After all, those tantalizing bubbles in your champagne represent a tradition of courage, a spirit of hope, and the lesson that if you continue to persevere against the odds, you might just make magic. *À votre santé!*

acknowledgments

I couldn't do what I do without the dream duo of Holly Root, my brilliant literary agent, and Abby Zidle, my equally brilliant editor. I don't say it often enough, but I adore you both, and I can't imagine being on this journey without either of you. I firmly believe I'm the luckiest author in the world.

To my dear Kristin Dwyer (I love you, lady!), Meagan Harris, and Michelle Podberezniak: Thank you so much for being such rock stars at handling publicity. Heather Baror-Shapiro and Dana Spector, you are beyond amazing, and I'm so grateful to be working with both of you. To Andy Cohen: what a long, wild ride this has been, my dear friend! I can't wait for the next step in our adventure! And to Danielle Noe: Thanks for all your ad help!

Jen Bergstrom: Thanks for all the support and kindness! Have I mentioned lately that I love being a Gallery author? I adore my whole Gallery team, including Diana Velasquez, Wendy Sheanin, Jen Long, Mackenzie Hickey, Nancy Tonik, Faren Bachelis, Lisa

Litwack, Chelsea McGuckin, Anabel Jimenez, Sara Quaranta, Ali Lacavaro, and Aimée Bell. I owe Carolyn Reidy a big debt of gratitude, too.

A special thanks to the Target book club team for making *The Room on Rue Amélie* a Target pick—and also for having such a dangerously tantalizing store, where I (over)shop at least once a week—as well as to Writer's Block, my wonderful local indie bookstore in Winter Park, Florida, and its delightful owner, Lauren Zimmerman! And to all of you out there who are working hard running independent stores, especially LeAnne Rollins of Writer's Block, and Cathy Graham, Serena Wyckoff, and Jean Lewis of the charming Copperfish Books in Punta Gorda, Florida: Thank you so much for creating friendly, welcoming, engaging places for book lovers in your communities. Thank you, too, to Lisa Proto, the best Barnes & Noble bookseller in the business!

Thanks to those who helped me research this book, most of whom are mentioned in the author's note. And thanks to all my wonderful foreign publishers. I feel so fortunate to have my books available in so many different languages. Each time I receive an email from a reader in Israel, Italy, Germany, Holland, China, Russia, or elsewhere around the globe, I'm reminded of what a gift it is to get to connect with people whose lives might not otherwise intersect with mine. It's something I'll never take for granted.

Every summer, I get together with an amazing group of writers to spend a week together—usually in Swan Valley, Idaho—and I don't think I'd be half the writer I am without the support of those talented storytellers. I adore each and every one of my Swan Valley sisters and brother: Wendy Toliver, Linda Gerber, Allison van Diepen, Emily Wing Smith, Alyson Noël, and Jay Asher.

I'm also so grateful to all the women and men who make up the online community of book bloggers, book lovers, and authors who love to read. It's such a supportive group, and I know I should participate more often, rather than (mostly) just lurking. But please do know that I'm always following along, and I'm really thankful for all your support and camaraderie, even if I don't always say it enough. A special shout-out to Melissa Amster, Jenny O'Regan, the buzzy Kristy Barrett, Aestas, Amy Bromberg, Lorelai, Brenda Janowitz, Liz Fenton, Lisa Steinke, Hailey Fish, Elizabeth Silver, Jen Cannon, Lloyd Russell, Kim Jackson, Karen Trosterud, Andrea Peskind Katz, Nancy Harris, Bobbi Dumas, Jenny Collins Belk, Sharlene Martin Moore, and so many more!

A huge thank-you to all of you who have been a part of my son's life and have made him feel so safe and loved while I'm working, especially Lauren, Bridget, Dinorah, Dayana, Rachel, Debbie, and Cindy.

To all my dear friends and all our amazing neighbors: I'm so lucky to be surrounded by such an awesome group of supportive, wonderful people.

And, of course, to my mom (Carol), dad (Rick), Janine, Wanda, Mark, Karen, Barry, William, James, Dave, Johanna, Brittany, Jarryd, Chloe, Donna, Courtney, and the whole family (especially my World War II research buddy, Grandpa Trouba): I love you all!

To Jason and Noah: I spend so much time and energy writing words for other people that I sometimes wonder if I fail to save enough of them to tell the two of you just how much you mean to me. I love you both so very deeply, and I'm profoundly grateful that I get to spend my life with you.

And finally to you, the reader: Thank you for spending a bit of your valuable time with me. It's an honor, and I'm more grateful than I could ever say. *Merci beaucoup.*

the winemaker's wife

KRISTIN HARMEL

This reading group guide for The Winemaker's Wife *includes an introduction, discussion questions, and ideas for enhancing your book club. The suggested questions are intended to help your reading group find new and interesting angles and topics for your discussion. We hope that these ideas will enrich your conversation and increase your enjoyment of the book.*

introduction

The year is 1940, and the Germans are quickly approaching the champagne-producing regions of northern France. As Inès, a young bride, rushes to inform her husband, the owner of a champagne house, of the Nazis' impending approach, she has no idea how much her life will change over the course of the next few years.

Many years later, Liv is recovering from a failed marriage and doesn't know how she'll start anew. But her eccentric elderly grandmother, Edith, has just the ticket—literally. She whisks Liv off to France, but won't tell Liv what she's doing there or how Edith is connected to the city of Reims.

These two stories in *The Winemaker's Wife* intertwine to tell a gripping narrative of love, loss, the tragedy of war, and the hope that comes from the smallest resistance against evil, set against the lush backdrop of northern France's champagne vineyards.

topics and questions for discussion

1. This novel takes place in the champagne-producing region of France. How does the location play into the plot? Is the setting crucial to the story, or could this book have taken place at any vineyard during World War II?

2. Inès struggles with her place at the Maison Chauveau. She feels disrespected by her husband and left out of everything important. Did you feel sympathy for Inès's predicament, or were you frustrated by her focus on her own problems? Or a mix of both?

3. Michel is not very attentive to Inès and doesn't notice her attempts to be useful. However, he pays very close attention to Céline. Why do you think Michel was so frustrated with Inès?

4. Inès looks inward for much of the novel, and as a result, she misses a lot of the horror happening around her. How did you feel about her spending time with a Nazi collaborator? How do you think Inès justified it to herself?

5. Much of *The Winemaker's Wife* revolves around characters being complacent in a time of crisis; therefore, it's easy for one to be willfully blind to what's really happening. Are there other times in history where this same observation applies?

6. Liv has her own struggles, including dealing with the end of her marriage. How does her situation compare with Inès's predicament?

7. Céline goes through an emotional journey over the course of the novel, worrying about her family and her own safety. Her story, sadly, is dictated by the times she lived in. Did you feel satisfied with the way it turned out, or did you want Céline's story to go differently?

8. Michel feels that he must defy the Nazis in any way he can. How did you feel about his resistance, and with his knowing that he was putting others at the Maison Chauveau in harm's way?

9. Inès tries to help the Resistance, but those around her accuse her of only wanting to prove that she's useful—in essence, still having selfish motives. How did you separate her motives from her actions? Is there something inherently selfish in every generous act?

10. Discuss what you learned about champagne making in *The Winemaker's Wife*. How much did you know before you read the novel, and what did you learn from it?

11. Harmel surprises the reader with a twist, revealing new truths about modern-day Edith's identity. Did you suspect that this was the case? Did it impact your understanding of the character of Inès?

12. The selfishness Inès displays has dire consequences at the end of the book. Do you think her work in the Resistance redeemed her?

enhance your book club

1. Buy a selection of champagne to sip while you discuss *The Winemaker's Wife*. Can you tell a difference between different champagne houses? What about the differences between varying vintages?

2. Read Tilar J. Mazzeo's *The Widow Clicquot*, a history of Veuve Clicquot (and a woman who's mentioned in *The Winemaker's Wife*), and compare it with the information presented about champagne making in this book. Discuss how important history and culture is to French winemaking.

3. Read *Wine and War* by Don and Petie Kladstrup, which is about French winemakers who resisted the Nazis. Discuss the Resistance techniques depicted in both books and whether they were effective.

4. Research French dishes that were popular in the 1940s. Have each member bring a dish to share, to celebrate the cuisine present in the novel.

DON'T MISS THE NEWEST NOVEL FROM
KRISTIN HARMEL

THE Forest OF Vanishing Stars

AVAILABLE SUMMER 2021 FROM GALLERY BOOKS

KEEP READING FOR A SNEAK PEEK . . .

one

1922

The old woman watched from the shadows outside Behaimstrasse 72, waiting for the lights inside to blink out. The apartment's balcony dripped with crimson roses, and ivy climbed the iron rails, but the young couple who lived there—the power-hungry Siegfried Jüttner and his aloof wife, Alwine—weren't the ones who tended the plants. That was left to their maid, for the nurturing of life was something only those with some goodness could do.

The old woman had been watching the Jüttners for nearly two years now, and she knew things about them, things that were important to the task she was about to undertake.

She knew, for example, that Herr Jüttner had been one of the first men in Berlin to join the National Socialist German Workers' Party, a new political movement that was slowly gaining a foothold in the war-shattered country. She knew he'd been inspired to do so while on holiday in Munich nearly three years earlier, after seeing an angry young man named Adolf Hitler give a rousing speech in the Hofbräukeller. She knew that after hearing that speech, Herr Jüttner had walked twenty minutes back to the elegant Hotel Vier Jahreszeiten, had awoken his sleeping young wife, and had lain with her, though at first she had objected, for she had been dreaming of a young man she had once loved, a man who had died in the Great War.

The old woman knew, too, that the baby conceived on that autumn-scented Bavarian night, a girl the Jüttners had named Inge, had a birthmark in the shape of a dove on the inside of her left wrist.

She also knew that the girl's second birthday was the following day, the sixth of July, 1922. And she knew, as surely as she knew that the bell-shaped buds of lily of the valley and the twilight petals of aconite could kill a man, that the girl must not be allowed to remain with the Jüttners.

That was why she had come.

The old woman, who was called Jerusza, had always known things other people didn't. For example, she had known it the moment Fréderic Chopin had died in 1849, for she had awoken from a deep slumber, the notes of his "Revolutionary Étude" marching through her head in an aggrieved parade. She had felt the earth tremble upon the births of Marie Curie in 1867 and Albert Einstein in 1879. And on a sweltering late June day in 1914, two months after she had turned seventy-four, she had felt it deep in her jugular vein, weeks before the news reached her, that the heir to the Austro-Hungarian throne had been felled by an assassin's bullet, cracking the fragile balance of the world. She had known then that war was brewing, just as she knew it now. She could see it in the dark clouds that hulked on the horizon.

Jerusza's mother, who had killed herself with a brew of poisons in 1860, used to tell her that the knowing of impossible things was a gift from God, passed down through maternal blood of only the most fortunate Jewish women. Jerusza, the last of a bloodline that had stretched for centuries, was certain at times that it was a curse instead, but whatever it was, it had been her burden all her life to follow the voices that echoed through the forests. The leaves whispered in the trees; the flowers told tales as old as time; the rivers rushed with news of places far away. If one listened closely enough, nature always spilled her secrets, which were, of course, the secrets of God. And now, it was God who had brought Jerusza here, to a fog-cloaked Berlin street corner, where she would be responsible for changing the fate of a child, and perhaps a piece of the world, too.

Jerusza had been alive for eighty-two years, nearly twice as long as the typical German lived. When people looked at her—if they bothered to look at all—they were visibly startled by her wizened features, her hands gnarled by decades of hard living. Most of the time, though, strangers simply ignored her, just as Siegfried and Alwine Jüttner had done each of the hundreds of times they had passed her on the street. Her age made her particularly invisible to those who cared most about appearance and power; they assumed she was useless to them, a waste of time, a waste of space. After all, surely a woman as old as she would be dead soon. But Jerusza, who had spent her whole life sustained by the plants and herbs in the darkest spots of the deepest forests, knew that she would live nearly twenty years more, to the age of 102, and that she would die on a spring Tuesday just after the last thaw of 1942.

The Jüttners' maid, the timid daughter of a dead sailor, had gone home two hours before, and it was a few minutes past ten o'clock when the Jüttners finally turned off their lights. Jerusza exhaled. Darkness was her shield; it always had been. She squinted at the closed windows and could just make out the shape of the little girl's infant bed in the room to the right, beyond pale custard curtains. She knew exactly where it was, had been into the room many times when the family wasn't there. She had run her fingers along the pine rails, had felt the power splintering from the curves. Wood had memory, of course, and the first time Jerusza had touched the bed where the baby slept, she had been nearly overcome by a warm, white wash of light.

It was the same light that had brought her here from the forest two years earlier. She had first seen it in June 1920, shining above the treetops like a personal aurora borealis, beckoning her north. She hated the city, abhorred being in a place built by man rather than God, but she knew she had no choice. Her feet had carried her straight to Behaimstrasse 72, to bear witness as the raven-haired Frau Jüttner nursed the baby for the first time. Jerusza had seen the baby glowing, even then a light in the darkness no one knew was coming.

She didn't want a child; she never had. Perhaps that was why it had taken her so long to act. But nature makes no mistakes, and now, as the sky filled with a cloud of silent blackbirds over the twinkling city, she knew the time had come.

It was easy to climb up the ladder of the modern building's fire escape, easier still to push open the Jüttners' unlatched window and slip quietly inside. The child was awake, silently watching, her extraordinary eyes—one twilight blue and one forest green—glimmering in the darkness. Her hair was black as night, her lips the startling red of corn poppies.

"*Ikh bin gekimen dikh tsu nemen,*" Jerusza whispered in Yiddish, a language the girl would not yet know. *I have come for you.* She was startled to realize that her heart was racing.

She didn't expect a reply, but the child's lips parted, and she reached out her left hand, palm upturned, the dove-shaped birthmark shimmering in the darkness. She said something soft, something that a lesser person would have dismissed as the meaningless babble of a little girl, but to Jerusza, it was unmistakable. "*Dus zent ir,*" said the girl in Yiddish. *It is you.*

"*Yo, dus bin ikh,*" Jerusza agreed. And with that, she picked up the baby, who didn't cry out, and, tucking her close against the brittle curves of her body, climbed out the window and shimmied down the iron rail, her feet hitting the sidewalk without a sound.

From the folds of Jerusza's cloak, the baby watched soundlessly, her mismatched ocean eyes round, as Berlin vanished behind them and the forest to the north swallowed them whole.

1928

The girl from Berlin was eight years old when Jerusza first taught her how to kill a man.

Of course Jerusza had discarded the child's given name as soon as they'd reached the crisp edge of the woods six years earlier. Inge meant "the daughter of a heroic father," and that was a lie. The child had no parent now but the forest itself.

Furthermore, Jerusza had known, from the moment she first saw the light over Berlin, that the child was to be called Yona, which meant "dove" in Hebrew. She had known it even before she saw the girl's birthmark, which hadn't faded with time but had grown stronger, darker, a sign that this child was special, that she was fated for something great.

The right name was vital, and the old woman couldn't call Yona anything other than what she was. She expected the same in return, of course, a respect for one's true identity. Jerusza meant "owned inheritance"—a reference to the magic she had received from her own bloodline, and a tribute to being owned by the forest itself—and it was the only thing she allowed Yona to call her. "Mother" meant something different, something that Jerusza never would be, never wanted to be.

"There are hundreds of ways to take a life," Jerusza told the girl on a fading July afternoon soon after the child's eighth birthday. "And you must know them all."

Yona looked up from whittling a tiny wren from a piece of wood. She had taken to carving creatures for company, which Jerusza did not understand, for she herself valued solitude above all else, but it seemed a harmless enough pursuit. Yona's hair, the color of the deepest starless night, tumbled down her back, rolling over birdlike shoulders. Her eyes—endless and unsettling—were misty with confusion. The sun was low in the sky, and her shadow stretched behind her all the way to the edge of the clearing, as if trying to escape into the trees.

"But you've always told me that life is precious, that it is God's gift to man, that it must be protected," the girl said.

"Yes. But the most important life to protect is your own."

Jerusza flattened her palm and sliced the edge of her hand across her own windpipe. "If someone comes for you, a hard blow here, if delivered correctly, can be fatal."

Yona blinked a few times, her long lashes dusting her cheeks, which were preternaturally pale, always pale, though the sun beat down on them relentlessly. As she set the wooden wren on the ground beside her, her hands shook. "But who would come for me?"

Jerusza stared at the child with disgust. Her head was in the clouds, despite Jerusza's teachings. "You foolish child!" she snapped. The girl shrank away from her. It was good that the girl was afraid; terrible things were coming. "Your question is the wrong one, as usual. There will come a day when you'll be glad I have taught you what I know."

It wasn't an answer, but the girl wouldn't cross her. Jerusza was strong as a mountain chamois, clever as a hooded crow, vindictive as a magpie. She had been on the earth for nearly nine decades now, and she knew the girl was frightened by her age and her wisdom. Jerusza liked it that way; the child should be clear that Jerusza was not a mother. She was a teacher, nothing more.

"But, Jerusza, I don't know if I could take a life," Yona said at last, her voice small. "How would I live with myself?"

Jerusza snorted. It was hard to believe the girl could still be so naive. "I've killed four men and a woman, child. And I live with myself just fine."

Yona's eyes widened, but she didn't speak again until the light had faded from the sky and the day's lessons had ended. "Who did you kill, Jerusza?" she whispered in the darkness as they lay on their backs on the forest floor beneath a roof of spruce bark they'd built themselves just the week before. They moved every month or two, building a new hut from the gifts the forest gave them, always leaving a crack in their hastily hewn bark ceilings to see the stars when there was no threat of rain. Tonight, the heavens were clear, and Jerusza could see the Little Dipper, the Big Dipper, and Draco, the dragon, crawling across the sky. Life changed all the time, but the stars were ever constant.

"A farmer, two soldiers, a blacksmith, and the woman who murdered my father," Jerusza replied without looking at Yona. "All would have killed me themselves if I'd given them a chance. You must never give someone that opportunity, Yona. Forget that lesson, and you will die. Now get some rest."

By the next full moon, Yona knew that a kick just to the right of the base of the spine could puncture a kidney. A horizontal blow with the edge of the hand to the bridge of the nose could crush the facial bones deep into the skull, causing a brain hemorrhage. A hard toe kick to the temple, once a man was down, could swiftly end a life. A quick headlock behind a seated man, combined with a sharp backward jerk, could snap a neck. A knife sliced upward, from wrist to inner elbow along the radial artery, could drain a man of his blood in minutes.

But the universe was about balance, and so for each method of death, Yona taught the girl a way to dispense healing, too. Bilberries could restore circulation to a failing heart or resuscitate a dying kidney. Catswort, when ground into a paste, could stop bleeding. Burdock root could remove poison from the bloodstream. Crushed elderberries could bring down a deadly fever.

Life and death. Death and life. Two things that mattered little, for in the end, souls outlived the body and became one with an infinite God. But Yona didn't understand that, not yet. She didn't yet know that she had been born for the sake of repairing the world, for the sake of *tikkun olam*, and that each *mitzvah* she was called to perform would lift up divine sparks of light.

If only the forest alone could sustain them, but as the girl grew, she needed clothing, milk to strengthen her bones, shoes so her feet weren't shredded by the forest floor in the summer or frozen to death in the winter. When Yona was young, Jerusza sometimes left her alone in the woods for a day and a night, scaring her into staying put with tales of werewolves that ate little girls, while she ventured alone into nearby towns to take the things they needed. But as the girl began to ask more questions, there was no choice but to begin taking her along, to show her the perils of the outside world, to remind her that no one could be trusted.

It was a cold winter's night in 1931, snow drifting down from a black sky, when Jerusza pulled the wide-eyed child into a town called Grajewo in northeastern Poland. And though Jerusza had explicitly told her to remain silent, Yona couldn't seem to keep her words in. As they crept through the darkness toward a farmhouse, the girl peppered her with questions: *What is that roof made of? Why do the horses sleep in a barn and not in a field? How did they make these roads? What is that on the flag?*

Finally, Jerusza whirled on her. "Enough, child! There is nothing here for you, nothing but despair and danger! Yearning for a life you don't understand is like staring at the sun; your foolishness will destroy you."

Yona was startled into silence for a time, but after Jerusza had slipped through the back door of the house and reemerged carrying a pair of boots, trousers, and a wool coat that would see Yona through at least a few winters, Yona refused to follow when Jerusza beckoned.

"What is it now?" Jerusza demanded, irritated.

"What are they doing?" Yona pointed through the window of the farmhouse, to where the family was gathered around a table. It was the first night of Hanukkah, and this family was Jewish; it was why Jerusza had chosen this house, for she knew they would be occupied while she took their things. Now the father of the family stood, his face illuminated by the candle burning on the family's menorah, and though his voice was inaudible, it was clear he was singing, his eyes closed. Jerusza didn't like the look in Yona's expression as she watched; it was one of longing and enchantment, and those types of feelings led only to ill-conceived ideas of flight.

"The practice of dullards," she said finally. "Nothing there for you. Come now."

Yona still wouldn't budge. "But they look happy. They are celebrating Hanukkah?"

Of course the girl already knew they were. Jerusza carved a menorah each year from wood, simply because her mother had commanded it years before. Hanukkah wasn't among the most important Jewish holidays, but it celebrated survival, and that was something anyone who lived in the woods could respect. Still, the girl was being foolish. Jerusza narrowed her eyes. "They are repeating words that have likely lost all meaning for them, Yona. Repetition is for people who don't want to think for themselves, people who have no imagination. How can you find God in moments that have become rote?"

Neither of them said anything for a moment. "But what if

in the repetition, they find comfort?" Yona eventually asked, her voice small. "What if they find magic?"

"How on earth would repetition be magic?" They still needed to procure a few jugs of milk from the barn, and Jerusza was losing patience.

"Well, God makes the same trees come alive each year, doesn't he?" Yona said slowly. "He makes the same seasons come and go, the same flowers bloom, the same birds call. And there's magic in that, isn't there?"

Jerusza was stunned into silence. The girl had not bested her at her own game before. "*Never* question me," she snapped at last. "Now, shut up and come along."

It was inevitable that Yona would begin wondering about the world outside the woods. Jerusza had always known the time would come, and now it was heavy upon her to ensure that when the girl thought of civilization, she regarded it with the proper fear.

Jerusza had been teaching Yona all the languages she knew since she had taken her, and the child could speak fluent Yiddish, Polish, Belarusian, Russian, and German, as well as snippets of French and English. *One must know the words of one's enemies*, Jerusza always told her, and she was gratified by the fear she could see in Yona's eyes.

But she had more to teach, so on their forays into towns, she began to steal books, too. She taught the child to read, to understand science, to work with numbers. She insisted that Yona know the Torah and the Talmud, but she also brought her the Christian Bible and even the Muslim Quran, for God was everywhere, and the search for him was endless. It had consumed Jerusza's whole life, and it had brought her to that dark street corner in Berlin in the summer of 1922, where she'd been compelled to steal this child, who had become such a thorn in her side.

And though Yona irritated her more often than not, even Jerusza had to admit that the girl was bright, sensitive, intuitive. She drank the books down like cool water and listened with rapt attention whenever Jerusza deigned to impart her secrets. By the time Yona was fourteen, she knew more about the world than most men who'd been educated in universities. More important, she knew the mysteries of the forest, all the ways to survive.

As the girl's eyes opened to the world, though, Jerusza insisted upon only two things: One, Yona must always obey her. And two, she must always stay hidden in the forest, away from those who might hurt her.

Sometimes Yona asked why. Who would want to hurt her? What would they try to do?

But Jerusza never answered, for the truth was, she wasn't sure. She knew only that in the early-morning hours of July 6, 1922, as she hurried with a two-year-old child into the forest, she heard a voice from the sky, sharp and clear. *One day*, the voice said, *if she is not careful, her past will return—and it will cost her everything. The only safe place is the forest.*

It was the same voice that had told her to take the girl in the first place, the voice that had always whispered to Jerusza in the trees. Jerusza had spent most of her life thinking the voice belonged to God. But now, in the twilight of her life, she was no longer sure. What if the voice in her head belonged to her alone? What if it was the legacy of her mother's madness, a spark of insanity rather than a higher calling?

But each time those questions bubbled to the surface, Jerusza pushed them away. The voice from above had spoken, and who knew what fate awaited her if she failed to listen.

Violet the Velvet Rabbit

by Janey Louise Jones
illustrated by Jennie Poh

PICTURE WINDOW BOOKS
a capstone imprint

Superfairies is published by Picture Window Books
A Capstone Imprint
1710 Roe Crest Drive
North Mankato, Minnesota 56003
www.mycapstone.com

Library of Congress Cataloging-in-Publication data is available on the Library of Congress website.

ISBN: 978-1-4795-8644-8 (library binding)
ISBN: 978-1-4795-8648-6 (paperback)
ISBN: 978-1-4795-8652-3 (eBook PDF)

Summary: A velvet rabbit takes on a dare to ski down Snowdrop Slope, but soon she's dangling over a deep valley. The Superfairies must save her, because she can't hold on much longer.

Designer: Alison Thiele

For my sisters, Sticky Toffee and Nana x
– Jennie Poh

Printed and bound in US.
007522CGS16